POINT

"A dark, believable vision of a (near) future Britain, but more importantly an intelligent, slick and brilliantly executed novel with a quite unexpected but superbly scripted ending. 5*****"

SFBook.com

... writer. He ...
new again."

Robert J Sawyer

"Blackthorne is such a fine ...
off the page, a trained killer whose anger and grief at his daughter's condition is brilliantly portrayed; the depiction of his simmering rage, barely held in check, and how he channels it, provides a masterclass in characterisation"

The Guardian

"An entertainingly gnarly conspiracy thriller that also features plenty of full-tilt action set-pieces."

SFX

"Thomas Blackthorne (a *nom-de-plume* of John Meaney) has created in *Edge* a near-future Britain which is in many respects hardly distinguishable from the present state of that green and pleasant land. It is a country of privatised surveillance, economic angst, and fears of arbitrary terrorism – like today, except more so. *Edge* is an exceptionally well-written story and one featuring a memorable character in Josh Cumberland."

SFSite

ALSO BY THOMAS BLACKTHORNE

Edge

THOMAS BLACKTHORNE

Point

ANGRY
ROBOT

ANGRY ROBOT

A member of the Osprey Group
Midland House, West Way
Botley, Oxford
OX2 0HP
UK

www.angryrobotbooks.com
Baker's dozen

An Angry Robot paperback original 2011
1

A catalogue record for this book is available
from the British Library.

ISBN: 978 0 85766 078 7
EBook ISBN: 978 0 85766 080 0

Set in Meridien by THL Design

Printed in the UK by CPI Mackays, Chatham, ME5 8TD.

To my brother Colm and his missus Leslie:
gigatonnes of love and respect forever.

"Give Me What I Want", lyrics by Aled Phillips,
used by kind permission of Notting Hill
Music (UK) Ltd.

[ONE]

It was the beginning of June, and snow was falling on London.

They called it the most interesting of times, because a month earlier, the prime minister Billy Church (aka Fat Billy) had created the institution of Midsummer Christmas by Act of Parliament. Its first occurrence would be in a month's time, on the third of July. He could have chosen the fourth, or any day at all. Pundits debated the symbolism.

Whether the broken, former United States would hold an Independence Day this year, no one knew. Former West Coast cities were blackened ash, while thousands of refugees a month were dying of radiation sickness. Meanwhile, after the coldest recorded winter on record, snow continued to fall on London as official summer began.

At least the snow was mostly white, though ash remained in the stratosphere around the globe.

Indoors in the warmth, Josh and Suzanne lay snuggled on the couch beneath an orange blanket, watching a party political broadcast by the leader of the TechnoDemocratic Party, the Right Honourable Sharon Caldwell, MP. She was scientifically trained, an outspoken atheist, a lesbian, and determined to win the general election in order to save the country.

Clearly, she was doomed.

Suzanne said, "I bet Fat Billy will hold the election on Mid-summer Christmas Day."

The prime minister had still not announced the election date, though his term of office was due to expire. Like most PMs through history, he would choose the timing with care.

"Probably." Josh ran his finger along Suzanne's smooth chocolatté skin. "Maybe the people deserve him."

"They don't deserve you." She kissed him. "What you did. You're too good for them."

Josh Cumberland was no politician. He was ex-Ghost Force, and last summer he had forced his way onto the live finals of *Knife Edge*, and battled his way through professional knife fighters purely to take the stage, so viewers would see the damning data that he and his friends webcast in realtime.

Those files showed more than the prime minister making covert deals with the Tyndall Industries; they also contained video footage of virapharm labs in Africa where living children formed incubators for new strains of drugs and nanoviral engineering tools.

But that had been the day that Armageddon came to Tri-State CalOrWashington, with mushroom clouds blooming, while President Brand declared: "The Sodom and Gomorrah that infested our sacred land are now burned from the Earth."

Political scandal at home was nothing compared to the disaster taking place six thousand miles away. Afterwards, the stories about Billy Church slid and blurred, because his political team had no lack of influence engineers: superb psychologists who brought science to the art of spindoctoring.

Suzanne pointed her phone at the wallscreen, increasing the volume.

"Before the ongoing Fimbulwinter," Sharon Caldwell was saying on screen, "everyone moaned about disappearing forests, while continuing to wipe their arses with toilet paper. Can't anyone see the contradiction?"

Josh smiled; Suzanne chuckled.

"If you balance a pencil on its point," Caldwell went on, "it can tip in any direction. When it does fall, it falls fast. That's where we are today, and not just with the weather. The geopolitical climate is just as bad."

Beside Josh, Suzanne was shaking her head.

"Every word intelligent," she said, "and none of it persuasive."

"About the only thing I can agree on with our current prime minister" – on screen, Caldwell looked grim – "is the nuclear reactor programme. But with one proviso. If we'd begun it years ago, say when Billy Church came to office, or preferably before, it would have been a damn sight less dangerous. Cracked cores or meltdown are deadly, and they should–"

"Don't think of a blue elephant," said Josh. "Especially not a blue elephant wearing a yellow tutu, hopping on one leg and singing 'Happy Birthday'."

"Very good." Suzanne patted his leg. "You have been paying attention."

Caldwell's use of psychosemantics was pitiful. Her most sensory-specific words, however factual, described the things she did *not* want. Viewers would subconsciously associate fear-images with reactors – and even worse, with Caldwell herself.

She went on: "The prime minister may have switched on the lights in Oxford Street, but this isn't Midsummer Christmas, it's midsummer madness. The only thing to do is–"

"Switch off." Suzanne pointed her phone. "Sadly."

The screen went dark.

"Now what" – Josh slid his hand under her blouse – "can we possibly do to entertain ourselves?"

From the bedroom, his phone chimed.

"I have a desperate desire to pee." Suzanne shifted her feet to the floor, pulling back the blanket. "And you've a call to answer."

Josh padded to the bedroom, smiling. He retrieved his phone from the bedside table and checked the sender ID: *Hammond*.

Vertigo pulled at him.

No.

It was a vmail message, not realtime.

He shouldn't be calling at all.

How could there be news? For so long, nothing had changed.

"I'm sorry to have to send you this," said Hammond in the small display. "Your daughter's condition deteriorated catastrophically overnight, with no prior changes to the regime of care that we–"

Fluorescence pulsed across his vision. His ears filled with the surf-like wash of stress.

"–in theatre since 4pm, but there was nothing we could do. I'm sure you understand there will have to be a post-mortem examination. If you want to see Sophie before then, please call back. Her mother is with her now."

Maria. With Sophie.

No, with a corpse.

His daughter was gone, had been gone for over a year. Soft tidal shifts in the base of her brain were the only activity in her persistent vegetative state. Machines kept her organs alive, but the real Sophie, his beautiful, sweet girl, was ten years old forever, her eleventh birthday a travesty. Maria had brought balloons to the bedside; he had stayed away.

"Josh?"

And he had been cuddling with his lover while his daughter died.

Sophie. My poor, sweet Sophie.

Staring into emptiness, a blackness that went to infinity, he dropped the phone back on the table. Moving to the cupboard where he kept his clothes, he pulled out a tracksuit. He dressed like an automaton.

Sophie. Gone.

Really gone. Dissipated, evaporated, blown away by chance.

The world is not benign, and never was.

"Josh, what's going on?"

The dagger he fastened at the small of his back was inscribed *William Rex, Dieu et mon droit*; but there was no God, only the harshness of death.

Out on the landing, he checked the fastenings on his shoes. Behind him the door to the flat, to Suzanne's flat, clicked into place. Then he was going down the stairs, moving fast.

And into the chill night.

Sophie. My baby girl.

He began to run through the snow.

Call it a passage of grief.

Snow, chill wind, a dark June night like Moscow in December. The pounding of his feet and heart. The sick desolation of a parent without a child, for Sophie's universe was gone.

He ran past cheery lights, ordinary Christmas decorations and new Midsummer Christmas banners. Gaudy bioluminescence decorated shops and houses.

Rowdy young men spilled from a pub, some of them armed. He jogged across the street and ran on, wanting no trouble. He had a dagger sheathed at the small of his back, but no phone: not the normal priority.

At some point he reached Embankment, having started from Queens Park. The Thames was black and glittering. He jogged past frozen turbines, their vanes ice-locked. Then he sped up, ran fast to Westminster Bridge where he slowed, plodding out across the bridge.

At the midpoint, he stopped.

"Good King Wenceslas" sounded behind him, children and adults singing. He wanted to yell at them to stop, but what was the point? Sophie was lying on a cold table waiting for the scalpel. That was the reality that lay in wait for all these kids, sooner or later. Let them retain their illusions for now.

His hands were tight on the freezing balustrade.

"You all right, pal?"

Sounds from a distant world.

Another voice: "That's a thin tracksuit, for this weather."

Cheerful conversation from a different reality.

"Look, you're not thinking of jumping, are you?"

His fingers were whitened clamps on the rail. He *could* fling himself over. The black waves would hit like a metal hammer. If the impact did not get him, the freezing temperature would. Oblivion courtesy of thermodynamics.

"Why don't you–"

Heavy hand, clamping his left shoulder.

No!

"–come with *uughhh*–"

He spun, the rage detonating in coordinated torque, the thrust and twist of body weight, powering from his feet, through his torso, more than the arm delivering impact – *Sophie* – of fist to throat – *she's dead* – and the crunch of collapsing larynx – *you fucker* – as the man in scarlet dropped. Down and dying, but Josh followed, knee-first to target the liver – *you bastard* – but there was padding in place – *what's this?* – and he raised his arm to hammer down as a child's voice sounded.

"He's killing Santa!"

His muscles locked, his mind lurching into gear.

What?

White cotton beard askew. Bulging eyes and struggling mouth. Cheeks darkening even in the night – if it were daytime, the skin would be purple. A wheezing croak from his crushed throat. Other men were yelling, not daring to approach.

He's dying.

To choke is to die in panic.

Medics can't help.

Even if someone had rung for assistance, it would not help. The end was seconds away.

Shit. Do it.

He had to stop the choking. Such an awful way to die.

You have to.

He ripped his knife free from the small of his back – light glinting on silver – and used his left hand and body weight to pinion the struggling man – weaker struggles now – and lowered the knife point-first, sighting along the blade.

"Leave him alone you–"

And rammed down.

Got you.

Into the base of the throat.

Careful.

Enlarging the cut before he withdrew.

Then he glanced up and saw the adults and children properly: half the grown-ups in Salvation Army uniform, their instruments of polished brass. Whipping upward from his crouch, Josh snatched away a trumpet, ripped off the mouthpiece, and knelt down beside the stricken Santa. Then he leaned over, put the mouthpiece against the hole he had cut, and pressed down.

Santa's chest rose, sucking air through the metal mouthpiece at the bottom of his neck, below the crushed larynx.

Done it.

As he stood up, blue lights strobed along the Embankment to the north, and sirens sounded from the south. Whether police or paramedics arrived first did not matter: either would have the training to keep the Santa safe.

Everyone turned to look at the approaching emergency vehicles, and timing was everything as Josh slipped behind the group, caught hold of the railing, and rolled over.

Dropping.

[TWO]

His hands were claws because they had to be. He hung in shadow beneath the bridge, like a frozen bat on the underside; but he could not flit away: he needed to wait.

"–happened to him?" said a voice overhead.

Police officer.

You could tell from the tone.

"Disappeared," someone said.

"Like a bleedin' ninja, or one of them magicians, like."

The sniffling kids were gone, led away by murmuring adults. You might call them traumatised, but not if you had seen what Josh had seen: in Africa, in Siberia, in post-Deathquake Japan.

Like claws.

He could not let go, that was the thing.

Like steel.

Only failure of will could stop him now, but the stubborn aggression that had kept him alive so many times before was active again. If only it had neared the surface earlier, he might have avoided the despairing stance on the bridge, hands on the rail as if contemplating the jump – *was I really thinking of it?* – leaving it to the emergency response centre of the brain, the amygdala, to react when the hand clapped his shoulder, and that was it: the

14

craziness that could have turned worse, into murder.

Black Thames beneath; but he would not let go.

Like steel.

Entering endurance-trance in order to survive.

There were voices in Suzanne's head, howling self-accusation. She was a neuropsych therapist and supposedly good at her job. It would not have taken expert verbal technique to short-circuit Josh's reaction, then lead him into a psychological space where he could grieve as he needed to.

Où es tu, Josh?

When her thoughts reverted to her native French, she was in trouble.

Calme-toi.

She needed to breathe, to calm down. There must be some way she could help Josh.

Call Tony.

She paused, thinking it through. Tony Gore had helped during last year's infiltration of the *Knife Edge* final. If the authorities were targeting her for surveillance… but she was not engaged in illegal activities now, and neither was Josh. She needed to make that call.

When she picked up the phone it showed a message waiting, but the pane read *Message from: Adam.* She minimised it.

"Call Tony," she told the phone.

"Which Tony, please?"

Merde.

"Call Tony Gore, urgent."

While she waited, she pointed the phone at the wallscreen, transferring the display. When Tony appeared, his face was larger than lifesize.

"Suzanne. Hey, doll. What's wrong?"

"I don't know for sure that it's bad."

"But you're ringing me at three in the morning, flagged urgent."

"It's Josh… Sophie died today."

Yesterday, technically. Was it really 3am?

"Hang on." Tony turned to one side. "Amber? Josh's daughter died."

There a swing of motion, and Amber, Tony's wife, was on screen, rubbing her face.

"Josh? Oh, Suzanne. Awful news. How is he?"

"He's distraught. It's why I needed to talk."

Amber blinked. As an ex-soldier's wife, she was used to hearing about tragedy and people going off the rails. The image tilted, then Tony was back on.

"What's he done, Suzanne?"

"Ran off into the night in thin clothes. Hours ago. Without his phone."

"Shit."

Civilian phones were DNA-tagged and GPS-linked, but people like Josh and Tony were not so easily found. Their handsets broadcast subversion code that altered the data inside the surveillance nets. Ordinary police could not have found Josh, even if they tried – which they would not, unless Suzanne used her authority to declare him at risk of self-harm.

Irrelevant. Josh had left his phone behind.

"Running is therapeutic," said Tony.

"It's been five hours."

Josh might still be running. During Tony's time in the Regiment, he had been able to run for longer than that. Josh had kept the discipline on leaving the army, that was all.

"What about his state of mind?"

"He was on the edge of losing it," said Suzanne. "Presenting all the signs. But how that might manifest, I couldn't tell."

Five hours ago.

"I'll call you back." Tony's face tightened. "Try to rest, sweetheart. Our Josh is a survivor."

"Yes…"

"Out."

The screen blanked out, as did her thoughts, leaving only feelings: sadness and fear, swirling together, corkscrewing through her body, unnerving her.

The Regiment was not perfect, but they had soldiering skills that others lacked for two reasons: training and resources. They could spend hours firing the latest weapons, using ten thousand euros worth of smartshells or nanofléchettes in a session. They could slip through enemy forces, because guile was a primary focus of their discipline, along with extreme physicality.

With hands like steel claws, he remained beneath the bridge.

Listen.

No one remained above, no humans, but spyballs and motion sensors were something else. He had escaped immediate capture; now it was time to evade the enemy.

Police. Not hostiles.

For his own sake, he needed to get clear, to think. Treat it as an exfiltration exercise through enemy territory, provided he remembered not to harm anyone who tried to arrest him. Things were bad enough already.

How could I screw up like that?

The answer was: reflex-fast, no conscious thought involved.

Shut up.

Pressing his tongue against the roof of his mouth, he stilled his mind.

When he moved, screams sounded, but only along his sinews as they cracked into motion. Then he was crawling to the end of the bridge – avoiding spycams – where he hung in place for minutes, before using counterpressure to climb around the end struts, then clamber onto the stairs.

He was in a surveillance blindzone.

An automated street-cleaning drone moved like a giant louse along the kerbside, its lights strobing orange. It would have anti-vandal countermeasures, but for urban infiltration the Regiment's training was all-inclusive: he knew how to avoid tripping the detectors.

Pre-dawn was smearing turquoise to the east. There was no foot traffic, no vehicle in sight besides the drone.

Now.

Two lunging steps and a shoulder-roll, and he was inside the carapace, clinging once more, squeezing his eyes to slits against the grit and noise.

Phase one of his evasion was under way.

There is an insomniac state of mind where someone thinks they are awake, while in fact tumbling through a series of microsleeps: undetected, unsatisfying, a safety mechanism for avoiding break-down. Suzanne flitted in and out of grey drowsiness, worrying about Josh, her knowledge of neurology no help at all.

When the door chime sounded, a rush of acid filled her stomach.

Josh.

But the wallscreen, switching to building surveillance, showed three bulky men on the landing outside her door. They had already passed through the locked ground-floor entrance. Two wore police uniform, while the third was dressed in a suit and overcoat.

"Adam?"

He had left a message on her phone, hadn't he?

"Oh, God."

She pressed the release, and electromag locks clicked open. When she pulled back the door, she blinked her sore eyes, un-able to read their expressions.

Bad news?

Adam said: "Can we come in, Suzanne?"

"Of… course. Yes."

She was panicking, but she could not speak freely in front of the uniformed officers, not unless she could be sure they knew who Adam Priest was: not a civil servant in the Department of Trade and Industry as his ID declared, but a serving officer in MI5.

"I'm Inspector Edwards." The larger officer held up his phone, showing the official sigil. After a second, it echoed on the wallscreen. "And this is Inspector Calvin."

The smaller man showed his ID the same way.

"Is Josh all right?" said Suzanne.

Inspector was a high rank; she was almost sure of it.

"Ma'am?"

"My... boyfriend. He's in a state of distress – his daughter died – and he went out running. I'm worried about him."

"And his name is Josh?"

"Josh Cumberland." She nodded towards Adam. "You can tell them, can't you?"

"I already have," said Adam. "I could tell *you* I'd just bumped into the officers by chance, but you probably wouldn't believe me."

Suzanne had no answer. There were implications here, but she was too tired to unravel them.

"Coffee, ma'am?" asked Inspector Calvin. "I could make some all round."

Suzanne said, "I'll just–"

"I'll do it." Inspector Calvin nodded towards the kitchen alcove. "No problem."

"Do you think he's in danger?" asked Adam.

"I'm afraid–" Suzanne blew out a breath. "He might turn that violence inwards."

Then she wondered whether she had heard correctly. Had Adam said he's *in* danger, or he's *a* danger? She closed her eyes, her nostrils feeling odd as she inhaled, dragging alertness into her mind.

Something was wrong, but not what she had feared.

"Where would he run?" said Adam. "Any particular place?"

Inspector Edwards was checking his phone. He was behind Suzanne, a gloomy reflection in the now-dark wallscreen. He looked up – at Adam? – and shook his head.

Adam's eyes gave the tiniest flicker.

Do they know each other?

"He likes exploring new routes," said Suzanne. "No special place."

"So is Josh very fit?" asked Adam. "I mean, the way he was in the military."

There had been a time, after last year's *Knife Edge* final, when Josh had been recuperating from cut- and stab-wounds: a snarling patient who was hell to live with as he forced himself back to full activity.

"He ran fifty kilometres last Sunday," said Suzanne.

"Some kind of marathon race?" Inspector Calvin was working the coffee machine. "I've always wanted to try that."

"Longer. But just a training run."

"By himself?" asked Adam. "That's disciplined."

"He is," said Suzanne.

From the microexpressions on the three men's faces, they disagreed. Their reactions were out of kilter, unless... unless Josh had done something. Not self-harm. Something else. Something not disciplined at all.

Josh. Please.

Vast reservoirs of energy inside him made Josh an electrifying athlete and lover; but the same energy could detonate as violence. Her memories of him fighting would have been awful, had she not used therapeutic techniques on herself, so that the images were distant, flattened, and blurred, losing their impact.

"Here you are, Dr Duchesne." Inspector Calvin had brought two mugs. "Mr Witten."

"Cheers," said Adam.

Suzanne looked. There were no other coffee mugs.

"Aren't you and your colleague–?"

"We'll leave you in peace, ma'am."

Inspector Calvin smiled at Adam, and said: "Steve."

"See you later, Ron."

The two men left. When they were gone, the flat's security system caused the electromag locks to snap home.

"Do police inspectors wear uniforms?" asked Suzanne. "I thought they were plainclothes."

"That's only the detectives," said Adam.

"Oh. But one of them called you Steve. Is that, what, a cover identity?"

"It's my real name. It's *Adam* that's my cover." Steve/Adam gave an asymmetric shrug. "Sorry."

"I thought Philip Broomhall was your friend."

"He is. He also knows me as Adam Priest, and I'd be grateful if you allow him to continue."

"But you're really… Steve Witten, is that it? And you don't work for the DTI."

"I think you knew that already." His face was lean, his grin cheeky, like a kid's. "You know, in China, it's no big deal. People change their names throughout their lives."

She realised there was no ring on his left hand.

Don't look at his finger.

Last year the wedding band had been white gold. Now there was only a depression in the skin.

"What's happened to Josh?" she said.

Adam – no, Steve – sipped from a retro mug labelled *Psychologists Do It Thoughtfully*. When he put the mug down, he kept his face blank.

"As far as I know, he's alive, uninjured, and somewhere on the streets of London."

"And what else?"

"I have a lot more to say, Suzanne. The thing is, I came here to ask for help. My timing may be awful, but I have to show you this."

He raised his phone and angled it towards the wallscreen.

"If this is official," said Suzanne, "then shouldn't you be checking for eavesdroppers, or something?"

"We already did." Steve/Adam's mouth twitched. "You're clean."

Dead people showed on screen.

"Oh, no," said Suzanne.

"Right," said Steve.

Sprawled, limbs angled and twisted, all of them teenagers, arranged in what might have been a circle before they slumped at random and died. Those with long-sleeved garments had the left sleeves pushed up, revealing inner forearms and the longitudinal gashes in soft flesh.

The pool of blood they lay in was almost black.

"Suicide pact." Suzanne felt phlegm in her throat. "Thirteen teenagers. With drugs or alcohol in their systems?"

"That's what the experts expected," said Steve.

"Oh. The post-mortem's been done?"

"A while back."

Suzanne could not look away. There was movement in the image, only because the camera's operator was alive and changing angles. The dead things on the floor would never move again, not of their own volition.

"Thirteen," she said. "Possibly a significant number."

"Besides being unlucky, are there any associations or meanings you know of?"

"I don't think so." Her face felt strange, tightening as if to weep, while her eyes were dry but stinging. "Thirteen dead kids. Awful."

"No." Sad and soft, Steve's voice lowered. "Not thirteen."

"I make it–"

"One hundred and sixty-two," he said. "We thought when it reached thirteen times thirteen, the deaths would stop. Today we found out we were wrong."

"Oh, God. Oh no."

So many teenagers, unaware that their isolation was shared by billions, including every adult in the past, for everyone lives through it. Or takes the despairing way out.

"We've done everything to keep this quiet," said Steve. "That's why, if you agree to help, you'll need to sign the Official–"

"Keep it *quiet*?"

"Yes. To stop it spreading."

Suzanne blinked at the awfulness on screen.

"That's impossible. Burying news like this."

"You'd be surprised, but it's not easy."

Awful, awful, awful.

"Thought contagion," she said. "Memetic cascade. A crazy idea that spreads like a fad."

"That's what we think."

"Spreading even though you've buried the news."

"Right." Steve's voice was like grating bones. "And when it gets out, what's going to happen then?"

That was the worst thought of all.

"An epidemic," said Suzanne.

Whenever a suicide is reported in the news, fatal traffic accidents increase, because they are not truly accidents. Even the death wish is contagious.

"Exactly."

"A suicide epidemic."

Steve said nothing.

I didn't even know your real name.

And now this, when Josh was gone, and surely needed her. *Yet you expect me to help.*

Their flesh was white-grey in the image. Every eye was opaque, creamy with death as proteins decayed.

"I'll do what I can," she said.

Because she did not have a job – she had a calling, and helping people was it.

I have to.

For the first time in years, the silver scars on her arms began to burn.

[THREE]

Tottenham Court Road, and the crowds were thinning out. In an alley between a small cinema and a block of shops, four black-garbed employees were smoking from ganja masks and shooting up nicotine. As Josh passed the opening, they began to stow away their gear, ready to go back inside.

An opportunity.

He loitered in a surveillance blindspot until they entered the building. Then he ran with a loping stride to the closing emergency door.

And caught it before the gap closed.

Good.

He was crouched, but rising would take him into a spyball's field of view. Shifting his weight, he jammed one foot into the opening, then pulled off his tracksuit top. He flung the garment up, obscuring the lens, then rolled inside, grabbing the top as it fell.

Now he was in. Pulling on the top, he continued down a bleak corridor, into the heart of the cinema. The recording of his entry would be suspicious but not definitive. Alert for more spyballs, he entered a plusher corridor, where paying customers would tread.

A small red sign shone:

CINEMA 4, NOW SHOWING: THE KOBRA MANIFESTO

He slipped inside and found a seat. The sparse audience was mostly white-haired. Senior citizens' matinee.

On the viewstage, the GoogleHoloMovies logo faded, as an old guy shook his head, presumably at the inaccuracy. All 3-D movies played out in a magnetically contained volume of sparklemist, though holographic cameras were sometimes used in the recording.

Josh closed his eyes as the music began, and allowed himself to sleep. At some point he woke to see terrorists on an airliner and the hero in action, but exhaustion overcame his interest – he had enjoyed all but one of the others in the series – and he slept once more.

Then the lights came up, and everyone was getting out of their seats, heading for the exit. Staff members stood by, ready to clean up spilled popcorn or cicada crumbs.

Better go.

He could slip into another showing, but that would also end at some time. His short sleep was enough for now. Out into the foyer, then the brightness of the street, he walked with his head down and gait altered, trying to keep to blindzones, wondering where he might steal some food.

In enemy territory, survival is a function of skill and opportunism.

"We call them Cutter Circles," said Steve, formerly Adam.

It was a descriptive term, yet it failed to capture the pressure of grief inside Suzanne's head, like fingers squeezing her brain. Each image was worse than the previous: group after group of teenagers, thirteen in every circle, each with their left radial artery sliced longitudinally open by the person next to them.

She tried to imagine the emotional atmosphere in each location at the moment the victims cut each other.

They would have synchronised the cutting, making the incision righthanded in their neighbour's flesh at the same time as a blade pierced their own left inner forearm.

What about Josh?

She rubbed her cheekbone and eye.

"I'm sorry. I can't concentrate."

Outside the window, snow was falling again.

"So much for summer," she added.

"Josh attacked someone," said Steve.

"*What?*"

Steve had almost coughed out the words, as if giving up a struggle to hold them in.

"There's surveillance footage" – he held up his hand – "which I can *not* show you, OK? But someone innocently touched Josh's shoulder, and he reacted with a potentially lethal strike."

"Oh, no."

"When the man was down, Josh took out a knife, which the bystanders misinterpreted but were wise enough to stand clear of. Josh used it to perform an emergency tracheotomy."

Suzanne tried to visualise the scene.

"He saved the man?"

"With the aid of a trumpet mouthpiece. How bizarre is that? He's resourceful, which is why the police can't find him. Neither can we."

Suzanne walked to the wallscreen, then turned her back to it.

"Why are you here?" she said.

"For the obvious reason. Our own experts aren't getting anywhere on Cutter Circles. I want you on board as a civilian consultant. It's not unknown."

"And I have to sign the Official Secrets Act. I got that. I don't respond to blackmail."

Steve shook his head.

"I'll do everything I can to kill charges against Josh. Regardless of what you choose."

"Hmm. Clever."

"Look, it's that or I make it conditional on your assistance. Those are my choices, so I'm going for the more benign. Whether you call it friendship or manipulation is up to you, Dr Duchesne. I'm helping Josh either way."

She had to agree.

"I'm tired," she said, hoping he would leave soon. "But tell me, how do the groups communicate?"

"The Circles? We don't know."

"What do they have in common? Forums, even passive websites. What's the common factor?"

"We don't know."

"It's the first thing you should—"

"Well, that's sort of my point, Suzanne. We're good at this, and we're getting nowhere."

"Oh."

Her phone vibrated, then stopped. Steve held up his own handset.

"You've now got directions to Thames House, plus an entry pass to get you in."

She blinked.

"It's that easy to get inside spy HQ?"

"Only through the front door. If you were an enemy, you wouldn't want to be there."

"I see."

"We need you, Suzanne."

If she were less tired, she might read his microexpressions and gauge the harmonics of his voice, and determine just how personal this request was.

One hundred and sixty-two dead teenagers.

She would have to do it.

Josh. Be OK.

If he was with her, she could do the work more easily; but she would do it regardless.

"I'll help," she said.

And so, a refuge.

It was called going to ground, and he did so with supplies – stolen food, bottled water and plastic bags – plus a phone but no torch. By the phone's light, he set things up. At some point, an attenuated pitter-patter sounded, then stopped as he looked up. Twin glitters reflected in his direction.

Mouse.

Josh gave his fellow lurker a silent salute, then got back to his hacking. Since Web 3.0, every apparent hyperlink was a bidirectional XLink, which formed part of his reverse-search strategy. There was a backdoor into MetNet that he had found last year – when Sergeant Petra Osbourne slipped one of his querybots into the system – and that also helped. But he was not running a surveillance sweep, not this time.

He was trying to determine whether anyone else was running a sweep, with himself as the target.

Working with a reflected clone of his best querybot, he created success parameters, and set a selection framework running. Species-oriented programming could take many iterations before useful code evolved. He would leave it to cook.

When he shut down the phone, his hiding place was in darkness, even the mouse unseen.

Sophie.

Closing his eyes made her face clearer, her eyes like tunnels into void.

Why did you leave me, Daddy?

He could not allow himself to cry.

Steve left soon after extracting Suzanne's promise to come in to Thames House at the start of next week. Alone in the flat, Suzanne tried autohypnosis and listening to music, but no more than a few microsleeps resulted. She gave up and made herself a cappuccino.

Maybe I'll sleep well tonight.

If Josh was found. Or not. What she ought to hope for was his continuing invisibility, meaning he was free, even if she had no way to help him.

I need your hugs, Josh Cumberland.

It had always been two-way support, their relationship. Instead, what she ought to do was talk to a friend, and Carol Klugmann was first choice. But that needed a phone, and if it was here in front of her, then she was hallucinating over it, because she could not see it.

"If I was my phone, where would I be?"

She went into the bedroom, then froze. There was no phone on either bedside table. Her own, she might have misplaced – but Josh's phone had been right there on his side of the bed.

Bastards.

One of the police inspectors, probably Calvin with his friendly smile, had taken it away. Or were they police? Maybe they worked for Steve – MI5 operators with the ability to pass for police officers, down to official ID.

She had been going to buy Josh an emotifone for Midsummer Christmas. Would he even be back by next month?

You have to come back.

Or was he out of her life forever?

She went back into the lounge. Her phone was on the floor beside the couch, where she had already looked.

Josh. I don't want you in prison.

Maybe he ought to stay lost.

Every choice is awful.

She called Carol.

"Girlfriend, what is it?" was Carol's greeting.

"Josh is... Carol?"

"I'll be right there." As always, Carol's round, sensual face was warm. Her modulated Texan tones were melted chocolate. "You are at home, right?" she added.

"Yes."

"Then Auntie Carol will be with you soon. Just breathe."

"Thank you."

"I'll bring cream cakes."

"I don't–"

"For me, anyhow. I know what your kitchen's like."

Suzanne half-sobbed. "Sorry," she said.

"Breathe. Forget the cakes, I'm coming now."

"Th–"

The phone display darkened.

Thank you, Carol.

She was not alone in her life. But to open her defences the way she had with Josh and then for this to happen–

"*Bâtard!*"

And then she cried.

[FOUR]

Carlsen did not like the poster-sized pictures of himself that advertised the place, but other than that his gym and even this too-small overstuffed office were perfect. His media image was modest, sort of, but he still did not take it seriously: Fireman Carlsen was the famous fighter, while he himself was a human being, Matt to his family and closest friends.

He farted.

"See? Only human."

There was no one in the office to hear him. From the gym next door sounded the thumps of training. Good.

Sorry, Zak. I'm going to say no.

Forty years old meant he was entering his fifth decade of life. He was the oldest fighter in the Knifefight Challenge Federation. On screen, his flat-chested, muscular physique looked harder and denser than a decade earlier; and the secret was simple: he loved lifting weights, running, grappling, and weaponwork.

The simple life.

It could get even simpler.

Just run the gym and train his fighters, and let the next generation have the arena and the fun. Some people would say it was time he grew up. Engineering degrees including a Master's from Imperial, and he fought for a living.

Except maybe it was time to stop.

While I still love it.

His desktop beeped and glowed, becoming a display screen. Zak Tyndall's features sharpened into view.

"Captain Invincible," he said. "You know your fans need you."

Tyndall was CEO of the Federation. His father Zebediah had stepped back from day-to-day control of other companies within Tyndall Industries, handing everything over to Zak. But the Knifefight Challenge Federation had always been Zak's baby.

"Captain Getting-Older," said Carlsen. "Captain Standing-Back-To-Let-The-Younger-Guys-Develop."

"Maybe next season. After last year" – Zak meant the abortive *Knife Edge* final – "we need to get back on an even keel. Don't you agree?"

The last sentence sounded more like a statement, and Carlsen found himself nodding in time with Zak.

"You sure need to get it kickstarted."

This year's reality show should have commenced three months ago, but the whole thing had been in doubt. Now it seemed Zak was pushing ahead.

"How better," said Zak, "than with two legends of the fight game coaching the two teams?"

"Legends."

"You and Jason Krill, my man."

"Krill?" said Carlsen. "No. He's a fighter all right, but a *coach*? He'll cut his team to pieces."

"He'll have good assistants," said Zak. "As will you, but in your case just to lighten the workload a little. You'll be in training too, of course."

Carlsen wanted to say no.

"What assistants?" he asked instead. "For Krill, I mean."

"Dan Schaeffer for weapons and trapping, Lewis Chiang for

kickboxing, Dmitri Yushenko for sambo and conditioning."

"Nice."

"While you can have anyone you want."

Carlsen stared up to one side.

I could back out now.

But in his mind's eye, he saw a big, bearded man with a loud laugh.

"That bloody Viking," he said. "Without Siggy, I'm not doing it."

"Funnily enough," said Zak, "Sigmund said the same to me. That he'd come on the show provided you were the coach."

"Well."

It would be good to work with Sigmund again.

I'm addicted, and Zak's the main pusher in town.

Hooked on adrenaline and blood. Fighting legal and capable opponents.

"So, Matt," said Zak. "Shall I send the contract to your lovely lawyers?"

"Don't bully them too much, Zak. They earn a millionth of what you do."

"Then you're on board for the new season?"

Carlsen felt his back muscles flare. "I'm on board."

"Welcome back, Captain Invincible."

"Thanks, Zak."

The desktop reset to blank opacity.

Nothing like being decisive.

He had known Zak was going to call, and had made a swift and irreversible decision, just as imagined – except it was the opposite decision.

I belong here.

Not just in the arena, but going through the daily sweat in the fight gym, pushing himself always, because fighting was not just a process – it was where he lived.

Home.

• • • •

Suzanne went out with Carol, via a coffee-and-cake shop to a tourist site she had often seen but never entered: the London Eye. Their capsule was nearing the apex of its circular journey when everything shuddered to a halt. Several people yelped. Others among the men glanced at Carol's voluptuous form jiggling with the movement. Then they collected themselves, and peered out through the plexiglass, checking for signs of catastrophic failure.

High up in the air, high enough to see across the city, and now it had stopped. It was nothing to do with people climbing into or descending from a capsule at ground level – they did so while the Wheel continued to move at its normal slow pace.

Some of their fellow passengers were pale and beginning to shiver.

"Maybe," said Carol, "we got us some phobias to cure."

"We could tell them not to think of the framework twisting and screeching as it collapses," said Suzanne. "Or the screaming from the capsules as they drop."

Her sense of humour was back. Or maybe it was unconscious pretence: let Carol think that the session at home had been everything she needed to regain calm and not worry about Josh.

"I'm thinking about those cream doughnuts."

"I don't think the difference in weight," said Suzanne, "is actually relevant here."

"No, I mean the ones I *didn't* eat this morning. Happiness postponed ain't nothing much when there's no *later*, see?"

"Like all those men" – Suzanne nodded around the capsule – "that you haven't been to bed with yet."

"And thrown away spent," said Carol.

"You're going to hell, you know."

"If it existed, I surely would be."

Outside and below, London resembled Moscow in winter: caked snow, Thames like steel.

A woman screamed, half a second before the capsule jolted.

This time, it oscillated, like the dipping of a boat in a swell.

Suzanne and Carol moved forward together.

"We're going to–" started the woman.

"Eventually," said Carol. "You'll look back on this and laugh, or you can do it now, because this is my friend Suzanne–"

Holding out her hand as if to shake, Suzanne drew close to the woman, whose own hand came up in reflexive response.

"–who would like you to–"

Twisting the outstretched hand, no pain involved, Suzanne pressed it against the woman's face and said: "Sleep."

"–and our voice will go with you as–"

Suzanne took over, following Carol's words.

"…you go deeper and deeper into this relaxed state…"

"–here and now as the muscles in your face and neck relax and–"

"…your shoulders become soft because with each breath in you take…"

The run-on sentences with ambiguous words – *here* and *now* formed a command to listen, marked out with shifting tones – created a powerful induction of trance. Under fMRI, the woman's brain would show profound change: the precuneus nucleus in overdrive, the anterior cingulate taking a rest.

Suzanne and Carol began speaking in parallel, not sequence.

"–descending deeper into the security of your ground self because–"

"…full circle as life carries you and supports you…"

"–everything fine as you let go of old behaviours you have done for the last time–"

They circled the woman, like witches or shamanic healers from some tribal era, while their technique was a modern re-boot based on neuroscience and psycholinguistics. Then they stood still, and Suzanne recited an abbreviated story about finding confidence – into the woman's left ear for right-brain processing – while Carol gave explicit instructions.

"–because you are always in control–"

Suzanne guessed the woman might be an artist, maybe an inveterate reader who was used to getting lost in a book, intelligent and imaginative enough to enter trance fast.

Then they brought her back to wakefulness.

"–rise up like a balloon–"

"…five…"

"–for you can–"

"…three…"

"–know how to have–"

"…one!"

"–won!"

The woman's face was shining when she opened her eyes. Her smile, directed at everyone, radiated charisma. Many of the group appeared relaxed – affected by the trancework – while others stared at the woman, surprised at the change in her appearance.

"I've never seen anything like–"

Then there was a lurch, and the woman laughed as the capsule restarted its motion.

Carol winked at Suzanne.

"Once we're down, we need to return to that coffee shop."

"For those cream doughnuts," said Suzanne.

"No, for that barista guy that served us. You think he can handle the hot stuff? Think his nozzle can take it?"

"Going to hell, Dr Klugmann."

"I certainly hope so, Dr Duchesne."

A yell and a thump sounded from beyond his office wall. A big throw, cleanly executed. Maybe Little Pete slamming Big Andy into the mat. Carlsen smiled, stabbed his thumb at the desk display – sealing the agreement – and sent it back to his lawyers. Then he ambled out into the gym.

Blue mats, hanging bags, scarred dummies. Racks of weights: dumb-bells, and fixed barbells stood on end. Battered kettlebells. Leather jump-ropes coiled on shelves alongside armour. Weapon cupboards, still locked: the fighters had brought their own training knives.

A dozen fighters were working out, including his hardcore regulars who helped with the teaching.

"I'm an old man," he said, "trying to kip in his office. Can't you keep the noise down?"

"Sorry, Boss." Big Andy whipped Little Pete into the mat. "My bad."

Angie, a length of rattan cane in either hand, called: "Matt needs his beauty sleep." Then she got back to work on the reaction dummy, her arms like whips, snaking around attack-cables flicked out by the dummy.

"If anyone needs beauty sleep" – Little Pete shot in low, his hands hooked behind Big Andy's knees, driving forwards – "that's Matt for sure."

Big Andy slammed back, scissoring his legs around Little Pete's waist, using his hands to parry the downward hammer fists. It was the guard position, dangerous with knives involved – you offered up the femoral arteries – but workable if you knew what you were doing.

Both men were barbarians on the weights, built like monsters. Big Andy's massive legs squeezed, targeting Little Pete's kidneys.

"Good work," said Carlsen.

From his office a beep sounded. Incoming call. He had powered off his desk system, but his phone was still hooked up to it. Never mind. He let the sound fade from his attention as he focused on the *tat-bang-tat, tat-bang-tat* of Joey working fist-and-knife combos on the bag, the *da-da-da, da-da-da* of Olga making the speed-ball dance, the crash as Saul dropped his deadlift bar. Pete and Andy grunting as they rolled. The whoosh of escrima sticks: Angie's high-speed patterns as they cut through air.

Little Pete passed Big Andy's guard – good timing – to attack from side mount with a knee to the ribs, then switching as Andy defended, whipping his legs around to enclose that massive neck, trapping one arm: a classic triangle choke, misnamed because it targeted the carotid artery, which made it a strangle.

Andy's hand, trapped under his own body, fluttered. His eyes rolled back.

"He tapped," called Carlsen.

"Oh." Little Pete rolled clear. "Sorry, pal."

Big Andy was having a little snooze.

"I've got him."

Angie sat him upright and began massaging the back of his neck. At the same time, a wailing sounded from Carlsen's office.

"That'll be the phone," said Little Pete.

Big Andy's eyelids fluttered.

"Woke him up, anyhow." Carlsen headed across the mats. "Let's find out who it is."

Only eight people were able to call him with the high-priority status that the wailing tone indicated. Inside the office, he transferred the display to the desktop screen, and opened the link.

"Hey, big bro."

She did not sound happy.

"Inge." Carlsen stared at his sister. "How's the arsehole?"

But Inge shook her head. Her ex was not the problem.

"Kat didn't come home last night. Stayed with a friend and didn't call me."

"Where is she now?"

"In school. It's not like–Bloody hell, Matt. She's not dropped out or run away, but it's like we're disconnected, you know?"

"I did worse when *I* was fifteen. You might remember."

"Yeah." She sniffed, and her mouth twitched. "You did. But you were like clear-headed on the inside, wild on the outside."

"Wild."

"You straightened up. I don't think Kat's got your strength."

Some people might think his current life was far from sane. But his discipline was immense.

"She'll sort herself out."

"*Scheisse.*" Inge sounded like an echo of their mother. "I don't think so. Not without help."

"You want me to talk to her?"

In the desktop image, Inge rubbed her face.

"She looks up to you."

"Then I'll be there, but not without payment."

The twitch in Inge's mouth extended to a partial smile.

"Curry or sweet and sour?"

"You choose."

"See you later, bro."

"Later."

The desktop blanked out.

"Bloody hell, Kat," he said. "Don't you go making my mistakes."

From outside came the sound of his fighters training.

Discipline. That's the difference.

His best friend, and he took it everywhere. But how could he persuade his niece of that?

Or I could just listen to her. Lead by example.

Whatever Inge cooked would be soya-based, for his sake. At around the same age as Kat was now, even before his army days, he had discovered Shaolin monks who lived and taught in a damp brick building in the heart of Brixton. They had shown him how peace-loving vegetarians could be hard, muscular bastards and pitiless fighters.

He had been trying to live up to their ideals ever since.

Some day, I'll get it right.

A yell and a thump sounded, and he grinned.

[FIVE]

"Remember Button B?" Steve Witten's grandfather used to ask. "Or how '1001 cleans a big, big carpet, for less than half a crown'?"

As a boy, Steve always shook his head.

"Of course not," Grandad would say. "You'll hardly remember phone boxes, and definitely not real money like thruppenny bits. Never mind the little details, like the brown flex cord, or the directory on the shelf, back when you could trust people not to steal them."

Grandad's point had been that the mass of detail surrounding everyone evaporates over time. Now, from the back seat as his car passed Parliament, Steve thought about continuity in a changing world, and whether his profession was the best use of his life.

He himself could remember television with remote controls, pushing the red button, earrings, nose-studs, *Little Britain* on the telly, rap on the radio – God, radios – train tickets, station barriers, Oyster cards, ASBOs, happy slapping, girl gangs, Islamic terrorists, Mars bars, shirts worn outside trousers, running shoes as fashion, knives in schoolyards – well, that still happened – racism, Bluetooth, bookshops serving coffee, petrol pumps, air miles, ballpoint pens, Post-it Notes, stamps, licking envelopes, Jelly Babies, golf, child-rapist priests, *Big Brother*, kebabs, dancing the macarena, and pigeons in Trafalgar Square.

All of them were gone, and he was pushing forty, not eighty.

How far did things have to change before he was no longer fighting for the country he grew up in? Of all the things that had disappeared, he missed only bookshops with coffee, and maybe Jelly Babies. Among the things that younger people took for granted, eating insects was the worst.

In the back seat beside him, Trin was munching a toffee cicada. Seeing him look, she offered the open bag.

"Revolting habit," he said.

"Nutritious. Likewise tasty."

"If you say so."

She was his number two, and he trusted her.

"Locust breath," he added.

"I'll eat a mint before we go in."

"If it turns McIntosh's stomach as much as mine," he said, "feel free to breathe all over her."

Trin leaned forward to the driver. "You didn't hear that, Carl."

"Sorry?" Carl shrugged. "I missed that. Someone was crunching cicadas. Nasty."

Steve smiled. "Good man."

They drove past the Admiralty Building, then turned into a cobbled courtyard out of sight from the street. Carl stopped, braked, then double-checked.

"Secure," he said.

Among the cobbles, cracks appeared: a jagged loop, as if they were parked on a huge jigsaw piece. Then the ensemble began to descend.

"I love this bit," added Carl.

"Me too," said Steve.

Trin put away her bag of cicadas.

"Boys," she said.

"Thunderbirds are go." Steve noticed Trin's expression. "Never mind."

Once in the underground garage, Carl drove slowly, and pulled up near a bank of lifts. Ceiling-mounted guns swivelled. After a moment, Steve opened his door and got out. Trin exited from her side.

The lift in which they descended looked ordinary, save for the nozzles overhead, the rows of tiny holes at waist- and ankle-height, and the lack of controls: you went to whichever floor Security decided. When they stopped, the doors opened on to a blue-carpeted corridor.

Steve and Trin walked side by side to the seventh ceramic door on the left, waited two seconds as it slid open – it could slam shut much faster – and entered the small outer office.

Flora McIntosh's secretary looked up from his desk display.

"Please go right in, Mr Witten."

"Thank you."

They went through.

McIntosh was sitting behind her desk. Steve positioned one of the visitor's chairs and sat opposite her, while Trin took a flanking position to his left.

"Special Branch arrested a member of Tyndall Industries yesterday," said McIntosh.

"Really?"

"You're paid to have your finger on the pulse, aren't you, Steve?"

"If you mean Briggs, then I'm sure our boys had compelling evidence to set up an arrest."

"Where would they have got it from?"

"I couldn't tell you," said Steve.

It was true. He could not tell McIntosh what he had done, or he would be censured, putting his job at risk. Mind games like this helped to subvert whatever sensors, perhaps in the chair, might be observing him.

"The Home Secretary has enough on his plate," said McIntosh, "without worrying about our foremost corporation suffering body blows. Not when they're trying to launch the programme that will stave off the Dark Ages."

"You mean the nuclear reactors," said Steve.

"I mean the power stations that will keep this country running when everything else gives out."

The past year's global freeze had resulted in greater energy demands, while many of the alternative sources failed to cope with the new conditions: witness frozen turbines on the Thames.

"If our other strategies had been better planned," he said, "with more quality, more quantity and more time, we would not be in a panic."

"Our predecessors' shortsightedness," said McIntosh, "is off the point."

"It's our own foresight that concerns me. Too much, too fast, starting too late."

McIntosh stared.

"You will keep your hands off Tyndall Industries."

"Yes, ma'am."

Briggs, now under arrest, had been a director of two major companies within the corporation. His dealings with African politicians had come into the open, and while the majority of the laws he had broken were not British, some were. Whether the case would reach court, that was another matter. Already, lawyers were in action.

That the Tyndalls were major contributors to the incumbent LabCon Party, via personal and corporate donations, ought to have no bearing on the Crown Prosecution Service's ability to bring the case, or on the resources available to the investigating officers. But if Steve had not briefed Special Branch contacts via back channels, they could never have made the move.

And even if they succeeded, Briggs would be a scapegoat who deserved what he got, but the bastard Tyndalls, father and son, would once more have demonstrated that different standards applied to them. To the rich and corrupt.

"You've been quiet." McIntosh turned to Trin. "Are you here as a silent observer? Say nothing, do what you're told?"

"I was just wondering, ma'am."

"Wondering what?"

"Whether you have a sister called Fauna." Trin showed no expression. "Just a thought."

McIntosh held still.

And laughed.

"I like you," she said. "I might take an interest in your career from now on."

Trin nodded.

"All right." McIntosh turned to Steve. "What's this thing you're working on now?"

"The Cutter Circles," said Steve. "Suicide cult, if only we could find a cult. We're backing the official police investigation, assuming police identities as required. Only two commanders know about our involvement."

"So you've called off your anti-Tyndall crusade?"

"There's no crusade, and my team is working on this one operation, nothing else. The nation's teenagers are dying, and no one knows why."

"You want to keep the country safe."

This conversation was on new ground.

"Yes," he said.

"So do I. Believe me, I grew up with the same negative associations to nuclear reactors as you did." McIntosh pressed her hands atop the desk. "Civil breakdown would be worse, when the energy fails."

"We have something in common, then."

"Don't we just," said McIntosh.

"We're both patriots."

"In point of fact, yes."

● ● ● ●

It was dark and there was no one to hear besides the mouse. Josh worked his Hindu push-ups in near silence all the same. The squats would be more challenging, but so long as he used the phone's inbuilt scanner, he could stop if someone entered within earshot.

Sometimes, an observation post required you to lie still for a couple of days. At least here he could keep his body in condition, provided he was careful.

The body is like iron.

In his head, he sounded out the training chant.

The more that you beat it…

It was a way to keep the rhythm.

…the harder it becomes.

His motion was fluid, powerful, and without pause.

Suzanne cancelled her appointments for the next few days. None of her clients was suicidal or otherwise at risk. If they had been, she would have passed them over to Carol. For herself, she could not summon the kind of resourceful mood that was required for her work.

It was on the fifth evening since Josh's disappearance that Tony Gore and Big Tel came to visit. The door chime made her flinch, but she recognised them on the security display. By the time the two guys entered, she had made herself calm.

"Hey, Suze," said Tony. "There's no news, but we thought we'd pop in, all right?"

She double-secured the door with mag locks, because they would expect her to. Tony waved his phone around.

"All clear," he said.

"But you haven't found him yet?"

"Sorry," said Tony.

Big Tel winked.

"He'll be all right, babe. He really will."

"I hope so."

"If we had news to get to *him*," said Tony, "have you any idea how we'd do it?"

Inside her, something tightened.

"What do you mean?"

"He ever mention anything like that?"

"I'd have thought you guys" – she looked from Tony to Tel and back – "would have communication arrangements."

"We do," said Tony. "I've dropped a message in a couple of places, but I don't think he's looked."

She realised Tel was staring at her.

"You need some grub, Doc. You got anything in the kitchen?"

"I don't–Probably."

"And a cuppa," said Tony. "We all need a cuppa, and a sit-down."

"Oh." Suzanne waved at the couch and chair. "Of course."

Trained to observe social interaction, and take part or take control as appropriate, she felt clumsy today, wrong-footed in the guys' presence. Good job they were friends.

You are Josh's friends, aren't you?

The military induced extreme loyalty to the people you served alongside. That much she had learned from Josh. What he had learned from her was a deeper appreciation of the army's training methods: marching as a form of hypnosis, human-shaped targets as cognitive-behavioural desensitization, combat discipline as operant conditioning. He showed no signs of resentment based on his increased understanding.

Tel carried over a plate of cheese-and-tomato rolls and mugs of tea.

"Never make a decision on an empty stomach," he said. "Assuming you can help it."

"That's a very sensible rule," said Tony. "What have you done with the real Big Tel?"

"Sensible is my middle name."

"In between *never* and *at all*, I presume."

Their presence was very… masculine. Also relaxed and protective. She felt webs of tension ease inside her.

"I think I'm hungry," she said.

The tea and roll were good – basic but good – and she was
warm inside and thinking clearly by the time she finished.

"You see the hardcopy books over there?" She pointed to a
shelf. "Sun Tzu's *The Art of War*. If you flick through it, you'll
find a coffee-stained page. Just the one."

Tony put down his mug and fetched the thin volume, flicking through until he found the page.

"Keep following the lines down," said Suzanne, "converting
characters into digits – A into 0, B into 1, C into 2 – until you
have a full IP address. Anything over J, you count again, like
K is 0, L is 1."

Big Tel was grinning.

"Smart," he said. "Modulo 10. Is that everything?"

"Then it's slash, followed by the Japanese for roundhouse
kick, which I keep forgetting. You can look it up on–"

"*Mawashi geri*," said Tony.

"What he said." Big Tel raised his tea mug in toast.

"But Josh told me I could only ever use it once. That's why
I haven't–I mean, I was saving it in case I needed to tell him
something specific. He must know I need him back."

Tel leaned over and patted her knee. It was maybe the least
sexual gesture she had ever received.

"He's not daft."

Tony, with an unfurled keypad, was working his phone,
glancing at *The Art of War*. His fingers moved fast. Then he shut
everything down, folded up the keypad, put it back in his
pocket, and Velcroed his phone to his wristband.

"Let's hope he checks that one." He looked at Tel. "Meanwhile, we've got a task to carry out."

"I'm ready," said Tel.

"What is it?" asked Suzanne. "Something to do with Josh?"

Tony shook his head.

"We'd rather not say."

She took that as a Yes. Also as a request not to press for details.

"Good luck," she said.

"Good planning," said Tony. "But we'll take the luck as well."

"Ta lots." Big Tel winked.

"Thank for the tea and food," she said.

"Yeah. You look after yourself while we're not here, right?"

Suzanne, still sitting, gave them a salute.

"I promise."

It was a shame that hospitals needed security. Standing in a parking alcove, clad in dark blue, Tony was invisible to the guards walking past with stun-batons on their hips, and to the spyballs overhead. The images they were recording were not reality.

Big Tel's taxi had slowed long enough for him to slip out. By the time Tel returned, Tony planned to be back in position for pick-up. Meanwhile, it was time to act as if this were the old days. He entered a space between two buttresses, checked his gekkomere gauntlets, then pressed himself into the corner where two walls met, and pulled himself up.

In the Regiment, he had climbed with heavy equipment. Nowadays, there was bulk around his waist, not strapped on his back; but the strength was still there. He ascended using counterpressure as much as the technology, reaching the fourth-floor window in decent time.

Same old drill. Easy.

He touched his phone, and the window's electromag locks clicked open. A tug, then a sideways roll took him over the sill and down to the floor, where he crouched.

No nurses, doctors, patients or guards in sight. Likewise no police officers.

Then voices sounded.

Two men.

So there were police on duty, further down the corridor. But he was already inside their line of defence. He scanned as he moved, finding no more obstacles, and pushed open the door to the private room. Monitors were beeping, so he closed the door before the changing sound level alerted the officers.

The man in the bed did not react.

Wakey, wakey, you fucker.

Tony had two daughters, Pearl and Jade, and there was no hesitation when he slipped the black-bladed commando dagger from its sheath and pressed the point into the supine man's throat.

"*Ugh…*"

"If you press charges, I'll be back to press this in." Tony twisted the dagger. "You know what I'm talking about, don't you, fucker?"

"N– yes."

The voice sounded odd because of the tube in the front of the throat.

Too bad.

There was a closet alcove with no door. The bastard's Santa outfit was hanging there beside his normal clothes.

"Did you think no one would find out what you are?"

"N-no."

Urine-scent wafted upward.

Danger.

He spun, dagger before him, as the door opened. The man who came in was dressed like himself, with the addition of a hood that failed to hide his features. Tiger stripes covered the left side of his face. The man looked from Tony to the figure in the bed.

"H-how many?" Fear laced the voice from the bed. "What are you–?" The bastard sniffed. He was crying.

"You've told him," said the stranger, "what'll happen if he presses charges over a certain incident on a bridge?"

"Yeah," said Tony.

"Mind if I say my piece?"

"Go ahead."

Tony moved to one side, still alert, as the newcomer took the patient's throat between his gloved thumb and fingers.

"Stay silent, and never misbehave again." A squeeze. "Ever."

"*Ugh.*"

"Good." The man with the half tiger-face released his grip, stepped back, and nodded to Tony. "Nice meeting you."

"Likewise."

Tiger Face slipped out first. Tony looked at the sobbing shape in the bed, then exited.

The other guy's feet were visible in a gap in the corridor ceiling. Then he was out of sight, and a tile moved back in place. Nice work. Crawling through ceiling spaces and air ducts was as easy as it looked in webmovies, but doing it *in silence* was near-impossible. The bastard things amplified sound.

He listened, but Tiger Face was good: not even the faintest thump.

Then Tony headed back to the window he had used, slipped over the sill, and fastened it in place. All done. Descending was easier than climbing. In what seemed like seconds he was back on the ground, in shadow.

Grinning because of the unexpected encounter, while another part of him raged inside, because the bastard in the bed deserved to die.

Not now. Not here.

He had a rendezvous to make with Tel.

Pearl. Jade. If anything happened to you–

And he had a family to go home to.

In the bed, Federico's finger trembled over the call button. Those bloody coppers were supposed to be on guard, weren't they?

"I was only looking."

The monitors flickered and beeped as before.

Since the last time, since they had let him out... he had not done anything, besides look and think the thoughts he could not help.

The door swung inward.

They've come back to finish me off.

But it was one of the police officers, not those ninja bastards or whatever.

"Officer," he forced out. "There were two–"

A big hand smacked against his forehead.

"I can hurt you without leaving a mark," said the officer. "Strangle you with a pillow, maybe."

"No."

"But I forgot. You're rehabilitated, aren't you?"

"Y-yes."

"Watch the steps when you're discharged. It's real easy to fall down and break something."

Federico was pissing himself again.

Like when he was a kid, and Father came in to, to–

"Or you could just kill yourself," said the policeman.

And reached down to twist.

It hurts.

And continued. By the time the policeman left, suicide had never been so attractive.

I'm despicable.

When they let him out of here, he would do it.

It'll stop everything.

Perhaps he would even use the Millennium Bridge. It would almost be poetic.

And the awfulness would end.

[SIX]

Sitting in darkness, this was what Josh read on the *mawashigeri* page:

YOUR VICTIM A KNOWN PAEDOPHILE.

He had expected a plea from Suzanne, not this.

PROSECUTION UNLIKELY.

It was signed *T*, which was non-specific, but he would bet on Tony Gore. The sender had attached large files, so Josh received them into a secure, sandboxed cache, opened the manifest file, and used introspective dissection bots to compare the stated contents to what was there. Everything seemed in order, so he ran the code, finding police records for one Federico Ryan, whose personal history was an ongoing tragedy that he dragged onto victims of his own, instead of finding the strength to fight his past.

But there was an addendum that worried Josh. There were two versions of a video log – each containing six segments, from different viewpoints – showing the incident on the bridge, the Santa touching his shoulder and the events that followed. The second version showed something similar, in which the knifeman – Josh, in reality – slipped and flailed out by accident instead of punching the throat with intent, while the knifeman's features were not Josh's.

There was a tiny text file attached, and its contents were a single sentence.

You have friends.

It was a nice sentiment, but the author was not Tony. Josh was almost sure of that.

Is the hunt really over?

Until he showed himself, he could not know for sure.

Suzanne was sitting cross-legged on her couch, hands clasped, feeling battered. Petra Osbourne was sitting in the armchair, while Tony Gore stood at the window.

"Are you going to be in trouble?" she asked Petra.

"If someone found out I'd been passing police data to this miscreant" – Petra nodded towards Tony – "then I would be. Won't happen."

"It's not enough, is it?" Suzanne so wanted Josh to be off the hook. "Just because the victim's a bad person, that doesn't excuse an assault."

"If the bastard won't press charges, it helps." Petra frowned. "Shit. Usually I'm encouraging victims to overcome their fear. This is topsy-turvy."

Tony was staring out of the window.

"Can you see something?" Suzanne asked.

"Er, no."

Tony came back into the centre of the room, sniffed, glanced up, then shook his head.

"Paranoid," he added.

There was a ripping sound from the bedroom, then a thump.

"What the f–?"

Petra was half out of the chair, and Tony was already at the bedroom door, by the time Suzanne started to react.

"Oh, for fuck's sake," said Tony.

He stood aside to let Suzanne and Petra see.

My ceiling.

A rectangle hung diagonally down, dangling shreds of plaster. Then a familiar head popped through upside down–

"No."

–and lowered, jackknifed, and dropped to the floor.

Josh smiled at her.

Right there.

Josh standing in the bedroom.

Josh!

"Jesus, pal." Tony sheathed a knife that Suzanne had not seen him draw. "Jesus."

Suzanne made her trembling legs take her forward.

"Sorry," said Josh. "It was the safest place to–"

Her hand arced up without thought. It was a hard slap.

"No!" shouted Tony.

Josh's half-formed fist froze. About to hit her?

"How could you?" said Suzanne.

Tony tried to explain something, but she twisted away and stalked back into the lounge, her mouth pressed shut in a downturned arc, holding back the scream. Arms folded tight, she stood, nose almost pressing the window, not watching the room, not caring.

Letting him into her life, through all her shields, and now this?

Bastard.

How could he have let her suffer this way? Torturing herself, imagining awful events, while all the time he was there above her.

"–for days," she heard Tony say. "Classic."

Sneakiness was the quality Josh said he had learned in his bloody Regiment. Now she knew what it meant, and did not like it.

"Very tactical," she said to the window. "Now piss off."

"Look." Josh's voice. "It was for your–"

"Is *piss off* too technical for you?"

Silence condensed in the room behind her. She did not turn to look.

"I should go," said Josh.

"Maybe–" That was Tony.

Petra murmured something.

Scuffles of sound, indecipherable in detail, indicated preparations for leaving. Then the men were at the door – somehow she knew – and Petra's hand was on her shoulder.

"You want me to stay?"

Suzanne shook her head.

"Take care of yourself, then."

It took another minute before everyone was gone, and the door clicked into place.

You're a bastard, Josh Cumberland.

She was crying. When had that started?

Bastard.

Her inner world was like a mine whose beams had cracked, where gravelly dust poured down, and cataclysm threatened. The only salvation was extensive shoring-up.

If she could find the strength for it.

Tony's car was a cheap Chinese import, supercharged inside, inconspicuous on the outside. Josh sat in the front passenger seat, feeling reality slide past, focusing on nothing. Especially not on what an idiot he was.

"Fuck it," he said.

"You certainly did," said Tony. "Right up."

"Yeah…"

It was a while before Josh added: "This isn't the way to Docklands."

"Gave up the flat. Got something new for September."

Graduate training for the investment banks meant that the freelance trainers, unless they lived in London, needed somewhere to stay. Tony liked to make the arrangements himself, taking the hassle away from the trainers. Just one of the reasons they liked to work with him.

"That's where we're going?"

"No, a hotel near Earls Court. We're running a bunch of courses there, got a couple of rooms for free when we booked the facilities."

It was always useful to have somewhere to dump equipment and chill out when the conference rooms were locked, even if no trainers needed to stay overnight.

"What courses?" If they were technical, he was surprised Tony had not asked him.

"Assertiveness, negotiation skills. Project management for non-project managers. Like that."

Not his kind of thing, then.

"Lofty Young could teach 'em assertiveness."

"I don't think they allow rocket launchers in the hotel."

"Uh-huh."

A mile later, Josh added: "I'm an arsehole, aren't I?"

"And full of poo," said Tony.

"Shit."

"I was too polite to say that."

Josh shook his head, wanting to smile – but inside a clear voice sounded, a child's voice that cried: *He's killing Santa!*

Bloody wonderful.

Someone was waiting in the room. The man sat cross-legged on the unused bed. His suit appeared expensive, and he looked like a banker, but only at first sight.

"Adam," said Josh.

He put down his rucksack. It contained the belongings

he had retrieved from the flat, packed fast and without much thought.

"That's right."

Tony closed the door and came in, stepping past the rucksack.

"This is Adam Priest," said Josh. "The man from the DTI who put Philip Broomhall on to Geordie."

Most of the work that Josh did was systems security training, and most of that he did for Tony. Geordie's agency operated in a different world. Last year, Josh had taken on the job of finding Broomhall's son as a way of breaking free from his own stress. It had led to meeting Suzanne, penetrating the *Knife Edge* final, and failing to bring down the government.

"Right," said Tony. "The Department of Trade and Industry. Of course."

He shook hands with Adam.

"Is Josh doing training for you at the moment?" asked Adam.

So he knew their working arrangements.

"Some stuff is coming up," said Tony.

Josh pulled out his phone – the phone that he had retrieved from the bedside table when Suzanne was out, the day after he went on the run – and pulled up one of his apps.

"The room's clean," he said. "So what's going on?"

"You're in the clear." Adam held up a phone showing the words: *You have friends.*

"What does that mean?" asked Tony.

"The evidence got tampered with," said Josh.

"Yes, that's right." Adam gave Tony a fingertip salute. "Along with the witness, twice over."

"Tiger Face is one of yours, is he?" Tony turned to Josh.

"Don't ask."

"I won't," said Josh. "I'd rather ask Adam why he's here."

"Maybe it's Mr Gore I want to talk to."

"You want Josh to do something for you," said Tony. "Talk about obvious."

"A friend of a friend needs someone tracked down." Adam got up from the bed and opened the minibar. "Drink, anyone?"

"That's supposed to be locked," said Tony.

"Really? I'm having a tonic water. Anyone join me?"

"No," said Josh. "If you work for Five, you've got operators by the hundred you can deploy. Why me?"

"Because it's off the books," said Tony. "Below the radar. Am I right?"

"Of course." Adam raised his plastic glass in toast. "To deniability."

"No," said Josh. "Your own officers can provide deniability."

"That depends on who I'm denying it to."

Josh looked at Tony, who shook his head.

"Dangerous games," Tony said.

"There's nothing intrinsically illegal in the task." Adam sat on the bed once more. "Plus, the disappearance might be as innocent as it seems, not engineered by the Tyndalls at all."

Those fuckers.

But Josh held his words inside. He had already screwed up one conversation tonight. No need for a second.

"Seems to me," he said instead, "*I'm* below the Tyndalls' radar, or they'd have got to me already. Or tried to."

If Adam thought mentioning their name would trigger a gung-ho revenge response, he had better reconsider.

"Isn't that the Ghost Force speciality?" asked Adam. "Under the radar, in and out with no one the wiser?"

Tony was smiling.

"That's not a bad point," he said.

Last year he had encouraged Josh to take the job with Geordie. His reasoning had been this: Josh needed action to straighten out his mind.

"I'm not looking for an assignment," Josh said.

"The missing person is a scientist-turned-nuclear engineer, who handed in his resignation by vmail. Told his landlady he was off to Scotland. Hiking solo. No friends or colleagues have seen him."

"Remind me what the word *solo* means," said Tony.

Adam shook his head.

"He was working for Tyndall Industries," said Josh. "Right?"

"For one of their competitors."

"Ah."

"His ultimate employer was a man called Jack Hardin. Why don't you chat to him, then decide?"

Josh looked at Tony, who gave a tiny lateral dip of his head. Call it agreement.

"Give me the details." said Josh.

"All right." Adam held up his phone. "Ready?"

On his own phone, Josh enabled redfang.

"OK." Then, "Got it."

"Good," said Adam. "By the way, Jack Hardin doesn't know me as Adam. He thinks my name is Robert Weber."

"Robert."

"Actually, Robbie to my friends, including Jack."

"Friends," said Josh, "who don't know your real name."

"All part of the job. So, we've covered everything."

Adam got up, went into the en suite bathroom, and poured the last of his tonic water into the sink. Then he tossed the plastic glass into the wastebin.

"Tidy man," said Tony.

From a soldier, especially special forces, it was a compliment.

"Nice meeting you," Adam said to Tony. "Josh, good luck."

"Your mission," murmured Josh, "should you decide to accept it..."

"Excuse me?"

"I mean thanks. I'll make the call, but no other promises."

"Fair enough. Cheers."

Adam went out into the corridor, nodded, then closed the door.

"Interesting," said Tony. "You'll give me a shout if you need anything, right?"

"If I take the job," said Josh.

"Come off it." Tony crossed to the minibar. "You'll take it. You know you will."

"Maybe I'll–"

"Son of a bitch," said Tony.

"What is it?"

Tony tugged at the minibar.

"Bastard thing's locked."

They looked at the door that Adam had just left by.

Then they began to laugh.

[SEVEN]

At 8am in his underwear, Josh was on his two hundred and seventh Hindu push-up, his buttocks high and chest low at the start of the rep, when the door opened.

"Oh my... Blimey," said a woman's voice.

Josh twisted to his feet.

"I'm using the room to stay in," he said. "I'm a trainer."

"Training to good effect, looks like." The woman's gaze passed up and down. "I'm Yvette."

"Nice to meet you. Do you need something?"

A twitch passed across her face.

"Just... my box of teaching materials." She pointed to the shelf above Josh's rucksack. "There."

Josh handed it to her.

"That's everything?"

His sweat was beginning to cool.

"Unfortunately." She grinned. "At least you made my day."

Then she went out and the door clicked shut. He checked the inner security bolt. The magnet was loose. He had remembered to lock it, but not checked the mechanism.

Sharpen up, Cumberland.

He took his position again, hands and feet on the floor and

arse uppermost – to a yoga student, the down-dog pose – grunted, shook his head, then dipped his chest towards the ground, getting the motion to flow once more.

Forty-three more push-ups and five hundred squats later, he held a wrestler's neck bridge for four minutes, then bridged forward for an equal time. That done, he used the bathroom door edge-on for a hundred reps of rowing – feet either side of the door in a lean-back squat, gripping the doorknobs – and finished with two hundred crunches. Enough for now. He stretched, drank from a litre bottle of water liberated from the minibar – Adam was not the only one with useful tricks – entered the en suite, and showered.

At 8.45am he was dressed and ready to leave. He checked the window, and disabled the safety catch. Now it would swing wide open if pushed. From his rucksack, he took an ordinary-looking leather belt, unhooked a fibre from inside, twisted a hook free of the buckle, and fastened it inside the window-sill. Then he tugged the rucksack onto his back and shrugged, settling the weight.

If someone pinged him when he went online, his safeguards would alert him. It would take only seconds to abseil out of here – the first step in getting clear.

He powered on his phone.

First he checked his various shield apps. Then, protected, he went to his normal mail service, while a secondary pane loaded up with news headlines, according to his pre-set heuristic filters. Last night, he had accessed only secure portals for a matter of seconds; now he was using his phone like a civilian, but with safeguards loaded and executing.

No flaring of red, no howling alarm.

Safe so far.

Then he examined the first text pane.

No…

And dropped the phone.

• • • •

When Tony came in at half past nine, he found Josh sitting on the floor, forearms on knees, chin on chest, a rucksack on his back.

"Hey, mate. What is it?"

Josh looked up, his eyes filled with void.

"Sophie," he said.

"You were a good father. There was no way to–"

"I missed her funeral."

Tony could not speak.

"Five days in a *fucking* attic and I thought I was being clever and all the time they were, they were–"

Then sobbing broke through Josh's voice, and he gave himself up to tears.

[EIGHT]

He had been telling himself for over a year that Sophie was gone. Now she really was.

Oh, my baby girl.

Suzanne could tell him whether he had mourned already or was starting now, but he did not want to talk to her. Everything bad that she might be thinking about him was true. What if the Santa he had struck had been a good man, or at least law-abiding? What if the tracheotomy had not worked?

He wondered if the authorities had given the mouthpiece back to the trumpeter.

After Tony departed, Josh left his rucksack at the hotel and went out to walk, without destination. It was nearly 6pm when he used his phone again, checked Jack Hardin's details from the data Adam had redfanged, and made the call he had committed to..

Partly, it was because he was a professional; partly it was something to do.

Just the call.

He had promised no more than that.

"My name is Josh Cumberland–"

"Of course." Hardin's features were square. "I've heard good things about you. Do you know Kent at all?"

"Er… Yes. A bit."

"I'm in Tunbridge Wells tomorrow. Can you get there for 2 o'clock?"

He might as well.

"Yes," said Josh. "Just for an initial chat. I'm committing to nothing more."

"That's fair. Here's the location."

Josh's phone beeped, receiving the attachment.

"I've got it. I look forward to meeting you."

He heard the lack of emotion in his own voice.

"Excellent," said Hardin. "See you then."

The video pane blinked out of existence.

I should've said no.

It would have taken too much energy.

The next day he retrieved his car from Queen's Park – staying clear of the flat – and drove to Kent, where he parked in the Langton Park and Ride and rode the shuttle bus into town. Early, he spent an hour in the Regency-era Pantiles, drinking cappuccinos in a coffee shop beneath a colonnade, opposite a crooked black-and-white, two-storey building that was built when Shakespeare was alive.

He had not worked out this morning.

At 1.55pm he presented himself at a glass-walled reception in a transformed Georgian townhouse, now offices shared by a law firm, accountants, and a yacht designer. Normally Josh would have checked them all in advance; today he had not bothered.

"Please go right through, Mr Cumberland."

There were bioluminescent posters and 3-D models labelled *Mall of the Future*. Sketches of things not yet built. What existed was a lift that took Josh down to grey concrete caverns, walled with slabs, where the air was cold and tasted dusty.

"If you would, sir."

One of the workers – Josh had scarcely noticed them – was proffering a white hard-hat. Josh settled the thing on his head.

"And this way, please."

He passed through dusty interiors with paste-on bioluminescent strips providing uneven light. Then a steel door opened, revealing the site office. Someone, perhaps a foreman, was leaving. From behind a metal desk, Jack Hardin waved Josh in.

The pressure change popped his ears as the heavy door shut.

"You can hear yourself think in here," said Hardin. "Better than out there."

"Impressive development," said Josh.

Under other circumstances, he would have read through all the details last night, and checked them again while he waited in the coffee shop before the meeting.

"You ever been to Toronto, Josh?" asked Hardin. "Or Calgary, anywhere like that?"

"No, I haven't."

"Big underground malls, almost cities in their own right. There are examples in Singapore and Mumbai, but we're talking about protection from arctic conditions here. Way of the future."

The climate was changing, and Hardin was making money.

He's not the only one.

Those bastard Tyndalls, for a start.

"Your missing guy," said Josh, "works on reactors, is that right?"

"Alex Evans." Hardin waved his phone. "Everything's here. Good man, bit of a late bloomer despite his PhD."

"What do you mean?"

He did not want to accept the data from Hardin's phone. Not if he was going to turn the job down.

"Had what you might call a solid career, then he came up with two *very* nice tricks in old-fashioned areas. One in coolant systems and the other in neutron deceleration. That's inside the core."

"Uh-huh."

"Look, we're not talking Nobel Prize stuff here," said Hardin. "At least, I don't think we are. But Evans could've resigned, waited for two years before doing anything – going to a competitor within two years is forbidden in the employment contract – then applied for patents in his own name. In his position, I might have done just that."

"So why didn't he?"

"Maybe he's a different kind of man to me." Hardin shrugged his fleshy shoulders. "Or perhaps it's just getting the work done that he cares about. But I think he believed in the power station programme, because without electricity the country will be in crisis. A two-year delay would place us at risk."

"But he didn't do that."

"His managers told him that we would look after him. At the end of the year, something good was going to happen."

Josh looked around the site office. Hardin looked at home here, more than he would at black-tie City dinners, gladhanding the politicians.

"In those words? Nothing specific?"

"Maybe not those words," said Hardin. "But about that vague, because we haven't decided on *anybody's* bonuses yet. Not even mine."

"And promotion?"

"Maybe. Some people don't consider extra responsibility as a reward. We would have looked carefully at that."

It sounded like an enlightened view of the workplace. But Hardin would know how to give the right impression. To get this far took many skills, and presenting corporate challenges in the best light was one of them.

"How much of the power station programme is yours?" said Josh.

"What do you mean? Nationally?"

"Yes. What's your slice of the pie compared to, say, the Tyndalls'?"

"Those bastards."

"A small cut, then."

"Relatively. Four percent or a little more, depending on which numbers you divide up, and how. It's still lucrative."

"But you'd rather it was bigger."

"Of course."

The Tyndalls had influence beyond most entrepreneurs. Josh had not tried to track their covert dealings over the past year, not after the first few months of disappointment as both they and Billy Church's government continued to flourish.

"You think your competitors might have got to Evans?"

"Maybe," said Hardin. "I've been waiting for news like that to pop up. Evans working for one of the other guys, and lawyers putting counterclaims through the courts to stop us invoking the clauses in his contract."

"But it hasn't happened."

"No."

It did not sound like any kind of job for him, never mind one worth doing. "And the police aren't looking."

"The thing is," said Hardin, "if someone's influencing Evans and it's not in the open, then something criminal might be happening."

"And you think it's the Tyndalls."

Hardin looked down at the metal desk, appearing to examine a newish scratch.

"I didn't say it's them."

Gritty harmonics in his voice told otherwise.

"Go back to the police," said Josh. "What's the point in you being rich, if you can't exert special influence?"

Hardin looked up.

"Excuse me," he said. "But I can. Why else do you think you're here?"

It was an excellent point.

"Do you pay your invoices on time?"

"Always."

"Then I'll take the job," said Josh.

Next morning, from a budget hotel room in Reading, he got to work. With keypad unfurled and the room's wallscreen co-opted, he set up his infiltration ware. It was a year since he had done this for real. Then, his attempt to uncover the Tyn-dalls' activities had been strictly illegal. Plus, the intelligence services had been on the alert, and he had needed to bypass their monitors, hence his need for Petra's help.

For a minor part of that op, he had worked in a different mode, requiring no assistance. Today that was all he needed.

People leaving special forces seemed to end up with weaponry and other kit that was *not* listed as missing in any quartermaster's database. Someone sensible had decided to endorse that almost-policy by offering facilities to personnel who had entered civvie street, on the basis that it was better this way, where MetaWatch (using an array of GCHQ substa-tions) could track their activities.

First, Josh needed access to police interviews of Jack Hardin's employees, colleagues of the missing Alex Evans. He could talk to them directly, but police officers knew their jobs: he was unlikely to learn anything new, not by conversation.

Suzanne could.

Well maybe, but she was nothing to do with this.

Go away.

The first stage was the most delicate. He needed to find out whether creating a search for Alex Evans would in itself trigger an alarm.

If he did find observer components in place, he would at-tempt to dissect them, to analyse the callback definition: backtracking to their human operator.

There was a strong possibility that, if such observers existed, they were primed to communicate with systems inside MI5, set up by colleagues of Adam Priest – maybe even his superiors – working in opposition to him.

He ran what checks he could, triggering no detectable response. Either no one was monitoring for someone hunting Alex Rhys Evans, PhD, or their monitors were too sophisticated for him to get a handle on. Either way, it was time to begin the search.

From the interview transcripts, none of Evans' colleagues had registered suspicious prior behaviour on his part, though nearly half of them were surprised at the way he left. He had said he wanted to go climbing in Scotland; it was his resignation that startled everyone.

It was hard to read between the lines, but the officers did not appear to be grilling the co-workers. Perhaps the interviews only happened because of Hardin's influence. Urgency was missing from everything he read. Still, the police had been competent.

The word *outdoorsman* appeared twice in the report, along with remarks about bashing around in the mountains, or preferring a windy tent to a proper bed. At his home in Wraysbury – there were images appended – the rooms were tidy, save for a clutter of climbing and camping gear, and a collection of old hardcopy science texts, mostly physics, along with some history books.

One day – or night – Evans had slipped away from his home, and that was that.

Let's see how you did it.

Using his security-cleared portals, Josh slipped querybots into the municipal street surveillance system. His initial scan results came back fast. Also, negative. No images of Alex Rhys Evans, PhD, leaving his home during the forty-eight hour period in question.

"The dog didn't bark that night," he said aloud.

Surveillance showed the cleaning lady arrive in the unoccupied flat, exactly as in the report. At that point, Evans had already disappeared. The previous footage of Evans, from two days earlier, showed him entering, not leaving.

There would be blindzones, so Josh set up a secondary, wider search and set it running. But the coverage near Evans' home was good. He *might* have left unobserved by chance; but already it appeared likely he had used subterfuge to get clear. If a wider search also came back negative, it increased the likelihood that deliberate deception was involved.

So this is a real job.

Something to get him through the days without thinking of Sophie, over and over again, except in the quiet times when thoughts were inescapable.

Evans might need peace and solitude. Josh needed to keep busy.

Time to move.

Enough of the virtual. Time for the real.

He pulled on his running gear and limbered up. Yesterday's break from training had not been a planned rest day – it had been a failure of discipline.

I missed Sophie's funeral.

Yes, but he had to keep going, and this was the way to do it. He would run hard and long, and punish himself with pain; but he would explore the streets around Evans' abandoned home while still fresh, able to observe minutiae, getting a proper feel for the difficulty of determining the blindzones and slipping through them.

He gekko-tagged his phone to his sleeve, and left.

[NINE]

The Parisian hotel, on the elegant avenue Carnot, was more like a block of upmarket apartments, with uniformed concierges and housekeepers, but no restaurant in-house. Instead, each suite came with its own kitchen, including Richie's, as well as a lounge and a minimalist European bathroom.

It made him feel grown-up.

Dad's suite was on the next floor up, adding to the sense of independence. Plus, these few days were a working holiday as far as Dad was concerned; he kept disappearing off into meetings in various parts of Paris, leaving Richie to spend time alone.

Company would be nice. He looked at his phone, wondering what Opal would be up to now. She still lived in a Vauxhall squat, but one whose standards continued to rise the longer the local authorities left them alone. What had changed was her attendance at a girls' school in Westminster, paid for by Dad.

Opal had accepted only because one of the housemates, Brian, persuaded her that reverse snobbery would be stupid.

Besides, she had been injured during the chase which resulted in Josh's grabbing Richie. They had not realised then that Josh was a friend; but the point was that Opal could have been killed. And she had been Richie's protector. So if Richie's dad wanted to pay for her education – so Brian had said – she would be an idiot to say anything but yes.

At school, from what Richie knew, she experienced trouble fitting in with the kids, but was polite to the teachers and determined in her studies. Slightly built, she had an agile strength from the parkour and gekrunning, and that helped.

On her visits to the Broomhalls' house, she trained alongside Richie in close-quarter fighting – classical wing chun and escrima, plus grapple-and-kickbox extensions that maintained the old principles: the impenetrable wedge defence and centreline attacks of wing chun, plus the blindsiding, weapon disarms, and limb destructions of escrima.

(The schoolyard had provided two real-life tests of her ability, the second against three much bigger girls. She doubted there would be a third.)

Their teacher was Lexa Armstrong, the Broomhall's live-in driver and former soldier. Lexa had her own suite right here, on the floor below. At the moment, she and Dad were somewhere south of the city, with Lexa driving the hired HyperJag. Dad was negotiating some deal with textile distributors; or perhaps that had been yesterday.

The corporate world seemed boring. But Richie had seen the harsh side of life during his time on the streets, and no longer took material comfort for granted. The act of eating food was a treasure.

And time spent in Opal's company was a miracle.

I wonder what she's doing now?

When the door chime sounded, he assumed it was Housekeeping, but checked the viewscreen anyway. Lexa had instilled careful habits in him.

Impossible.

He opened the door, and Opal grinned at him.

"Hey," she said.

"Bloody hell."

A gym bag was dangling from her hand.

"Um, I need to drop this off," she said. "In Lexa's room. There's an extra bed, apparently."

"Oh."

"Thought I'd come and see you first."

"Right."

Richie swallowed. Then he reached out and hugged her.

She felt slender and warm.

There was a single route into and out of Evans' home – ingress and egress as the training manuals said – that maintained a passage through surveillance blindzones. That night, Josh used it to pass through neighbours' gardens, open a side window, and slide inside.

With his phone scanning, he searched every room, starting with the ceiling.

Hardcopy texts; functional furniture; casual clothes in the wardrobe, also a single suit, not new; a pair of old, patched wellies, a torn kagoul, and a half-deflated inflatable leek – the only whimsical note – abandoned in the large, near-empty below-stairs cupboard; not much food in the kitchen.

No secret caches. No stored porn.

"Outdoorsman," muttered Josh.

He made a second sweep of every room, standing in the centre, trying to focus on overall patterns, looking for anomalies. Nothing untoward. Everything was normal, normal, normal.

Dr Evans, why did you piss off in the night?

Or maybe daytime. With the lack of surveillance it could have been at any hour; and that was the point.

"Ah," said Josh. "Shit."

He had missed something.

Sharpen up, all right?

Back to the wardrobe. He checked again, verifying his memory. Two Welsh rugby shirts with the three-feather symbol.

Likewise the bookshelves: Feynman's three-volume *Lectures on Physics*, Head First String Theory, five biographies of Owain Glyndwr, three indecipherable books in Welsh, the *Mabinogion*.

The inflatable leek was the giveaway.

You lying git, Dr Evans.

He had told everyone he was off to Scotland for some climbing. But his heart belonged to Wales.

"Land of my fathers, isn't it, boyo?" said Josh.

Tony would have said he sounded like a Pakistani.

Never mind.

This was a solo assignment, with no need to involve his friends. Pity.

Back in his hotel room, Josh widened his search westward. He had wondered why Evans had buggered off, and still had no idea. But he might know *where* he had gone, thanks to the leek.

"Got you."

Twenty minutes after submitting a revised search, one of his querybots came back with a .87 probability match. Bath services, westbound side, M4: a man climbing down from the passenger door of a lorry. Three days ago at dusk.

Long gone.

But Josh needed to move. Although it was midnight, he gathered up his things, packed his rucksack in under five minutes, and slung it over one shoulder. Another five minutes, and he had checked out, was sitting in his car, about to place the phone into its dashboard slot.

Slow down.

That was always Lofty Young's advice in the Regiment. When the pressure is on, it is time to take care.

Earlier, he had scanned for software watchers – others observing anyone who looked for Evans – and found nothing.

Doesn't mean there aren't any.

It seemed unlikely, but if an adverse party had caused Evans to disappear – can anyone spell Tyndall? – then it was time to move less openly. Smiling, Josh slotted the phone in, activated heads-up, and got to work.

He booked a ticket from King's Cross to Edinburgh on the UltraMag, departure at 11.15 in the morning. Then he used a false ID to book airship passage from City Airport to Glasgow.

Double feint, on expenses. Good enough.

Subversion ware running – M4 surveillance was about to show him heading east towards London – Josh put the car into gear and rolled forward. By the time he was out on the west-bound carriageway, he was already at the speed limit.

He kept it that way as he drove through the night.

Sophie.

Driving, and trying not to think.

My beautiful girl.

Eyes of blue. What colour had her coffin been?

No.

Time to drive, nothing else.

Two in the morning, and he was checking in at the motorway lodge. A solitary young man, his name badge reading Barry, manned the desk. The system required little in the way of human intervention, hence the wallscreen full of complicated graphs labelled with ideograms.

"Studying?" asked Josh. "What's your subject?"

"Economics with Mandarin."

"That's the way to get ahead."

Meanwhile his phone had completed check-in and had the key code for room 470.

"Could I ask about a friend of mine?" added Josh. "May I?"

"Sure."

Josh used his phone to pop an image of Evans on screen.

"Might have been here three nights ago. Would you have been on duty?"

"Yeah, but I don't remember him. Sorry."

"Silly bugger went hitch-hiking with his phone offline. He's probably OK."

Barry shrugged. "Sorry."

"Never mind. I'll go to my room."

"Goodnight, sir."

From the car he fetched not just his rucksack but a kettle-bell, wrapped in a cloth shopping bag to look less strange. He lugged them in – Barry did not look up from his studying – and was sweating by the time he reached the bedroom.

Nuts.

At least he would be set up for a workout when he woke. Now, he checked the cost per shower, and decided against it. Partly because it was antisocial at this hour, partly not to waste the client's money.

The tickets for the feint had been necessary, not whimsical.

If I were Evans, what would I do?

If he had false ID, Evans might have checked in here. Could he have acquired anonymity ware? Some dodgy, lesser version of the utilities Josh used? Certainly he could have slipped past Barry without being remembered.

Then what?

Whether he had a room or not, Evans might have been hungry. Only a lobby vending-machine provided anything to eat in the lodge. In the main service area, there would be fast food joints, perhaps a way to get in via blindzones.

He went to check, found one likely way in, and decided on the pizza joint – still open in a blaze of light – as the place Evans would have chosen. Wearing a hat and with good timing, entering as part of a group, he could have avoided showing his face to the spycams.

Despite the hour, Josh decided he could manage a pizza slice.

The joint had an internal window that in theory looked onto the mall-like aisle, but swarmed with adverts – bioluminescent posters and video loops – that disrupted visibility. Josh took one of the seats next to it, on the basis that Evans might have sat here.

"Hiya." A waitress came up, touchpad in hand. "Do you know what you want yet, love?"

"Hiya." Josh looked down at the menu displayed inside the tabletop. "I could murder a cappuccino."

"Not planning on sleeping tonight?"

"Can you do decaf?"

"We can do that."

"OK, then. Just don't tell my mates."

"Our secret," said the waitress. "Anything to eat?"

"What's this?" Josh pointed at the tabletop. "The Fat Billy?"

"We used to call it the Heart Attack special."

"Ah. Maybe I'll have the spinach instead, and a salad."

"All right." The waitress used her touchpad. "Anything else?"

"Not to eat." Josh held up his phone, displaying his best still of Evans. "I think my mate Alex ate here three nights back. Do you remember him?"

"I'm not–Why are you asking?"

Josh blew out a breath.

"Actually, cause he's not been in touch. Silly bugger likes clambering round mountains without a phone."

"Oh. We get so many– Hmm." The waitress turned. "Sian? Come here a minute, will you?"

A plump blonde waitress came over.

"How be?" she said to Josh. "What's happening here?"

She was Welsh, a valley girl – *here* sounded like *yuh*.

"Your brief encounter," said the first waitress, pointing at Josh's phone.

"Oh, right." Sian beamed at Josh. "Spoke Welsh, didn't he? We had a right old chat." A pause. "We did."

That trailing confirmation reminded Josh of Taff – real name Dafydd – in the Regiment.

"How did you find out?" said Josh. "He didn't order in Welsh, did he?"

"Course not. He heard me on the phone to my mam. I was coming off break, see."

"So did he say where he was going?"

"The mountains, he said." Sian put her chubby hands on her hips. "Exactly where to, I don't know."

She started to frown, so Josh backed off the subject. Instead he asked whether she had gone to Welsh school – which she had, meaning lessons were in *Cymraeg* – and stayed with inconsequential chat until the first waitress came back with his food.

"I'll leave you to it," said Sian. "Enjoy."

"Will do. Nice meeting you."

He ate the pizza as a celebration of achieving step one in his mission, then ambled back to the lodge. After brushing his teeth, he sat down on the bed and lay back, his motion becoming one long tumble into sleep.

Next morning he felt good. His day began with juice and cappuccino in his room, fetched from the services. Then he used an abbreviated body weight workout to get fully warm, before taking hold of his kettlebell and going through the full routine: low-rep windmills, presses, one-legged squats and Turkish get-ups, then the high-rep swings and snatches.

Afterwards, he stretched and mixed himself a pea-and-soya protein shake for breakfast. Then he showered, sluicing off the sweat – and his whole body felt alive as he dressed in clean clothes and unfolded the keyboard for his phone. He linked to the room's wall display, ready for some serious work.

Two hours later, he wished he had not bothered.

Shit shit shit.

Nothing.

Evans, you bastard.

That one sighting was an aberration, perhaps because Evans was tired. Despite expanded search parameters, none of the querybots came back with a hint of where Evans had gone next.

Could he be an operator?

But all the bio data indicated Evans was a civilian scientist, a geek who liked the outdoors. He avoided surveillance by thinking physics, not spec ops. After misleading colleagues by talking about Scotland, would he really have thrown in another feint? Headed for Wales, then switched, maybe doubling back?

If he had, he had left no traces.

Clever bastard.

Tossing a coin would not help, because if Evans had switched, his choices were approximately infinite.

I need help.

But it was not Tony Gore or Petra Osbourne, or any of his London friends who came to mind.

It's not that far.

He lugged his things out to his car – checking out as he passed through the lobby – and was en route in minutes. But he did not cross the border into Wales; instead, he headed north, and soon enough was hurtling through the countryside towards Hereford.

Heading home.

To the Regiment that continued to define his world.

[TEN]

This was the secret world. Suzanne enjoyed occasional web-movies that featured spies, often fanciful. Yet here in the foyer of Thames House, the building was tangible and the people were real. Also normal-looking, turning up for an ordinary day at work.

Only the layers of shielding and the uniformed security officers – genial guys in their forties and fifties: retired military and police – told her that she was in a different kind of place. Her phone went into an armoured chute, while the officers joked with her. Then she followed a group of visitors that seemed at ease here, passing through scanner after scanner, deeper and deeper into the building, telling officers at three different desks what she was here for – though if she had not been on their list, she could not have walked through the front door – and finally entered a lounge where she could wait for Steve.

There was a drinks machine, so she fetched a hot chocolate and sipped. Tasteless, but a comfort all the same.

Could she really help these people?

Remember the teenagers.

The victims were past help, but the point was that any kind of fad could spread as easily as hairstyles or tattooing, and suicide epidemics were not unknown in history. She was not sure, but didn't the South Sea Islands have a case of–?

She reached for her phone to check online, but she had surrendered it.

"Suzanne." It was Steve. "You came. Brilliant."

Their handshake was prolonged.

"Come on," added Steve. "Let's get you through security."

"I thought" – she gestured to the door she had entered by – "that was it."

"Sort of the outer half." Steve held out a yellow beanie hat. "I'm afraid you have to wear this."

"Um, all right." She pulled it on. "Does it suit me?"

"Gorgeous. Er… Anyhow, you can't take it off now. Not until you leave the building. It's got sensors inside that–"

"You're kidding."

"Sorry. Thing is, you've got level one clearance only. That means there's stuff we can't talk about when you're around."

"And this" – she pointed at her head – "is the signal, right? To watch what you say."

"Yeah, I'm really sorry that–"

"Actually, I think it's quite clever." She touched his upper arm. "A really good idea."

For her protection, too. These people were serious, and she did not want to learn things she was not supposed to, or wander into some forbidden area. She had no idea what the consequences would be; nor did she feel like asking, not in the middle of this forbidding place where others had total control, more complete than in any prison.

If she wanted to leave but they disagreed, there was no way out.

"Let's go meet the guys," said Steve.

Josh was familiar with the deceptive, layered security of the intelligence services. During his time with Ghost Force he had worked joint ops with MI6, visiting their Vauxhall Cross HQ a dozen times or more. There, the protection was formidable, but you never saw a gun, although weaponry was everywhere: inside walls, ceilings, and even floors, and always to hand for those who might need it.

Here in Sterling Lines, security was overt and a thousand times more reassuring, at least by his standards. The guys at the gate bore heavy-duty weapons and knew how to use them. It was not just about keeping intruders out; it was about destroying them.

The grin on Josh's face proved everything he had learned about subconscious association. This was home, and he was glad to be here.

Carpark 3 was near the parade ground. Josh got out of the car and leaned against it, arms folded.

"Help you?" said an approaching trooper.

Beside him another man checked his combat phone.

"Josh Cumberland," he said. "Ex-Regiment, right?"

"Only legally." Josh tapped his temple. "In here, I've never left."

They grinned at him.

"I believe that's what other regiments call a parade ground," he added. "Use it much?"

"Yeah, right."

By the standards of ordinary military, special forces were a disgrace when it came to proper army discipline, in the form of marching, saluting, and parading. They had no time for it.

"Recognise him?" said the other trooper.

A lanky, grey-haired runner was cutting across the parade ground, moving fast.

"Hell, yes." Josh raised his voice. "No need for a Zimmer frame yet?"

Lofty Young trotted to a halt.

"Cumberland, you cheeky young bugger."

He clapped Josh's shoulder with a hand that felt like granite.

"Um, Lofty?" said one of the troopers. "Where's the rest of 'em?"

"They sort of gave up."

"Bloody hell, Lofty. Are they lost?"

"I'm sure they'll find their way."

The nearer trooper looked at Josh.

"Two dozen Airborne Rangers, about my age, come to visit. And Lofty's run the poor fuckers into the ground somewhere."

The Rangers were the US equivalent of the SFSG, infantry support for spec ops. Or had been, before the United States deteriorated and the command structure fractured.

I wonder what they're doing here.

Lofty must be over fifty-five, possibly nearing sixty.

"Let's walk, lad," he said to Josh. "I need to rehydrate."

At the mess, they stayed long enough to pick up two bottles of electrolyte-replacement fluid. Then they walked on, heading for the Killing House.

"Before you broke the Rangers," said Josh, "what were they here for?"

"A bit of extra training. Usual kind of thing."

"The usual, right. I'll forget I heard anything."

"Good lad."

Even now, countries around the world prized British training for their own special forces. A long time ago, Lofty had explained that Britain had been at war – officially or secretly – *every single day* for over five centuries. Practise anything that much, you get good at it.

"Henry V took France," he had added, "with his special-forces archers."

Sometimes, as an extension of foreign policy, the Regiment took down governments. Ghost Force preferred cyberspace, but in the previous century at Margaret Thatcher's direction, four unarmed members of the SAS – unarmed until they snatched weapons from the enemy – rescued the Gambian president's family from Marxist rebels. The coup collapsed; the president returned to office.

The British government could not be planning to help insurrection in America, could it? Say, by assisting disaffected former Rangers to move against President Brand?

None of my business.

Lofty led the way to an area of rough ground. Beyond, several ThermoRovers and SUVs were parked by the Killing House. Official visits were common: not just to be impressed by the Regiment's skill, but for high-profile VIPs to experience a rescue scenario with themselves as the hostage. Practice in case it happened for real.

"Who's visiting?" said Josh. "Or is that something else I should forget?"

"Take a look. They've done OK, looks like."

"Oh, her."

The Officer Commanding and Special Branch officers were escorting Sharon Caldwell, leader of the TechDems, along with her partner, Laura Collins. Some VIPs left shaking after their experience; Caldwell look composed.

"There's only one thing wrong with this picture," said Lofty.

The party were boarding the vehicles.

"What's that?"

"It's Fat Billy Church who's going to win the election, isn't it?"

"Sorry about that," said Josh.

If he'd done a better job last year – if only that insane Brand had held off his devastating actions for another day – Church's government would already have fallen. Not that Lofty could officially condone Josh's stunt in the *Knife Edge* final.

"Never mind," said Lofty. "Let's go see the gang."

He meant Ghost Force.

"Who ya gonna call?" said Josh.

Lofty joined in with:

"Ghost*busters.*"

From inside her vehicle, Sharon Caldwell glanced at them.

"You think she heard?" said Josh. "Audio pickup?"

"Never mind. The country is safe in our hands."

As the ThermoRover started up, Caldwell might have shaken her head.

Maybe, if you spent every day trying to save your country from corruption, humour was the last thing on your mind. Or maybe she was serious as a bastard by nature.

Lofty turned away from the vehicles, and Josh followed. Soon they were at the familiar low bunker with its armoured entranceway.

"Home, sweet home," said Josh.

A long descent later, they were in the underground command centre. After a series of blank, armoured ceramic doors, they stopped before a steel-and-glass barrier on which a high-res holographic logo shone.

GHOST FORCE

you didn't see us
we weren't there

As they waited for the barrier to draw back, Lofty asked a question.

"Are you fit, laddie? I mean properly fit?"

For *properly* read *to operational standards*.

"Why do you ask?"

That was not why he was here.

Lofty can't think that.

But the guys had taken Josh through security procedures in

record time, almost as if he had explicit clearance. As if he were expected.

"You've been gone a while," said Lofty. "If you want to rejoin the Regiment, you'll have to pass Selection a second time."

What?

"I didn't–"

"Starts next week, the summer intake." Lofty smiled at him. "Good timing, young Cumberland."

"Not so young," said Josh. "Not any more."

But inside his head, a different voice was talking.

Rejoin the Regiment?

His muscles bunched and twitched without conscious command.

Can I even get in?

Or was it coincidence that he had come here at this time – this specific time – for help?

Rejoin.

While deep in his mind, laughter sounded.

[ELEVEN]

The place reminded Suzanne of a neuropharm research group, when she interned in an Oxford science park during her studies. The office was open-plan, big enough to hold a meeting of perhaps twenty people; but Steve's team had exactly four members. Their workspaces were large, with multiple display screens in addition to desktop inlays.

Though they were busy, each paused their work and shook hands with Suzanne.

"I'm Trin," said a woman with short hair. "No one ever calls me Trinity."

"Good to meet you."

The others were Shireen: dark eyes, cut-glass accent; Carl: thin, could pass for a teenager; and Shane, with bodybuilder muscles and tiger-stripe tattoo covering half his face.

"We've had a new incident." Shane's muscular control, as he shook Suzanne's hand, was exact. "Did Steve tell you?"

She felt fragile, standing this close to him.

"He said it didn't stop when you thought it would. With thirteen times thirteen victims."

Steve had disappeared into a meeting.

"No, it didn't. There's a new Cutter Circle just this morning.

Number fifteen."

"Damn," said Suzanne.

"Let me show you the 3-D."

A list of glowing text elements hung in the air above a small viewstage. A 2-D projection showed on several of the workspace displays. Suzanne had not known the technology could be this small: civilians went to a cinema to see 3-D.

"Showing off," said Trin.

"Might be useful later," said Carl. "When we start plotting proximity graphs."

Shireen smiled at Suzanne.

"He means relationship nets. Social-interaction phase spaces."

"Er, right," said Suzanne.

What the hell am I doing here?

Then she focused on the list because these were *people,* the teenage victims. Whatever she could do to help, she would.

Aaronson, David, known as Dave, 17

Baldcock, Tony, 17

Carlsen, Katherine, known as Kat, 18

Cooke, Paul, 17

Gordon, James, 19

Lalvani, Adrienne, 17

Mason, Kevin, 18

Morgan, Gwyn, 17

O'Dowde, Finbar, 18

O'Toole, Mary, 16

Singh, Rajesh, 17

Trent, Magnus Harald, known as Harry, 19

Zweig, Colin, 18

They all stared at the list.

"First thoughts, people?" said Trin.

Shireen pointed. "Top of the list, name starts with A.

The last one is Z. Have we seen that before?"

"No," said Carl. "Also, it's a low ratio of girls. Only four this time."

"Even lower," said Shane. "Gwyn is a guy. *Was*."

"Bollocks." Carl tapped one of his desktop inlays. "How could I miss that?"

"Two Irish names." Trin checked a screen. "A first-generation immigrant, Catholic, from Kerry, plus a fourth-generation Wiccan from Hull. Not much in common."

Besides being teenage and dead. No one made any smart remarks.

"Age spread, sixteen to nineteen." Carl tapped a screen. "Usual. Preliminary tox rep indicates no alcohol, nicotine, ganja. One of them probably took cough medicine."

"And that's also usual?" said Suzanne.

"In the Cutter Circles," answered Trin, "it definitely is."

"Right."

Trin's words implied she knew this was highly *un*usual for teenage suicide in general.

"Histories of self-harm or parental abuse?" said Suzanne.

Shakes of the head.

"None uncovered yet." Shane pointed at the 3-D list. "Other Circles show a higher than average number of kids with anorexia or other self-harm behaviours."

"Right," said Trin. "The thing is, it's not *much* higher than you'd get with a random pick of teens. And it's a hell of a lot lower than you'd expect, given how the poor buggers ended up."

On the 3-D viewstage, a new image shone: pale corpses in a tangled circle, many with left hands palm-up, all with great longitudinal gashes in their soft inner wrists. Teen corpses lying on a carpet of dark blood.

"What's the political backdrop?" asked Trin. "Do we know yet?"

"Swings back the other way," said Shane.

"Shit."

"Another factor to rule out."

"Yeah. I guess." Trin turned to Suzanne. "We wondered if it might be occurring in certain constituencies or whatever. Whether the community would be LabCon, TechDem or smaller parties. No correlation."

"Right," said Suzanne.

I would never have thought of that.

Yet their guess did not work out. She was here to bring something different to the mix. But what?

Over the viewstage, the images of dead teenagers still hung. You might fancy their expressions were agonised or pleading, their eyes signalling a final call for help, for justice, for *something*. But these were dead things, already beginning to decay.

I'll help you.

Clearly the team comprised intelligence officers, not healthcare professionals. If they suspected the deaths had been engineered, they would want all the neuropsych expertise they could get.

I'll find out.

Whatever had happened to the teenagers, she would help the team work it out.

And forget Josh.

Because her problems could only be a distraction, she needed to push them away for as long as it took to do this.

Right.

In the display, the dead things remained unmoving.

Carlsen, pushing open the front door of Inge's house, knew only one thing.

I should have insisted.

And he had promised Inge, that was the thing. Promised he would help Kat.

I should have tracked her down.

It would never happen now.

• • • •

Shane whirled back to his desk, his fingers fluttering through intricate gestures – CSL, Command Sign Language, the display manipulation method of choice for many academics – as new panes blossomed on his workspace screens.

"Crap," he said.

"What is it?" Trin moved over to him. "A new factor?"

"Not across the sample pop." Shane tapped a screen. "Katherine Carlsen, one of the victims. Her uncle is Fireman Carlsen."

"Who?" said Trin.

"Bloody hell." Carl looked over. "Everyone's heard of Fireman Carlsen. Even–Er, Suzanne? You know who he is, right?"

Suzanne looked at him.

"I've sort of met the guy," she said.

She had been wearing a light disguise and impersonating a police officer, pretending to arrest Josh in order to spirit him away from the Barbican Centre during the *Knife Edge* final. Carlsen had been right there, but she had not talked to him.

"Poor bastard," said Shane. "I wonder if he and his niece were close?"

There was a uniformed policewoman sitting on the couch next to Inge. Just for a second, as Carlsen entered, Inge looked up and something flared inside her – *it's a mistake* – but then she saw it was him. The spark diminished, replaced by hopeless void.

"She's gone," said Inge. "She killed herself."

"I know."

"How could–"

And then the sobbing overwhelmed her words, and Carlsen was crying too as he hugged her, because she was his sister and he was the big brother always on hand to help and protect – except that this time he hadn't done it, had he? He was supposed to talk to Kat, but she had begged off, claiming an arranged visit to a friend's place.

I should've, should've–

If only he had pushed he might have found out what was happening, and saved her.

The officers he had talked to had not wanted to share the details. But they were fight fans and he was insistent, so they gave in. What they related was so awful, he wished he had not heard.

Not just Kat. Twelve others with her.

The door security system chimed. The policewoman stood up.

"I'll check it," she said.

Her physical movement was competent, her voice was low and calm. She went out, then her voice echoed back from the hallway.

"Oh, for God's sake."

Carlsen squeezed Inge's shoulder, then stood up and went out.

"What's going on?"

The policewoman pointed to the display. It showed a group of people on the front path, and more beyond the low hedge, on the pavement.

She said, "You don't know any of them, I suppose?"

"No."

"Reporters or fans," she said. "Maybe both."

His supporters. Reporters interested in him. So much for helping his sister.

"I'll send them away," he said.

"No– Please, sir."

But he had already pulled the front door open and stepped outside. It was gloomy and thin snow was falling. The crowd looked cold but eager.

"Go away," he said.

The man at the front was bulky, even bigger than Carlsen, though much of it was fat.

"You gotta tell us, Fireman. How did she die? They're saying– *Mmph.*"

Carlsen's fist twisted into the neck of the man's shirt, forearm rotating into the carotid, forming half a cross-strangle. He pulled down with his other hand, turned the man around, and walked him through the crowd. Out on the wet pavement, he took the bastard over his hip to the ground.

Someone pointed at Carlsen.

"Officer, he assaulted that man. You saw it."

"I saw nothing," said the policewoman. "Everyone, clear this area now."

"But the cameras–"

There were spycams on walls and lampposts along the street.

"Won't show a bloody thing." The policewoman unhitched her stun-baton. "What part of *fuck off* don't you bastards understand?"

The people began to back away.

Jesus Christ.

Carlsen watched as they moved faster, anything to get away from the officer striding forward with her stun-baton cocked over her shoulder.

One of them, a teenage girl not much older than Kat, held her phone high as she back-pedalled out to the middle of the road. Then she turned, pocketed her phone and strode away. Maybe he should follow and snatch the thing from her.

But if she had been webcasting in realtime, it was too late.

"Disperse," called the policewoman, "or I'll have Riot Suppression here in seconds."

The group broke apart, some of them running in order to get away. Carlsen stood at the front gate while they disappeared into the gloom.

"You'd better come back in," said the policewoman. "See to your sister."

"All right," said Carlsen. "Can I ask you something?"

"Sure."

"What's your name?"

"I'm Constable Milton."

Carlsen looked down the street, sniffed in a breath, and turned back to her.

"I meant your first name."

Her fearless eyes closed, then opened.

"Sandra," she said.

"Thank you, Sandra."

"You're welcome."

Jayne Feng increased her stride length, hoping she could move fast without it being too obvious on surveillance. By the time she reached her bedsit, she was sweating inside her clothes.

She hated paying the extra fees for baths – her landlady had installed a commercial system to control the shared bathroom – but she would splurge tonight. If this footage was as good as she thought, then with editing and well-written background, she could submit it to one of the news portals. Maybe even to Google-Reuters, where it would not just earn her money – it would launch her career.

Ever since the Munich Catastrophe, when over a hundred people died and thousands were disabled following inaccurate treatment guidelines on a medical wiki, *accreditation* and *verification* were the buzzwords that mattered online. No one trusted online information unless it was peer-reviewed and double-checked. The mediwiki publishers remained in jail, symbol of the modern Web.

While the thing Jayne wanted most was a career in journalism.

The best way was to attain Google-Reuters accreditation, and her best chance of doing that was right here, *provided* she submitted an exclusive, timely and accurate report on the death by blade of Fireman Carlsen's niece.

You can do it, girl.

Her bed/sitting-room was large, though shabby, lit by wall-lights and featuring a bay window whose curtains drew straight across, forming an alcove. Had she left the curtains closed earlier? Well, she must have.

She raised her phone, activating the camera, linking to her vmail app.

Then the screen blackened, along with the room.

"No," said a male voice.

A gloved hand pulled the curtain back. A wide-shouldered shadow stood there, scarcely visible against the dark street outside.

Where streetlights flickered and went out.

"S-stay there." Her thumb pressed the emergency button on her phone. "Back."

The phone was lifeless.

"I'm not going to rape you."

His words knifed through her lower belly.

Oh, God.

Urine leaked into her panties.

As the man reached up to his forehead, she realised he was hooded. He pulled the hood back. In grey shadow, half his face was striped like a tiger's, his eyes predatory.

"Reporters are a good thing," he said. "Especially when they know their duty."

"Wh–?"

She threw herself towards the door, but the electromag locks snapped shut.

"Every good journalist knows how to listen. And when."

The big gloved hand manoeuvred her shoulder, causing her to stumble backwards, then drop to a sitting position on the bed.

Please don't rape me.

Police officers had given a talk during her last year in school, and some of the accompanying images had been graphic. What they had destroyed was the myth of lying back and taking it, because that resulted in scarred victims, disfigured for life inside as well as on the surface, assuming they lived at all. So often the aftermath of rape is a smashed face, if not lethal strangulation.

"Fight back," the officers had said. "Fight back and get clear. Always."

The words and pictures had stayed with her; but they did not help, because her resolve was gone.

"If you thought I was a rapist," the man said now, "you should have hit me with your phone, clawed at my face, gone for a knife – you've a carving-knife in your cutlery drawer, you know – and done anything to go through me and get away."

The words were a surreal jolt, juxtaposed with her memory of police advice.

"Who–?"

"I'm a friend."

No, he was an intruder here to frighten her. But maybe *only* to frighten.

"My preliminary report…"

"Went to our servers," said the man. "Nothing's going viral. Not tonight."

She noted the *our*. He served a larger organization.

The government.

"Why are you here? Why me and why–"

"You'll stay quiet about this evening." The man's bulk was all muscle. "And perhaps we'll put something your way. Something Google-Reuters might find impressive."

Slick ice wrapped her intestines.

How can he know?

But he did. Focus on that.

"I'll do what you want."

Her eyes were drying. Cold tears had streaked down her face, unperceived until now.

"Good."

The man moved like a tiger.

"How will I know when–?"

Something happened.

Hours later, she woke up, feeling no pain. She crawled into bed, pulled up the duvet, and slid back into sleep.

[TWELVE]

It was late, but Suzanne had nothing to go home to. Shane had slipped out earlier, calling an ops team to come with him. They appeared to have no problem with her overhearing such conversations, though their use of earbeads meant she caught only one side.

Shane had said something about Carlsen. He also used the word *op*, part of Josh's vocabulary.

He's not around.

Like not thinking about a blue elephant, Josh's name was in her mind, triggering worlds of associated memory.

Forget him.

She focused on the words, or tried to.

"–not viral," Shireen was saying to someone. "All right, it's contained. Nice work."

The term made Suzanne look up. Viral as in networks, not medicine. Dinner party conversations between Josh and Petra Osbourne's lover, Yukiko, often turned to complex systems and networks. Also to insults.

"That's interesting," Suzanne said.

Shireen turned. Trin paused several moving displays and said, "What's that?".

"You're blocking the news about the Cutter Circles," said Suzanne.

"We prefer freedom from fear to freedom of the press."

"No, I mean…" Suzanne paused to work through the mental steps. "You're blocking the news, therefore you're scanning for it. For any signs of memetic contagion."

"Right," said Trin.

"But the Cutter Circles are still occurring," said Suzanne. "I know you've not identified the channels of communication, or any nexus points that link them… Still, the Circles keep happening. The idea is spreading even under a news blackout."

"With most of the victims," said Carl, "it's been a surprise that any members of a Circle know any of the others."

"So they've not been meeting up in person. In coffee shops or after-school clubs."

"Hardly."

"Or online."

"That's not a…" Trin paused. "What are you getting at, Suzanne?"

"These people live all over the place." Suzanne pointed at a map that showed all Cutter Circle outbreaks to date. "In any one Circle, they live close, but the different Circles are spread all over."

"So the idea spreads via the Web. That's what we've been assuming all the–"

"But they're also far apart psychologically," said Suzanne. "That's why there are no obvious links. Different interests, different outlooks."

Trin was frowning. "And this helps how?"

"Look, there are a few sites nearly everyone visits, and a vast number with scarcely ever a visitor." Suzanne had known some of this network stuff for years; recent conversations with Yukiko delivered up the rest. "You must be monitoring the nexus points, where everybody goes."

"Could be."

"All right," said Suzanne. "They're not meeting in person, the victims. So they're maybe not meeting at all, even online. They're just accessing some common service."

"But not a major Web portal. It's some minor thing we haven't identified yet."

"Maybe. I guess what I'm asking is *why* you haven't found it. It seems to me that you guys are good."

Shireen grimaced. "We thought we were."

·"Maybe you are. Maybe you aren't the only ones."

Shireen blinked. "You mean someone else is burying traces? Destroying whatever links the teenagers together?"

"Destroying records of their access, yes."

Carl was grinning at Suzanne.

"That's paranoid," he said. "Welcome to our reality."

·"Ha. Well, that's all my thoughts so far. Not much help."

"We're glad you're here."

"Thank you." Suzanne looked at her empty coffee cup. "Er, anyone up for escort duty?"

As a yellow-beanie wearer, she could not wander the building without someone accompanying her, even for toilet breaks.

"Sure," said Shireen. "I'll–"

"No, it's all right." That was Trin. "I need a break too."

"Thanks," said Suzanne.

But as Trin held open the door for her, she wondered what it was that Trin wanted to talk about, away from the rest of her team.

Lofty led the way to Major O'Driscoll's office. In a corridor midway, he stopped.

"I've got something to do. Wait there."

"Something to do?"

"The heads are there." Lofty had come via the Royal Marines and SBS originally, and it sometimes showed in his choice of words. "I'm either going for a piss and a fart, or a short explosive crap. I'll let you know later which it was."

"Information overload. With respect."

After Lofty had disappeared, Josh stood relaxed, keeping alert for one of those *Not now, Cato* moments – it was not beyond Lofty to have arranged a sudden ambush for laughs. But nothing happened until Lofty came back.

"All right," he said. "Let's get you re-upped, laddie."

An American term, hence the sarcastic tone.

"I must be mad," said Josh.

"Course you are. Why you're here, ain't it?"

Once inside the major's office, their language became more formal. Mervyn O'Driscoll was Officer Commanding, Z Squadron. His direct responsibilities were the seventy-two people reporting to him (a twenty percent increase over the traditional squadron size); but the nature of special operations meant that the responsibilities were much higher than the number of people would suggest.

It accounted both for the lines in his face and the ready laughter, because without humour he could not thrive. He also competed annually in the Marathon des Sables – despite its name, a traditional ultramarathon across the Sahara – unless he was on active deployment.

"So you can't stay away," he said to Josh. "We get some of that."

"Yes, sir."

"Even though the regs state you need to go through Selection once more."

There were circumstances where this did not apply, for instance when someone resigned from the army in order to take part in a deniable operation. Perhaps a year later, they might rejoin and slip back into service with no comments from any quarter.

"I'll muddle through, sir."

O'Driscoll grinned at him.

"I'm sure you will. Is there anything you need to clear up first? Before getting clear of civvie street."

Josh looked at Lofty, who glanced up at the ceiling.

"Er… I'm working on something," Josh said. "A Geordie Biggs-style op, but I'm doing it directly for the end client."

"Knowing Geordie," said O'Driscoll, "that could be anything."

"A missing person, sir. Resigned from his job and disappeared. It was a planned disappearance."

"Planned by him, you mean?"

"It's looking that way."

O'Driscoll looked at Lofty. "You know Selection starts next week."

"That's right," said Lofty.

"And Josh really ought to be on it."

"Definitely."

"So if your lads and lasses helped him out now, he'd get this thing sorted and be ready in time, wouldn't he?"

"I'd say so," Lofty said.

"So I'm ordering you to help Josh."

"Yes, sir."

"Which is exactly what you wanted me to say."

"Yes, sir."

"Uh-huh." O'Driscoll turned back to Josh. "At least it keeps me humble. Good luck and good hunting, anyhow. Because we want you back."

Josh said, "Thank you, sir."

They shook hands, making the commitment.

Suzanne came out of the cubicle and washed her hands. Trin was waiting with her arms crossed, waiting to talk. It was obvious.

"How can I help you, Trin?"

Trin blinked, her shoulders rocking back.

"You knew I was after a quiet word?"

"If I hadn't known, then I wouldn't be the right person for you to relax and feel comfortable talking with me now."

Suzanne's syntax was deliberately odd, partly to deliver the correct suggestion, partly to make use of the oddness itself. Her tone subtly marked the words she wanted to emphasise – *relax, feel comfortable, now.*

The loosening across Trin's body was immediate.

"You, er…" Trin glanced down. "You know about neurology, right?"

"That's right."

"My son, Tommy. Thing is, it runs in the family, and my grandad died of it, all alone, still in his thirties."

"What's the condition?" asked Suzanne.

"Epilepsy. He… They did the tests this morning."

"It's treatable," said Suzanne. "These days, it's all very different."

"My grandad. He was an engineer. Electronics. The drugs made his brain dull – my mum used to tell me – so he often wouldn't take them. Then one day he was alone and, and…"

Trin's eyes were triangulating on a point in space, responding not to empty air but the geometry of imagination, mediated by the entorhinal cortex and its spatiotemporal grid.

Suzanne wiped her hand back and forth through the air, in the exact location of Trin's virtual mental image. Trin blinked and stumbled back.

"No one uses drugs any more," said Suzanne.

Perhaps the medics had tried to explain that. Under stress, hearing is the first sense to lose acuity. Suzanne used her body language and voice to evoke relaxation in herself, and Trin followed. Mirror neurons in action.

"We use pulsed ultrasound," Suzanne went on. "Along with laser pulses, but it's primarily the ultrasound that does the work."

In essence, the lasers were part of the scanning, while the ultrasound directly controlled the neurons.

"I thought flashing lights cause fits to happen."

"That's right, but the lasers avoid that, while the ultra-sound changes everything for the better, allowing the patient to feel good."

"Oh," said Trin. "Oh."

"What will it be like," said Suzanne, gesturing, "knowing Tommy is fully healthy?"

"I... It'd be like" – Trin's spine straightened – "a weight off my shoulders."

"That's right," said Suzanne. "Remember that."

"Yes, I..." Trin stopped, then: "How did you do that? Everything feels different."

Suzanne smiled.

"Magic," she said.

When they re-entered the office area, Steve was there, his eyes widening as he saw Trin. She appeared to be taller, and glowing.

He smiled at Suzanne, and mouthed: *Well done.*

Was he congratulating her on the basis of good intuition and what he saw now? Or were there spycams in the ladies' loo, here in MI5?

Does it matter?

She smiled back.

[THIRTEEN]

The commitment changed everything. In the subterranean control room beneath Sterling Lines – every tunnel and armoured chamber on spring-loaded supports and gimbals, so it would keep steady even if missiles were exploding overhead – Josh watched Ghost Force operators at work. He felt at home. These were his comrades, his band of brothers and sisters.

A red-headed man looked up from his console.

"Hey, Josh."

"Hey, Ginge."

"Welcome back, you old bastard."

"Thanks. I've a little old Selection to get through first."

"Piece of piss," said Ginge.

"Walk in the park," called out another operator. "For someone like you."

"Cheers," said Josh.

It was a lie, but one he appreciated.

Behind him, Lofty said: "I'm taking the Ranger boys out for another little stroll in the morning. What say you tag along, keep an eye on the youngsters?"

"A stroll," said Josh. "Why not?"

Several smiles showed around the room. They must have

heard about Lofty running the Americans into the ground, though he was twice their age.

"Isis," Lofty said. "Got a minute?"

"Sure, Boss."

A black-skinned woman with good shoulders paused everything on her console, then came over. Lofty extracted a phone from his pocket, and handed it to Josh.

It was Josh's own phone.

"Oh. Cheers."

Lofty pointed from him to the young woman.

"Josh, Isis."

They nodded and said "hi".

"Josh has a missing-person case," Lofty added. "Shall we take a look?"

"Definitely." Isis pointed back at her console – her shoulder-flash was SBS: she had started as a Royal Marine – and it came to life. "Redfang now, if you like."

"Here you are." Josh worked his phone. "And that… is the lot."

It included his querybots in ultra-compressed archive files, the retrieved footage from the motorway services, and the negative results from street surveillance around Evans' home. Isis checked over the files, getting a feel for the search's scope.

There was no such thing as a Ghost Force shoulder-flash, so that the badges on view were SAS, SBS, or SRR. As the former SCS there had been a badge, but after the C changed what it stood for several times over – Computing, Cyberwarfare, simply Cyber – the force became a covert detachment once more.

The real badges were invisible: processors woven into their clothing. But the deepest signifiers were in the mind: attitude and capability.

"There we go." Isis turned back from her console. "Easy."

"You've found Evans?" said Josh.

"Of course I have." Isis grinned. "What did you expect?"

"Right, Josh," said Lofty. "What did you expect?"

"Humility, maybe?"

"Boy," said Isis, "are *you* in the wrong fuckin' place."

Lofty led the way to the Quartermaster's Store, beyond armoured doors labelled Q13. Inside, they stopped at a ceramic counter. Behind it stood a lean-bodied man, almost as grizzled as Lofty.

"Alfie, this is young Cumberland," Lofty said. "I think he should be taking the piss."

"What?" said Josh.

"P-I-S-S. Pulse Interference Scanning System, like the old BatEars but better." The quartermaster, Alfie, shook his head. "There's so much gear lying around unrecorded when it ought to be in my inventory. It's a disgrace."

"He'll bring it back in one piece," said Lofty.

"Good." Alfie looked around. "You know, I'm sure there ought to be another box of whisperdrones someplace. Thing is, no one gives a monkey's if *they* disappear."

Josh and Lofty grinned.

"Good man," said Lofty.

"Back in a mo," said Alfie.

He disappeared into the stores proper. Lofty scrunched up his forehead.

"Blimey," said Josh. "Steady on with that thinking lark. You don't want to strain nothing."

"My whole life is a strain. I was wondering whether an EMP bomb would help."

"Bloody hell, Lofty. My man is holed up in a pub, not a bloody fortress."

"Yeah, but it's a Welsh pub."

"True. I think I'll manage, though."

Alfie returned with a large duffel bag, and swung it onto the counter without effort. Josh was not fooled. He braced himself for a heavy load, and hauled the bag onto his shoulder. It weighed more than Suzanne.

Forget her.

He had work to do, and this was it.

"Cheers," he said. "Both of you."

"Remember," said Lofty. "Guile before strength."

"And smile when you waste the fuckers," said Alfie.

Josh grinned.

"I will."

"And come back safe," said Lofty. "Because you owe me a run, right?"

"The morning jog with the Rangers," said Josh. "Sorry I'll be missing that."

"Poor little buggers," said Alfie.

"Yeah. I could save them the pain" – Lofty looked at Josh – "if I was somewhere else, doing something else."

This was not what Josh had expected.

"Thanks," he said. "Really. But I can sort this one solo."

"Fair enough."

But it was the offer that made the difference: the knowledge that he was among men and women who would watch his back, as he would watch theirs. This was what civilians would never understand.

Maybe it's a form of dependency.

That was a new voice in his mind.

Shut up.

He hitched the heavy bag. The strap was digging into his shoulder. "It's the best thing," he said.

"What's that?"

"To drife your enemies before you" – he laid on the Teutonic accent – "and hear zer lamentation of zer women."

"You're a sick man," said Alfie.

"One of us," said Lofty.

Josh's guts settled.

"I'll be back," he said.

[FOURTEEN]

Dad had another meeting today, this time in the centre of the city. He was travelling by Métro, so Lexa had no driving to do.

"Come on, *mes enfants*," she told Richie and Opal over breakfast. "Let's explore Paris."

"Sac-ray blue," said Richie.

"All right," said Opal.

They began by exploring the oldest quarter, on what was really a separate island in the Seine – the Île de la Cité. Wonderful buildings, some three centuries old, the earliest going back nine hundred years. Cobbled lanes. It reminded Richie of the Three Musketeers, and he said so.

"Old Alexandre Dumas," said Lexa, "used to wander down these very streets."

Richie did not believe her. "Really?"

"For his monthly booze-and-marijuana sessions with Baudelaire. Out of their heads, the pair of them."

"Yeah, yeah," said Opal. "Who's Baudelaire when he's at home?"

"Some old writer," said Lexa.

Meanwhile, Richie was working his phone.

"Bloody hell." He turned it towards Opal. "Lexa's right."

Lexa squeezed their shoulders.

"Thing is," she said, "Lexa is always right."

Richie had seen drivers in other cars dropping off pupils at St Michael's. They were not friends of the people they drove, merely employees.

Ever since last year, something had changed. Though Lexa had always been terrific.

She's brilliant.

They stopped at a small café, where Richie and Opal ordered hot chocolate. Off in one corner, as Richie spoke, a group of people with guttural voices muttered something. Lexa's face tightened. There was another remark, then laughter.

Lexa crossed to their table, and delivered a low-voiced fluent speech which caused faces to whiten. She came back and sat down beside Opal.

"What did you say?" asked Richie.

"Just making conversation."

"They were insulting us," said Opal.

"Because they're country bumpkins." Lexa glanced at the other table. "Parisians have good manners."

"You sounded fluent." Richie had been discovering how little his schooling had prepared him for the live experience of language. "Where'd you learn?"

"In the *Légion étrangère*," said Lexa.

"You were in the French Foreign Legion?"

"Not bad for a Brummie girl from Selly Oak, eh?"

The group she had talked to were leaving, looking everywhere but in the direction of their table. After a while, Lexa wandered over to the counter to talk to the staff. Just chatting.

Just leaving Richie and Opal alone.

"She's like Josh," said Opal. "You think she ought to marry him?"

"Er… What?" Hot choco swirled in Richie's stomach. "What do you mean?"

"I know Josh and Suzanne are together, but they're like different, don't you think?"

"Er..."

Opal looked at him, then shook her head. She began to spoon the remnants of choco from the bottom of her mug.

Later, they were crossing the snow-patched Pont Neuf when Opal broke away, took two long strides, jumped onto a rail – landing crouched – and threw herself backward, in a half-somersault, half-cartwheel, to land back on her feet.

"All that adrenaline and frustration," said Lexa.

"Frustration?" said Richie.

Lexa shook her head, much as Opal had done in the café.

"No." Lexa reached forward. "That's too–"

But Opal was back up on the rail – where it curved around a lamppost, while beyond was the drop to cold grey waves – then she took hold of the lamppost with opposing grips, and raised her body to the horizontal. It was called the flag: a hard move for any free runner.

Her hand slipped.

All that painted metal was ice-slick. With the first slip everything was lost: she tumbled, her limbs tangled; splayed, and something dropped clear as she nearly went over, into the Seine. But she grabbed hold of the rail, then Lexa's fist was twisted in her sleeve, holding her.

"Are you all right?" Richie was stammering. "O-Opal?"

Lexa stepped clear, leaving him and Opal face to face.

"Opal, I thought you–"

Then her arms were around his neck, and she kissed him, her tongue a shocking sweet explosion. Time collapsed. His world folded up, encapsulating the moment.

Opal.

And then they were standing apart, hands on each other's arms. Lexa was staring off across the city.

He could look only at Opal, and she at him.

"Hmm." Lexa was doing something with her phone. "Never mind."

Opal twitched, smiled, then turned to Lexa.

"Sorry," she said.

"Well done, girl," said Lexa. "That was worth a phone."

Richie was blinking.

"Phone?"

"*It's fallen in the water,*" said Lexa in a high-pitched voice. Then: "Never mind. Before my time, never mind yours."

"What was?" asked Opal.

"Neddy Seagoon. Richie, you need to take your girlfriend shopping."

"I–"

Beside him, Opal's face was pink.

"Come on, you two. Somewhere posh like Galeries Lafayette. Buy her a replacement."

"He doesn't have to buy me a–" Opal started.

"Yeah, he does," said Lexa.

"Yeah, I do," said Richie.

Opal's hand took hold of his. He swallowed.

"*Allons-y,*" said Lexa.

He drove along a meandering road – an A road according to the heads-up map – over peaks cloaked with bracken, gorse, and snow, taking switchbacks where rockfall had created scree slopes on the inner side. The outer edges crumbled over long drops.

Finally, halfway up a valley with pine forest covering the ridges, he pulled in to park in front of a co-op store. Collapsing the driver's seat, he reclined as if resting, then twisted around to pull down the rear seat, revealing the boot's interior. He hauled forward the duffel bag containing the PISS apparatus.

He reached inside, pressed buttons, then pulled out what looked like a pair of sunglasses, and put them on. He raised the seat once more.

Across the valley sat a white-painted pub called the *Glyndwr Arms*. Of course Evans would have chosen it. As Josh worked the PISS, skeletal lines of light overlaid the building. Pastel ghost-figures of customers and staff appeared, while text-only transcripts of their dialogue began to scroll in separate panes.

Just an ordinary pub with ordinary conversation. The Blues were in trouble again, the older folk hated the new lyrics to Hymns and Arias, and the pub's Guinness tasted off. Olwen was having an affair with Kev in the toy factory.

Much of the data came from resonance in the building's wiring, a surveillance source few people knew about. No one used Evans' name, but a lone figure was sitting on a bed in one of the guest bedrooms. At ground level, the bar and lounge were less than half full. Three people sat in tactical positions, backs to walls, one foot in front of the other: able to drive upwards or sideways from the seated equivalent of a sprinter's crouch.

Two wore flat knives in calf sheaths and ceramic gas pistols in concealed holsters. The third carried no weapons as far as the PISS was concerned. Sitting at a good logistical location did not necessarily mean the person was an operator.

Which way to enter?

There was the gymnastic option, up the outside of the building; or he could go inside like an ordinary punter, provided he was careful not to look like a professional entering a hostile environment. Call it disguising the vibrations that every predator transmits and is sensitive to.

Think tunnel vision, slouched gait, closed-in awareness.

I am harmless.

He crossed the road, head down, paying little attention to the world.

Soft and unaware.

In his mind he pictured a hard day in the corporate workplace, leaving him filled with real exhaustion that was stress rather than muscular fatigue. Tiredness after a sedentary day is a call to exercise, to get the blood flowing; but he did not know that because he was locked in a certain life, overwhelmed by domestic trivia, stumbling through existence.

Not looking at the watchers as he entered the bar.

"How be?" said the barmaid.

"All right," he said back. "Or I'll be all right with a pint of Brains inside me."

Josh kept his voice deep, harder to distinguish against the ambient noise of conversation.

"Fabulous. What we're here for." And, after less than a minute: "There you are."

"Thank you."

It took fifteen minutes to manoeuvre through the saloon, making brief conversation with several locals – their natural friendliness would make it hard for the watchers to realise that Josh was a stranger here – and timing the next bit with precision. As several standing drinkers moved to let one of the barmaids through – she had two fistfuls of empties – Josh moved towards the head of the stairs leading to the basement-level toilets, then slipped into the upward staircase and around the first bend, out of sight.

He checked his phone. The pub's financial subsystem contained one room booking for tonight. The name was Rees and the payment method was cash: suspect in an urban hotel, business as usual in a valley pub.

Slowing down, he used his remote link to the PISS to check that none of the suspected watchers was following. Likewise, that the single occupant remained where he had been, sitting on his bed. At the top landing, an uneven hallway led to four numbered doors.

Room 3 contained Rees, who with luck was really Alex Rhys Evans.

Odd pulsating music sounded from inside the door, reasonably loud. Good. As Josh turned the old-fashioned doorknob it was almost silent. He pushed inwards with care, testing for the pressure of a mechanical lock – his phone showed no electromagnets – but the door opened.

Evans was sitting on the bed, staring at a wallscreen that pulsed with a moving mosaic of greens and purples and silvers, swirling and strobing, bright enough to get lost in, revolving like a vortex–

Falling.
–that pulled him in and down forever.
To black nothing.

The store levels encircled a central atrium down which silken banners hung, dripping with bioluminescent script, advertising products that Richie had never heard of. The air was scented with expensive fragrance, for only the most exclusive brands had franchises here. On the fourth floor, gold-plated handsets were the highlight of the phone display.

Opal was shaking her head.

"It is for you?" The saleswoman wore black gloves for handling the merchandise. "You would like a phone, yes?"

"I guess. But nothing like–Like that."

The saleswoman glanced in Lexa's direction, then checked out Richie. His clothes looked plain, but the fabric was expensive, and a platinum bracelet showed from under his cuff. He adjusted his sleeve.

"Nothing expensively vulgar," said the saleswoman. "Maybe something new."

"Perhaps we should go somewhere–"

Opal stopped, her attention snagged by a small silver phone with red highlights.

"All the young people want these." The saleswoman's gloved hand was inside the display case, withdrawing the handset. "It features our own extra, a world music library pre-loaded for the emotifone engine to play."

Lexa was smiling and shaking her head. To someone of her age, Richie supposed, a phone responding to your emotional state was a pointless accessory. But with earbeads and a decent music library, you had a soundtrack for life, not to mention easy access to the webmovies that suited your mood.

Mal James had been the first boy at school to get one, and Mal was one of the good guys.

"Suzanne asked me about buying one for Josh," Richie said. "A Midsummer Christmas present."

"Did she get one?" asked Lexa.

"I don't know, actually."

Opal held up the shining phone.

"Richie, are you sure about this?"

Off to one side, Lexa was looking at the floor, front teeth biting lower lip, eyes tense.

"Er, of course." He pulled out his own phone to access the payment app. "How much is it?"

Within a minute, sale and setup were complete, the saleswoman smiling as Opal created her DNA-tagged user profile. Richie turned to look for Lexa, but then his phone vibrated.

Thank U ♥ *0*

He smiled at Opal, feeling he might cry because she was perfect.

"Come on, kidders." Lexa was standing beside them. "Time we went."

As they descended in the glass-walled lift, Lexa's tone changed to a hard tension he had not heard before.

"You know I love you both." She pushed out a breath. "But life is complicated. That's code for fucked up, but you're too young for language like that."

Richie tried to smile.

"Boys are stupid," said Opal.

"Even when they're too old to be called boys." Lexa's mouth twisted: a sine wave of regret. "Throwing yourself at them like a kamikaze doesn't work either. Because they never had time to fall in love with you. Lust turning into love is a fairy tale."

The lift opened on the ground floor. Halfway across the

marble-floored foyer, Lexa's phone buzzed, and the three of them stopped.

"On our way back," Lexa said into the phone. "Fifteen minutes."

Opal glared at Richie.

"All right, Boss," added Lexa.

She tagged her phone to her belt, and shrugged.

"See?" said Opal.

"What?" said Richie.

"Don't you even–?"

"No, look." Lexa's hand was on Richie's shoulder. "Forget it, all right?"

"Er…" said Richie.

They went outside, the cold air a contrast to the scents from the perfume – no, the *fragrance* counters. Perfume was a down-market term. Who had told him that? "Bloody hell," he said.

For so long, memories of Mum had been a blank. Now, Richie remembered not just her face on the day she mentioned perfume, but the stink of booze on Dad's mouth in the mornings following her death, his unshaven face when he worked from home, and the shivering sessions after long business meetings. During the days when he forgot he had a son.

Not Lexa and Dad.

Days that continued until Josh and Suzanne came into their lives last year. Lexa had played a part in that. Since then she had loosened up in some way. But perhaps Dad still saw her as an employee, though a trusted one.

Maybe Lexa had a different view.

Opal had said that boys were stupid, but the truth was that girls were complex and lived in a different universe, one that he had no way to navigate or even understand. As Opal and Lexa walked beside him, Richie wondered how they could be so different, and what – if anything – he could say to Dad.

While all around, Paris existed in all its richness, a city that had known so many stories of romance and complication.

[FIFTEEN]

Harsh pile pressed into Josh's nose, cheek, and lips, while his eyes remained closed. Waking up felt effortful.

"Fucking hell."

His voice slurred with sleepiness.

"Bastards."

He opened one eye.

Shit.

Face down on the carpet, sunlight around him, and the smell of bacon drifting through the closed door. Evans' bedroom. Was he still–?

On hands and knees, Josh checked. The bed was unoccupied, made up but creased, and the room felt empty. Wonderful.

Anaesthetic?

He could feel no pinprick pain from a gas-launched dart. A vapour spray was the most likely mechanism. Had it been Evans or one of the watchers from the bar? He remembered entering the room and, and–

Darkness had dropped on him.

Evans, then.

He would have to have a word with the bastard. First, it was necessary to stand steadily and wait for the world to settle. It did not take long. The room was en suite, so he used the bathroom, including the shower. Then he went down to breakfast.

A small table was already laid out, with a plastic tag bearing the numeral 3. Josh sat down, wondering whether he might try pretending he was Evans or just a friend who had crashed in Evans' vacant room and was willing to pay for breakfast. But the woman who bustled out from the back had not been here last night; she just took Josh's breakfast order, and came back with beans on toast and a coffee pot.

In the bar, washed glasses stood on cloths atop the counter. Was this the kind of pub where the owner poured slops back into the barrels once the customers were gone? It was hard to tell.

Working his phone, he checked his car. The PISS system remained inside, and the vehicle was unharmed.

So what happened last night?

The watchers – either two or three of them – might have been protecting Evans, planning to kill him, or simply observing, perhaps with a brief to intervene if a third party – like Josh Cumberland – turned up. Or the X scenario, the alternative he had not figured out.

In the pub system, he could find no footage of Evans leaving. Nor could he distinguish the features of the three possible operatives, though the images of other customers were clear. At least he now knew they were all male. And professional, including the one he had doubted, not detecting any weaponry.

"Breakfast all right, love?" The woman poked her head round the door. "Anything else I can get you?"

"Perfect, thanks," said Josh. "I've got everything I need."

Apart from a nuclear scientist and a trio of covert operatives whose affiliation was unknown.

"You're here another night, isn't it?"

"That's right."

Not really, because Evans was not coming back. There had been no luggage in his room.

"Busy tonight, mind. *Knife Edge* on the big screen, see."

She gestured towards the massive wallscreen in the lounge bar.

"Everyone'll be wearing team colours. You for Bloods or Blades?"

"Er, not really my thing."

"Well, never mind, love." She winked at him. "That's all right."

Then she went back into the kitchen.

She forgives me for not being a supporter.

Smiling, Josh resumed demolishing breakfast, loading up on protein and carbs because Evans was an outdoorsman, and if he was really going to ground then it would be in the mountains, inside the cover of pine-forested slopes. A mountain trek was on today's agenda.

Time to find the bastard.

Also to shut him down before he could retaliate. Forget about questioning until Evans was secured and unable to fight or get away.

Good.

Little remained on the plate by the time Josh felt full.

"Thanks," he said, not too loudly.

He slipped out of the pub.

An hour later, he rested below a pine-covered ridgeline. On his back, the Bergen was heavy, its system communicating with the whisperdrones he had released earlier. On his phone display, the tracking data glowed.

There was a new hit: 0.97 probability match.

Got you.

His whisperdrones were unarmed, of so-called apoptotic design: built to land and dissolve after four hours flight. He could not use them as weapons, only to track Evans unobserved or else fly them into his visual range in order to panic him.

With the head start Evans had, it was better to keep him unaware of pursuit.

There was no sign of the other three men.

Move your arse, Cumberland.

Lofty's voice in his head.

With a forward lean to counteract the Bergen's mass, Josh got into motion again, the yomping/tabbing gait that was faster than a walk, zigzagging among pine trunks, clean air filling him, his skin coming alive. A peregrine falcon hovered high above, then flashed out of sight in a killing dive.

Josh's feet had an intelligence of their own, or that was how it seemed as he trusted himself to four billion years of evolution, moving through the terrain faster than logical analysis, knowing the dangers of a fall but also that he could maintain this pace and keep his footing.

Think of Evans.

The objective, sharp and focused in his mind, impelled every part of him forward, allowing doubts and residual fatigue to drop away.

It was another hour and ten minutes before Evans stopped, by which time the gap was eight hundred horizontal metres in his phone's aerial display, something over a kilometre across the actual terrain. If Evans had countersurveillance kit, this would be the time to slow right down; but instead, Evans – as observed by a transparent whisperdrone he did not look up to see – shucked off his backpack amid tangled gorse, then strode to the edge of a precipice and looked down.

And continued to look.

Shit.

This was not good. Slipping out of his Bergen, Josh dropped it into bracken, hiding it.

Oh, fucking shit.

Now he could run, and did.

Come on.

Trees, and his route became an uphill slalom, zigzagging once more. His phone was in his left hand, still hooked in to his whisperdrone.

Nine hundred metres.

Faster.

Eight hundred.

Out in the open, trees behind him, pain beginning to envelop him as anaerobic sprinting became impossible, his short-burst time elapsed and the lactic-acid system taking over.

Seven.

Now Evans was a blurred silhouette – blurred because of wind and stress-condition vision and the need to run – *faster* – up the broken slope, amid gorse and bloody snow patches, so much for summer, and the bastard was close – *check distance* – with five hundred metres the gap, ninety seconds minimum on this gradient, and just how long does it take a man to jump?

Run faster.

Four hundred metres.

The phone was irrelevant as the countdown continued in his mind and his sinews screamed because of what he was putting them through, thighs powering him upslope, inhaling fire, or that was how it seemed: there's a reason they hold sprint races on the flat for one hundred metres, the emergency boosters of physiology good for no more; but he was less than three hundred metres from his target – and the bastard knew someone was coming.

Evans had flinched.

Fuck's sake run harder.

Two hundred metres, the universe a fireball of pain, Evans a watery image turning to process the danger of Josh's approach, but what could be worse than a drop into void?

Harder.

One hundred metres.

Everything hurting as Evans' lips moved, and whether Josh heard him or reconstructed the words later, he would never know; but it would always seem those final words were clear.

Fifty metres.

"You'll be sorry."
Twenty, but Evans was turning.
One second from grabbing the bastard.
Got–
Movement.
–nothing.
As Evans jumped.

[SIXTEEN]

It took twenty minutes to climb down to the body.

Partly because Josh was taking care; partly to regain his emotional balance. Every now and then an ex-spec ops man – rarely a woman – would take a step out of a light aircraft with no parachute. One of his old mates, Franco, had done just that, leaving his wife – suddenly his widow – to land the bloody thing.

"He just smiled at me," she said. "Then opened the hatch and rolled right out."

One last adrenaline rush in a civilian life grown boring.

I could have helped you.

Whether he meant Franco or Evans, Josh was not sure. Maybe it was both.

Tell me why.

He bypassed an outcrop of gorse, descended a near-vertical slab, and reached the broken, splayed thing whose spilled, fatty, decomposing brain once held a mind. Josh's phone detected no concealed devices – not even a phone – so that meant a manual check: pockets, fabric linings, belt, bootsoles, the lot.

Nothing.

It made no sense, suicide, except that it had looked so tempting

– had it not? – when he had peered over the bridge and into the Thames, so black and promising oblivion, which meant this corpse had recently been a soul brother, perhaps: someone he could have talked to, formed a bond with, and saved from death.

He crouched with one hand hooked over a jagged lip in the rock-face, his other hand dangling free, keeping watch over the dead man, thoughts swirling for an unknown duration.

Then he raised his phone.

"Emergency services," he told it.

There was a beep. A human operator looked out from the display.

"What is the nature–?"

"Mountain casualty." Josh turned his phonecam towards the corpse. "He's dead."

After that, the process got rolling.

I'm sorry.

Call it an end to civilian life. Whimpering disaster, a sign that his only home was in the Regiment, among professionals, where his game would sharpen because it had to.

Where he could remain busy enough to forget his failures.

Another funeral. Another death by blade.

But this was Kat, baby-turned-teenager, child-turned-schoolgirl-turned-corpse, his niece, and it was not right. But Inge, Carlsen's little sister, now a bereaved mother, was devastated, needing his support; so his own grief would have to wait.

"–shadow of the valley of death," said the black-cloaked priest, "where I will fear no evils."

Carlsen held Inge's shoulders and wished there was some way he could strike out, some physical action to dissipate his rage. He scanned the mourners: distraught faces, and the stony features of Police Constable Sandra Milton, wearing a black coat. This was June, but snow patches lay among the graves.

Kat would be cold in her coffin.

After the words and the staring at the box down in the hole, as the mourners turned away, someone touched Carlsen's arm.

"Excuse me?"

She was a teenager, Asian, pale.

"Yes?" he said.

"I'm Mandy, and I–"

"A friend of Kat's?"

"Yes. I don't know–And the knives. I mean, I know you–"

What was this? Another political nutter?

"My brother wanted your autograph," she went on. "But he's too young to understand. The thing is, Kat really hated knives, you know?"

"I..." His guts curled inward. "Hated them?"

Her eyes, Mandy's eyes, were leaking tears.

"She wouldn't tell you because of–you know. Who you are."

"I don't know what to say. But I'm glad you told me."

"Yes, I–Sorry."

She stumbled off towards two waiting women, one of them clearly her mother. Carlsen nodded to them, and went back to Inge's side.

There was no need to tell me that.

So his niece had died hating his profession. Did this new knowledge make things any worse? It was the death that mattered.

He helped Inge into the hearse. About to climb in, he stopped.

Black coat, strong features. Someone approaching.

He stepped away from the car.

"I'm sorry for your loss," said Sandra Milton. "And could you glance over my left shoulder for a moment?"

He did so, then his attention went back to her. What was this?

"In the grey BMW," Sandra went on, "there's a blond man and a–"

"Woman with brown skin. I recognise her, almost. I... don't know."

"Don't worry. They're not civilians. Probably Special Branch.

I don't know them."

"If you think they're police, why don't you–?"

But the grey car was already moving, the chocolatté-skinned woman looking back at him. The driver was a stranger.

Carlsen stared into Sandra's eyes.

"My niece was scared of knives," he found himself telling her. "I just found out."

"I'm sorry."

"Makes you wonder how she managed to kill herself like that, doesn't it?"

"I–"

Sandra stopped, face tightening.

"My sister needs me." He moved to the hearse, then looked back. "Will you come to the house?"

Again they stared at each other, faces serious.

"Yes, I will."

Sandra Milton was the last of the mourners to leave. She had never met Kat, and she wished she had met Matt "Fireman" Carlsen in some other way, but reality does not let you choose the context of your life. One of her teachers used to tell her that.

Whatever was going on, there were twelve dead teenagers in addition to Katherine Carlsen, and the hint of a lot more – of other suicide groups – beyond that. There were new faces among the detectives, allegedly temporary transfers from other forces; but the rumour was that they were Special Branch, or maybe even spooks.

Sharing information about an ongoing investigation – sharing it with a civilian – was totally forbidden.

"Matt Carlsen," she said to the graveyard.

Her parents, both of them teachers, had raised her in the old regime of political correctness; but she believed in self-honesty.

Carlsen was a real man, and she wanted him.

• • • •

For Suzanne, in the passenger seat of the BMW, a mental montage of mourners' faces overlaid the reality of the motorway. Beside her, Steve was focused on his driving.

"They saw us watching," she said. "That woman in the black coat."

"She's a police officer." Steve gestured at the windscreen, though he had switched off the heads-up. "I checked."

"Carlsen saw me before. At the thing last year."

"If he remembered you, who would he think you were?"

She smiled. His questioning technique resembled her own.

"A Special Branch officer, arresting Josh."

"So we'll keep an eye on Constable Milton." Steve steered over to the fast lane. "If she asks the wrong questions, we'll have a quiet word."

Since the woman was a police officer, Suzanne assumed that *have a quiet word* was reasonably literal, not a euphemism for threat or violence.

"Too bad Josh didn't succeed," added Steve. "The Tyndalls have friends in high places, but if the news had come out a day earlier—"

"The West Coast catastrophe was genuinely more important."

"Of course. Does Josh take his failure that calmly?"

Suzanne's shoulders shifted, her poise disturbed.

"You're using judgmental language."

"Yes, and how does Josh see it?"

She relaxed, mouth twitching. He really had a feel for psychosemantics.

"As a failure, just as you said." Then she had an intuition, and went with it. "Does the list of Tyndall's friends include your boss, by any chance?"

Eyebrow raised, Steve said: "Clearly you're the expert I thought you were. Trin's booked her son in for pulse treatment, by the way."

It was an oblique way of answering yes while closing off the topic.

Better at language games than Josh.

Her stomach seemed to curl up and squeeze.

Then Steve pulled across to the nearside lane. Up ahead it became the M25 slip road, arching up and over the M4 they were on now.

"Little diversion," he said. "A country hotel. Mansion style, in Surrey."

"Steve, I really don't think–"

"It's a professional conference. We're only attending one session."

A conference for spooks?

"Do I have clearance? I mean, if they're discussing intelligence results and–"

"Oh, no," said Steve. "It's not that sort of conference."

The car banked a little with the rising, curving road.

"Neuropsychs," he added. "You'll be right at home."

They parked on gravel among shining, expensive cars. Acres of lawn were edged with trees. Stone fountains decorated formal gardens. Faux turrets and battlements decorated the extensive building and its colonnades.

In the car, Suzanne watched an archived news item on the heads-up.

"Diplomatic visit," said Steve. "Day before yesterday. The Foreign Secretary and her delegation. Note that President Brand is standing right there on the tarmac to greet her."

Not just the president, but half of his inner cabinet, the so-called Twelve Apostles.

The scrolling text and video reported only the facts. Editorial comment panes were available but unnecessary: President Brand was a pariah, the former US a rogue state, and here was the United Kingdom sending one of its highest politicians to visit.

Brand must be loving it: a public relations coup.

"If you were going to explain a bit more," said Suzanne, "what would you tell me now?"

Steve smiled.

"Your Jedi mind tricks will not work with me, old woman."

"Excuse me, did you say *old*?"

"Yes, but I didn't mean it." He pointed at the image. "The Foreign Secretary's entourage. See the bald guy with the goatee?"

"Even with my old eyes, yes."

"Sorry. You're very beau–Anyway. Um, the bald guy. Expert in the techniques you explained to us in Thames House."

Suzanne tried to ignore what he had nearly said.

"In what you called mindbending?" she asked.

"Exactly. He's called Badakian."

"I sort of know that name."

"Well," said Steve. "I wondered if you would."

They went in to the hotel's foyer – it was big on chandeliers and marble – and picked up name badges from a desk. Steve was registered as Dr Don Duncan, Suzanne under her real name.

A glowing sign announced the next seminar.

Professor Rashid Badakian
"ENTERING THE SCHIZOID WORLD"

Steve nodded towards it.

"You think that means he's nuts?"

"Probably." Suzanne was not going to rise to any bait about insane therapists. "Doesn't he run self-realization programmes, that sort of thing?"

"That's the man. Gospel-church atmosphere, teams of assistants trained by himself, not academically qualified."

So how did that translate into political influence, accompanying the Foreign Secretary abroad? Or perhaps it made sense: scientific, rational techniques and research were less glamorous to those segments of the public that had been failed by the school system, never taught to think critically.

"There can be benefit to that atmosphere," she said, "for rapid personal change. But it also allows charismatic leaders to install delusional belief systems."

Which might make Badakian an expert in more than a technical, academic sense.

"I take it his PhD and professorship are genuine?" she added. "Guru-type figures like the authority that titles grant them, while often not having what it takes to earn the qualifications."

"In his case, they're real."

Steve's tone was tight. She wanted to ask more, but people were drifting over to tables set up for coffee: too many eavesdroppers. Also, Steve kept looking at the coffee urns.

"Need a caffeine fix?" she said.

"Don't tell me, you can cure that."

"If you want me to."

"I'd rather get a cup of coffee and a Jammie Dodger."

"Then I'll join you."

Off to one side, a shaven-headed man was surrounded by a ring of men and women. Professor Badakian's suit looked expensive; his coterie looked to be intent on everything he said, and there was a glow to his appearance, though there was something lizard-like, swift and calculating, about his movements and expression. Suzanne knew how charismatic auras arise: partly from increased bloodflow to the speaker's skin, partly from the physiological reaction of the observer, sniffing the airborne molecular messages that humans are not conscious of.

Dogs smelling a pack leader probably saw him the same way.

When Badakian moved away, presumably to get ready for his talk, a near-tangible absence remained in that part of the room.

A bell sounded – Steve murmured something about Pavlov – and everyone headed for the seminar room. Suzanne followed Steve's lead, and sat near the back. Behind them, two neuropsychs, a man and a woman, were talking about Badakian.

"You read the *PsychoPsych's* thing on Badakian?" asked the man.

"Might be sour grapes," said the woman. "The man makes money. That doesn't make him a charlatan."

"I met one of the assistants from his self-help programme. Most of Badakian's rhetorical metaphors are stories about his own feats. He apparently claims he disproved quantum physics at a science conference, by asking where computers and electric kettles come from, if thought processes are random."

"That's nonsense," said the woman.

"It presupposes a scientifically illiterate audience. He tells the story to create a certain mood, one of rejecting authority. That helps the delegates knock down the limiting beliefs in their minds, but only if they don't recognise how outrageous a falsehood he's telling them."

Suzanne noticed that Steve was looking down, apparently at nothing. Listening in to the gossip, just like her.

"And he's another one," the man went on, "to appropriate Korzybski's dictum that the map is not the territory, while failing to complete the original sentence."

"The usefulness of a map lies in its structural similarity to reality," said the woman. "But even the abbreviated rule implies there is a territory, therefore a real world, not just their own beliefs."

Suzanne slipped a throat mic around her neck, then selected *Steve* (renamed from *Adam*) from her phone's contact list, though he was sitting next to her. He already wore an earbead, so he did not need to make any overt movement when he received her subvocalised call.

"New Age therapists," she said in her throat, "make it seem that all beliefs are equally valid. It's more postmodern nonsense, but the point is, if a client presents a limitation in their worldview – they're too old or stupid or bad to change jobs or fix their relationship, whatever – then that limitation is probably true only because they think it is."

Steve gave a micro-nod.

"When these non-medical therapists start believing in magical systems," Suzanne went on, "they justify their schizoid delusions with these notions of arbitrary reality. They get away with it because a client never says that their life is awful just because they can't, I don't know, teleport to Jupiter right now."

"Because they really can't," came Steve's reply in her earbead. "Are Badakian's assistants really that stupid?"

"Maintaining an inner circle of true believers," Suzanne subvocalised, "is one of the symptoms of cult behaviour. Likewise a leader whose every word is true."

"That's interesting."

Then everyone was applauding as an MC introduced Professor Badakian. Suzanne killed the comm link and prepared to watch and listen.

There was a demonstration as part of Badakian's talk, and it was impressive. Working with two patients that were borderline schizophrenic, he used pulsed ultrasound technology combined with hypnotic patterns that were new to Suzanne. He seemed accepting of the patients' worldviews, and by the end of the session, both confided that the voices and visions remained in their heads, but they were able to converse in normal tones, and describe ordinary goals like getting new jobs and living with their families once more.

They were functional, not "cured", and Badakian's point appeared to be that that was good enough. For sure, his skill was sufficient to elicit applause from the delegates. In one of his self-help sessions, presumably, the atmosphere would be rapturous.

It would be interesting to interview the patients tomorrow, and again in six months time.

"If he can alter a schizophrenic's subjective world," muttered the man behind Suzanne, "then how easily can he induce schizoid beliefs in his happy-clappy delegates?"

"But he's teaching those psychological techniques, surely, on his programme," said the woman.

"And do you really think the majority of delegates analyse what's going on?"

That was an interesting point, which Suzanne would raise later with Steve. Some of Badakian's delegates would learn the techniques, be empowered by them, and use them to understand the process they had been through. This was *not* cult behaviour. Also, their average age and income level was likely to be higher than a normal cult, whose members tended to be younger, therefore more gullible.

Like teenagers.

Sickness swirled through her.

Could that be why Steve had brought her here? Something more than learning new techniques of what he called mindbending?

This isn't just technical.

Was there an actual link between Badakian and the Cutter Circles? Was this some kind of lead that Steve was following up, with herself along as an expert observer?

From the tension in his face, this was a question for later.

Applause attenuated as delegates stood up, and soon they were heading back to the breakout area where hotel waiters once more stood behind coffee urns, waiting for the rush.

It didn't seem that long.

A distorted time sense was characteristic of trance. Perhaps everyone in the audience had been in some kind of altered state. Badakian was probably that good.

Steve took her arm and led her through a gap between groups of delegates, directly to Badakian.

"Amazing talk, Professor," said Steve. "My colleague and I were fascinated."

Badakian's eyes seemed to enlarge.

"Of course you were." He reached out, and Suzanne's hand was drawn forward. "Nice to meet you, Bella."

His smile was that of a hunting lizard.

Bella!

Suzanne felt her bladder begin to leak, and recovered enough to squeeze things shut.

No.

Then she was released as Badakian's attention moved to Steve.

"Confusing, isn't it?" Badakian said. "Don, Robbie, Steve. Keeping them straight is really hard, so perhaps you should let it go."

"Er..."

Then a group of grey-haired neuropsychs approached, one carrying a cup of coffee for Badakian. Of course there would be no waiting in the queue for the great professor. Badakian turned to them.

Sweat coated Steve's face. "Let's get out of here," he said.

Suzanne rubbed her eyes.

"Ladies' room for me," she said. "I'll meet you at the car."

"All right."

As they stumbled away in opposite directions, she wondered if Steve was half as scared as she was.

He called me Bella.

She hurried, not knowing which was more imminent: pissing in her panties or throwing up.

How could he know?

She was a rationalist; but Badakian was a demon.

[SEVENTEEN]

An hour before the ghosts came for him, Josh knew something was wrong. From various angles, he took pictures of the dead body splayed on the outcrop that had killed it. Then he moved away, into forest cover, and waited for the emergency services to come.

His call would have been untraceable, his features false.

Close questioning of the locals might throw up some weird results for the police – back in the pub, the woman who had served Josh breakfast would fail to recognise pictures of Alex Rhys Evans (deceased), though it was Evans who supposedly had slept overnight in room 3.

They used a chopper, its sound thunderous, to retrieve the corpse. Presumably someone went down on a winch cable; but Josh did not hang around to see it. Instead, he circled around to retrieve his Bergen, then moved deeper into Forestry Commission land, surrounded by dark pines, breathing in the forest air that should have been calming.

Shadows that might have been grey or translucent, slippery or shimmering, flitted among the trees at the edges of his vision, disappearing when he stopped to look. His head was thick with increased blood pressure, his breathing too heavy for the level of exertion.

Downslope, still among trees, he moved.

Things out there.

It was not the way he normally thought. Once back in Hereford, there would be medical checks before he started Selection. They would sort him out.

An invisible foot took him in the ribs.

Ghosts.

But the pain caused him to squeeze his eyes shut as he curled over, while reflex drove him to grab fabric, twisting his hands into fists as he rotated, taking the tangible yet unseen entity over his hip. He kicked out, then backed away.

No such thing as ghosts.

Something disturbed pine needles on the ground, and then a knife flashed. This time he half-slitted his eyes as he slapped at the weapon – palm to side of blade – and grabbed invisible clothing as he punched – *jaw* – and again – *throat* – and then again, pumping his fist into the ghost's throat, almost hearing the squawk that accompanied its going limp; and then he released the thing, letting it drop.

Sounds of shuffling along the slope.

Away from me.

Yes, the sound was diminishing.

Get clear.

It was instinct, a trained mode of operation, and he let the automatic part of the brain take over as he ran through forest, moving fast despite the Bergen's weight.

Then he was at a cold, foaming stream. He climbed upslope, bypassing a dead sheep, then drank where the water was pure and wonderful.

Back inside cover, he sat down with his back against a tree, and slept.

When he woke, he did not remember leaving the scene of Evans' death. It was a surprise to feel the Bergen's straps snug around his shoulders. When he checked his phone, he found pictures of the body – he recalled taking them – and a record of his call to the emergency services. Nothing to Jack Hardin, who had hired him to find Evans.

Didn't expect me to find his corpse.

There was also a sharp pain in his ribs, and a tear along one sleeve that looked like a knife cut. Yet there had been no confrontation, had there? He did not even remember falling.

Must have hit my head.

He felt for bruising, detected nothing.

His phone displayed a contour map, showing him the route back to his car. An hour's clambering, maybe more. Good. It was time to leave this life behind and get back to the Regiment, his home.

Debrief first.

He dictated a report to Hardin, apologizing for not getting to Evans before the poor bastard threw himself over the edge. After thinking about it, Josh deleted that last bit – he did not want Hardin to think there could be liability here – then replaced it with objective facts. Suicide, nothing more.

Then he attached pictures of the body and sent the lot to Hardin.

Job done.

Not satisfactorily, but over all the same.

Good.

Time to get going and forget the past.

Suzanne and Steve did not discuss Badakian. Steve drove, muscular tension clamping his face, not sharing his thoughts. That was all right, because she did not want to discuss this, not yet.

It was two hours later when they reached Whitehall. Steve used the courtyard entrance to the subterranean car park which led towards Thames House, far below the level of tourists and Londoners tramping the streets overhead.

American tourists used to be common at this time of year.

Once in the team room, Steve told her he had a meeting to attend, and they could talk later. Then he said: "You believe in telepathy, Suzanne?"

"Definitely not." The tremble in her voice was new. "We'll talk."

"Yes."

Shane looked at them without commenting. Trin, Shireen and Carl were discussing something at the far end of the room.

So, Badakian.

Autism? Is that it?

Suzanne returned to the workstation she had used before, feeling it was hers – territoriality is a given in human behaviour – and thought back to the confrontation. On Badakian's part, everything had been calculated to increase his control over others. When Steve had said he was glad to meet Badakian, the response had been: "Of course you are." Modesty would have entailed a drawing-back, a suggestion of weakness.

Also normal humanity, but that was lacking in Badakian.

So he's a sociopath.

Such people can make effective generals or politicians, manoeuvring individuals like inanimate resources, while charisma and control strategies are part of their nature. But picking up on secret thoughts was something else.

I haven't told anyone about Bella.

That was what they called her in school, the nickname that should have been a compliment but instead became a nasty thing, insult and sarcasm; but the point was that this had happened years ago, and it was surely never written down in any record.

Her hands-on contact with autism was limited, but she remembered a case study of a young girl with frequent insomnia who complained about the shouting. She lived with her parents in a quiet street; but it turned out that over half a kilometre away, in another house, a feuding couple used to argue every night.

The poor girl had been unable to shut out a sound that no normal person could have heard. While functional in other ways, perhaps Badakian had senses like this. Probably his personal traits derived from an atypical spread of characteristics.

That's creepy.

Even though she was trained in reading body language, from microexpressions to behavioural clusters, still she found this thought disturbing: that Badakian could read the subvocalizations that most people assumed were silent self-talk, a major part of their thinking process that they always considered private, the one thing that no one else could sense.

Some people with eidetic memories are dysfunctional, their minds crowded with perpetual detail, lacking the ability to forget. What must it be like to be overwhelmed with sensation on every sensory channel, unable to filter out the normal minimum?

I can't feel sorry for him.

She reached for the workstation, about to check on Badakian's past.

"Fucking hell," said Trin.

Shane, Carl, and Shireen joined her. Then Shane looked back at Suzanne.

"You'd better read this too," he said.

The workstation in front of Suzanne, along with other screens, including the big wall display, blossomed with glowing news text.

TECHDEMS SUICIDE WAVE
Teenage cult killers belong
to Young TechDems

Suzanne found herself blinking, taken aback. Had someone else found the common link?

But the TechDems?

A link that led back to a mainstream political party – it seemed unlikely.

"Is that a real report?" she said.

"Yeah," said Carl. "And it's not the only one. Look here."

SUICIDE CIRCLES LINK
TO PARTY MEMBERSHIP
Statistical correlation between teen suicide
and TechnoDemocratic membership

Two more secondary panes popped up.

TECHDEMS KILL OUR KIDS
Suicide cult epidemic

And:

CUTTER CIRCLE KILLERS
MURDER EACH OTHER
– AND THEY'RE ALL TECHDEMS!

Shane's fingers were a blur, his half-face tiger tattoo darkening, or seeming to, as he worked the information streams. Then he stopped.

"We've a live news conference. Here."

The Home Secretary's lined face seemed stone-like, less flabby than usual.

"–no comment to make on the disgraceful and criminal acts purportedly carried out by the TechnoDemocratic party. I have, within the last few minutes, instructed the Crown Prosecution Service to investigate, with utmost urgency, the allegations. His Majesty the King fully supports our every effort to safeguard democracy in this appalling–"

A smaller pane pulled another headline from a tabloid site.

TECHDEM SUICIDE COVER-UP
HUNDREDS OF TEENAGERS DEAD
"They buried the news along with our children," says mother.

Shane pointed at this one.

"We're fucked. The country is fucked."

The air felt ten degrees colder.

So they're exposing the cover-up.

It was to protect people, to stop the mind-epidemic spreading. But a headline like that might cause a very different set of ideas to sweep across the country.

Shireen said: "No one could believe we deliberately–"

"You don't get it," said Trin. "We are guilty. We did cover things up."

"To stop it spreading, not protect whoever did it."

"The public won't make that distinction. If all those deaths are linked to the TechnoDemocratic Party, they'll say we must have known all along."

"You were stopping a memetic contagion from spreading," said Suzanne. "A teenage suicide fad, the same mechanism as hula hoops or Rubik's cube, or dyeing your eyeballs green."

"I did that," said Shane.

"You would," said Carl.

But Trin was putting up a new display, sheaves of tabular data highlighted here and there. From the headings, she and Shireen had extracted the lists from the TechDem membership database.

"That's really not possible," said Shane.

Suzanne could not process the detail as fast as the others, but it looked genuine.

She said: "I'm surprised you didn't spot this."

"Not half as surprised as we are," said Shireen.

"You mean the data was different when you checked."

Shane drilled through data with merciless speed, panes popping up like artillery bursts.

"It's true now," he said. "And it used to be true. But during the time between, it wasn't."

To Suzanne it sounded like a hypnotic induction designed to confuse; but the others were nodding.

"Someone altered it," said Trin, "at least in our view of the data, only while we were looking. The rest of the time, the evidence was there for anyone to see."

Except they had not even glimpsed it.

"Have you seen this?" said Carl.

He was talking to Steve, who was standing inside the doorway, his face like ice.

"Emergency legislation is going through Parliament," Steve said. "Right now."

"What do you mean?" said Trin.

Steve looked around at all of them, then spoke to Suzanne as if she had asked the question.

"We're on the brink of martial law," he said. "With Fat Billy Church taking absolute control."

In Paris, the snow was an elegant decoration; in London it had been a nuisance. Richie, leaning out from his wrought-iron balcony, looked along avenue Carnot to the great stone archway of the Arc de Triomphe at the boulevard's end, at the centre of a flat roundabout. It reminded him of Marble Arch in London. He just stared at it, then down at the people – there, an elegant woman walking a poodle – realizing how much there was to explore.

Dad was at another meeting.

Opal might want to walk around a bit.

A part of him wanted more than a walk, but drew back from imagining exactly what those other things might be. A vibration ran up and down his arms, like soliton waves in a constrained channel – *forget the physics* – as he walked to his door, went out into the corridor, and counted the paces downstairs to Opal's door.

He rang the bell. The apartments were glorified hotel suites, too elegant to expect someone to knock. But either way, there was no answer.

Raising his phone to call her, he leaned against the door.

It swung open.

Opal?

Atavistic senses can be trusted – both Lexa and Josh had taught him that, backed up by Suzanne. Four billion years of evolution have granted senses that are inaccessible to the conscious mind. He *knew* the apartment was empty.

His thumb pressed her name on his contacts list, and a phone began to buzz. It was right here on the couch; but there was no Opal to answer it.

Behind him, the wind moved a window, just a fraction. It was unlocked.

Oh, no.

The phone display had brightened on receiving his call request. He killed the outgoing comm on his own phone, while on Opal's handset, a tiny missed-call pane showed the figure 1. The main display showed the text she had been reading.

Thank you for your application, and congratulations. You are approved for membership of the Young TechDems.

Making Britain sane and rational!

Politics? That did not seem like Opal.

He walked to the half-open window.

Outside, the city murmured, filled with life but offering no answers. Then, not knowing why, he pushed the window fully open and leaned out. There was a drainpipe off to one side, leading up to a leaded roof, edged with black guttering.

A gutter that glistened with viscous blood.

"Opal!"

A drop fell past his face.

[EIGHTEEN]

A thunderflash exploded. Men yelled on every side.

Josh was already on his feet beside his bed. He had been asleep; now he was standing, the process automatic. Adrenaline hammered through him. His combat phone displayed the time as 3.00am. Dead on the hour.

"Right, you *FUCKERS!*" Torch beams splayed through the darkness. "Hey, Josh. How's tricks?"

"Good. You're looking fit, Dave."

"Yeah. You other bastards, *outside now! Move-move-move!*"

From other cots, men were rolling, some caught up in their blankets. In the torch beams, faces were briefly visible: pale and shocked. One had his teeth bared. Everyone was pulling on clothes fast, except for Josh, already dressed.

He snagged his camouflage fleece and strode out, his soft-soled combat boots silent. All around was din and clamour. As a group, the Selection candidates jogged outside and stood in ragged lines, darkness and cold surrounding them.

"You fucker," someone whispered to Josh. "Coulda warned us."

Last night, Josh had ignored remarks about sleeping with his boots on.

"He kinda did though, didn't he?" said someone else.

"Respect, guv."

"Cheers," said Josh.

"Any other advice you can give us?"

"Yeah. The best thing I ever learned."

An old-timer once told him; now it was time to pass it on.

"What's that?"

"When it really hurts, start smiling."

Shakes of the head and chuckling were his answer.

Sophie.

That was not the kind of hurt to smile through.

Why am I here?

Because this was home and Sophie was dead, why else?

What else was left for him?

"Right," called one of the instructors, a shadow in darkness. "We're going for a little five K jog, boys and girls."

All told, there were thirty-five candidates in the group.

"Move off."

They got into motion at a slow pace, made easier by the adrenaline jolt from waking up that way. Josh scanned the darkness. Thirty-four fellow candidates, six instructors. A large group to be moving through the pre-dawn.

But they were in the open, and keeping to a well-trodden path until eyes adjusted, and something inside Josh settled. Stress in the workplace means adrenaline in the bloodstream but no way to change the situation; here the dangers were real but action was immediate.

Call it extreme therapy.

"It's only five K," muttered someone.

"Maybe," said Josh. "Don't count on it."

"We're all insane, aren't we?"

"Blimey," said a woman. "I hope so, or we'll never get through it."

Laughs rippled around the group.

"Come on, you lot," called an instructor.

All of the training-wing guys were running easily. Their brief included being fitter than the rest of Special Forces at their peak. They would not mind the smart remarks – in fact, they would be looking for people who used humour under pressure.

A female candidate moved up between Josh and the two men, matching their pace.

"The night after Guy Fawkes," she said, "Little Johnny's teacher asked the kids to say what they got up to."

"You what?" muttered one of the others.

"Little Johnny put up his hand and said, 'Last night I stuffed a firework up my friend's arsehole, miss.'"

A few chuckles sounded.

"But the teacher said, 'No, Johnny. Rectum.' And Little Johnny said–"

"Faster, you lot."

"–'Wrecked 'em, miss? Damn near blew 'em off.'"

Everyone laughed as the pace increased.

At 6am, Suzanne was beneath the English Channel, travelling first class in the EuroLev, her ticket paid for by Philip Broomhall. Outside the window was blackness, hiding the tunnel walls. She sipped from her coffee. Whether it was the plastic cup or the coffee blend, she could not tell, but something gave it a faint, nasty tang. On the pull-down table lay a damaged croissant – she had broken off a piece before realizing she could not eat.

Opal. What have you done to yourself?

But the medical report was clear enough.

Un coup donné près de l'artère radiale, it read. One thrust close to the radial artery.

This was not like Opal. What could have triggered such a radical change?

"We need you," Philip had said on the phone. "Richie as well as Opal. Actually, Opal's asleep right now."

"A sedative?"

"Kind of. The doctor placed a sort of headband and visor on Opal's head. I couldn't understand the terms he used to describe to it. He's French, of course."

"Pulsed ultrasound," Suzanne had said. "With laser-scan feedback."

"That'll be it. Weird-looking device, but it seems to work."

"Good. And they've kept her in the hospital?"

"Yes, under constant observation. Look, if you can get to Paris, then come here to the hotel, and we'll go on together. Is that all right?"

"Of course it is."

Philip Broomhall could afford to pay for the best of private treatment, including the "constant observation" he had mentioned. In fact it was a euphemism.

Suicide watch.

Later she would gather everything she could by way of background. Young Richie was observant; that should help. Likewise Lexa, Philip's down-to-Earth ex-military driver, who apparently was with them. For now, the best thing would be to rest, except that Suzanne did not sleep well in trains, not even this one.

Therapist, hypnotise thyself.

Autohypnosis was a breeze, but not when Steve kept returning to her thoughts. Late yesterday afternoon, he had sent her home from Thames House, explaining that the op was entering a new phase and he would rather she kept clear. She took it to mean that he was concerned for her well-being. Trin had hinted that Steve was going to make payments for Suzanne's time out of a covert slush fund, keeping her name dissociated from this particular operation.

At least I can help Opal.

It was not just that she was a civilian, out of place in the MI5 world – she was a neuropsych therapist, a professional doing what she loved, glad to make a difference.

Her phone beeped. She blinked, looked around at the other passengers – most were trying to sleep – and slipped on her throat mic, then popped in her earbeads.

"Hello, Steve," she subvocalised.

On her phone display, Steve smiled.

"I knew you'd be awake. I expect you'll be glad to be back in Paris."

Did that mean he was monitoring her? Hacking in to the EuroLev's internal spycams? She had received Philip Broomhall's call after returning home yesterday, and told no one else.

"And you're up early," she said.

"We can talk quite openly. This comm link is not just encrypted, it's effectively invisible in the Web."

Much of the Web was what Josh called dark-cloud computing: beyond the perceptions of ordinary users.

I'm thinking of Josh again.

"Is there a specific reason for going to this trouble?"

"I want someone outside the team to know… I mean, outside the core team."

"That's OK, Steve. I know what you mean."

"Professor Badakian doesn't just make state visits as an advisor."

Suzanne blinked, remembering the news footage: the official delegation alighting on American soil, Badakian trailing the Foreign Secretary. President Brand and half of his cabinet members there to greet them.

Steve went on: "Badakian is a non-employee working closely with certain aspects of the intelligence services. Like yourself, but long-term, with a brief to design training programmes and operational procedures."

Around Suzanne, the other passengers were lost in attempted sleep, paying no attention to her. She swallowed, then subvocalised the question she could not avoid. "What kind of training and procedures?"

"Interrogation techniques. He has clearance high enough to have directed or carried out the questioning of certain strategic individuals. Names you would recognise from the news."

"You mean torture."

"Not necessarily. Full interrogation. That covers a lot of ground."

"And you're telling me why, exactly?"

"Because," he said, "we're moving against people with a lot of power."

Going up against his own bosses?

"You're frightened."

"Yes. I'm keeping some things from Trin and the others, and this is one of them. Anyway, good luck with your young patient. Opal, is that her name?"

"That's right, but I'm interested in–"

"Have a successful day."

The phone display blanked out.

For the third time, the group reached a hillside rendezvous point – an RV – just as the truck moved off. They kept doing that: promising a pick-up, then driving away before the candidates got there. One of the men broke pace, walked a little, then stopped.

"This is shit," he said.

He sat down on the ground.

"Come on," said Josh.

One of the instructors was female, her face pale in the breaking dawn.

"Leave him," she said. "Everyone else, just trot over the hill, and it's over. Really. Two minutes, and you're on your way to breakfast."

From the sound, the truck had pulled up again, just out of sight, its engine idling. The man on the ground looked up.

"Not you," said the instructor. "You're on your way back to your unit."

"But–"

"It's RTU for you." She looked around. "Anyone else need their mummies to hold their hands?"

"No, Boss," said someone.

"Then get going and reach that fucking truck."

"Yes, ma'am."

Josh resumed running, along with his thirty-three remaining fellow candidates.

[NINETEEN]

Philip's face was tight. Richie was pale, sitting by Opal's bed. Lexa, arms crossed, looked as if she wanted to hit someone. Nurses popped in from time to time.

Suzanne took in the situation, including Opal's bandaged forearm and the output from various monitors. The pulsed ultrasound apparatus – a thick metal headband with opaque visor – remained on Opal's face. Her breathing was slow and her neural activity, as displayed on the monitors, was consistent with natural sleep.

The paramedics had found her on the roof, with her inner forearm cut, missing the radial artery. Suzanne's old scars felt warm.

"Bastards," said Lexa. "And I was thinking of voting for them."

"Who's that?" asked Suzanne.

Philip held out a phone.

Thank you for your application, and congratulations. You are approved for membership of the Young TechDems.

Making Britain sane and rational!

Opal's phone, then. Of course Philip would have kept track of the news.

"Is everything you read believable?" asked Suzanne.

Lexa looked at her. "You know something about this?"

"Yes."

"Well, what–?"

"Let's get Opal better," Suzanne said. "And worry later about the rest of it."

"That's not good en–"

"Wait," said Philip. "Is this anything to do with Adam?"

For Adam read Steve.

"It might be," said Suzanne.

"Your friend in the Ministry?" Lexa asked Philip.

"That's the one."

Perhaps it had become obvious to Philip that Steve/Adam was something other than a DTI official. Maybe it was Lexa who had pointed out that civil servants in the Department of Trade and Industry tend not to have contacts with ex-special forces personnel working in the security field.

"You can fix Opal?" Lexa was staring at Suzanne now. "You can, can't you?"

Thinking of people as broken mechanisms was counterproductive; but that was Lexa's view of Opal's condition.

"Yes," said Suzanne. "Yes, I can."

Something moved inside her stomach as she spoke. Whatever had been done to Opal, the manipulation must have been designed by Badakian, assuming Steve and her own instincts were correct. The thing was, Badakian might be a monster, but he was a true expert in the field she considered her own.

Better than her in all the ways that did not require human warmth.

Forget it. Whatever he did, I can undo it.

And it was clearly a rehearsal that Opal had engaged in: the first step in a sequence of self-harming incidents designed to increase her willingness to join a Cutter Circle, presumably on her return to London. So remaining in Paris would help.

Suzanne had the advantage of being here in person, working one-on-one with poor Opal. Whatever Badakian had done

– assuming it was him – must be remote and generalised, not geared towards a specific person. That was disturbing; but the point was that getting immediate feedback to her own words and actions meant that everything would be focused on what Opal needed from second to second.

The thing she had to fight against was this: self-harm required discipline, and it did not matter whether it was cutting or anorexia – it was the sufferer's only way of maintaining control in a world perceived as both chaotic and threatening, a world in which they were powerless. In which everyone else controlled them.

Meaning that any intervention, to Opal, would seem part of that terrible world, just further proof that she could not control her life except by ending it.

On the bed, still sleeping, Opal turned her head and moaned. Philip squeezed her phone as if to crush it. Then he put it down.

"It's a new phone," said Richie. "I bought it for her."

Lexa put her hand on his shoulder.

"She was showing off for you in the first place." Lexa looked up. "Doing parkour stuff on the Pont Neuf. Her old phone dropped into the Seine."

Suzanne blinked at the perfect pronunciation: parkour, Pont Neuf, Seine.

"Lexa might be a Brummie," said Philip. "But she used to be in the French Foreign Legion, would you believe that?"

When he and Lexa looked at each other, Suzanne felt another internal jolt. Something had changed between these two.

And I'm jealous, because I've lost Josh.

It was the first time she had thought of it as a loss. She felt awful.

"Would you say Opal's attached to her phone?" she asked. "You know the way some people can't stop fiddling with them."

"Er… I guess," said Richie.

"Give it me." Suzanne took the phone, walked to the bedside, and pressed the phone into Opal's hand. "Just let her hold it."

She wanted to know what she was dealing with.

"But–" Philip looked about to leap forward, then: "Well, we're here to stop anything happening, aren't we?"

"And she's not wearing earbeads," said Lexa. "She can't hear anything that we won't."

Richie stared at them.

"She's asleep," he said. "She can't work the phone while she's asleep."

"Ah. True," said Philip.

Suzanne patted Opal's hand. Perhaps the feel of the phone was a comfort, because something softened in Opal's features. Behind the visor, her eyes remained closed.

Something bright moved across the phone display.

"What's that?" Suzanne asked.

A heart-shaped icon, shaded lilac to blue, bore a down-turned smiley, denoting a frown, but one that was slowly changing. The arc representing the mouth beginning to straighten, while the shade became less blue.

"It's an emotifone," said Richie. "It responds to – you know – how you feel."

"Fuck me," said Lexa.

Philip looked at her, swallowing.

Oh, boy.

Suzanne would have liked to point out that Philip and Lexa had just exchanged messages on two levels, that Lexa's words might really be an invitation. But that was a secondary thought, and she brushed it away.

Because the important thing was a phone that sensed the user's neurological state. Suzanne had thought she had the therapeutic advantage, because she was here in person, so much more empowered than some kind of recording that would look and sound the same to anyone. But responsive software in a handset that could read its user – if it was designed by someone clever enough, it might be more effective than a human therapist who lacked electronic sensors to read the client's neurophysiology.

Steve needed to know this.

"That's part of it. Emotifones." Lexa was watching Suzanne. "I'm right, aren't I?"

Tears formed in Richie's eyes. "You mean it's *my* fault?"

"No," said Lexa.

"No," said Suzanne.

"Then whose is it?" asked Richie. "I was the one who bought her–"

"I know who it is," said Suzanne. "I know exactly."

"What?" Philip stared at her. "How can you?"

She blew out a breath. "Make a phone call," she said. "To your friend in the DTI."

"To Adam?"

"That's not his real name."

Lexa was pointing at the phone. "You really think we should let her hold that thing?"

"Maybe not." Suzanne pulled it from Opal's limp hand. "That's better."

At Suzanne's touch, the emoticon faded. She was not the DNA-registered owner, and the inbuilt biometric scanner knew that. The phone took itself offline.

You'll be OK, Opal.

Suzanne had been at the periphery of one victim's funeral: the niece of Fireman Carlsen. It demonstrated the human cost; but here and now, the whole monstrous thing had become personal. Opal a victim, and an identifiable person responsible.

Badakian.

She was scared of him, but there was something else as well. Something new.

For the first time in her life, she had an enemy.

[TWENTY]

There was a new sign in front of Carlsen's gym. It was biolu-minescent, and bright.

Welcome to
the FIRE-PIT!
Home of Team Fireman

Sandra, in her police uniform – she was due to go on duty in an hour – stood beside Carlsen in the car park, staring up the sign.

"Tasteful," she said. "Brighter than the sun, maybe. But discreet."

"Discreet?" said Carlsen.

Angie, who helped out with the admin in return for a small salary and use of the facilities, had arranged the details. Well, arranged the whole thing.

"Could've been a blade with dripping blood," said Sandra. "Maybe a loudspeaker playing screams."

"Good point."

Sandra slipped her arm in his.

"So, are you going to show me around?"

"Anything you say, Officer. Just don't cuff me."

"Not until later, Fireman."

As they went inside, Carlsen wondered what she would make of the place. To him, the grey and blue mats smelled of fighting, the scent of home. In the conditioning area, Angie was performing kettlebell swings. Seeing Carlsen and Sandra, she switched to an intricate flip, throwing the kettlebell and catching it. For a beginner it would have meant a fractured skull.

Showing off.

On the mats, two hulking men were rolling, working their weapons-free grappling.

"That's Big Andy." Carlsen pointed. "And the *really* huge one is Little Pete. Don't ask."

The kettlebell thumped on the ground. Angie came over, her bare feet silent on the mat, her toes curling when she stopped.

"You here to train?" she asked Sandra.

It was a strange way to address a policewoman in uniform. But then Sandra had entered with her arm still inside Carlsen's.

"Maybe later," said Sandra.

"Er… Sandra, Angie." Carlsen gestured. "Angie's a fighter, trains here. And, um, Sandra's a friend."

"Right." Angie exhaled. "I've got a workout to do."

"Don't let us stop you," said Sandra.

Carlsen watched as Angie made her way over to the heavy bags. She stopped in front of a long banana bag, one that reached almost to the ground. Angie ripped in a low kick, and then another. Either would have shattered a knee for life, had the bag been a person.

"Ferocious," said Sandra.

"Yeah. I don't know what–"

"And jealous." Sandra squeezed his arm. "You didn't even know, did you?"

"Know what?"

"How she feels about you."

"What do you mean? She just trains here every day and… Oh."

"Mmm," said Sandra. "Exactly."

A soft beeping sounded.

"That sounds like a security alarm," added Sandra. "At this time of day?"

Carlsen pointed to the office.

"There's a screen in there."

"So let's take a butcher's."

On the mat, Andy and Pete had paused in their grappling.

"Did she say *butcher's*?" said Andy.

"It means taking a look, old chap," said Pete. "It's how one speaks in the jolly old East End."

"Is it really, old thing?"

"Yeah, too fuckin' right." Pete waved to Sandra. "Morning, Officer."

"Morning." She grinned at him, then tugged Carlsen's sleeve. "Alarm. Check. Let's do it."

They went in to the office. Carlsen had not thought how small and grubby it looked, not until now.

"Here we are." Sandra tapped the desk, and the battered screen lit up. "That's the car park out front, isn't it?"

"Er, yeah."

There were some twenty people gathered there, knotted together in a group. Their expressions were serious, and some were muttering. Some bore what might have been placards, currently upside down with no writing visible; others simply carried sticks. Most had knives sheathed at their hips.

"They don't look like athletes," said Sandra. "You got a beginners' class starting, or something?"

"No, I don't. What are they doing here?"

"I don't know." Sandra ran her fingers along her equipment belt, checking the holstered stun-baton, cuffs, and spray canister. "You stay here."

"What do you–?"

"I'm going out to chat with them."

Carlsen shrugged his big shoulders.

"You have to be kidding."

"It's my job." She smiled at him. "And I'm actually good at it."

"Bloody hell."

He went out with her into the main gym, then stopped and watched her cross the mat, then leave by the exit.

I don't think so.

There were weapons in the wall-cabinets, from sponge-coated blades through wooden and ceramic knives, all the way to live steel. And he could armour up before going out.

"Shit."

He shrugged again, then headed after Sandra.

They removed the pulsed ultrasound device from Opal's head, and allowed her to sleep naturally. Suzanne chatted to the doctor and nurses, who were open about their diagnosis, perhaps because this was an expensive private room and Philip Broomhall was paying for it. Lexa joined in the conversation, her terse but flawless French impressive, and relayed summaries to Philip and Richie.

When Opal came round, it was Lexa who summoned Suzanne from the visitors' lounge.

"Hello," Suzanne said. "They say you're feeling better now, and that's right, is it?"

Her greeting might parse as a question, but her subtle use of frequency and timbre marked out two phrases – *you're feeling better* and *that's right* – as covert posthypnotic suggestions.

"Yes." Opal's facial muscles trembled into a smile. "Yes, I am."

"Good."

Suzanne made adjustments to the angle of her own shoulders, and used peripheral vision to latch on to the movement of Opal's collarbones beneath the thin nightdress. It was part of her training, to find the easiest visual indicator of breathing, because matching her voice to Opal's respiration would magnify the effect of her words.

These were the minutiae of persuasion. Badakian must use them all the time because his charisma and skills derived from a psychopathology of control. The thought of being like him was repulsive, so Suzanne pushed away the mental imagery, reminding herself that she was here to help Opal.

So she chatted with Opal about Paris, before beginning the trance induction proper. When Opal went into trance, she went fast, with eyelids fluttering, respiration softening.

"–and I want to thank your unconscious for looking out for your security, for trying to protect you–"

For this, Suzanne required a deeper trance than normal, and the repeated use of *your unconscious* was part of that, because she marked it out as a command – *you're unconscious* – amid the unbroken single sentence that was the first phase of the session.

One of her lecturers, Judy O'Brien, had written: *There are parts of the brain specializing in, say, recognizing numerical digits or alphabetic characters. Since evolution* cannot *be that specialised, this compartmentalization must be learned, and the six layers of neocortex that define humanity are particularly plastic in this way.*

And she had added: *In therapy, to identify modules of the mind with distinct goals and subconscious behaviours is more than metaphor – it is neurologically accurate,* provided *you recognise the shifting, distributed, and malleable nature of those modules.*

The language might have been technical, but for Suzanne the guidelines were so clear that she brought them to mind every time a session might prove difficult, or when she felt a particular pressure to get things right.

Because this was Opal, who needed help in unexpected circumstances.

"–thank the part of you responsible for the cutting because it had a purpose–"

This was the crux of it: casting the behaviour in a goal-oriented light. Just as a drinker gets benefit from a single occasional drink but destroys their life with alcoholic addiction, every odd-seeming behaviour can be considered to have a goal that is reasonable in some context.

"–and before you make those changes, I want to talk to the part of you that made these choices. If you agree to this, raise this finger" – she touched Opal's right forefinger – "for *yes*, and this" – the left forefinger – "for *no*. Do you agree to this conversation?"

Like some horror movie about possession, a trembling, hesitant motion pulled the right forefinger upward. Had the motion been smooth, Suzanne would have had to regroup. But this was true subconscious movement, an ideomotor response.

"Thank you," she said. "And I want to ask that part of you, why it made the choice it did. Does it know the reason why?"

After a few moments, the hesitant *yes* motion repeated.

Good. We're getting somewhere.

The next stage was–

"*Madame?*" came from the doorway.

"*Je suis* Docteur *Duchesne.*" Suzanne stared at the man. "*Il faut qu'on laisse–*"

But he was not going to allow her to remain alone with Opal.

"*Je regrette, mais il n'est pas possible que vous restiez ici.*"

Suzanne said, "*Mais c'est nécessaire.*"

And it really was necessary, but there were two men in suits behind the doctor, and they did not look like medics.

"Please come with us," said one of them in English. "Immediately."

"*La Police Judiciaire?*" she said to the doctor.

The man nodded.

Merde.

"Just sleep," she told Opal. "Sleep and be calm."

Then she got up and followed the men, hoping that Opal would remain at rest, that her young brain, her neocortex that was so superior to any computer, would begin to knit itself back together in useful ways, to discard the implanted drive towards self-harm.

Merde alors.

They showed her to a consulting room, but as she took a chair all she could think of was that a minute's delay, maybe two, would have allowed her to identify and eradicate that self-harm impulse in Opal's mind. But these were policemen, so she had to talk to them.

She did not have time for this.

Carlsen felt his mouth-muscles pull back, some part of him needing to rend with his teeth like a hunting cat, while his hands clenched around knives that were not there. They were in the car park, some two dozen people gathered as a mob, and he wanted to kill them all.

Their placards, now upraised, read:

CUTTER CIRCLES – WHY DIDN'T YOU TELL US?

Along with:

STOP THIS MADNESS NOW!

Kat was in the ground, one more dead teenager, and yes, he himself was a symbol of fighting with knives, but the two things were so very different. He would have done anything to save his niece. And these bastards dared to protest *here*, in front of *his* gym? In theory, a mob could defeat one man by pressing forward, using the mass of the group; but in practice, he could outmanoeuvre and kill enough of them to terrify the rest, then hunt them down as they ran away.

And he so wanted to do that, to rip them apart, to lose himself in slaughter.

"Everyone calm down." Sandra, in police uniform, held up her hand. "Mr Carlsen thanks you all for being here today, because you may not know this yet, but *Fireman Carlsen agrees with you*. In fact he is on your side."

Something tumbled inside his stomach.

I do what?

But her words had produced an effect: the people had stopped advancing.

"As a role model for young people," Sandra went on, "Mr Carlsen keeps his fighting in the gym where it belongs, in controlled competition with a referee and medics attending. His own niece, Katherine, was the victim of something very different.

"That is why he is leading a new charitable venture, called, er, Keep Blades in the Arena, which aims to promote the education of young people, and add self discipline to their lives."

Carlsen realised there was someone amid the mob with a phonecam: a young woman with part-Oriental features he recognised from Kat's funeral. She nodded at him, smiling.

Like she's on my side.

What was going on?

"Fireman?" Sandra was looking at him. "Matt?"

"Er…"

He looked at the faces. They were confused, skin blotched, their feelings at war with themselves. Grieving, wanting to vent anger, hurting the way a teenager must hurt if they can deal with the world only by ending it. By ending themselves.

I'm a fighter.

Sometimes the choice is clear: wimp out or step up.

Not some motivational speaker.

He breathed in through his nose, sniffing a little.

"Officer Milton is right," he said. "If you'll help, maybe we can get this thing off the ground, to, er… " He glanced at Sandra. "To Keep Blades in the Arena. All right? With your support, we'll start with the schools…"

His voice became easier, more fluent as he went on.

And all the while, Sandra's smile grew wider.

[TWENTY-ONE]

Josh ran with the others, rods of pain in his back, the steel handles of the targeting system digging into his hands. The two with him were Kyle and Danie, the woman who had told the joke about Little Johnny and the firework. Between them they were carrying the apparatus at a run. All around, other trios with similar devices were "stumblerunning" – Danie's word – across the ground.

"It's not for... real, is it?" gasped Kyle. "Into action with... something like... this?"

"Can be," said Josh.

He remembered a live operation in Siberia, infiltrating a military cordon with what was effectively an ancestor of the PISS system. First the boffins made things that worked, *then* they refined their design to make them easier to deploy. But no one waited for the refinement when a piece of kit could make the difference between success or catastrophe.

In Siberia, he had slipped a disc. Because of a problem with the anaesthetic, the battlefield microsurgery hurt like a bugger, worse than the injury.

Not this time.

Then they were at the RV, able to lower the dummy device onto the ground, and lean back, sucking in cool air.

"Holy shit," said Kyle.

"Papal diarrhoea," said Danie.

"Huh?"

"That's the Catholic version."

"You're fucking… insane."

One of the instructors, a wide-shouldered woman with cropped red hair, strode forward.

"Wouldn't you know it?" she said. "The truck failed to make the RV, so it's off to the fallback point."

Josh grabbed the nearest handle at the same time as Danie and Kyle grabbed theirs."Shall we have a little stroll?" he said.

"Why not?" said Danie.

"Jolly fine idea," said Kyle.

He tightened his midsection, commanded his lower back to remain hardened and flat, and hauled up.

Piece of piss.

When you can lie to yourself, everything is so much easier.

"Maybe" – Danie's teeth were gritted – "a stumblerun's in order."

"No staggering out of step," said Kyle. "Remember, *synchronised* staggering, everyone."

"Let's stagger off," said Josh.

The instructor winked at them – at him – as they got back into motion.

That night, while the other candidates went off to a lecture on systems security – Josh could have taught it in his sleep – a staff trooper pulled Josh to one side.

"Lofty wants a word," he said. "Room 7."

"Got it. Thanks."

Inside room 7 it was not just Lofty waiting for him: there was Jan Black, the redheaded instructor, and Brummie Ingrams, who had a good reputation in the Regiment, though Josh had had few dealings with him.

"Take a seat," said Lofty. "And tell us how you're doing."

Josh manoeuvred the chair into position and took his time sitting down, while he tried to work out the meaning of this little chat. And whether there was something he ought to tell them, as opposed to saying what he thought they wanted to hear.

This was Selection and his major goal – his only goal – was to get through it, to become part of the Regiment once more.

Tell them how great you're feeling.

But instead, he found himself rolling up one sleeve, to show healing cuts on his forearm. Minor, but the problem was he did not remember getting them. They looked like knife wounds, and he had not been fighting.

"I'd like to know how these happened," he said. "Something to do with chasing Evans, maybe."

Lofty looked at the other two.

"I told you," he said. "Brighter than he looks."

Brummie smirked, but made none of the obvious comments.

"I'm not sure I even remember Evans jumping off the edge," said Josh. "Not really. I sort of remember remembering him. Like seeing myself imagining something."

He was not sure the words reflected what was happening in his head, never mind how much sense they made to others; but the three of them nodded. On returning to Hereford from Wales, he had debriefed with Lofty and the OC, and related all that happened. Clearly Jan and Brummie had been familiarised with the op, if you could call it that.

"What happened after that?" said Jan. "Before you turned up here, that is."

"I made my way back to the car." Josh closed his eyes. "After I sent a report to Hardin. That was Evans' employer."

"You sent the report." Jan looked interested. "Do you still remember editing it? Creating it?"

"I…"

Of course he must have created the files and zipped them

into a transmissible archive. No one else could have done it.

"…can't."

Lofty said, "Josh, can you move your seat there, please? Facing the wallscreen."

It was a big screen. The others shifted their chairs, angling away from it.

"All right." Josh moved his chair, and settled back. "What's the movie?"

With a screen this big, you could get lost in it.

"You know," said Jan, "when my mum died, Dad scarcely left the house for six months. I was lethargic too, for about the same time. Like, I was running every day, but there was no energy in it."

"You're talking about Sophie." Sinews and tendons tightened throughout Josh's body. "Don't."

Did everyone know his personal secrets? His entire life?

They have no right.

Lofty was doing something behind his desk.

"Maybe you ought to delay Selection." Brummie, speaking up at last. "If it's too soon–"

"She went a year ago." Josh's voice tightened into snarling. "What part of *persistent fucking vegetative state* don't you understand?"

His hands were claws on the arms of the chair.

Remember.

Were they trying to enrage him?

Remember he's a fourth dan.

Brummie was an Olympic medallist in judo, one of the strongest men in the Regiment. If you wanted to subdue someone violent without hurting them – too much – Brummie would be a good man to have available. Was that why he was here?

I'll take out his eyes.

The rage was building now. Josh strained, but electromag cords from nowhere were around his wrists and ankles–

"What the fuck?"

–binding him to the chair, but he would not put up with this, as he strained and shook, because no piece of furniture was unbreakable, and he would get loose. He would.

I'll have all your eyes.

That was when he noticed them putting on dark glasses, all three of them, and pushing earbeads into their ears. What was going on?

I'll tear your–

Green and silver, pulsing.

–liver with my teeth, spleen with my–

Like expanding snowflakes, over and over.

Brightening.

–fingernails, and crush your eyeballs in–

Pulsing, while the humming grew louder.

–my–

Washing, throbbing through him.

–fists.

And then darkness as tension let go and his head slumped forward, and there was time to think how strange this was before he slept.

When he woke up, the bindings were gone, and so was his rage. What he had was a hangover-headache that owed nothing to alcohol. It was an awful lot different from the warm aftermath of trance sessions with Suzanne.

"Fuck me," he said.

Brummie, Jan, and Lofty had removed their shades. Brummie was in the process of popping out his earbeads.

"Anti-sound." He waved a bead. "Clever stuff. Dead silent."

The wallscreen was dead.

"What was that?" said Josh.

"You should know," said Lofty. "It was your second time round with one of these."

"What do you–? Shit."

In the pub, the *Glyndwr Arms*.

Holy crap.

Entering Evans' room, with Evans sitting spellbound on the bed, and something pulsing on the wallscreen opposite him.

"I thought I'd been sprayed."

He meant a narcotic aerosol, designed to put the target to sleep for hours. It had been the next morning when he woke, and the absence of bruising or pain had meant he had not been thumped unconscious, so an aerosol had been a good second guess.

Just wrong, that was all.

And I'm a good subject.

Suzanne had put him into trance so often that he was used to going there. Shame it had not sorted him out, because the rage was still inside him, though under control.

Because these three were not his enemy.

"How many guys attacked you in the forest?" asked Lofty.

"Two." Josh looked down at his injured forearm. "Bloody hell."

"And what was it they said before they came at you?" said Jan.

"I have no–"

"One of them spoke, right?"

"Yeah. It was…"

Then sounds issued from Josh's mouth.

Now that was weird.

He looked at Jan, who was raising her combat phone.

"Can you repeat that?" she said.

More complex noise came from inside him. Speaking in tongues.

Holy crap.

"Armenian." Jan examined her phone display. "Translates roughly as *kill the fucker*."

"You're making that up," said Lofty.

"No. Honestly." She turned the phone to face him. "See?"

"I've fought some Armenians in competition," said Brummie.

"Trained with them a little, too. Good guys, very serious. Intense."

Speaking in tongues aside, what bothered Josh was the co-incidence of the software they had just used – taking him into trance via a light display that pulsed in odd ways – so similar to the device used against him in the pub.

"Where did you get that from?" He waved at the screen. "It's powerful stuff."

Lofty's face was like granite.

"We got the PulseTrance from QinetiQ," he said. "Via the MOD. This one contains focusing collimators that direct pulsed ultrasound right into your head. It ain't the lights so much as the sound you can't hear that twists your brain. Clever, ain't it?"

"Er, yeah."

"The real question is, where did your Armenian friends get one?"

Jan said: "The guys who attacked Josh came from one country. That doesn't mean the entire opposition is Armenian."

Josh blinked at her. "That's good thinking."

Brummie was frowning. On the rugby pitch – where Josh had seen him in action – and on the judo mat – archived Web footage only – Brummie went into a berserker mode that owed more to the unofficial Navy Gunners' motto (*I may not be intelligent, but I can lift heavy weights*) than to the Ghost Force dictum of *You didn't see us. We weren't there.* He could hack software too, but he had famously raged at an instructor who had tried to claim that indeterminacy and even the abandonment of causality could be useful in software engineering.

What the instructor had meant was that in massively distributed and parallel architectures, the more you can treat processes as black boxes with self-directed behaviour *so long as someone else is designing them*, the easier it is to specify how they behave when put together.

It was technical, but the point was that Brummie was impatient with anything that sounded like mumbo-jumbo. Right now, he was shaking his head and looking sceptical.

"Search online," Josh told him, "for stuff on trance states, precuneus nucleus, anterior cingulate. Also visualization techniques, entorhinal cortex, and grid cells. Maybe a bit of neocortex feedback while you're at it."

"You what?"

"The brain does computation. It just isn't a computer, not like the ones people design. But it's as technical as software engineering, this voodoo stuff."

"Oh. Right. Got it."

"It's just..." Josh looked at the darkened wallscreen once more. "I didn't really think it was this precise."

He meant software, as opposed to a human hypnotherapist. Suzanne could produce amazing results just by using her voice, but only in realtime, by phase-locking her body language and breathing to the client's, and using her trained perceptions to pick up a plethora of non-verbal feedback from the client – microexpressions, skin lividity, even the degree of lip tumescence.

A piece of software was necessarily dumber and incapable of getting the realtime feedback... or was it?

Josh ran his fingers around the arms of his chair. Then he dug his thumbnail into a thin depression and popped back a small rectangle of false wood. Inside the opening, optoelectronics glimmered.

"That's how you did it," he said.

"Right," said Lofty. "And you won't have caught the news at all, will you?"

"News?"

During Selection, every candidate's entire world was physical endurance and pain. There was no time for external considerations.

"If war had broken out," Josh went on, "I guess we'd have heard. But that's about it."

Jan shook her head.

"It's politics," she said. "Except it isn't. Not really."

The wallscreen came to life again. Josh flinched in his seat.

"Just normal stuff." Lofty grinned at Brummie. "No more mindbending. Guaranteed."

Brummie looked more relieved than Josh felt.

Words brightened on screen. Headlines from news feeds.

SUICIDE CIRCLES LINK
TO PARTY MEMBERSHIP
Statistical correlation between teen suicide
and TechnoDemocratic membership

As Josh leaned forward to look at the detail, a second pane blossomed.

TECHDEMS SUICIDE LINK
Over 170 teenagers kill themselves
"May have spread abroad," claims OneEarth Party
spokesperson

This was surreal and nasty. But from the URIs, these were major news sites, sourced from Google-Reuters-accredited reporters. Unless Lofty and co. were showing fake data for some purpose of their own; but Josh did not think so.

"Mindbending software on the Young TechDems website," said Lofty. "It's insane, and Special Branch and GCHQ are investigating. They'll call us in if they need us."

"Holy fuck," said Josh. "That *is* insane. Plus, why would they risk it?"

"Probably never thought of failure modes." Brummie gestured. "Hired some neuropsych team to create subliminal mindbending software. Designed it to make idle enquirers into rabid party supporters. Get the young folk talking about it to their friends. More and more of them visit the website, and there you go. Instant election swing."

"Christ."

"Except it went so deep, it turned some of them suicidal. The thing is, the police tried to keep a lid on things to stop it spreading like a, what, a psychological epidemic. So there were an awful lot of deaths before the news broke."

Josh nodded. Suzanne knew about this stuff, and could have explained it in terms of memes, replicating ideas responding to selection pressures.

"So it probably took a while for the bastard neuropsychs to realise," Lofty went on, "that their young supporters were killing themselves. And when they *did* realise, they were too scared to own up, so even more teenagers died. And now the TechDems are really in the shit."

"But no arrests or anything?" said Josh.

Lofty shrugged.

"Not our operation, but people are getting busy, I'll tell you that much."

Jan tapped the screen.

"Maybe they did understand that failure meant the possibility of inducing depression to the point of suicide. Perhaps they got the risk assessment wrong, and thought the failure wouldn't happen."

The basic axes for plotting risk assessment were probability of failure versus the consequences of failure. And a good basis for disaster was to underestimate the likelihood of a failure whose consequence was fatal.

A little-used website that drops one connection in a thousand is good enough, so long as the potential user is willing to retry. A plane engine that fails one in every thousand hours – even every thousand flights – is useless. These were basic principles, known to Josh's corporate clients in Docklands as well as to Sandhurst graduates.

"Nasty failure mode," said Josh. "Suicide."

In a peripheral pane, opinion polls showed rising numbers of potential OneEarth voters in the forthcoming Midsummer Christmas general election, enough to push the TechDems out of their projected second place, even if their support stopped plummeting and stabilised at the current level. The prediction was, quite naturally, that the decline would continue and that the party was dead.

"Suicide for their party, too," added Josh.

"Like your mad Welsh scientist," said Brummie.

Jan nodded at the screen, then at Josh.

"Maybe not so mad," she said. "At least, not before he was got at by rogue military software in the hands of Armenian mercs. Or whoever the bloody hell they were."

Josh rubbed his face.

"Crap. I'm sorry, guys."

His brief had been to turn up for Selection, nothing more. Most people came straight from fulltime service in some other part of the armed forces; their intention was to leave their old units behind, not drag their past with them.

"Come off it," said Brummie. "Some unknown buggers running around with this whatyoucallit, voodoo shit? I don't care if it's technical or not, it's fucking frightening. If someone can make a victim top themselves, we need to put the bad guys out of business."

No doubt Lofty would have fired off messages to his favoured contacts in Whitehall.

"Yeah, look..." Josh was trying not to slip into the old brainstorming role. "Rules are, I still have to get through Selection, right?"

It seemed indecent to bring the conversation back to himself, but he needed to understand what was going on. Instructors were treating him as an equal. A small hope brightened: that he could rejoin without the testing. But some other part of his mind was not so pleased. He had geared himself up for the Selection ordeal.

Or perhaps it was something else: a *need* to go through Selection once more in order to regain lost confidence.

"This isn't an op," said Lofty.

"Not yet, anyway," said Jan.

Josh needed to do this right, to focus and not weaken, because to let his defences down would be to lose everything, to break down or give in to rage. If he was going to kill it should be with His Majesty's sanction: the targets, people who needed to be stopped, not civilians dressed like Santa who happened to be nearby.

"I presume it's still thirty hours for the final waltz?" he said.

He meant the final mountain ultramarathon that completed Selection; but the thing was that fitness was not the only criterion: there were people who passed all the physical tests before the final stage, but were still RTUed because their minds or attitudes were wrong.

Jan folded her arms. As a training-wing instructor, she was not about to give away secrets; but in this case there was no confidential information beyond the exact route, and that was not what Josh had asked about. Still, his question had reminded everyone why he was here.

"I'm sure you won't take that long," she said.

Lofty had produced his combat phone, and was reading something from the display.

"Your girlfriend, Dr Duchesne" – he waved the phone – "seems to be an expert in this field. Mindbending and therapy."

The term *mindbending* occasionally surfaced in regard to interrogation techniques, but presumably that was not what Lofty was thinking of.

"We're not… having a good time of it," said Josh. "I'm not sure she's still my… whatever. Anything."

Jan and Brummie both gave small shrugs, mouths downturned.

"Sorry, pal," said Brummie.

"Thanks."

Relationships as a casualty were nothing strange in any part of the services, certainly not in the Regiment.

"You think she'd be willing to give technical advice, all the same?" asked Lofty.

"I don't–"

"Because" – Lofty worked his phone – "she's got the right stuff, wouldn't you say?"

A large still image snapped into being on the wallscreen. It was a shot from last year's *Knife Edge* final, with Josh – his features only mildly altered by disguise – cuffed and under escort from an arresting officer: a chocolatté-skinned woman, allegedly from Special Branch.

"That's your girlfriend?" said Jan.

"That's Suzanne," said Josh.

"But she is just a civilian, is she?" asked Brummie. "Takes guts, doing that."

She was also more beautiful than showed in the picture. The make-up had altered the shape of her eyes and made her lips appear thinner.

"Just between the four of us," said Jan, "you got help from Taffy C on this?"

Taff was one of the best make-up experts in the theatrical business, a raging queen who had spent time in Sterling Lines teaching his skills to Ghost Force operatives going undercover.

("I'll spend time under the covers with any of you boys," he always said.)

"No comment." Josh smiled. "But did you know that actresses just strip off in theatre changing rooms with no hesitation? Bare boobs everywhere. And the rest."

Jan grinned at him.

"So how is the old pouf?" said Brummie. "We haven't seen him for ages."

"Same as ever," said Josh.

The memories of bare flesh had been a visual flash in his mind's eye, before returning to thoughts of Suzanne.

Am I mad to leave her?

Because throwing himself into Selection was throwing himself away from her. However hard it was to understand his own intent, that much was obvious.

It was a question of which need was greater.

"So you don't think Dr Duchesne – Suzanne – would help?" said Lofty. "Is that it?"

Josh blew out an exhalation.

It's Lofty. He won't let go of anything.

The man was a bloody Rottweiler, when it came down to basics.

"Maybe she will," said Josh. "I'm just not sure I'm the right person to ask her. Not right now."

That was some kind of turning-point.

What have I just done?

It was here in the room with his friends, but it felt like a betrayal.

Suzanne. Am I screwing up?

His path had seemed clear. Was Lofty trying to distract him, as some form of test?

You know better than that.

Brummie moved his big shoulders as if getting ready for a fight.

"Maybe Jan should contact Dr Duchesne," he said. "Make sure you start by saying Josh is OK, in case she thinks he's a casualty or something."

"Suzanne doesn't know I'm here," said Josh.

Jan blinked.

"Oh."

Clearly she recognised that for the bad sign it was.

"I'll do it," said Lofty.

"Come off it." Brummie shook his head. "No offence, Lofty, but scaring the shit out of the poor woman isn't the objective, is it?"

Jan said, "Lofty doesn't look scary to civilians. Not to women, anyway."

Brummie gave a mock wolf-whistle.

"Please don't tell us you fancy Lofty."

"He'll be the father of my children," she said, "provided I want to give birth to Rottweilers."

Josh laughed.

"What?" said Lofty.

"Rottweilers," said Josh. "It was like she read my– Never mind."

Then the still image onscreen, of Suzanne leading him from the Barbican Centre arena, came back into his awareness.

What am I doing here?

It was not a question he could afford to ask. This was a time of single focus – it had to be.

Passing Selection, that's what.

Something clanged into place inside him.

"You're OK, aren't you?" said Jan.

It was not really a question.

"I am now," said Josh.

This was home, and he was committed to it.

"Good man," said Lofty. "Now piss off, and leave us to our devious planning."

"Yes, Boss."

Josh left the room smiling, then jogged back to barracks, enjoying the night air, knowing that tomorrow had somehow simplified: learn, absorb, and take all the shit they could throw at him, in the knowledge that he could take it and survive.

More than that: win through.

Because once more, he had purpose.

[TWENTY-TWO]

When Opal woke, the room was monstrous. *They* were everywhere, they and their tools – the adults of darkness, the monsters of chaos who pervaded the world. It spun her head, revolting her: the smell and roughness of the sheets, the wrongness of the beeping monitors, the tightened bandage on her arm.

Their world was dark and cynical and senseless. The worst of it was that you knew they had once been teenagers too, the adults, and look what they had done when they turned.

You could be nice to other people or not, but the city was different, monstrously different. Unknowable, self-centred, inhabitants living in a world of incomprehensible work and uncaring institutions: everyone in their own nasty world and no one reaching out.

She did not want to be like that, or live in a world that was. *There are other ways.*

Of course there were, and her first steps into parkour and then gekrunning had offered a way to fight back, not by violence but by maintaining control, because if she could control herself no matter how much pain she felt, then she could hold out against them, against the chaos, and survive. But they were stronger than she had thought, the adults.

Witness the Fimbulwinter, the climate turned upside down.

Still they just got on with things as though the world that cradled them did not matter.

Evil adults everywhere.

It was as if demons possessed them, dark creatures that rose from the oceans at night and crept the streets unseen, slipping into bedrooms and sliding inside adult bodies, possessing their hosts and turning them away from the simplicities of childhood, transforming them into these *entities* that were everywhere: on the streets, in the buildings, right here in this hospital.

Doctors and nurses were the worst of all, prodding and not caring. If you were in their control then that was it: they could do what they wanted with you.

Her phone was on a chair at the far end of the room.

Things snagged at her, the wires they had plugged into her. It hurt when she pulled free of them, but pain was a kind of liberty. Her choice.

Monitors beeped, but the power buttons were right there on the fronts of the boxes, and she switched them off. Then her hand was on her phone, and things were better.

They'll be coming.

She was better, but that was temporary unless she could get out of here without them stopping her. Her earbeads were with the phone, so she popped them in and set the phone going, keeping it clutched in one hand as she searched for her clothes, feeling the music start up, adjusting to her, becoming one with her.

The door.

Any adult could come straight in, and that would be the end of it. One-handed, she lifted a chair – dragging it would make a noise – then leaned it against the door, fitting the back of it under the door handle.

Now the clothes.

There was a shallow wardrobe with her clothes hanging up, and she changed without losing her grasp on the phone.

In her head, the rhythm of the music quickened because her excitement was rising.

This was the soundtrack of her life.

Breaking free.

She used the gekko tags to fasten her phone inside her clothes, pressed against her skin at the hip, waistband snug to ensure it would not slip.

And now the window.

From what she could see outside, the hospital was one of those grand old buildings from centuries past, and Richie had said something – *Richie will be worried* – about the centre of the city being designed by some old baron and no one daring to change it – *no, he won't* – so that only the outskirts were modern – *he's becoming one of them* – but that closed-in thinking meant the windows were old-fashioned too.

You could swing them wide open if you wanted.

The handles moved without squeaking, but the thing as a whole was heavy and stiff. Before it would move, she had to jerk her full body weight against it. Then the hinges did more than squeak: they screeched like living things.

"Opal?" came someone's voice.

Someone she should know, but the music was quickening, growing louder, because the action was intensifying. In seconds they would realise the door was jammed and begin breaking in. Her remaining time would collapse.

She had to get out now.

Run free.

Her hands were on the sill, then she vaulted into a crouch, ready to leap into space. She looked down, seeing the long drop to a courtyard, then twisted her head, tracking the line of a drainpipe upwards. The roof was grey lead; it looked like fun to run on.

In the building opposite, someone noticed her, their hands pressing against their window from the inside. They could not reach her but they could make a call so this was it: launch into freedom, or surrender.

She swung herself out onto the wall.

Suzanne slammed the door open. Something – a chair – held her back then toppled. Jammed under the handle, but not quite right.

"Opal."

Damn the policemen, who had delayed her so much and then lost interest when they realised she had arrived in France just this morning. Whatever they were investigating, they assumed you had to be physically present in the country, and yet this was cybercrime or even cyberterrorism, so you would think they might know better.

The empty bed was an accusation.

Where the bloody hell was Opal?

A shadow dropped from the roof overhead – *mon Dieu, c'est impossible* – and arced like a panther through the air, across the narrow gap to the roof opposite – *Opal, you idiot* – and hit, rolling forward over one shoulder and continuing to her feet, straight into the run. There was a raised housing, aircon vents or something, and she vaulted over it, ran along the roof to the next building, and was gone.

"Opal!"

But the girl was already out of sight.

What will I tell Richie?

No, Opal's safety was the major concern. Suzanne ran from the room and grabbed one of the police officers, who appeared to be chatting up a nurse.

"*La fille s'est échapée,*" she said, "*par la fenêtre et sur les toits.*"

It sounded insane – through the window and across the rooftops – so she used the Leveller posture from the Satir categories – shoulders level and hands pressing down – as she slowed and lowered her voice, adding authority to her words.

"*Elle est experte en parcours.*"

That fired a reaction. The officer strode across to Opal's room while ripping his phone from his waistband.

"*On a un problème,*" he said, and began issuing instructions.

Suzanne watched him, then raised her phone. Her call went through an imperceptible series of software barriers – no one called an MI5 operator without their location being pinpointed – reaching only a mailbox.

"Steve," she said. "I might need your help, if you can spare it."

Then she moved back into the corridor, pulled her throat mic from her pocket and looped it over her head, and subvocalised the rest: everything she knew about Opal's case.

Including the emotifones, in case Philip had not told him.

Being outside the UK, Paris was beyond Steve's operational remit, as far as she understood. But Steve might have contacts in France that he could use, or ways of hacking in to public surveillance.

Then she went to find Richie, Philip, and Lexa, to break the news of Opal's flight.

Jean-Pierre Gascoigne had left school as soon as he could, despite pleas to go on to university. What he always loved was painting and books, and he found himself working in a Left Bank gallery-bookshop. There he sold reasonably priced paintings and old hardcopy books, sometimes giving advice to customers who could not decide between first editions of Sartre or Camus.

Jean-Pierre hated both of them: learned helplessness and depression masquerading as literature.

But he could neither paint nor write; he needed some other vocation. A part-time psychology degree sharpened his interest in aberrant behaviour and the criminal mind. When he joined the Police Judiciaire it seemed a logical step, however much it disconcerted his friends in the bookshop trade. And so he found his meaning in life, in a way that limp-minded existentialists would never comprehend.

After being stationed in several rough districts – including the *banlieue* of Clichy-sous-Bois where he grew up – he was now back in the rarefied atmosphere of the Rive Gauche and the Île de la Cité. Today, he was pretending to watch trizep airships float high over the steel-grey Seine, while tourists took pictures of Notre-Dame. In fact he was keeping an eye out for sneak-thieves targeting foreign visitors. This year's numbers were down, both for prey and predator: fewer marks meant fewer opportunities to rob them, partly because thinner crowds made for easier surveillance.

Some of his fellow officers vied for large arrest numbers, but Jean-Pierre was happy if his presence discouraged crime and the public remained safe. That was his goal: to help everyone get on with their ordinary lives. So when the call came through about a depressed and suicidal girl freerunning across the rooftops, it caused him to snap upright, processing the contradictions in the alert.

Exercise beats psychotherapy for mental health, because a listless body may contain high levels of stress hormones like cortisol, but a body in motion is pumped with all the biochemical factors of confidence and joy. It was hard to reconcile suicidal intentions with the abbreviated video segments of a young teenager throwing herself across the urban architecture. What she ought to feel was exhilarated.

Interesting.

He was keeping on eye on the tourists from the northern end of the Place du Parvis, when he spotted the lithe girl heading this way at a sprint across the wide Pont au Double, avoiding pedestrians, pouring on the speed. It had to be her.

The only way to intercept her was to match her speed. He broke into a run, heading at right angles to her route, which was taking her past the façade of Notre-Dame. She was at the nearest of the three Gothic-arch main doorways when she saw him, and her response was to haul to her right, into the rue du Cloître alongside the cathedral.

She was fit, but she had been running a while, while he was sprinting fresh. He pelted past the pavement seats of the nearest café. On his left, above the cafés, apartments rose for six storeys. Curlicued iron balconies, shuttered windows. On the right, behind a tall railing, stood the north wall of the cathedral, with its row of arched windows, Gothic magnificence rising high. Here, a chase seemed incongruous, but it was not the first time.

Got–

She twisted away, in front of a doorway – had she intended to enter? – then ran across the street, and leaped for the railings.

Impossible.

Then she was crouched on top, ready to leap onto the cathedral wall.

No.

He ran to follow, ripping out his phone, and calling for help.

Opal leaped from the railing to the stonework and clung in place for a moment. Glancing back, she could see the policeman was following. Further down the street, a lorry had stopped, delivering crates of booze to one of the cafés. That was her chance.

She scrambled up the cathedral window, swung out onto a buttress, climbed up a little further, and grabbed hold of a gargoyle. Dangling one-handed, level with the fifth-floor apartments opposite, she looked down to check the policeman.

No.

He was hauling himself up onto the railing.

But *they* were over there, on the other side of the street in the loft, waiting for her. She felt them. Felt twelve black ropes of nothingness tugging at her, pulling her into their web where they would bring it all to an end. Striking back at this dreadful world. It was going to be a proclamation: *See what you made us do?*

The pain would be least of it.

And we can rest.

They would be at peace, all thirteen of them, in a place where there is no suffering, looking down with ironic smiles as the living cursed themselves for their mistakes and indifference, realizing at last what terrible people they were: hypocrites who did not care for others. Let the world suffer then.

The policeman threw himself from the railing onto the stonework below, clinging as if about to perform a Cat, and even before he started to spider up, she realised something.

He's a freerunner.

This was Paris, birthplace of parkour, but you did not expect this from the police. For a moment she remained hanging from the gargoyle, then she jackknifed up to a sort of ledge that ran above the windows, and began to run along it, Kong-vaulting over obstacles – decorative stonework – moving fast until she was level with the parked truck–

Hurry, hurry, the beat in her earbeads commanded.

–which was her only hope, but what if the others were not waiting for her? The time was almost here–

Faster.

–and this was insane, but danger was irrelevant now, so she took the risk and threw herself off the cathedral wall–

Push.

–to sail over the railings and land with a thumping roll atop the truck, then shoulder-roll once more, grabbing a binding and swinging herself over the edge, down to the pavement. She ran for the doorway that called to her.

Hurry, we're waiting.

The policeman lunged back off the stonework to perform a one-handed cartwheel on the railing, dropping to the road and shoulder-rolling once, coming to his feet.

No...

She pushed her way inside and commenced her run up the

staircase, pushing hard despite the fire in her legs: hamstrings and thighs and calves filled with pain.

Black sweetness of death, we're waiting for you.

Top floor.

Policeman running behind her – he was fit – getting close, but the front door she needed was right there and unlocked – *because we need you to complete us* – and she thumped it inward with a crash and skidded across the polished parquet floor as the policeman caught up, and her friends were waiting for her but they–

No.

–forever, that was it, and her chance was gone and everything was over–

No, you can't!

–and she pulled a knife from an outstretched hand, turning with the blade in her grip, and she tried to lash out, but her feet slid and then she was falling–

Please no.

–amid the corpses, pain incandescent as her arm twisted in ways it was not meant to, and then the knife was gone and a hard force pressed her face-first into the floor, immobilizing her. The stuff got into her mouth, so she closed her eyes and tried to spit.

Then she was shaking, pinned in place, a butterfly specimen fluttering but wanting to die.

Jean-Pierre kept the wristlock in place, the toe of his boot pressed into the girl's shoulder-blade. It was impossible for her to move. He had stripped the knife from her grasp and thrown it aside, although it was evidence that ought to be carefully handled. But he had a suicidal yet athletic girl locked in a pool of blood, her face pressed into it, while all around lay splayed corpses, laid out in a circle, freshly dead.

The blood was lukewarm but cooling.

He dragged the girl up by her collar, led her slipping through the blood pool until they reached clear floorboards, then sat her down. She was trembling now, the kind of vibration he had seen before in shock victims. But she had surprised him already, so he could not let go of her until she was secured.

"I am sorry," he said in English.

Pulling mag-ties from his belt, he cast around for something to bind her to, and picked the old fireplace. It had iron scroll-work like the balcony outside the window, and the mag-tie looped around it nicely. The other end of the tie fastened around the girl's wrist.

She was not struggling. The vibration of shock was still running through her, and her abdomen was cramping, pulling her into a foetal curl. But he could not take the chance of her recovering movement. He double-checked the mag-ties.

Then he could no longer avoid looking at the crime scene.

Ah, dear God in heaven.

Twelve teenagers who would never become adults, their worlds ended – or if his parents' beliefs were correct, continued for an infinite duration in the ongoing torture chambers of hell. But the reality was dead meat in a pool of blood, cadavers about to rot.

He stared around the room because he had to, burning every detail into his head while he moved his phonecam around, capturing a pale, dissociated electronic image of a tangible tragedy. Perhaps the dead things had, when their brains carried thought, held some imagined picture of beautiful corpses, with no notion of the carrion appearance and the stench of shit and piss, because death is always nasty.

Then his phone beeped, a welcome signal of his colleagues' arrival. Soon this would be a forensic scene, the dead things poked and prodded before pathologists hauled them away and cut them up. But he had a live girl right here, her eyelids fluttering in weird ways.

Leaning close, he could hear music from her earbeads.

Shit.

If hell had an anthem, it was what he heard right now.

What is that?

Then he carried out what might have been the most unprofessional act of his career, or the most professional, acting on instinct. He pulled the earbeads from her ears, placed them on the floorboards, and stamped down with his heel – once, twice – crushing them to silent fragments.

Earbeads were nothing by themselves, so he ran his fingertips along her clothing – she moaned – and found the hard lump inside her waistband. Extracting the phone, he stopped, then thumbed the power button, switching off the device.

The girl's features smoothed out, including the skin around her closed eyelids. Her mouth moved. Then she began to snore, a soft and innocent sound.

Boot-steps were thumping below. Jean-Pierre got ready to make his report.

[TWENTY-THREE]

Warm classroom, droning voice: the antithesis of effective training, in the corporate world that Josh had spent so much time in. But this was Selection, where the objective was not to make people feel good: it was to test them.

His fellow candidates were nodding off, while others struggled for attentiveness. They each had small vertical screens on their desks, bearing static diagrams that Jan changed barely every five minutes. Her voice was a monotone as she delivered acronyms and figures. She posed no questions, asked for no opinions.

"MetaZ comes from the union of CSP and Z" – Jan recited the facts – "meaning the combination of a formal modelling language whose basic concepts are events and processes with another based on logical schemas that define a system or any subcomponent in terms of state, therefore behaviour in terms of pre- and post-conditions. Since all modelling is an abstraction, we require a language that offers an algebra of manipulation such that we can reason about that which is less detailed than the software code that will implement our design."

Josh knew the notation and found it interesting, also challenging. Every piece of military smartkit was designed with symbolic-logic rigour, because software failure meant deaths.

Had he been teaching this, he would have found anecdotes to keep people on the edge of their seats.

He was pretty certain Jan could have done the same, had she wanted to.

Under the desk, he used his combat phone to access Black-Web layers unseen by civilians, then scrolled through search results for *PulseTrance* + *QinetiQ*. Several entries were marked with *Badakian algorithm* among the major keywords. He selected one at random.

Jan was saying: "Species-oriented programming, belonging in some sense to all three previous paradigms – OO, functional, and stone-age procedural – requires meta-algorithms to enable the evolutionary changes in a mutual-web phase-space that defines the–"

The point of true algebraic notations was the ability to manipulate the model and know your reasoning was mathematically correct. It applied to the subject of Jan's lecture, and it increasingly applied to neuroengineering. The Badakian algorithm concerned Hawkins-network neocortical neurons, while the references to practical usage were all about pulsed ultrasound and neuronal activation.

Where Badakia was, Josh did not know or care.

Nor was he about to learn neuroscience without three or four years to spare, so he shut down the phone just as Jan's tone of voice changed, becoming energetic.

"–clearly, and the notion of composition is paramount, or you would not be able to reason about separate components of the model in isolation before bolting them together, and that is the end" – she looked and sounded cheerful – "of the one-hour lecture."

Several of the candidates blinked and smiled.

"So phase two is the exam on what you've just learned."

Every screen went white, then filled with a list of questions.

"You have one hour," added Jan, "to complete the test."

Swallowing and pale faces on every side.

"Your time starts now."

Ten minutes after the exam had finished, everyone stood in front of the barracks, lined up but not at what most soldiers would recognise as attention. Special forces had little time for military niceties.

There were now six beds standing on end in the candidates' rooms, marking those who had been RTUed.

Jan was among the instructors standing in front of them, her voice now filled with the energy that had been deliberately missing during her lecture. She pointed at a yellow beacon standing almost as tall as her.

"This will be your target," she said, "during the final test. Up a mountain, naturally. You will have exactly thirty hours to complete the mountain route, and if that sounds like a long time, then you haven't seen the distance or the landscape, because you won't have time to sleep. And you *will* have an eighty-kilo load to carry."

No one groaned. By this stage, they knew better.

Yellow beacon.

Josh stared at it, remembering his quiet triumph the first time he made it through.

I did it once.

He was younger then, with less confusion in his life; but he must have learned some lessons in the meantime.

Second time is easy.

An image held in the mind is the way to succeed at anything. He had known that before meeting Suzanne; now he had a clearer idea of the underlying process. The yellow beacon would glow in his mind and he would use affirming mantras to reinforce his determination to reach it on the final day.

Easy.

It was the end goal, and reaching it meant he had no choice but to pass every intervening test on the way. That was how he was going to win through.

"Your objective is to take an enemy installation guarded by an élite regiment," Jan went on, "who in this case are the Paras, bless 'em. As usual in these things, they'll be expecting you, but not know when. You'll be working as two fifteen-person squads, cooperatively, with each squad containing five three-person patrols."

Some phones beeped.

"Patrol and squad leaders, you have your dispositions. Read them as you walk to the truck."

Then every phone buzzed.

"And there's the trucks' locations. Read as you walk."

They got into motion.

At first the pace was easy, because they wore no Bergens. Someone would be issuing them equipment later, perhaps aboard the trucks. Josh flicked through the preliminary briefing material – talk about light on detail – and found that he was leading a patrol consisting of Danie, Kyle, and himself. The three of them were part of Red Squad.

"Who else is Red Squad?" he called out, raising his own hand.

Fourteen others responded, including Danie and Kyle.

"We're Green," said someone else. "Right?"

Nods answered the question.

Hmm. Interesting.

Most of the candidates looked satisfied that they had identified the two squads. No one, however, had proclaimed themselves squad leaders. Maybe it was because their initial orders told them to keep it quiet. Or maybe there was something else going on.

We like devious minds, don't we?

But however hard and necessary this was – with the possibility of dying – it remained an exercise. As he walked, Josh pulled up the material he had been reading earlier.

The trials and reports on the Badakian algorithm indicated something that might be powerful, particularly combined with subliminal commands over time. Most of Suzanne's methods fell under the category of brief therapy; but there was nothing to stop someone using many iterations of treatment to produce a deeper effect.

Still, can it really be possible?

He used voice mode to enter search arguments to the Black-Web correlation engine.

"Mindbending. Badakian algorithm. Brainwashing. Suicide cults."

Then he tapped the phone.

"Commence now."

Danie came up beside him, her stride as easy as his.

"Suicide cults?" she said.

"Cheery bastard, aren't I?"

"Not so fucking miserable as all that."

"If that was a compliment," said Josh, "then ta lots."

"That was me wondering what you're working on."

Josh gestured at the landscape all around. Their fellow candidates who were moving faster now, in the distance-eating lope known as yomping or tabbing, depending on your origin.

"Passing Selection, that's all."

"Yeah." Danie punched his arm at the lower shoulder, the deltoid insertion. "Lying git."

"Ouch."

"Is this something that would help the rest of us?"

"No." Josh glanced at the others, none of whom were listening in. "It's something external. Just wondering... My, er, girlfriend is a neuropsych, and she uses hypnosis."

"I'm not after your aging body, Cumberland. I don't mind if you got a girlfriend."

"She might be my ex-girlfriend. And I've already got an ex-wife."

They were tabbing uphill now.

"And your little bit of research?" Danie's breathing was still calm. "Why the suicide stuff?"

"Cause I came across some unpleasant people who use what you might call electronic hypnosis. I think one of their victims threw himself off a cliff, but that's so *not* what you use hypnosis for."

For a second, Danie broke pace.

"I can't imagine how it could work." Josh slowed to match her. "Or whether there's something else, some kind of drug you have to administer, a depressant or something."

They got the pace going again.

"You're not a fight fan, then?" she said.

Perhaps her breathing was a little altered. Josh was definitely aware of the gradient, plus the accumulated exhaustion of the previous few days.

Yellow beacon.

All he had to do was remember that.

"I'd say I am." Josh raised his phone. "I've not been online since we got here, though. Not outside BlackWeb material."

Not like a normal person.

"Fireman Carlsen," said Danie. "His niece did the wrist-cutting thing, died a few days back."

"Suicide?" said Josh. "It happens, but it's not what I was thinking about. Not that kind of case."

"Cutter Circles. Groups of thirteen kids, doing the *wup*" – Danie mimed cutting her wrist – "on the person next to them. Cosy."

That was what the headlines were about, the ones that Lofty, Jan, and Brummie had shown him. But knowing that Fireman Carlsen's niece was a victim, that brought it home – into the particular, to actual people.

But this was coincidence. In his first year in the army, a maths instructor had drilled them in probability thinking precisely because people are naturally bad at it. Given a random group of fifty-six people gathered in a room, the chances that some two of them will share a birthday is ninety-nine percent – so counterintuitive that they had to work the proof half a dozen times before Josh and his colleagues were convinced.

Evans had committed suicide. So had a lot of teenagers. That implied no startling failure of random chance. For sure, Evans would not have applied to join the Young TechDems – he was too old.

That's crazy.

Josh slowed down.

They wouldn't have done it.

Or was that part of the reason for Lofty discussing the Cutter Circles? Because they had not had time to talk about the political dimension. The reality was that another form of suicide had just occurred: the self-destruction of the TechnoDemocratic Party.

Just days before Midsummer Christmas and the general election.

Talk about coincidence.

"You've seen the stuff about the Young TechDems' website?" said Josh.

"Yeah." said Danie. "If you use mindbending software, you shouldn't be too surprised if it goes wrong. A failure rate of one in a thousand is madness if you've got hundreds of thousands of visitors to your site."

She thought like a software engineer, reasoning in the same way that Lofty, Jan, and Brummie had last night. Not just Regiment material, then – she was a natural for Ghost Force.

She's got to get through Selection first.

And so did he.

"Up the pace, people," called Jan from the front.

They were running now. Danie ran beside Josh, keeping up. This was still an endurance pace, and she had breath enough for conversation.

"You think they'll call in the Regiment?" she said.

"For what?"

"The TechDems thing, of course."

"No, they–"

His running pace broke.

Holy fuck.

And he stumbled to a stop.

No. That would be insane.

It was other people's investigation: Special Branch and GCHQ. Lofty had said so last night. But if they began with a false assumption, it could skew the results, couldn't it? Even to the extent of blaming the wrong people.

In his mind's eye, he saw Evans turning to him, and saying once more his final words.

"You'll be sorry."

And then the silent drop, followed by the thud and muffled crunch.

It's impossible. Has to be.

Jan was coming back this way. Danie, confused, had also stopped running.

"Come on, Josh," she said. "Just fucking come on, will you?"

But it was not what she thought.

"Run on." Jan tapped Danie's shoulder. "Move it."

"Yes, Boss."

Danie recommenced her run.

"What's the matter?" said Jan. "You want to be RTUed?"

In his case there was no unit to return to, unless you counted civvie street as a unit.

"What if they've got it wrong?" he said.

"Who? What wrong?"

"GCHQ. Special Branch."

"The Cutter Circles?" said Jan.

"What if the suicides aren't a failure mode?" said Josh.

She stared at him.

"What do you mean?"

Surely Jan knew what he meant. She just did not want to accept it.

Nobody would.

He said: "What if suicides – spectacular group suicides – are the *objective*? The sunny day scenario. The goal of the system."

"Impossible."

"Not if someone else put the software on the TechDems site. Someone psychotic who didn't care about the human price."

"Jesus Christ," she said. "You can't mean it."

"You know I do."

"Sweet Jesus Christ on a fucking crutch."

"That too."

"OK." Jan raised her phone. "I'm calling Lofty now."

"Good."

"And you'd better get running, Josh."

"Yes, Boss."

"Run fast" – she forced a small smile – "or you'll get my boot up your arse."

"I'm going."

He resumed his tabbing pace, then accelerated to an easy run, while Jan's voice diminished behind him. She remained in place as she talked – she used Lofty's name – enunciating her words carefully enough so that he could still hear.

Delivering Josh's idea just as he had worded it.

What if suicides – spectacular group suicides – are the objective?

It was nasty. It was evil.

And if it was the same thing that had been done to Dr Alex Rhys Evans, it was a connection that he, Josh Cumberland, had made. It was beginning to feel personal.

No. It's nothing to do with me.

As he ran, he tried to focus on the mental image of a yellow beacon, but it was difficult.

Murderous fucking bastards, whoever you are.

Instead, he imagined ripping throats out and smashing limbs, breaking skulls with his hands and elbows, with his feet and shins and knees. The enemy were white-coated men with no faces, and he tore them apart in his imagination.

Raging with blood-joy and the need to kill them all.

[TWENTY-FOUR]

Carlsen was not one for ceremony. His arrival was quiet.

Once inside the *Knife Edge* house, though, the cameras would be on them, because this was part of the show: the arrival of the coaches, meeting the hungry pro fighters who were in there, waiting to find out which team they were in. All the while, Zak Tyndall would be grinning and acting like an impresario.

Carlsen stood outside the near-mansion, checking the grounds. This was Berkshire and not so far from the infamous M25; but beyond the walls stretched woodland, looking surprisingly rural. If you walked in any direction, you would soon hit a road and buildings; yet here it might have been true countryside, say Scotland or further abroad.

An engineer by training, he found it natural to imagine the web of rail and road that linked people into one complex system, shunting individuals like blood cells in arteries and veins. But the natural world was greyer than it ought to be for this time of year, and he knew that the world's climate was on the point of another transition, depending on the mean size of airborne particulates at high altitude.

The ash was fine enough to remain aloft for this long. If it did not start falling out of the atmosphere soon, it would be the start of a new ice age; but the crops would fail long before the big freeze proper. By rights, food wars should have started already, but gene-tweaked crops – from companies like Tyndall Bio – were managing to grow.

It put into perspective the spectacle of two men facing each other with knives.

Kat. Why did you cut yourself?

Worse: allowed someone else to cut her left inner wrist, while she passed on the favour to someone on her right. What state of mind did someone have to be in for ritual suicide?

"Hey, you big gorilla." The voice sounded Scandinavian. "You can't stand there thinking. Fighters got no brains, right?"

Carlsen was grinning as he turned.

"Siggy, you Viking berserker."

"Ach, Matt, you half-blood."

Carlsen's mother had been German, so Sigmund had once, during a drunken post-fight celebration, declared him an honorary half-Viking.

"Still wasting away, I see."

Sigmund's neck was the thickest that Carlsen had seen in a lifetime among fighters. His trapezius muscles looked like concrete loaves atop his shoulders, and the rest of his body was massive to match. He was in his fifties, but in a barehanded fight – or with sticks for that matter – he would crush Carlsen.

They hugged. Sigmund's hammer fist thumped Carlsen's upper back.

"Is the circus in town yet?" Carlsen asked.

"Yeah. Listen." Sigmund stepped back, gripping Carlsen's shoulders, one massive hand grasping each deltoid. "You watch out for Krill. That one, he is cold."

"My contract's only for coaching. It's not every year that the coaches fight each other, you know that."

"*Ja*, and I know that Cutter Krill likes blood."

Carlsen looked at him. "I'll remember."

"Good. Because I don't want to be changing your diapers for you, boy."

"Nappies," said Carlsen. "We call them nappies here."

"Don't make runny shit smell sweeter."

"Jesus, Siggy." Carlsen began to chuckle. "I've missed you, man."

"*Ja*. The madhouse, no one could miss. Come see."

Once inside, the spycams were everywhere. Somewhere in Milton Keynes, a small production team were probably already splicing the realtime footage into one-, two- and three-thread versions of the show. Premium-rate viewers had pseudo-realtime access (with a five-second delay) to every spycam in the house, along with a building blueprint and PoV selection tree, allowing them to switch points of view at will, or display them in parallel.

Why they would want to, Carlsen had no idea. But his job was to coach a team of fighters, and the way to do that was to forget the viewers and act the way he always did.

"Arkady and Scott are having coffee," said Sigmund. "The kitchen's this way."

They walked along a corridor painted bright blue and white, hung with bioluminescent artwork that made Carlsen's head ache. It was striking and tasteless. No wonder the fighters tended to go a little nuts, incarcerated here for weeks on end with nothing to do but train, go through two or three elimination fights, and get on each other's nerves.

At least the coaching team got to go home every night, or at least to a hotel where they could interact with normal human beings.

"Hey, Matt."

"Hey, Scott," said Carlsen, then grinned at the fourth man. "Arkady."

They shook hands, while Sigmund poured coffee for Carlsen.

"The fighters' kitchen is already a mess," said Scott. "Looks like we don't have a Miss Tidy this year."

Last year's Bloods had included a rigidly fussy gay fighter, Rory, whose neatness in the kitchen matched his precision with a blade.

"They said anything about the magic cupboards?" said Carlsen.

"Nah. Either they didn't notice or they already know." Sigmund shrugged his bulky shoulders. "Or they're too stupid to think about it."

The cupboards appeared to restock themselves. What happened was that junior members of the production team sneaked through acoustically insulated tunnels in the walls – many of the interior rooms were defined by false walls which would be removed when the series was over and the house became a luxury rental once more – replenishing and occasionally carrying out repairs (the spy-cams going offline in those rooms while work was in progress).

Three dozen trained fighters in close quarters occasionally resulted in collateral damage to furniture and fittings, despite Zak's annual warnings to *Keep it in the gym, guys.*

One year, a bright, zany fighter called Forry had lain in wait, then ripped open a larder as a production guy was restocking it from the rear, and dragged the poor man through the cupboard. Then he had run around the house with the guy on his shoulders, before stuffing him back into the cupboard and through to the tunnel.

It destroyed the magic-house illusion, but it was too good theatre to cut, so it had made the prime view-threads. Forry – Sergeant Fearless – had won the overall series, which made it all the better.

Arkady, Scott, and Sigmund updated Carlsen on the trivia of their lives. Then the mood changed.

"We were sorry to hear about your niece," said Arkady.

"Yes," said Sigmund.

"Sorry, man." Scott clapped Carlsen's shoulder. "Bad business."

The stinging in Carlsen's eyes was like salt sweat or a trickle of blood.

"Thanks, guys," he said.

After a few moments, Sigmund cleared his throat, like a bear coughing.

"You want to meet your babies?"

This year's fighters.

"Why not?" said Carlsen.

"Wait till you see the gym," said Scott. "All the latest gear."

"Oh."

"Plus the old-fashioned stuff that works," said Sigmund. "You'll see."

"Good."

They put their coffees down, and went to meet the fighters.

In Carlsen's view, barbells were good only for two things – dead lifts and clean-and-presses – while kettlebells were most useful for swings. Strength-wise, everything else could be achieved with dumb-bells.

Big, heavy dumb-bells.

As for the fancy new kit that used electromagnets to provide resistance in two directions – combining bench press and rows in one exercise, for instance – he despised it. Anything painted in bright colours that came with soft hand-grips was anathema. His idea of strength training was ripping things hard against gravity, using his whole body.

The more callused his palms became, the better.

This year the production team had provided two training centres, so the teams could work independently without scheduling problems. Carlsen moved through the shadowy spaces of the gym that would be his, nodding at the kit, in particular the profusion of racked dumb-bells. Punchbags, stab bags and grappling dummies hung next to the weapons cabinet.

Everything smelled new.

"We'll wear it in soon enough." Sigmund seemed to know what he was thinking. "Buckets of sweat, maybe a little blood. A few drops of piss. It'll feel like home."

"I hear you, you bloody Viking."

"Ha. The other gym's through here."

Applause rose as they entered the second gym. All of the fighters were gathered there, dressed in street clothes. Another group stood to one side: Jason Krill and his assistant coaches.

Krill's gaze was that of a blue-eyed reptile.

The cheers and clapping were real, because the fighters were pros from the smaller circuits like Blade in the Cage, and this was the big chance. In armoured, blunt-blade fights, they had proven their abilities against other contenders in pre-series tests – held in hotels across the country, their ballrooms made over into fight gyms for a day – while Zak and his advisers had pored through footage of their professional fights. For every man and woman here, there were hundreds who would kill for the chance of taking their place.

Carlsen had been like that.

Centuries ago, it feels like.

He grinned at them. Soon, after he and Krill got to observe the fighters in training and then pick the teams, half their number would be his boys and girls, his responsibility. He would do his best by them.

More applause sounded. Zak Tyndall had arrived, with his entourage of personal assistants.

"Hey, guys." Zak waved at everyone. "Good to see you."

Man of the people.

He was dressed in the most expensive of casual wear. When he wore a suit – as he sometimes did when a fight was on – it would be a made-to-measure garment that cost more than most folk earned in months.

Unlike his forebears in MMA, Zak's enthusiasm for fighting remained that of a spectator, or a financial speculator. In the old days, the small number of entrepreneurs who transformed the sport and made it global were genuine devotees who trained in combat arts. If they had made money it was because, in Carlsen's view, they deserved to: their initial risk had been huge.

Zak Tyndall projected the same type of persona, but in his

case it was faked for the cameras, a role that he stepped out of as soon as he left the fighters' house or the arena.

Call it the only game in town: the fight circuit that dwarfed all others, that paid the big money and let the talented, lucky few live their dream, while the rest went to the wayside.

It's not supposed to be easy.

That was the thing.

"–and Fireman Matt Carlsen," said Zak. "My friend, how are you doing?"

Zak had been making a speech while Carlsen's attention drifted off.

"Good." Carlsen walked forward to shake Zak's hand. "Good, Zak."

They shook hands and clasped shoulders.

"And Jason." Zak released Carlsen and greeted Krill. "How are you, buddy?"

"Great, Zak."

While Krill shook Zak's hand, his cold blue eyes triangulated on Carlsen, and his mouth widened as though he were about to snap forward, going for Carlsen's throat with his teeth.

You're a piece of work, aren't you, Krill?

This was going to be an interesting few weeks.

"So while we're here," said Zak. "I've an announcement."

Everyone sharpened their attention. Spontaneous announcements often involved cash incentives for performance either in training or the elimination fights, occasionally for something wild and off the wall.

"We weren't going to do this, not this year" – Zak smiled at Carlsen and nodded to Krill – "but with such legends in the room who've never faced each other, it's an opportunity we could hardly waste."

Eyes widened around the room. Carlsen's stomach felt gravity shift.

Zak, you manipulative bastard.

It was not supposed to happen. Retirement was not Carlsen's

plan, not yet, but he was already older than almost any other pro fighter. This he could do without.

"You know the tension is going to be high anyway." Zak's smile was predatorial. "And Ice Pick McGee is out of the game, after a great career."

Last year's other coach, Tom McGee, had announced his retirement days after the *Knife Edge* final and its strange events. He was seven years younger than Carlsen.

"So for a record purse" – again the smile – "I'm asking the Fireman to face the Cutter on the series finale. What do you say, guys?"

Krill was calm. Either he had been expecting the announcement – challenge, whatever – or he really was a reptile.

Sigmund said: "Uh-oh."

The thing was, Carlsen's own gym could do with a refit, but he did not truly need the money.

Inge does.

His sister had lost her long-term partner to drunkenness and promiscuity, and her daughter to a suicide cult. What she needed was some financial security, as well as counselling.

If he was going to do this, it would be for her.

"I don't know," he said. "Jason's one hell of a fighter, and I'm getting too old for this."

"I'll say," said Krill. "Too bad, though. I enjoy cutting old guys up."

Breath hissed in among the fighters.

"Not this time," said Carlsen.

"Pity." Krill shook his head, then turned to the fighters and shrugged. "And I pity the losers who end up on Carlsen's team."

Zak frowned, eyes half lidded.

Not used to not getting your own way.

Perhaps Zak should get used to it.

But not today.

"You missed my point," said Carlsen. "You won't be Cutter Krill, you'll be Carved-Up Krill before I'm finished with you."

Whoops sounded.

"Hoo-ya, Fireman!" called Scott.

Zak looked shocked. Carlsen was the Fireman, the hon-ourable Captain Invincible who never trash-talked his opponents.

"Do your best, old man," said Krill.

"Hang on to your liver," said Carlsen.

Cheers rang out through the gym, while Zak's smile widened, then widened again as his eyes glittered – perhaps with the thought of all that money he would make as the ratings soared.

"It's going to be a war!" he shouted.

The volume of cheering increased.

Jan had given both squads four hours to reach their respective lay-up points, but Josh pushed the pace, so that he arrived at the LUP with nearly fifty minutes to spare. Kyle and Danie were breathing hard.

After they settled into concealment, it was Danie who mur-mured: "Why the hurry, Boss?"

"Not that we're complaining." Kyle kept his voice low as well.

"It's deliberate," Josh told them. "Gives us longer to catch our breath."

A balancing act, but it was more than that. He wanted to check the disposition of every three-person team, and surveil the attack vectors. First, he established blip comm links with the other four teams in Red Squad. Three were still moving but on schedule; the fourth was in trouble, with one man down – a twisted ankle – and another whose morale was low.

"Do your best," Josh told the woman on the other end. "Ask them if they're able to continue. If the answer's no, then use red channel to notify the instructors, and come on solo."

"Roger that. And thanks."

Josh smiled. There was toughness in her voice, whatever her comrades' state.

Now check the situation.

He told Danie and Kyle to hold position, while he took a look ahead.

"Is that part of our orders?" said Danie.

"You'd be surprised what's missing from our orders," he said.

He wriggled out of cover, and commenced a commando crawl across cold ground, heading for a minor ridge. Once there, he used ultra-slow movement to raise his head just enough to see what lay below.

Then he began to slow his breathing.

Calm. That's right.

He had to relax.

Slower.

The point was to reach a kind of Zen state.

Slower still.

For an unknown but extended duration, he held himself in quietness, absorbing everything, and finally he got it: three snipers laid up in tall grass – there, there, and there. Professional. The Paras had not just posted sentries at the target installation – they intended to ambush the attackers on the way in.

Sorry, guys.

It was not going to happen that way.

Bad luck.

He reversed his crawl with infinitesimal speed, imperceptible even to graduates of sniper school. Out of their sight, he moved faster, heading back towards Kyle and Danie.

This was going to be interesting.

The fighters and coaches reassembled as before. Zak was flanked by female presenters who spoke directly to the cameras. They had already done some kind of "welcome to the *Knife Edge House*" spiel. Now it was time to choose the teams.

None of the fighters would be known to the viewing public, not yet, not as personalities. But Carlsen had watched them carefully in training, and he assumed Krill had paid equal attention. Most of the fighters were male. Two were American. One of the Americans, a pale giant called Anders, wore crosses tattooed on his deltoid muscles, revealed by his sleeveless training shirt. He was staring at Carlsen now, and nodding.

Willing Carlsen to pick him, it looked like.

Zak tossed a coin.

"Jason? You call."

"Heads."

"You win. First choice is yours. And you pick the colours."

Blue eyes, cold smile.

"I choose Anders," said Krill.

Pure devilment, if he had seen the way Anders had stared at Carlsen, and picked up on the intent just as Carlsen had.

Bastard.

But sweetness and happiness were not the name of the game.

"And Blades," added Krill. "We're Blades."

Anders frowned as he pulled on the silver training shirt that Krill handed over. Then he shook himself and said: "Thank you, Coach. I'll do my best for you."

"I know you will," said Krill.

They bumped fists, then Anders took his place standing beside Krill, massive arms folded, his expression becoming stone.

Carlsen picked up a red shirt, then scanned the fighters.

"It's official now," said one of the gorgeous presenters. "Jason 'Cutter' Krill now leads Blades, while Fireman Carlsen is coach for the Bloods."

Ignoring her, Carlsen smiled.

"Bob Kahn," he said. "You're Bloods."

"Yes, Coach."

A bear hug and a handshake, then Kahn pulled on the red shirt.

"You." Krill pointed at the other American, a woman. "Durkee."

Her face clamped with tension.

Think you're in the wrong team?

Carlsen thought it was too bad, that he would have liked to pick her for Bloods; but this was a show with rules that everybody knew, and she should have known the choice could go either way. Her compatriot Anders had clearly wanted to be in Bloods, but he had not shown the weird vibrating tension that grew stronger with every pace she took closer to Krill.

Not Krill.

Something flipped inside Carlsen a moment before it happened.

That's not the problem.

He had been a fighter for decades, developing unconscious skills at reading attacks before they happened. A voice screamed danger inside him as this slim, short female fighter stepped closer to her coach, the reptilian Jason Krill.

But he's not her–

And then she moved.

"Fundamentalist Christian bastard!" she yelled.

Her hand whipped fast–

"Blade!" shouted someone.

–to the side of Anders' neck.

Shit.

Carlsen lunged forward, but Krill was closer and very fast, slapping the weapon out of Durkee's grasp and snapping an elbow to her jaw, before reaping her leg from under her.

Blood spurted from Anders' carotid artery.

"Medics!" shouted Zak.

It was a good call but the medical team were on hand only for training sessions, and at full strength only during elimination fights. The coaching teams, Krill's and Carlsen's, converged on the fallen Anders. Med-kits appeared.

Carlsen put a leg-lock restraint on the woman, Durkee, but she was not struggling. She had her eyes closed and – if anything – looked peaceful.

What the hell?

While Anders' eyes were protruding and he was seconds

from death unless someone could clamp the artery and stem the blood loss.

Carlsen shuddered.

"Clamp," said Sigmund. "Got it."

Gleam of silver at the side of Anders' neck.

Zak came closer.

"Is he–?"

"Comatose." Krill looked at the woman, Durkee, in Carlsen's restraint hold. "Hang on to that little girl, Fireman."

This did not seem the time for smart remarks.

She said something about Christians.

Carlsen looked up at Zak.

"Where's Durkee from?" he said.

"Er, I don't know."

"California," said Scott. "Got a degree from Cornell, went back to LA afterwards. She's over here for a year, studying and fighting."

"West Coast," said Carlsen.

"Yeah. And an East Coast alma mater."

It was the bit of the country in the middle that was fundamentalist: witness their continued support for the insanity of President Brand.

"Madness," said Arkady. "It's madness."

Carlsen looked at the shocked presenters, then at Zak. The corner of Zak's mouth twitched.

Jesus H. Christ.

No one could be that heartless, that calculating.

He's thinking about the ratings.

None of this belonged in the broadcast, but Zak was going to include it.

"That's one hell of a start to the show," said Krill.

Expressions of shock showed all around.

This is mad.

Only Zak's shock was faked.

[TWENTY-FIVE]

When the other patrols arrived – including the lone woman, Jacqui, who had abandoned her two colleagues after summoning help for them – Josh set up a conference redfanged among the patrol leaders' phones, and asked the question that had occurred to him right at the start of the exercise.

"Is anyone designated as Red Squad leader?"

No one answered yes.

"I thought so," said Josh. "I'll volunteer, unless someone's got an attack plan already in place."

There was a ten-second pause before the first reply, from a patrol leader whose designation read *Jeff*.

"I'm with you, Josh."

One by one, the other patrol leaders agreed.

"Good. Who do we know in Green Squad?"

"Brian is clued up." This was Jeff again. "If they need a squad leader, he's good."

Clearly Jeff was clued up too, guessing what Josh was after.

"That's exactly what I was thinking of," said Josh. "Give me two minutes to call and coordinate, and I'll get back to you."

It turned out that Jeff's analysis was correct: Josh could tell, as soon as he talked to the man on the phone, that Brian was a good choice. A minute later, Brian called back to confirm that he had taken command, and suggested they coordinate their attacks on the installation.

"Roger that," said Josh. "What are your positions? I'm sending mine."

His patrols' coordinates showed as red stars on his phone's map display; five green stars now formed an approximate arc to the north-east, on the other side of the target.

"Bastard drone is good, though," said Brian.

"Surveillance drone? Just one?"

"Looks that way."

"Can you see snipers in place?" asked Josh.

"Snipers? Shit."

Josh had the expertise to spy them out. If Brian saw no one, the negative result could mean there were no snipers near his location – the Paras trusting the drone to safeguard that approach – or that their concealment skills were better than his perceptions.

"Is the drone armed?" said Josh.

"Mag-darts and 9-mil conventional ammo, looks like."

For the exercise, the darts would bear no toxin and the bullets would be blanks. Laser sighting beams would register on the attackers' uniforms, rendering them dead in theory.

"With microwave sensors?" said Josh.

"I haven't dared ping it."

"Hold back on that." Josh stared down, picturing the drone. "Do you have an estimate of its flight trajectory?"

Some kind of regular loop would be easier to judge than flights with random shifts.

"Roger that. Take a look."

It was a twisting loop, like an infinity symbol. The drone repeated its exact route over and over, scanning the ground below.

"Easier to triangulate from," said Josh.

"Say again?"

"A regular loop like that, it's easier for us to predict the flight path. But it's also easier for the drone to perform a triangulation fix. Picking up a signal's direction from two different points on the loop."

"We got two marksmen in our squad," said Brian. "Markspersons, I mean."

In Josh's squad, Danie was the highest scorer on the rifle range so far. She grinned at Josh.

"Hold on a minute," said Josh.

Infinity-symbol flight path over desolate ground. Microwave sensors. Onboard weaponry, darts and bullets.

"Oh, yeah." Josh was smiling now. "I got it."

"Got what?"

"Are you ready to move forward in ten minutes?"

"We're good," said Brian.

"So listen, I don't, repeat do *not* want you to attack the drone."

"We can't get around it."

"The drone needs to be shot down," said Josh.

"Then what–?"

"Let's get someone else to do it for us."

Towards the eastern apex of its flight, the drone sensed a momentary signal from the south-west. Some seconds later, nearing the western end of its predetermined loop, it picked up an identical blip from the southeast. It sent a zipblip of its own, the code that designated *Enemy acquired*.

The enemy was approximately due south, and close.

Five seconds later, it sent a second signal.

Enemy engaged.

Josh grinned as the rifle fire sounded. He thumbed the waiting *Go* icon on his phone, and was already running by the time acknowledgements flared. Both squads were using leapfrog sprints, patrols taking turns to cover and advance; but none of the gunshots were theirs, and that was the way Josh intended it to stay.

Sorry, guys.

All the Para snipers were "dead" – lying still to play the part – but one of them had squeezed off an expert shot to drill the drone. It responded to central command by drifting in to a controlled landing, simulating its demise.

"Result," said Kyle.

Red and Green Squads were circling north, and soon they were at the walls of the installation: a brick-and-girder monstrosity used purely for training such as this.

"Move-move-move," they heard.

The Paras were sending out one patrol to investigate their downed snipers, and another to form a defensive perimeter at about the same distance as the snipers' location.

Maybe they had no idea that Josh and twenty-three other special forces troopers – both squads having lost candidates on route to the LUPs – were on their doorstep and about to penetrate the walls. Or perhaps their commander did guess that the drone's targeting their own people meant the infiltration had started, in which case she had sent the two patrols out as a feint, while readying defences inside the building.

Time to find out.

Danie stood up and said: "Bang."

Simultaneous with her voice was the whispered flit of "toxic" mag-dart from her handgun.

"Ow," said the Para she had shot.

The dart's point had penetrated his armour, as it was supposed to. Luckily the only fluid it carried was dihydrogen oxide, famous for frightening the scientifically illiterate, but no one else.

"Night, night," said Danie.

Josh had been halfway through reacting when she fired; but the Para had been coming from his rear.

"Sorry about this," he told the Para.

"That's all right, mate. I walked right into it. At least I get a rest now."

"No." Josh levelled his Heckler & Koch IonPulse. "Sorry for this: take your clothes off."

"Say what?"

"Tunic and trousers, plus the armour, that's all we need. And" – with a nasty grin – "your beret."

"Fuck off," said the Para. "Shit."

The maroon beret, like the Regiment's sand-coloured counterpart, was a badge of honour, hard-won.

"We'll bring it back intact." Danie looked at Josh. "Right, Boss?"

"My word on it," said Josh.

The Para nodded, then shrugged.

"I'm dead anyhow, aren't I?"

He struggled out of his gear. Meanwhile, Danie stripped – the Para's expression brightened – and pulled on the borrowed uniform, then adjusted the maroon beret on her head.

"How do I look?"

"Fucking beautiful," said the Para, fully serious.

Danie held out her phone.

"Redfang me your ID," she said. "No funny stuff."

Love at first sight, spec ops style. The Para blipped his details to her, seeming to understand that she could not return the compliment, not right now. But she had his army number and could track him down.

Josh's phone vibrated. The others were at the ingress points, ready for the penetration phase.

"Go now," he said.

They blew the bolts off one door. On the rest, they used electronic subversion to set the electromag locks to open while the control systems continued to indicate a locked state. From eight different points, they ran through corridors whose spycams registered no movement, converging on the command centre where the "enemy" colonel presided over her troops.

There was a small – though heavy – control box that Josh and his squad needed to liberate: that was the principal objective. But nothing made the point more than kidnapping the enemy commander, so that formed Josh's other goal: to capture the colonel and force her to leave with them.

Danie's uniform got her through a checkpoint, one of several that formed an inner ring of defence. Once inside, she turned and shot the guards in the back.

"You're all dead," she told them. "Never mind, eh?"

Then Josh and the others joined her, and split up: some to take out other checkpoints from the rear, so Green Squad and the rest of Red Squad could join them, others to proceed to the command centre. Josh's nerves were roaring with fear and excitement, because this was so close to the real thing, to an operation right on the edge. He stopped three paces from the control room door, getting ready for the final stage of penetration.

Gunfire sounded.

Good.

And someone screamed.

That's not right.

In that moment, the exercise was blown to hell.

"Priority." The voice on his phone was accompanied by a flashing red icon. "Brian here. One of my guys is down. Lowry. Shot through the shoulder."

"Tell me more," said Josh.

"Really shot. Live ammunition."

"Shit."

Josh thought about it for maybe three seconds – the duration of a lethal hand-to-hand encounter – then signalled the abort.

"Stand down," he said into the phone. "We have a live casualty, everyone. Drop out of role."

Then he walked into the control room, pointed his gun at the colonel's head – "Bang" – then lowered it.

"We're standing down," he told her. "There's been a real casualty."

"What do you mean?" Her voice buzzed, and she raised her combat phone. "Fuck. Get the medics. Yes? Good."

She looked at Josh.

"Come with me," she said.

"Yes, sir. Ma'am."

It took less than a minute to reach an intersection of corridors where Lowry lay quietly – morphine – with his shoulder a bloody, splintered mess. One of the nearby Paras stared, his face white and bloodless.

One of his comrades had his weapon.

"Where are those *bloody*–? Good." The colonel waved her hand. "Here. Fast."

The medics rushed over.

"Chopper's fifteen minutes away, ma'am."

"Keep him breathing." She looked at the ashen-faced Para. "What happened, Briggs?"

"I checked, ma'am. I used the right mag."

His comrade ejected the magazine from what must be Briggs' weapon. A yellow X marked the mag.

"He's right, ma'am."

"Bad ammo?" The colonel's face became stone. "I'll have someone's balls for this."

Josh's phone vibrated. Danie calling.

"Trouble," she said. "Broken bones, two Paras injured. Maybe a torn-up knee. A couple of our guys are bruised and battered. They heard Paras say something about arrogant fuckers deserving what they got."

Josh felt his face match the colonel's.

"Take names, pull everyone back." He turned to the colonel. "Apologies, ma'am. Best if we get clear."

"All right, but make sure they don't cause trouble." She raised her phone. "My lot will keep discipline."

Josh nodded, and the colonel's mouth twitched – clearly she knew better than to expect a decent salute from special forces – then he headed out. Behind him, the colonel's hell-freezing tones spelled out concise orders about standing down.

She was terrific.

Balls.

But the exercise was a fuck-up.

Riding to the barracks in the back of a truck, Josh felt isolated from the others. Several of the patrol leaders – plus Jeff, who had led Green Squad – took care to tell him what a good job he had done. He thanked them, but it did not feel good to him.

There would be a post-mortem, the debriefing from hell. He knew what it would find: two Paras, not knowing the full situation, making smart remarks – because the Regiment really could appear arrogant to outsiders, riding roughshod over what other units considered necessary discipline, sometimes playing pranks or holding water-pistol fights while waiting to commence a live op.

Probably the Paras had thought that one of the Selection candidates had broken a leg or something, not been shot by one of their own with a failed blank acting like a live round. Josh should have left the wounded Lowry in the Paras' care and pulled everyone out immediately.

But there was more than that.

Evans. I should have found you earlier.

What he should have done then was snatch the poor bastard from his bedroom over the pub, and kicked the wallscreen into splinters if necessary, because Suzanne had hypnotised him often enough for him to pick up on the onset of trance: he should have realised what was happening.

I'm leaving it all to others.

Lofty had been talking to the powers that be, but beyond that Josh knew nothing. Were Special Branch and the spooks already investigating the possibility that the mindbending software was designed to induce suicide, rather than producing it as an accident, an unintended disaster? And if so, were they aware of the likelihood that Evans was a victim of the same people who had loosed this Cutter Circle craze among the nation's teenagers?

Danie got up from her place in the swaying truck, and came over to squash in beside Josh.

"You did good," she said.

"I'm not so sure."

"Yeah, you—"

"But I do know you're going to be outstanding. It's been a real pleasure, Danie."

He held out his hand.

"I don't like the sound of that," she said, shaking his hand. "You can't quit."

Her words made his shoulders tighten.

I hate quitting.

But sometimes you have to reconsider your objective.

"Maybe I'm acquiring another target," he said.

Danie thumped his leg with her fist.

"Then give the fuckers hell," she said. "Leave no one standing, right?"

He looked in her eyes as he grinned.

"I won't."

The truck slowed, approaching the barracks. Time was collapsing, but however hard the next few hours were going to be, Josh's decision was already made, fixed in his subconscious.

Some ninety minutes later, in the middle of debriefing, Jan mentioned that the Paras' training ammo came from Axe-Blade. Josh, not knowing the name, asked who they were.

"Old armaments company, new name," she said. "Re-branded when Tyndall Industries took them over."

The final doubts flowed out of Josh's mind.

[TWENTY-SIX]

The rue des Saussaies was a normal-looking Parisian street, not one of the great boulevards. Along one side ran a building that was almost plain by the standards of the city, with a dour edge to its squared-off lines that reminded Suzanne of municipal buildings in Edinburgh. The only clue to its identity was the words MINISTERE DE L'INTÉRIEUR carved into the lintel above the main gateway, its huge metal doors decorated with what looked like round shields.

The car stopped outside. This was the Direction Centrale de la Police Judiciaire, and the lone uniformed officer out front was the human face of a massive and powerful machine, with little sympathy for enemies of the state. The DCPJ was forbidding, and though Suzanne had been in the equally formidable Thames House, her status here was different, one of vulnerability. At least she had company.

Philip, Richie and Lexa came inside with her. Officers escorted them along a busy corridor – uniformed men and women, a few plainclothes detectives with scarlet armbands – to a waiting-room with armoured view-windows and obvious spycams. Besides more PJ officers, a lawyer from the British Embassy was already there. Though Nordic-looking, his name was Vasquez.

Suzanne hoped she did not need legal protection, not at this level. While Vasquez might do his utmost to aid Philip, her own status was different. This was her country, after all; and when it came down to it, she still loved the place.

As a group, they descended to a basement-level conference room with grey furnishings and a glittering black glass wall, presumably a display screen.

The questioning, in English, was led by a bland-looking inspector called Gagné, and a hard-faced female sergeant named Zanoni. Gagné allowed them to remain as a group, instead of questioning them individually.

In a gritty webmovie, the police would interrogate a criminal gang one by one, playing them off against each other, which made enough psychological sense for Suzanne to assume it approximated real procedure. Since Gagné made no attempt to separate the four of them, he was treating them as witnesses.

To what crime?

There was a flipside. This was no routine checking of an attempted suicide – the officers were too high-ranking, for a start – therefore they knew of Cutter Circles, and understood what must have happened to Opal.

"Mr Broomhall." Gagné's tone was polite. "If you could tell us, first, what you know of Opal Payne, and then what happened today."

"Yes, of course." Philip nodded to Vasquez, who nodded back. "Opal is a friend of my son's, who sometimes comes to visit us at home. This trip, part-vacation and part-business for me, seemed a good opportunity to–"

He related what he knew, with no surprises for Suzanne, and no evidence of surprise on the officers' faces. Then Gagné asked Lexa for her story, which did not take long. That done, with gentle questions, he extracted Richie's view of events. The boy's guilt for buying the offending phone was obvious.

As Richie spoke, Zanoni's face hardened even further, her

eyes focused on some target constructed in her mind.

Finally, Gagné asked Suzanne whether there was anything she could add from a professional standpoint. At that, Vasquez touched her on the arm.

"Refrain from speculation, Dr Duchesne. But do relate the facts."

So he was worried about her professional liability. But Opal's condition was implanted by phoneware using subliminal techniques, not triggered by Suzanne.

She told them what had happened since her arrival in Paris.

"Thank you," said Inspector Gagné finally. "We appreciate your coming here. A car will take you, Mr Broomhall, back to your hotel."

"Not just me, I hope," said Philip.

He glanced at Suzanne.

"Ah, of course not." Gagné smiled at Richie, then Lexa. "But Dr Duchesne, we would appreciate it if you could stay, because you are a professional in this area, and might help us understand more what is happening to these poor children."

Philip and Lexa frowned.

Vasquez, showing no surprise, said: "Your invitation includes me, I trust."

Zanoni's lips thinned.

"You're very welcome," said Gagné. "Of course we wish justice to be observed."

"I'll be fine," Suzanne told Philip. "You need to take care of Richie."

"And Lexa," Philip said.

"I'd say she can look after herself." Suzanne noted the hard look Lexa gave Zanoni. "But your friends in London will be worried."

Meaning a certain MI5 officer.

"Actually," said Philip, "I asked one of my new friends here in Paris to recommend people to help. With personal security,

I mean. This is someone who's about to sever his supplier-chain links with various Tyndall enterprises and replace them with contracts via yours truly."

He came to life when talking business. Or perhaps he was trying to tell her that anyone going up against the Tyndalls needed decent security in case of dirty tricks, therefore the recommendation would be for a good firm.

"What about the firm you used last year?" she asked.

Josh had praised them as real professionals.

"I figured locals already on hand and fluent in the language would be better."

"Seems fair enough."

The lines on Zanoni's face were deepening. Perhaps Suzanne had kept her waiting long enough.

"I'll be fine here," Suzanne added to Philip. "Take care, and I'll see you in a bit."

"If you're–"

"Go on, Philip. Get your son out of here."

That decided him.

"Then I *will* see you later."

He stared at Gagné, then Zanoni, before finally leading Richie and Lexa from the room.

"Shall we start again?" said Gagné.

Suzanne settled back in her chair, while Vasquez looked alert.

"Let's do that," she said.

The second phase felt tangible, something Suzanne could get a grip on, as the earlier hidden tension came out into the open. It was Zanoni who pointed her phone at the big wallscreen, causing a bleak image to appear.

Opal, in an armchair beside a hospital bed. Inside a different room from before.

"You moved her."

"To somewhere safer."

A secure psychiatric unit. The armchair included restraint straps, currently dangling free. A doctor was talking to Opal, while a large male nurse stood off to one side, almost out of view.

There was no sound.

"I'd like to be involved in her treatment," said Suzanne. "If you suspect me of something, then I suggest Dr Carol Klugmann in London, because Opal needs someone with fluent English."

Vasquez twitched a smile.

"Let's have some sound," said Gagné.

"–know the others were there?" The doctor's accent was heavy. "How did you know where to go?"

"I don't know." Opal's mouth curved down. Lines no fifteen year-old should show were deepening around forehead, cheeks and eyes. "I *knew* but I don't know how I knew."

The doctor blinked.

With verbal confusion like that, Suzanne could have induced hypnotic trance in the doctor within seconds.

"He's using the wrong approach," she said. "In her current neurophysiological state, she won't recall subliminal suggestion. The part of her brain that's conversing now is not the part with the stored knowledge."

"So it's impossible," said Gagné, "for Miss Opal to recall the techniques of persuasion, is that it?"

"In this fully conscious state?" said Suzanne. "Yes, it's impossible."

Zanoni shook her head.

"Hypnosis. Maybe I'm just too intelligent to be hypnotised."

The tone of her voice was the real communication: sceptical irony.

Good. I can use that.

Suzanne watched, then began to alter her breathing.

"Did you know the other twelve teenagers?" On screen, the doctor was trying again. "Did you know their names, perhaps?"

"No, I told–"

Gagné gestured, and Zanoni cut the sound. In the image, Opal showed obvious agitation. But Suzanne was focusing on Zanoni.

She's fit. Very fit.

Her leanness was that of an endurance athlete, different from the brittle thinness of anorexia.

"It's a matter of context," said Suzanne. "If you've ever been lost in a book or been driving for ages and suddenly wondered what had been happening, like your unconscious took over, that's all that trance means" – she slowed her voice – "not like the impression you get when you relax watching webmovies" – and again – "because any athlete knows how to go into trance in hard training when the normal conscious part of you just drifts away as a serious athlete has the habit to go into trance every day–"

Zanoni's eyes looked defocused.

"–and in a moment you may blink, *comme ça*, and again, *comme ça*, and as your muscles soften then *ma voix* descend *avec toi vers cet endroit confortable et plaisant...*"

Eyelids fluttering, Zanoni's head bowed.

Gagné looked on, bemused, as Suzanne gave her suggestions, then led Zanoni out of trance.

"*Lève-toi maintenant* and the thing is, Opal needs a different form of approach if you need to find out what happened to her. That's all I'm saying."

Zanoni blinked several times, then synched back into the conversation.

"And you think you should be the therapist, Dr Duchesne? Is that correct?"

She had forgotten the trancework.

"That's my recommendation."

Gagné stopped biting his lip.

"Look," he said. "I don't think we–"

Zanoni stood up, dragging her chair away from the table. She put one foot on it, bounced up, rotated on the spot, leaped down, hauled the chair forward and sat down.

"–need to, er... Zanoni? What was that?"

"What, sir?"

"Why did you do that with the chair?"

"Excuse me?" She looked down at the chair legs. "Do what?"

Beside Suzanne, Vasquez snorted.

He's no lawyer.

A real lawyer – or one who was just a lawyer, not something else as well – would have tried to stop her demonstration of hypnosis.

Suzanne said, "You're recording this interview. Can you play back on screen?"

Zanoni was frowning.

"Yes." Gagné pulled his own phone from his belt and worked it. "There."

The image of Opal snapped out of existence, replaced by a disconcerting perspective of this room from near the ceiling to Suzanne's right. Gagné had gauged the timestamp well.

"*–my recommendation,*" the on-screen Suzanne was saying.

"*Look.*" Gagné. "*I don't think we need to, er...*"

And the on-screen Zanoni did the thing with the chair, climbing onto it, turning around, then sitting back at the table as if nothing had happened.

"*C'est pas moi,*" said the real-life Zanoni. "You've faked my image."

She could not look away from the screen.

"Play it through again," Suzanne said to Gagné.

With a smile, Gagné muted the sound, then replayed the video sequence.

Then he winked at Suzanne.

Good.

Vasquez leaned close.

"Steve Witten would appreciate your passing on what you learn."

She kept her face free of reaction.

More than a lawyer.

After a second, she nodded.

They let her make one call before going to see Opal. Assuming she was under surveillance, she called Carol Klugmann. Perhaps she needed the kind of confidence boost that Carol could give.

"Hey." Carol was wearing one of her old *Keep Austin Weird* sweatshirts, tight across her massive bosom. "How're you doing, girlfriend?"

The tonality was different from normal.

"I wanted to *feel relaxed* and *feel confident*, so who else would I talk to?"

Suzanne automatically marked out feel relaxed and feel confident with her voice: slipping into therapist mode.

"Your Jedi mind tricks," said Carol, "will not work with me, old woman."

The same thing Steve had said.

"This is not the therapist you're looking for."

"Your thoughts betray you, young Suzanne."

"You win," said Suzanne. "So long as you tell me what's up."

In the display, Carol pointed to the ceiling.

"Opposite to going down, hun. Not that I have been, lately."

"Bad Carol. You need a sexual conquest, do you?"

"Only one?" But Carol's voice lacked its usual saucy energy. "Ah, not today. Matt's on some kind of arrest list back home."

It took a moment to process the words.

Matt. Her cousin.

He was Epsilon Force, stationed in the UK when he resigned from the disintegrating US Army. Josh had driven Matt to meet a stealth flight that took him back to the States.

"An arrest list?"

Perhaps she should not have made this call when under

police surveillance. But President Brand's America was a rogue state, unlikely to receive help from French authorities.

"Scuttlebutt is," said Carol, "they think Matt was involved in the assassination attempt. You know, the one that failed last month? Someone got through layers of security, through heavy duty systems, so they reckon it's ex-special forces guys. Whether they really think Matt was involved, or they're just checking possibilities, I don't know."

"You've not been in touch?"

Perhaps she should not ask this, not with possible eavesdroppers.

"No contact with any of my folks, not since last summer."

"Shit."

"Yeah, that's what the old country's fallen into."

Suzanne thought back over Carol's words. "I didn't know about any assassination attempt. You mean on Brand?"

"Yeah, but it's not on the news sites. I got it from, er, other friends back home."

Suzanne blinked.

"It *must* have been on the news. You can't hide–"

She stopped.

Can't hide important news like teenagers killing themselves?

Like boiling frogs, slow changes go unnoticed. When had such important events begun to go unreported? Was this new, or something that had gone on for decades?

Josh tried to change all this.

But it was too much for one person. For the man who had run from her life.

"Hold still," she told Carol. "I'm going to cheer you up now."

"Don't you dare."

"Too late. You can already sense that good feeling starting to move inside your stomach–"

"Fuck. Jesus fuck."

"–as it starts to intensify and–"

"I love you, girlfriend, in a non-gay way."

"–move up and down inside your body–"

They continued until they both felt better. Mutual therapy. After ending the call, Suzanne felt her smile attenuate, thinking of Josh, missing from her life.

"Dr Duchesne?" Zanoni was standing there. "This way, please, to the car. To see Opal."

Her voice was tight.

"Are you riding with me?"

"I don't–"

"Because I'd like to apologise," said Suzanne. "For using you to make a point."

"Hmm."

"And" – with a smile – "I could show you visualization techniques to enhance your athletic performance. What are you, a runner?"

"*Ouais*. Marathons and ultras."

Serious stuff.

"So are you interested, Sergeant Zanoni?"

"Maybe."

That was good enough.

Rule one: Do no harm.

She followed Zanoni out to the car.

[TWENTY-SEVEN]

Richie rode in the back seat of the unmarked car, wedged between Dad and Lexa, feeling safe. It made him feel hopeful about Opal, too. Suzanne was here, and Opal would therefore be all right.

The officer-driver dropped them off outside the hotel. Lexa shared a rapid conversation with him in French, at the end of which the officer grinned. Then she led the way inside, followed by him, with Dad behind. If they were intentionally keeping him in the centre, that was fine. Upstairs, standing outside Dad's apartment, were five men and one woman in suits, hard-looking and fit.

"The security," said Lexa. "*Vous êtes Français, monsieur?*"

"*Pour moi-même, la réponse est oui,*" said the smallest man. "*Je m'appele Gérard Thériault. Alors, je vous présente–*"

Richie thought he understood. The man speaking, Mr Thériault – now introducing the others by first name – was French, while some of the others were not. He caught the last two names: Nik, then the woman, Kari.

Lexa frowned.

Josh ought to be here.

He had thought that before, but this time it was like a commanding voice inside his mind.

Opal had pointed out that Lexa was like a female Josh.

Does Suzanne still love Josh?

It was weird to think about grown-ups this way, but Suzanne had not mentioned him, not once. He ought to ask Opal–

But she would not be answering questions until Suzanne had treated her, and the hospital had let her go. Sunk in thought, he half-heard the serious tone of Lexa and Dad discussing things, with the French security guy chiming in. Arrangements for guarding them, which seemed ridiculous, at least before Opal came back. She was the one who needed protection.

The police were guarding her now.

It's my fault.

Everyone said it wasn't, but who else had bought Opal the phone that had hypnotised her? If hypnosis was what it used – he wasn't sure about that.

I have to do something.

But it was Josh who could sort out a situation like this. Josh who could–

So that's what I can do.

Walking away from the adults, he worked his phone, pulling up the contacts list and adding a priority call status – category red – before selecting *Josh*. But the reply was an immediate *disconnected from network* message.

Maybe that was why no one had contacted him. He was offline, long term. Working on something secret? But last year's episode had been a one-off: Josh's normal work was in corporate training, wasn't it? Or was that part of his cover?

But there was another way. When under surveillance, Josh had used covert websites for communication. At some other point, after Lexa had taken himself and Opal through a wing chun training session, she had talked about military IDs and the separate networks that soldiers used on active deployment: comms layers sealed off from civilian use.

Putting those pieces of information together, and remembering the panes of source code that Josh had showed him so briefly, he thought it was possible to create a message archive on one of Josh's secure sites, then encapsulate the message in a search-bot that could respond to military challenge protocols and find Josh's message box.

First, he needed to work out what message to send. That seemed harder than the hacking exercise itself.

The security guards were leaving, stationing themselves outside. Richie sat down in an armchair, pulled out a pocket keyboard, unfurled it, and tagged it to his phone. He did not want to speak his message aloud, and putting on a throat mic to subvocalise would look suspicious. So old-fashioned text would have to do.

Hi, Josh. Opal's in trouble here in Paris, and I don't know if you've heard of this suicide thing, but

He stopped. Should he mention Suzanne first, or later? Or keep her name out of it?

"–of them are Armenians," Lexa was saying to Dad. "Look capable, though. Understood what I meant about deployment vectors."

"I'll take your word for it," said Dad. "I'm presuming that's a good thing."

"I know I'm just the driver, and you're busy counting all your money, but yes, I know about these–"

"You're not just my driver."

"Oh."

Richie pulled earbeads from his pocket.

None of my business.

Plus he did not know what to hope for. With music pounding in his ears, he focused on the text once more.

Hi, Josh. Opal's in trouble here in Paris, and I don't know if you've heard of this suicide thing, but Suzanne's treating her so she's going to be OK. She will be, right? What happened was I bought a phone and

The message had to be just right.

• • • •

After a couple of two-hour sessions with Opal, then long sessions of analysis and preparation to put together her report, Suzanne was tired, her head aching and her balance unsteady. It was Zanoni who insisted on her fellow officers taking Suzanne to dinner, then finding her a room at 11, rue des Saussaies – the DCPJ – that came with a cot to sleep in.

Zanoni also said she would get a message to Philip Broomhall, telling him that Suzanne would reappear next morning.

That night, Suzanne slept deeply for the first time since Josh had left her. She had no idea, the next morning, why her night should have been so restful, unless it was just giving in to exhaustion. Over breakfast with Zanoni and Gagné, she relished the chance to natter on in French about politics, climate change, everything but Cutter Circles and Opal.

Opal. At least you're going to be all right.

Unluckily for anyone wanting to use Opal as a witness, she now had amnesia for large parts of the last few days. That was not normal treatment methodology, but this was not a normal case. The easiest way to reverse brainwashing was to scrub it from the infected brain, and that was pretty much what Suzanne had done.

"*C'était merveilleux.*" She leaned back, gesturing at her empty espresso cup and the remains of two croissants. "*Merci bien.*"

"*De rien,*" said Gagné.

Breakfast over, he and Zanoni escorted Suzanne to a sort of boardroom to give a presentation of her report. Ten people were already there, including Vasquez, the lawyer from the British embassy. No one introduced the others, but that was all right: Gagné had already said they preferred to remain nameless.

Everyone settled, while Suzanne took her place at the head of the boardroom table. Behind her was a pale grey wallscreen, currently offline. She raised her phone, while off to one side Zanoni made adjustments, then smiled at her: ready to go.

Using a white background with a heavy black font, Suzanne displayed a short list of topics.

- **neurocognitive foundations**
- **subliminal perception and signal phase-locking**
- **psychopathology of suicide**
- **cult expansion: memetic cascades**

Whoever these people were, she could assume no background in neuroscience.

"I'm going to show you how Opal was given to create a massively false mental picture of the world, with imagined episodes of uncaring adults that cleverly used real events as their start point – in other words, the software tailored itself to the individual user.

"Before explaining the mechanism, you need to realise that computation is the basis of all your experience. Can I ask what colour this text is?"

The obvious answer was black, but her audience hesitated.

"Light grey," said the unnamed Englishman, and smiled. "Am I right?"

"Exactly right." Suzanne switched off the display. "It's a light grey screen, and that's the default colour. You can't project blackness, but" – she brought up the list once more – "the font *looks* black because even something as basic as the difference between black and pale grey – or even white – is calculated, comparing the intensity of light with the average brightness of the visual field."

For several minutes, she talked, then a bearded man near the front raised his hand.

"Excuse me?" His French intonation was light. "Is it really that easy to hypnotise someone? Just because they use their phone often?"

"*Absolument oui,*" said Zanoni from the corner. "She did it to me, but don't take my word for it. Just look."

She grinned, then winked at Suzanne.

"*Baise-moi!*" The man pushed his chair back. "What is this?"

Three of her audience were slumped in their chairs, including the Englishman.

"It's OK to be sceptical," said Suzanne. "And in my opinion you should be. I'm a scientist and the only thing I take on faith is that the universe behaves consistently. The rest is observation and deduction."

She did not need to say that an experimental fact was right here: three of their colleagues entranced with no overt hypnotic induction. Point made, she brought them out of it. All three yawned, smiled, then answered questions from the ones who had remained awake, all wanting to know what the experience was like.

Finally, they returned their attention to her.

"Tell us everything," the bearded man said. "We're ready to listen, Dr Duchesne."

"Thank you. This is everything I know–"

Her report included details of the stages of brainwashing: the steady induction of paranoid beliefs, the identification with a beleaguered group – the other twelve teenagers in particular – and the memory of self-cutting and other forms of voluntary pain that formed a self-discipline against the perceived cruelty and chaos of the world. In that context, self-harm became a logical response to an environment they could not affect.

"She did not know the other twelve, however?" said the bearded man.

"That's right," said Suzanne. "She did not. But she had memories of interacting with them, all the same. And when you think how a horror movie can you make you flinch, you realise that an imagined experience carries all the same emotional reactions as something real."

The Englishman at the back was frowning.

"So you could implant false memories in all of us right now, could you?"

"That would be very hard," she said. "And I'm sure you've

got video surveillance enabled in here. So you'd know, wouldn't you, if this was anything other than a safe environment?"

"True."

"In her mind, Opal had a months-long experience of gradually increasing paranoia, increasing bonding and identification with the group, and of increasing self-harm, some of which actually occurred. Which was lucky, by the way, in terms of her friends identifying that there was a problem."

"And the other twelve?" said Zanoni, asking her first question. "They also had false memories of interacting with Opal?"

"Yes, except that they would have found only in retrospect that it was her. I mean" – Suzanne slowed down – "the other people's identities would be a template. Think back to a vivid memory involving people, maybe something you saw in a movie. Think how complete it is. Now describe the colours of every garment in the shot – and tonight, dig up that old movie and check your memory."

"I see what you mean," said the Englishman, working his phone. "Damn. I didn't remember *that*."

"So it's a kind of fill-in-the-blanks, but it wouldn't appear that way to the victims. Because these teenagers *are* victims. We need to stop more of them suffering."

"Your analysis," said the bearded man, "will certainly help our people. Is there any more you can think of in the way of, what would you say, countermeasures?"

"To stop the spread? That's for your systems experts. Kill the software."

She meant people like Steven's MI5 team, the GCHQ gurus they mentioned, and Ghost Force operators just as Josh used to be.

"But for developing deprogramming ware, something to counteract the brainwashing, this information will form a start point. And of course I'll help."

The nameless Englishman glanced at Vasquez, who

nodded back.

"You must be exhausted, Dr Duchesne."

"Not at the moment. Later, I will be."

When she had finished her presentation, she would feel like collapsing.

Zanoni said, "Perhaps Dr Duchesne would like to return to her hotel."

"If you would make yourself available for another meeting," said the bearded man, "say in the late afternoon tomorrow, we would like that."

"My pleasure," said Suzanne.

There were pleasantries and handshakes, then the meeting broke up. Gagné told Suzanne how he appreciated her help, and nodded towards Zanoni.

"Thanks for *all* your help," he said.

Zanoni smiled.

"You're really welcome," said Suzanne.

"Especially for helping my running."

"Win medals for the department, Anne," Gagné said, "and I'll arrange a bonus for you. Somehow."

Vasquez had been standing nearby. Gagné turned to him.

"Your client has some scary skills," Gagné said.

Suzanne was not exactly his client.

"You're telling *me*," said Vasquez. "Very intimidating."

"So where would you like to go?" Zanoni asked Suzanne. "We'll drive you there."

"Um, back to the hotel, I guess. If that's where the Broomhalls went."

"I hear and obey." Zanoni raised her arms out straight, hands dangling at the wrist. "Your wish is my command."

Days-long tension broke as Suzanne laughed, joined by the others.

In the fighters' house, several rooms were set aside for

coaching and executive staff. Fighters entered only when invited, perhaps to discuss fight selection, sometimes to discuss their physical health – either to arrange a hospital visit or, sometimes, to deliver the bad news of a medical verdict, telling a fighter they were off the competition.

"Nice entry," said Krill, watching the biggest wallscreen. "Even if I say so myself."

"We're not thinking of viewing figures," said Zak Tyndall. "But you did take Durkee down nicely, Jason."

Carlsen shook his head. They had stopped Durkee only after she had stabbed the other American contender, Anders. Hardly good timing.

Anders had died in the ambulance.

"What do we know about her?" Carlsen asked. "Did she lose her family when President Brand nuked the West Coast?"

Zak scowled. Probably this bit would be edited before transmission. Even the premium-rate viewers, apparently, were now watching the show on a thirty-minute delay, not the usual five seconds.

"No idea," said Sigmund. "Unless your security people know different, Zak?"

Most people called him Mr Tyndall, but Zak liked to be a man of the people while on the show. Not that Sigmund cared much, either way.

"Not yet."

"So she might have had it in for Anders personally," said Carlsen, "or she might just have known that some guy from Alabama was going to be on the show. The bios were available beforehand, were they?"

He was a coach admitting that he had not paid attention to the public side of the show, but that was all right. Fighting, training and coaching were all that he was here for. Let the execs take care of the webcasting.

"So what's on the news?" asked Krill. "We famous yet?"

Zak raised his phone.

"My people are probably still putting it together. But let's see."

"So you're showing what happened?" said Carlsen. "Durkee attacking Anders?"

"Killing him, you mean," said Krill. "And the cops taking her away."

Carlsen had stayed inside – in the other gym – while the officers took her out to their vehicles; likewise as the paramedics left with their gurney, carrying Anders.

"Here's the main stories." Zak pulled up text-only panes. "Soon as the guys webcast what's happened, we'll be up there. Top spot, I reckon."

The first pane read:

POPE EXCOMMUNICATES AMERICA

Catholic primate casts former US from Church.

The Pope today announced that he has excommunicated the entire population of the former United States of America, effectively sundering their ties with the Roman Catholic Church and placing them in a state of mortal sin. This means… <read more text> <multimedia>

"Holy crap." That was Chiang, one of Krill's assistants. "My folks are Catholic."

Murder was always bad and always personal, at least to the victim's family. This news seemed abstract, even bizarre, but perhaps it might produce more ripples to affect the world than one dead fighter on a reality show.

GUR INVADES ROMANIA

Nuclear missiles a threat, says Russian Premier

Following last month's economic and strategic pact between Georgia, Russia, and the Ukraine, Premier Shtemenko appears to have directed a tripartite military incursion into the Romanian heartland. "We cannot continue to stand by," said Premier Shtemenko, "while rogue missile installations belonging to the collapsing regime of President Brand remain a threat upon our doorstep." The invasion force has… <read more text><multimedia>

Reading the second pane, Carlsen shook his head. If they were invading Romania, where would it stop? There were American missiles in other countries, weren't there?

"Maybe they'll go for Poland next," said Krill.

Sigmund was scowling.

"Kinda like some historical echo," added Krill. "Don't you think? Armies pouring into Poland always kicks off something big."

"Maybe they'll see sense," said Sigmund.

"Yeah. Hard not to worry, though." Krill looked at Zak. "Unless you're the kind of guy to sell arms to both sides, that kind of thing."

Zak spread his hands.

"I'm a peaceful man," he said. "We need the world to settle down."

Carlsen knew that real fighters laugh a lot when they're not training or in combat, and that soldiers who had served in conflicts were best placed to appreciate peace. Screwed-up hatred and directing people from afar to their deaths, that was for old guys in distant rooms.

People like Zak Tyndall?

Carlsen was not afraid of asking Zak outright about arms dealing, but tactically it was best to remain quiet and research later online. Then he could make some decision, because however much he wanted *Knife Edge* to succeed, things were not right.

His sister could do with the money, what with poor Kat in the ground, but there must be other ways of earning it.

Do what's right.

The Shaolin monks in Brixton had taught him that. He often thought that while their values might not be same as his – their view of the right thing to do might be different – he had always been certain they would never betray themselves. Every part of their minds and bodies moved in a single direction, together.

Perhaps they were better men than he was.

[TWENTY-EIGHT]

Josh was going to resign. As he completed his morning run
with the group, he knew it was going to happen. Had either
Jan or Lofty been among the instructors running with them –
at least one of the pair normally led the way – he might have
already done it.

I'm sorry, Lofty.

His old mentor might consider resignation a betrayal – or
worse, an act of weakness, of giving up under stress. Before
leaving, Josh had to clear the air.

As they ran back into barracks, he saw someone step into a
shiny ThermoRover: Sharon Caldwell, leader of the TechnoDemocratic Party. On the previous occasion, she had been doing
the usual VIP routine of experiencing the Killing House, seeing
special forces in action and receiving some training in being a
hostage while the guys extracted her to safety.

This time she was alone.

And her party organization was linked to the Cutter Circle
deaths – in fact *link* was too weak a term. If Josh was right,
then Caldwell's party was a victim, just like the teenagers. In
the kind of terrorist op that Ghost Force could investigate
better than anyone.

"You're looking good for an old guy," said Kyle in the showers. "Lean and mean and not a Zimmer frame in sight."

"If I had my Zimmer frame with me," said Josh, "I'd beat you to death with it."

A shower that sluiced away sweat felt better than a shower otherwise, for reasons Josh had never worked out. He concentrated on the simple pleasures of drying off, dressing in a clean uniform, and drinking electrolyte replacement fluid that tasted of lemon.

Then he presented himself to one of the sergeants.

"Request permission to see Lofty," said Josh.

The sergeant blew out a breath.

"You're breezing through Selection, Cumberland. That exercise fuck-up was someone else's fault."

"Yeah. That's not what it's about."

"Good. Cause if you're not here afterwards, I'm going to kick your arse."

Now it was Josh's turn to exhale aloud.

"I might have to tighten the old sphincter, then."

The sergeant used his phone to pass on the request. Seconds later, Josh's phone vibrated, with details shown on screen: he was to meet Lofty right now, in level minus five of the Ghost Force bunker.

Before closing it down, Josh checked his inbox for other messages, and found an error message in the log. It read *ProxyFailureException* but carried no further details beyond a timestamp.

Josh followed the sergeant's directions, and ten minutes later was in a steel-lined subterranean office, sitting himself down opposite a metal desk. Behind it sat Lofty. Off to one side, Jan worked her combat phone, bringing a wallscreen to life.

"No hypnosis this time, laddie." Lofty grinned at Josh. "You're safe."

"I need to talk to you about–"

"Shut up, Josh," said Jan. "And tell us afterwards, all right? We were going to call you, even if you hadn't asked to see Lofty."

"But– OK."

Lofty said: "You have a young friend called Richie Broomhall, is that right?"

That was a surprise.

"Sure I do. Last year, he was the lad I was looking for on the streets of London. A runaway. It kind of kicked off everything else that happened."

"And he's a bit of a hacker, is he?"

"Not by my reckoning," said Josh. "But he's a natural at science. Why do you mention him?"

"He tried to send you a message," said Jan. "Got through many layers of security, too."

"That's not– Oh." Josh looked at his phone. "I've a failure entry on my calls log."

"So he almost got a message to you," said Lofty. "All the way in to the Regiment net. You think he's our sort of person in the making?"

What a question.

"Never mind." Lofty nodded. "Jan? You want to explain?"

"It's not the message itself we're interested in." She pointed, and process diagrams appeared on screen. "He used a nice mix of stealthbots to deliver the archive file, that's the point."

Josh leaned closer.

"Where did he get them from?"

Richie, you're a bright lad.

Jan was smiling.

"Seems his dad got his IT experts to do some hacking of their own last summer. You'd almost think it had something to do with all that footage of Zak and Zebediah Tyndall splashed over our screens. Dirty labs in Africa, backhand deals with Billy Church in Number 10. That sort of thing."

Now Josh was smiling too.

"Richie nicked his dad's infiltration ware?" he said. "And tracked me down, so he must have worked out how military IDs operate."

"We're impressed," said Lofty. "But this is not a schoolboy's fan club."

Jan manipulated the display.

"So we backtracked into the Broomhall network, pulled out copies of every bit of infiltration ware, including the data and metadata files for their assault on Tyndall Industries. Portal interface schemas, password lists, architecture diagrams. The lot."

Shit. Richie had just dropped his father into deep trouble, because while much of the data was legally accessible – provided you knew how and where to look – some of it was not. Hacking foreign servers was a violation of the UN Systems Rights Charter. When legal authorities chose, they could use such violations as an excuse to come down heavily.

"Unfortunately" – Jan's voice lightened – "we lost the metadata showing that everything came from Broomhall's organization, so we've no evidence of him breaking the law."

"Shame," said Lofty.

"Careless." Josh grinned. "Too bad."

"So we were left in what you might call a quandary," said Jan. "All this great infiltration ware, and what should we do with it? So guess what we decided?"

"To use it for its original purpose?"

"Exactly," said Lofty. "Seems your pal Philip Broomhall is an honest man. Since last year's hack attack, he's steered cleared of Tyndall's systems."

Maybe because last year's episode was a failure. The Tyndalls were richer and more influential than ever. Billy Church was still prime minister, and about to tighten his hold further in the Midsummer Christmas general election.

Now only days away.

"That's Lofty's way of saying" – Jan pointed – "that what you're about to see is something only the three of us in this room know about."

"For now," said Lofty.

"Because we respect the chain of command," said Jan.

Which was why they were showing this to him instead of their superior officers. Right.

"Respect," said Josh.

A display pane grew large on screen: video with poor resolution and washed-out colour, showing two men, seated either side of a desk. Then a secondary pane overlaid it in part, filled with rolling text: a transcript file replacing audio output.

"The man in the visitor's chair," said Jan, "is Dr Alex Rhys Evans, now deceased."

"Fucking hell," said Josh.

Then he shut up.

CLIVE: Everyone appreciates a nice salary raise, if nothing else. We can deliver better remuneration than you're used to.

EVANS: That's not the only thing in life.

CLIVE: Of course not. The freedom to direct your own research, though– How interesting is that?

EVANS: You know it is. Very.

CLIVE: Your new design is… Well, some people are calling you a late bloomer. It must be gratifying to have done such good work.

EVANS: Work you shouldn't know about.

CLIVE: That's how the world goes these days.

EVANS: I won't break the conditions of my current contract.

CLIVE: Of course we wouldn't expect

Jan stilled the display.

"The other guy, Del Clive, is allegedly in Human Resources at the Burnham power plant. You know about Burnham?"

"Somewhere near Slough, isn't it?"

"Close enough. It's also where Tyndall Industries has placed its flagship mesoreactor, so-called. Fission in a smaller-but-safer installation, hence its location so close to a major town."

Evans had worked for Jack Hardin on *his* nuclear power

plant programme. So far it appeared that Evans had been job-hunting, looking for something else in his own field.

"The national grid is going to start failing soon," said Jan. "Blackouts are going to be common, unless we get more power plants online. Blame poor investment or poor engineering, but the wind turbines and ocean booms aren't doing their job. Not with the Fimbulwinter conditions, anyhow."

"Like we didn't know decades ago that this was coming," said Lofty. "Maybe no one predicted a global ash layer in the sky, but the rest of it was known."

Josh was re-reading the transcript.

"Evans isn't suicidal at this point, is he?"

"No." Jan blanked the display. "You can see the rest in a moment, if you like. It's not interesting. What caught our attention was some snippets from later, after Evans had taken a tour of the plant. Take a look."

New panes opened on screen.

Now Evans was sitting in an armchair, while another man – bald-headed, goatee, expensive suit – sat in its counterpart at an oblique angle. Evans' eyelids were fluttering, and his chin was beginning to dip forward.

"Tell me," said the stranger, "what you noticed."

Evans spoke with a slur.

"The key is flux resonance effect caused by the emergence of virtual cavities in the flow, but it's the failure mode that worries me. They underestimated the chances of breakdown, so the shutdown gates are inadequate to–"

Again Jan stopped the display.

"It gets technical on the reactor design, but Lofty and I are software engineers and we understand risk assessment and failure modes. Evans clearly spotted something, based on his own work, that's likely to go wrong. What happens next is that Evans is asked about the innovations he created for Hardin, and he spills the beans. That's *really* technical."

It was obvious why she and Lofty had missed the morning run. They had been working all night on this.

"And presumably it's also theft," said Josh.

"Right," said Lofty. "Tyndall Industries could not take the risk of Evans going public. So they brought in a mindbender."

The bald guy with the goatee.

"Looks ordinary enough," said Josh. "But there's something a bit scary about him."

"Good instincts." Jan gestured at the stilled image. "That's Professor Rashid Badakian, and according to Suzanne Duchesne, he's a psychopath. As well as being a leading neuropsych specialist."

"As in the Badakian algorithm?" Josh had searched the Web on that, but had looked at the mathematics, not the biography of its inventor. "Used by that PulseTrance thing you hypnotised me with?"

"The very man."

"But Suzanne—"

"Had a brush with him recently," said Lofty. "In fact, she's been mixing in interesting company."

Josh turned back to the display.

"Show me the rest."

"Read the transcript," said Jan. "Unless you want to drop back into a trance again."

"It's that powerful?"

Lofty said: "Show him the last bit. You know what I mean."

"Right." Jan worked a slider widget. "There."

On screen, the image jumped, then got back into motion.

"—and as you float back above your imaginary timeline," Badakian was saying, "you see all those instances of abuse, remember the feelings of dirtiness that always overwhelm you, because you know how the memories intensify and get worse the more you think of them, or try not to think about the slaps and the painful probing since you know it will always be with you – unless you stop the memories dead."

Josh shook his head as Jan stopped the footage.

"I don't believe that's possible," he said. "But if it is, it's nasty."

"That bit about a timeline," said Jan. "I didn't quite get."

"It's a metaphor," said Josh, "that lets people navigate through memories or imagined futures. Suzanne taught me. It's to do with visualization. Mental images have apparent positions in space. Events at different times are in different locations, usually along some line or arc."

"So this bastard is giving Evans, what? A false memory of an abusive childhood?"

"Looks like it," said Josh. "You said Suzanne's had a brush with him. What did you mean?"

"We backtracked her movements, because of the message from Richie Broomhall. Suzanne Duchesne popped up on surveillance at a hotel hosting a medical symposium, a couple of days back. She stayed for a single session, a lecture by Badakian, then went."

Josh's midsection tightened as if bracing against a punch.

"What was in Richie's message?"

"Wait a sec." Lofty nodded to Jan. "Show Josh the guy Suzanne was with."

"Just a–There."

A new pane showed a short sequence of Suzanne walking alongside a lean, pale man. Then it jumped to the start and looped through again.

"That's Adam Priest," said Josh. "He's MI5."

Lofty smiled. Jan shook her head.

"You just cost me a tenner," she said. "I bet Lofty you wouldn't know the guy."

"Adam Priest is a cover ID," said Lofty. "His default public cover."

"And his real name? Is it, er, Robert Weber?"

That was the name Jack Hardin knew him by.

"Who knows?" said Lofty. "His most common name in our circles is Stephen Witten, but you know what Five are like. He could be anybody."

"But what's he doing with Suzanne?" asked Josh.

His phone vibrated.

"That's the message," said Jan, "that your young friend nearly got through to you."

Josh opened it up.

Hi, Josh. Opal's in trouble here in Paris, and I don't know if you've heard of this suicide thing, but Suzanne's treating her so she's going to be OK. She will be, right? What happened was I bought a phone and it hypnotised her or something. She cut herself and then she jumped out of the hospital window and tried to meet up with twelve friends trying to kill themselves. Except they were already dead and they weren't friends because she never knew them.

Dad has been in touch with Mr Priest in London, which Lexa says is important but she won't say why. I thinks she's in love with Dad. I think Suzanne misses you.

Putting the phone down, Josh looked at Jan, then Lofty.

"Paris," he said.

"You're in the middle of Selection," said Jan. "Looks like you got a choice to make."

"No, I don't."

"Well, you can't–"

"He means," said Lofty, "he's already decided. Right, laddie?"

"Yeah. Sorry, Lofty."

"Come back and talk to us when it's all over. That's all we ask."

Josh did not deserve friends and comrades like these.

"I will."

"So what you have to bear in mind," said Jan, "is that Badakian is *persona grata* in certain sections of the intelligence services. They think he's a good guy."

"Because he taught them interrogation techniques?"

"And performed the interrogations, sometimes. And gave them the basis of PulseTrance technology. Plus, since he's obviously wrapped in with the Tyndalls, you have to figure on their influence as well."

Too many shadowy figures in Whitehall saw Zak and Zebediah Tyndall as establishment icons worth protecting.

"You can't hang onto this." Josh gestured towards the display. "I've got to make sure Suzanne's OK, but all this is too big."

What the hell was Suzanne mixed up in? Adam – or whoever he was – looked at her in ways that were not professional, but he had never made a move on her. It had to be business.

Really?

That was before Josh pissed off and left her. Perhaps things had changed while he had been clambering around Herefordshire and the Brecon Beacons.

"We agree," said Jan. "But we don't want to send it up the normal chain of command just yet. Not when the Tyndalls' allies can put their oar in."

"Shit."

"I'm going to double-check that there's nothing in here that leads back to Broomhall." Jan worked her phone, and the wall display blanked out. "A couple of hours at most. Then we'll use back channels to GCHQ, get them pulling the whole thing apart."

Random association made Josh wonder how the NSA was faring – GCHQ's American counterpart – given the current state of the US.

"It's like a critical mass," said Lofty. "Faced with enough evidence, nobody's going to stand in the way of taking down Badakian and the Tyndalls. Senior officers and bureaucrats will be running for cover. That, or claiming they were suspicious all along."

So the big guns of electronic intelligence were being brought to bear. Against them, Tyndall Industries and this Badakian arsehole stood no chance.

Finally.

But Josh's objectives had narrowed down to one thing.

Keeping Suzanne safe.

"Let's take a walk, laddie."

"I've got to pack my–"

"A little stroll through the Quartermaster's Store," said Lofty, "won't take too much time."

Jan was grinning.

"You guys are the best," said Josh.

"You're absolutely right," said Jan.

"Come on, laddie. Let's get you kitted out."

Suzanne arrived back at the hotel as Lexa and Richie were leaving. They were in the lobby, approaching the glass doors, as she stepped inside.

"Hi, you two."

"Hi, Suzanne. Are you all right? We were worried, with you being gone all night."

Lexa hugged her, for the first time ever.

"It was fine. I worked with Opal." Suzanne smiled at Richie. "She's going to be OK."

Masses of tension dissipated from his stance.

"Oh," he said. "That's great."

Lexa squeezed his shoulders.

"We'll celebrate," she said. "That hot choco you were looking forward to."

"OK."

"But let's escort Suzanne back upstairs before we do that, all right?"

"OK."

"No need," said Suzanne. "Philip's on the third floor, right?"

"Uh-huh." Lexa nodded. "See that guy outside on the pavement?"

"Yes, I–Is he watching us?"

"Sure is. He's one of Thériault's crew. They're the security that Phil hired."

Suzanne noted *Phil* rather than *Philip*. Another first. From the secretive smile on Richie's face, she decided he had noticed too.

Good.

Perhaps things were changing for the better. With the information she had given the Police Judiciaire – and whichever organizations the rest of her audience had represented – the authorities had the basis for countermeasures against the brainwashing ware. Now all she had to do was give the same information to the British intelligence services.

She would call Steve once she had talked to Philip.

"Come on, then." Lexa led the way into the lift, then held her finger over the button widgets on the touch panel. "*Quel étage*, Richie?"

"*Il faut monter*" – Richie's intonation was careful – "*trois étages.*" Suzanne knew his talent was not for languages.

"*Excellent,*" she told him, as Lexa pressed for the third floor.

Suzanne had a story she could tell about an American neuropsych in Paris, who had described a beautiful woman as having *un sot à triple étage*. The last four words translated as *totally dumb*, as in idiotic.

After the fight was over and doctors had stitched up the American's face, they worked out that his phone's free online dictionary had translated *sot à triple étage* as *consummate ass*. The American had assumed it was a compliment, not an outmoded British insult.

She was trying to work out how to tell the story in a way suitable for Richie's ears when the lift reached the third floor. Two hard-faced operatives in suits – one male, one female – checked them, then nodded.

The new security.

"Nik." Lexa nodded to the man, then the woman. "Kari."

They walked along the corridor to Philip's apartment, where Lexa pressed the buzzer. Another hard-faced man, this time of darker complexion, opened the door.

"*Voici Monsieur Thériault.*" Lexa gestured to Suzanne. "*Docteur Duchesne.*"

"*Enchanté.*"

Thériault led the way inside.

"He's the boss," said Richie. "Of the security team."

"Got you," said Suzanne.

Her feet stopped moving, though her mind seemed to carry on going.

Philip had company.

"St–Adam?" she said.

Philip knew Steve as Adam Priest.

"Suzanne." Steve was on his feet and halfway to hugging her when he stopped, then shook her hand instead. "You're all right, are you?"

"Yes. It's been… interesting. Everything's going to work out."

"Good."

Steve was in shirtsleeves, an elegant jacket draped over the back of his armchair. On the breakfast bar stood an empty *cafetière*, used plates and cups.

"Ahem." Philip got up from the couch. "You two need to catch up. I hadn't realised, Suzanne, that you and Adam had been working together."

He picked up a coat.

Suzanne said, "I meant to, er–"

"No problem. Lexa? You were taking Richie out for that choco."

"Sorry, Boss. Never quite made it, but we're on our way now."

Suzanne had never heard *boss* used as a form of endearment.

"I'll join you," said Philip. "If that's all right with you."

"Sure, Dad," said Richie.

"We'll let you." Lexa touched Suzanne's shoulder. "Take it easy."

"Yes. See you."

The security chief, Thériault, nodded to Steve. He followed the others out and closed the door behind him.

Suzanne and Steve were alone in the apartment.

"Um," she said.

So much for years of neuropsych training and practice.

What do I want to happen?

Steve's hands were on her upper arms.

Is this what I want?

His kiss was warm, then hot and liquid fire slid and coursed inside her as time paused, everything reduced to this, to him and her. Then he stepped back, and it felt like a gap opening in reality.

"Oh, my God," he said.

"S-Steve. I…" Then she kissed her fingertips, and placed them on Steve's mouth. "Yes."

Swallowing, he took another pace back, and bumped against the couch.

Josh left me.

Steve had always been fascinating, but she had not expected this.

"We have to" – he cleared his throat – "talk business, because I want to make sure you're OK. After that, we'll, er…"

"Go for a walk," she said. "Drink coffee. Or wine. Both. And I'll show you Paris."

"Yes. Yes."

So this was her, moving on.

Josh never brought me here.

Steve raised his phone and checked the display.

"Thériault and most of his crew are bracketing the Broomhalls," he said. "There's two of them left on this floor, the English pair. Nik Butler and Kari Sperring. Plus two more downstairs. If you're staying in Paris a while longer, I'd rather put my own people in place."

"You're here," she said.

"There is that."

"I don't think they're English, though. You spies with your cover names." She smiled. "Does your birth certificate read Steve Witten or something else? Maybe Throgmorton Murgatroyd?"

She had lived in England long enough to know the ridiculous old names people used to use. But Steve was not reacting to her teasing; instead, he was placing a call.

"*Monsieur Thériault?*" he said. "*Vos deux collègues Français aux noms Anglais, est-ce qu'ils sont–?"*

The volume was turned up loud enough for Suzanne to hear Thériault's answer directly.

"*En fait ils viennent d'Arménie, comme les deux autres–*"

"They're Armenian?" said Suzanne.

Steve turned to the nearest window. "Are you OK with heights? We need to climb down if possible."

He reached for his jacket.

"Heights?" said Suzanne. "Why would we–?"

A percussive bang blew the front door in. Waves of pressure knocked her to her knees.

The world blinked.

When reality came back, Steve was struggling to get up.

What is this?

Dark figures in suits – Kari and Nik – moved into the room, each with their empty left hands extended, their right hands tucked close to their chest, gripping a firearm. Nik swivelled and Steve spun away, his shoulder exploding into strawberry mist.

"No!"

Her yell was silent.

Eardrums.

But that was irrelevant as the two Armenians brought their guns to bear on her – *I'm dying* – and there was no way to evade – *this is it* – as Steve rolled to his feet and tore his jacket from the back of the armchair, continuing his spin as he ripped out a handgun of his own and fired. Nik's carotid artery tore open, then his left temple was a dark hole, and his body tumbled like dropped sticks.

Steve was trying to get a bead on Kari but she was fast, lunging to her right and swivelling, firing the gun hugged to her torso. For a second he seemed to keep it together, then he tipped forward, firing as he fell, and Kari's calf tore open, spectacular redness spurting. But she too could fire as she dropped.

No!

Three rounds into Steve's face—

Please, no.

–blasting him into meat.

I need to move.

Josh would have known what to do, but this was not her world and everything was awful, but she was a human being and the product of four billion years of evolution, filled with survival instincts and the mechanisms to effect them – so the time to move was *now*.

She rose to her feet, vision blackened at the edges, the floor seeming to twist beneath her. Motion occurred on her periphery – *Kari, on the ground* – as the female assassin raised her weapon – *run now* – and Suzanne leaped for the breakfast bar, dropping behind it as glass exploded.

There was a glass door in the front of the old-fashioned cooker, affording a reflected view of Kari crawling across the floor. Suzanne pulled back, keeping a sliver of the image in view.

Carving-knives.

Meeting Josh had begun with her treating Richie for hoplophobia, so how about this for irony? Kari was moving closer from behind the furniture. Soon she would be certain that Suzanne was crouched behind the counter. All Kari need do then was fire through the wood and that would be it: the end.

No.

Josh had taught her better than that.

In the reflection the gun was rising, but so was Suzanne, throwing herself up from the floor and onto the countertop, grabbing a knife with each hand – *Josh, help me now* – hoping her body remembered her lessons – *oh, God* – as momentum took her over the top and then she dropped, knees first onto Kari's back, twin knives descending like a matador's swords.

The first point scraped off Kari's shoulder-blade but the other went true, driven straight into the back of her neck, severing the spinal cord.

She's dead.

The corpse grew soft as she rolled off it.

Oh Jesus God I'm sorry God it's awful.

She was an atheist but not by upbringing.

Her hearing was still gone, but something made her turn to face the front door, now hanging in shards from wrecked hinges. Two more men in suits were entering, one sweeping to the side, scanning the room, while the other revolved towards her – *merde* – then twisted away, his hand rising as he fired into the ceiling – *what?* – with an arm around his throat – *Lexa* – and then the gun was in Lexa's hand as she fired twice – *pop-pop*, a distant sound to Suzanne's damaged ears – and the other killer was down.

Then Lexa hammered with the pistol's butt to the back of its owner's neck, knocking him forward. She pushed her foot against his head and yelled something.

To me?

Suzanne stumbled forward.

This is awful.

Then Lexa's hand was on her, strong and supporting, helping her away from hell.

Josh. Oh, Josh.

She needed him and he was not here, but Steve was dead and everything was senseless, blacking out; but Lexa was dragging her onward – *danger* – because who knew what might happen yet – *getting me clear* – and she tried to help by moving her feet, but it was very hard – *come on* – and somehow they staggered down the emergency stairs – *come on, help her* – and into a side alley.

Cold air. Walls. Traffic.

People.

It's the world.

Ground hard beneath her feet as she stumbled.

It still exists.

And she was still alive.

[TWENTY-NINE]

They stopped before reaching the boulevard, avenue Carnot, that ran left and right at the head of the alley. Lexa released Suzanne's arm.

"Can you move all right?"

Her voice still sounded distant, but clearer than before.

"Yes," said Suzanne. "I'm... I'm all right."

She was not, but her anti-trauma techniques would help. They worked against post-traumatic stress laid down for years and reinforced by many-times-daily revisiting of the memory. Remembering a trauma strengthens it, which is why exam revision works and why talking through a bad experience can make things worse.

"I need a few minutes," she added.

"By yourself?" said Lexa. "Just what I was going to suggest."

Cars, coming from the direction of the Place de l'Étoile, slowed opposite the alleyway. Sirens sounded, pulsing in Suzanne's still-recovering hearing.

"But the police–"

"We're going to talk to them now and tell them everything," said Lexa. "But *we* does not include *you*. What you have to do is disappear in the city, *n'est-ce pas*?"

"Those people. Nik and Kari shot Adam but they, they…"

"Take your time."

Suzanne closed her eyes.

Whirl it away.

In her mind she remembered the experience of crashing shots and blood, visual and visceral, so she fragmented the movie-like memory into shards, a sequence of stills, and pulled herself out of them, observing herself in the scene. Then she pushed the diminishing shards off into an imaginary distance. Sensitizing herself to the roiling feeling in her stomach, she imagined that turbulence reversing direction, neutralizing the neuropeptide flow of fearful, gutfelt memory.

For her, the visual and somatic senses were the realest part of her experience, so those were the ones she worked with. Amnesia was not an option.

"I'm OK." Her voice sounded clearer to herself. "You want me to disappear. Why?"

Lexa was blinking.

"You have to teach me that trick," she said. "Whatever you just did. But a hit squad just took out an MI5 officer – Phil might not know what Adam was, but I do. Phil and Josh tried to take down the Tyndalls, but it didn't work. The Tyndalls have powerful friends."

"I can't trust the police?"

"See, I don't know," said Lexa. "But how can you risk it?"

Suzanne lurched, then sniffed in a breath, regaining strength. "You said you're going to the police. With Philip and Richie."

"Right. The hitters made their move when you arrived, sweetheart. Me and my two boys are not the target."

Her boys. In all of this, Lexa found humour.

"Later on," said Suzanne, "*you* have to teach *me* how you do that."

"Do what?"

One of the sirens wailed to a stop.

"We have to decide now," said Suzanne. "I think I trust Zanoni and Gagné, the people we dealt with earlier."

"Then maybe you should try to contact them alone, somehow." Lexa stared out at the street. "I need to go."

"Yes."

"Are you sure you... Who could that be?"

"Who?" said Suzanne.

"Your phone is ringing."

"Oh." Suzanne pulled it out. "No. *C'est pas possible*."

The incoming-call ID read *Josh*.

"Hello? Josh?"

In her ear, the words were indistinct. Whatever her expression, Lexa must have realised what was happening. Lexa took hold of Suzanne's hand, turned it, and called into the phone: "Hey, Cumberland. Lexa here. Your girlfriend's got bad hearing temporarily. She also needs your help."

Whatever Josh's reply, it caused a grim smile.

"Yeah. So look, use text and you'll be fine."

Another exchange.

"Are you sure? London is just as bad."

A pause, then another smile.

"Josh Cumberland, you are one devious bastard. Respect."

She closed down the comms and released Suzanne's hand.

"Your boyfriend knows what he's doing."

Is he my boyfriend?

This was irrelevant.

"Doing what?"

"Get yourself to the Gare du Nord," said Lexa, "and onto the EuroLev to London. Josh is going to cover your tracks."

"Cover my tracks?"

"He'll alter your appearance in the Métro surveillance system. And add your name to the list of casualties in the police report."

"Casualties–"

Suzanne looked up at the hotel building.

"You've got to go now," said Lexa. "You really have to."

"Yes."

They hugged for the second time ever, then disengaged.

"Philip's a good man," said Suzanne.

"Yes. And so is Josh, kind of."

"Kind of. I know what you mean."

"Is he the one for you?" said Lexa. "Some part of your mind knows, right?"

"You want to swap jobs?"

"No, but I want you to be safe so we can swap girl talk later. Be safe, OK?"

Suzanne's eyes were blurring.

"Yes. You too."

She watched Lexa walked out onto the street, hurrying because Philip and Richie were waiting, worried for her sake.

Josh. Come to rescue me?

Sort of rescue, except that she had to make her way back to London first, while up in Philip's temporary apartment lay the corpses of Steve-aka-Adam and his killers. Something had been happening between her and Steve.

It was hard to remember now.

What am I doing?

She was sitting against the alley wall. Last time she had been conscious of her position and actions, she had been talking to Lexa. Perhaps she was hurt. She felt her skull, checked all over.

Physically intact.

Introspection was for later. For now she had to get away without being seen by the police, because the authorities might have been subverted by the Tyndalls.

Or Badakian.

The Armenian connection was significant. Badakian's cronies, or employees of his cronies from back home. Something like that. How else could a neuropsych rogue genius with a penchant for brainwashing have access to people with guns?

Not just people: professionals, who had moved fast and should by all rights have killed her. She was alive because of Steve and Lexa.

And myself.

Yes, she had killed one of them, but not by herself.

Come on.

Steve had died saving her. The least she could do was get a move on.

Yes, move.

She pulled herself to her feet, feeling the rough wall with her palms, reminding herself that the world was tangible and textured, something to hang on to.

Just get going.

Stopping at the corner, at the edge of the wide roundabout, she looked back down avenue Carnot. Underneath the chestnut trees, police cars were angled towards the hotel entrance. Most of the officers must be inside already; some were entering the coffee shop next door. No one was looking in her direction.

Je suis Parisienne.

She belonged here and that was the thing to focus on – Josh had taught her this, the art of open concealment – because by playing the part, believing it all the way down to her core, she became invisible.

Head down, she crossed over to the roundabout's centre where the Arc de Triomphe stood, and took the steps down to Charles de Gaulle-Étoile. It had been years since she lived here – no, she belonged here, remember – so she should have been unsurprised to remember the route, not needing to check the Métro map. She went down to the platform for line 2, Porte Dauphine-Nation, and caught an eastbound train.

No one in the carriage paid attention to her.

At Barbès-Rochechouart, she got out and changed trains. It was only one stop to Gare du Nord and she could have walked, but her legs were trembling.

Josh.

Soon she would be back in London. But was that any safer than here?

Josh was driving east on the M4, wipers going against the wet snowfall, keeping to the speed limit because that was the way to evade attention. His destination had been Burnham, with no hurry in his plans because his intent had been to spend at least a day – preferably several – scouting the nuclear power plant and its environs.

Suzanne. I thought you were safe.

Young Richie's call had caused him concern, but he had figured she was safer in Paris. Adam/Steve's feelings for her seemed obvious, and he had let himself believe that physical attraction was the only danger. Now, after calling Suzanne but speaking to Lexa, his arms were vibrating with the need to lash out, to tear throats and claw out eyes, and the toughest thing of all was retaining control.

In its dashboard slot, his phone beeped.

"Go on," he said.

A display pane opened in the heads-up.

"Josh Cumberland." It was a woman: short black hair, pale skin. "You don't know me, but I work for the man you know as Adam Priest."

"You mean Steve Witten."

"He told you?" She blinked. "I'm Trin, and Steve is, is…"

"I know." Josh pulled over to the nearside lane and slowed. "I'm sorry."

A small green icon appeared below the pane. His verification ware, including voice-stress analysis, concluded she was telling the truth. On screen, she rubbed her face.

"We've conflicting reports about Suzanne," she said.

"Do you know her?"

"She's part of our team, sort of. Steve's team."

Josh slowed right down.

She's what?

Since when had Suzanne started working with MI5?

"We need to get her clear of Paris," Trin went on. "I'm not convinced Steve was the target. She had analysed the Cutter Circle ware, we think, and presented a report to the Police Judiciaire and other organizations."

"A committee," said Josh.

"Yeah, exactly. Too many people, and somewhere a leak. Whether they'll manage to bury Suzanne's report, I don't know. I hear two Police Judiciaire detectives are playing hardball, refusing to disclose whether they made backup copies."

As in Lofty's office, Josh had the sense of too much happening.

"I just want to keep Suzanne safe," he said.

"Good. I want that too." Trin looked away for a moment. "I see your car is ghosted."

She meant invisible to surveillance. That she could tell that much was impressive: to most searchers he would not exist.

"Could be." Josh said.

"We'll help. What are your plans?"

"To keep Suzanne safe."

"That's an objective, not a plan. Whether you trust me or not, here's my callback tag. Any help you need, just signal."

"You as good as told me that the opposition have official help."

A lorry was crawling along in front of him. Josh matched its speed.

"Consider this off the books," said Trin.

"Then I'll think about it. And thank you."

"Good enough. Out."

The pane disappeared.

Assume she was telling the truth. She might be based in some distant substation, but the likelihood was that she was London-based, working out of Thames House or one of the covert sites. Meanwhile Lofty was in Hereford, with limits on how much force he could deploy without official sanction.

"Shit. I don't like this."

He dictated a message to Lofty and told his phone to send it. What Josh had requested was that Lofty check out this Trin to verify she was MI5. It might take hours.

I need something else.

He had ghostware in place to protect Suzanne during her EuroLev journey, altering her image in the onboard surveillance logs. Once she reached London, with its massive overlapping spycam nets, keeping her invisible was a bigger challenge. Trin's help would be welcome, if he could trust her.

"Call Petra," he told his phone.

The offline icon appeared. His only police contact was unavailable.

"Damn it."

Professional pride made Josh want to do this solo, but pragmatism and fear argued in favour of getting help. Massive help, if possible.

"Call Tony."

In the heads-up, Tony Gore smiled.

"You heard," he said.

"Heard what?"

"Amber's expecting again."

"Oh."

Desolation revolved inside Josh.

Sophie.

That void would always be there.

"Congratulations," he made himself say. "Well done you, on doing all the hard work."

"Yeah," said Tony. "These girls make such a fuss of just popping out the kid, right? A natural function, happens every day."

The lorry was turning off at the next junction. Josh would speed up a little then.

"Yeah. Tell Amber I disagreed with everything you told me."

"Uh-huh," said Tony. "Before I do, what aren't you telling me?"

"Nothing. I was just calling to chat."

What he could do was call Big Tel directly. If Tony knew there was an op happening – assuming Tel agreed to help – then he would want to take part. And him with a third child on the way.

"I'm sure you were."

"Well, of course I–"

"Was calling to chat about whatever unofficial op you're trying to pull off this time. Spill it, old mate. Come on."

Josh's diaphragm felt tense as he breathed.

"Suzanne's on her way from Paris. Arriving this afternoon. I'm worried there might be a hit team targeting her. Covert mercs."

"Jesus."

"Yeah. So look, I'm going to call Big Tel and the boys, and we'll–"

"No chance, mate. Not without me."

"But you can't–"

"I like Suzanne," said Tony.

That was clear enough.

"Tell me everything," Tony went on. "We're encrypted."

Josh did. When he was finished, he shut down the heads-up, and decided to trust his ghostware all the way, and forget about obeying the speed limit.

He moved over to the fast lane, flooring the acceleration.

[THIRTY]

Stone steps and the martial sculptures, Britannia high overhead, proud and determined with banners frozen in mid-ripple. The bronze plaque listing the names of the war dead: ex-railway employees who perished fighting fascism. This was Victory Arch, a monument to ordinary people finding courage in their lives: a mix of sculpture and architecture that no one created any more.

Underneath, commuters streamed, with no time to remember the past or the wider context of their lives. The station was Waterloo, the busiest of stations in its own right, even without the throngs of arrivals and departures at the EuroLev terminal, newly re-opened – at vast expense – following the St Pancras Collapse.

Hands pushed into the pockets of his black coat, Josh allowed himself to sink into morose thoughtfulness, reacting to the sculptures. It was not the act of an alert professional, but someone with time on their hands: a traveller whose train did not leave for hours. He carried a full-looking bag to reinforce the illusion.

The opposition might be scanning for someone who looked as if they were waiting to meet an arrival.

Suzanne. My God, Suzanne.

He dared not allow the excitement to rise, because he needed to do more than look harmless: he had work to do, running interference in the station's security systems. Job one was to disguise Suzanne's appearance when she arrived. He was already doing this in the EuroLev's onboard surveillance.

With his scanbot extending virtual tendrils through the station net, he dared not risk further intrusion. He would have preferred to search for opposition spotters by co-opting the station's spycams. But that was more likely to trip anti-intrusion countermeasures.

Spotter.

The first of the opposition was at a roast cicada-and-bagel stand just inside the concourse. Two more – *got you* – were nibbling baguettes, standing near a clump of genuine travellers. Their gazes scanned the surroundings in endless iteration. Between the three of them, they had two entrances covered: the big opening with the wide steps, and a pedestrian tunnel that led out towards the London Eye.

Josh's grandfather, as a young police constable, had been near Victoria Station when the IRA bombs went off. It was Josh's father, himself a policeman, who considered that event the beginning of London's ongoing quest to become the most highly surveilled city in the world.

Once, when Josh's dad was on duty in Waterloo, a tourist from New York had complained about having nowhere to "toss his trash", not realizing that in England *toss* meant masturbate, while *trash* was what rock bands did to hotel rooms. Josh's dad had smirked before telling the American that New Yorkers and Bostonians in Irish-American bars had paid for the bombs that blew up women and children in English railway stations and supermarkets, hence the lack of places where explosives might lie concealed.

In the bizarre way that such things happen, the American, name of Schultz, had talked with Josh's dad for a long time, and they ended up becoming friends who kept in sporadic touch from opposite sides of the Atlantic.

Schultz died in the North Tower on September eleventh, 2001.

Later, Josh's dad worked in one of London's major surveillance centres, promoted from the streets. He was off-duty, returning home, when he spotted the teenage gang trashing a mall, and went inside to intervene.

Ten minutes later, their boots had kicked him into oblivion, while shoppers stood back, too afraid to intervene. When the paramedics lifted Jeff Cumberland's corpse from the floor, his head separated from his body.

The teenagers fled. No one ever found out who they were.

Three years ago, right here on the Waterloo concourse, a similar gang, armed with steel rods, had turned on a police officer, kicking her to the floor. Commuters stabbed the gang members to death, every one of them.

And the police officer received a mild concussion and a bruised knee, returning to duty a week later.

Josh remembered all this as he ambled through the station, stopping to buy a cappuccino and a bar of Green & Black's dark chocolate – it had been his dad's favourite – while making occasional bored glances up at the giant display screens, then pretending to double-check the same information on his phone. He was tracking the EuroLev.

In less than an hour, Suzanne would be here.

He counted seven more spotters around the concourse. When he wandered outside, he pinpointed two more; but he dared not make a full scan of the streets, because it would be out of character for his persona.

Ten of the opposition inside. Guesstimate the same again outside.

Just for Suzanne?

They must be assuming she would have professional help, and in fact they were right. But thirty-one minutes before the EuroLev's scheduled arrival, Josh's phone gave an intermittent vibration, and everything changed.

"Sorry, mate." Big Tel's voice sounded in the tiny earbead Josh wore. "Bastards have clocked us. We're blown."

"Shit."

Tel was supposed to track the opposition vehicles.

"They don't know we realise that, mind. Want us to spring a trap, see how many we can take down?"

Josh had not intended to bring warfare to the streets of London. Hannah, Vikram, Tel and Tony had lives to lead, not waste them in an action that might not be necessary.

"No," he subvocalised, using his throat mic. "I've got it. Check your phone, look surprised, then everybody pull out and hack down to Ashford as fast as you can."

"Ashford? Why would–? Oh, nice."

"Yeah. Fake 'em out, see how many you can draw after you."

"Roger that. Give Suzanne my love. And get her clear of them bastards."

"Will do. Cheers, Tel."

The EuroLev had two stops on this side of the Channel: Ashford in Kent, then the terminus here in Waterloo. If the others made a feint towards Ashford, the opposition might follow on the presumption that Suzanne had got off early, and slipped through whatever surveillance they already had in place at the other station.

They could not be sure that Suzanne was on this particular train, or that she would travel back by EuroLev at all. Not if Josh's subversion ware was working as well as it seemed. The spotters were keeping a general watch, shifting up to maximum alertness on every EuroLev arrival. It seemed unlikely that, even if they believed Tel's feint to Ashford, they would draw everyone away from Waterloo.

Two minutes later, Josh's thinking was confirmed. Changes in body language among the spotters told him that they had received some form of urgent communication; but they remained in place around the concourse. Only a brief text from Big Tel

told Josh that some of the surveillance vehicles from the surrounding streets were now following Tel and the others.

Twenty-six minutes to arrival.

What was not clear was the spotters' intentions. Their goal
was likely to be stopping Suzanne from reaching Thames
House in person or making a call for help. Right now, her
phone was powered off and inside a protective pouch that
would shield it from pinging scans. If the opposition were
clued up, they would be on her case as soon as she switched
the thing on, ready with countermeasures to block her calls.

Beyond that, there were three possible, mutually exclusive
objectives: follow, snatch or terminate.

I won't let them harm you.

Eighteen minutes, and one of the spotters was looking this
way because Josh was moving too fast – *for God's sake* – so he
changed direction and headed for the toilets, making a brief gesture towards his stomach that he hoped looked unconscious.

It gave him the opportunity to empty his bladder, perform
shrugs and hip circles inside a cubicle, throw cold water on his
face, and retie his shoe laces in the usual double knots, but
tighter. He was ready.

Seven minutes.

On the concourse once more, he pretended to browse a juice
stand menu, back in his bored-traveller persona. He was now
at an oblique angle to the head of the escalators, by intention.
When Suzanne arrived, she would not see him.

He had to do it this way.

As a consummate psychologist, she could act a part; but a
year in Josh's company did not make her a trained tactician.
She was capable of pretending not to recognise Josh, but she
might not realise the necessity. Even a momentary expression
would be enough to condemn them both.

He loaded a short text in cache, ready to redfang the message as soon as she powered up her phone.

Three minutes.

Turning, he slouched away, then returned to the juice stand, trying to run his autohypnotic mantra – *bored, bored, bored* – while inside he was springing into adrenalized life, the amygdala beginning to kick in, the brain's emergency response system ready to take over from the conscious frontal lobes when things began to move too fast for rational thought.

One minute.

The spotters were looking alert because the feint towards Ashford meant that, unless Suzanne really was in Kent, she was likely to be here now.

Zero, and the buzz of Josh's phone told him she had powered up her own.

He redfanged his waiting message:

Make no calls. Leave Waterloo on foot, head for Charing Cross then AWAY from Thames House. Love, J.

It would show immediately on her phone's display.

The time to arrival was now in negative numbers. According to the board, the EuroLev had pulled in, while at the top of the escalators, a surge of people stepping onto the concourse must be the passengers from France. For Suzanne, the best place to be was in the centre of the disembarking group, but whether she would realise that or–

Minus four minutes and thirty-two seconds, and there she was. *Suzanne.*

He wanted to rush towards her, but pushed himself back instead, thinking of quietness, of invisibility, watching the spotters fan out and follow the stream of people towards the old exit.

Suzanne went down the stone steps under Victory Arch as Josh made his move.

He was into the crowd, folding back panels on his bag to change its colour, then reversing his black coat – he was now wearing burgundy – relying on movement and angles of sight. But these were professionals: if they recognised his face while noting the changed appearance, they would know him for a player and act against him.

There was only one obvious route and Suzanne appeared to be taking it, heading for the high steel footbridge that ran alongside the main railway bridge from Waterloo East to Charing Cross. Josh slipped away from the crowd, bearing right down a pedestrian underpass. Then he was in open air ten metres below street level, on the circular walkway that ringed the cylindrical Imax Ruin.

Last year he had chased Richie through here while gekrunners performed a night run; but he had to concentrate on here and now, so he jogged left, into the urine fragrance of Cardboard City, shedding first his bag and then his coat, then stopping briefly to unfasten the lower half of his trouser legs. He was now wearing shorts, like an ordinary urban jogger.

Rolling the detached trouser-legs into a cylinder, he walked faster, dodging among the cardboard boxes and their grimy inhabitants, part of London's homeless. From his pocket he took a black beanie, and pulled it down on his head. Then he shifted his pace to a jog, moving upslope, then faster, heading for the footbridge as so many office workers did, those for whom jogging was part of the daily commute.

He was ahead of Suzanne.

Slowing again, he worked his phone as if checking a text, while using his rear-view app, a simple tweak of webcam usage: spying over his own shoulder, zooming in. Suzanne's face looked tense. Two of the spotters were visible, hanging back.

Underneath the steel bridge, the Thames was grey and chill-looking. The night of Sophie's death, beneath the next footbridge upstream, he had stared into the waves, contemplating suicide. Now he was in action with Suzanne's life at stake, and a part of him was singing with animal joy, the thrill of risking everything.

You could not explain that in civilised company.

Objective: keep Suzanne safe.

Think of it like a professional op. He jogged down the stairs at the northern end of the bridge. With a minute or less to spare, he refastened the lower portion of his trouser legs, pulled off his sweater – another reversible garment – then tugged it back on, now showing olive green. His beanie reversed to show yellow and blue. He began to walk alongside Charing Cross Station towards Trafalgar Square.

Just a tourist, braving the cold summer of an unusual year, taking in the sights.

Keep going, Suzanne.

She passed him on the other side of the street. There was no way she could have failed to notice him, but the message had sunk in and she hid any reaction. Her pace was brisk. Behind her, seven spotters moved in a strung-out formation. No one was trying to get ahead, which suggested that other spotters were now mobile in vehicles.

A dark blue Tata Sparky hummed past, heading for Trafalgar Square. Three on board. The others would be taking different routes.

They were past a cut-off point, because if Suzanne had turned left and continued along the Embankment, the opposition would have assumed she was heading for Thames House directly. Now they would be wondering, perhaps considering the immediate danger had passed; but they were too professional to relax.

He dared not risk another redfang message, because at this proximity the spotters' phones might detect the resonance, even if they failed to decode the signal. Just knowing Suzanne was in communication – and with someone nearby – would be enough to make them close in.

The possibility of firearms changed everything.

They were into Trafalgar Square now, past the statue of Richard Dawkins. Suzanne turned right, passing along the north wall of St Martin-in-the-Fields. Perhaps she had some idea of what Josh had to do. She headed for the quieter streets of the West End.

She stopped, looking back towards the Square, so Josh took a chance. He walked openly north. From his peripheral vision, he saw her turn away smoothly and continue her route. He slowed, reached the edge of the Square, and waited to cross into St Martin's Lane.

Suzanne trailed him.

There was some kind of matinee at the London Coliseum, and he passed through a group of tuxedo- and gown-wearing theatregoers. They were good potential cover and distraction, but they were also civilians and therefore innocent. He walked on.

Follow the leader.

What he wanted was somewhere deserted – here in the middle of the busy West End – and time was shortening. If the opposition realised that Suzanne was following his lead, then they would close in regardless of who was around. Knowing the risk, he took a right turn off Charing Cross, a quiet alley that jogged left and onto Shaftesbury.

Very soon.

He crossed the road, then checked back. As Suzanne appeared, with seconds to spare before the spotters came into sight, he pointed to another side-street, then turned away and walked fast along Shaftesbury Avenue, towards its intersection with Charing Cross. When he was out of sight from Suzanne's watchers, he began to run.

"Sorry."

Pedestrians were in his way and he zigzagged around them, then poured on the speed, sprinting now, turning right and right again, coming into Phoenix Gardens from the north-west alleyway as Suzanne would be entering from the south. Surveillance was light and he loosed his subversion ware from his phone, using the simplest of all deceptions: the video log would loop on the past few seconds, over and over until he sent a cancel signal. Then he put his phone away because things were about to become primitive.

Happening now.

A centuries-old church and cemetery stood to the north of a quiet miniature garden protected by tall black iron railings. Buildings backed onto the silent alleys that formed three sides of a square, while the church blocked off the north. No one was around, not even workers taking illicit breaks from work.

Yes, now.

Wheelie-bins stood in a row and he used them for cover, sinking into a parallel squat he would not have to hold for long.

Wait.

Suzanne walked past, heading to his right, and he wanted to reach out for her – but his nerves were screaming with more than the effort of maintaining his static stance because the first of the opposition was right behind her, reaching into his pocket and coming out with a supple steel cord of a kind that Josh had seen before.

Garrotte.

The bastard was planning to slip it over Suzanne's neck using a cross-handed grip and then tighten it. Whether he intended to kill her directly or hold her in place while one of his comrades rammed a knife into her was irrelevant as Josh bounced down – myostatic reflex to increase explosiveness – then bounded up, slamming a thrust kick forward – *ribs* – to knock the guy back, then kicking with the other leg a fraction lower – *liver* – because that would drop him in agony – *got it* – and the fucker was down while Josh was spinning away but there were more of them and this was serious.

Two came side by side, one of them roaring in primate rage, but Josh was a reptile now, the ancient brain taking over as he slapped aside a knife-thrust and clawed into the bastard's eyes, driving the head back as Josh spun with his elbow high into the other's face, then hammered down to smash his knife-grip – *missed* – but the man held onto his weapon so Josh wrapped his forearm around the arm and pulled in close, elbow to his own body, and hooked his other hand behind the bastard's neck and rammed in a rising knee, then again – *yes* – and a third time to the same spot.

Black ink and yellow sparkles swirled across reality – he had taken a punch – but it was not the first time, and he went with the impact, getting sight of the fucker who had hit him.

The man had used the hilt of his knife, unable to bring his blade to bear. He would never get another chance.

Josh stepped diagonally, ripping a round kick into the knee, tearing the joint. The fucker was already falling when Josh rammed both thumbs into his eyes, kneed into the larynx to crush it, then tore his hands outwards, thumbs like steel hooks taking the eyeballs.

Let that make the others think.

A glance behind: Suzanne was pale but no one was near her. She might have moaned but Josh's hearing had shut down most of the way. Tunnel vision, auditory exclusion. He had in any case zero emotion to spare, because the reptile brain is lightning-fast and cold, a problem-solver.

Josh was calculating trajectories as he stripped the knife from the second fallen man.

Three more and they were professionals, but their bodies were a mass of targets, vulnerable points overlaid with imaginary crosshairs. The nearest launched himself forward with his knife glinting through complex arcs, but the man at the rear was unfastening a metal case – *gun* – of the kind that could take a firearm undetected through microwave-scanner surveillance.

The third was circling, also with a blade, hoping to take out Josh while the first man distracted him.

A knife to Josh's kidney would bring disaster, but that was not going to happen because he advanced left-right, using the diagonals to confuse, whipping the snatched knife through the same arcs as his opponent, following like the harmonic dance of *chi sao* – a flash memory of teaching Suzanne last year – then a fast reversal, a backhand hook to catch the wrist, a minor blood-spurt, slapping with his free hand to deflect the counterthrust, then cutting rapidly three times down the forearm to slice the bastard's grip open.

Then he drop-stepped into their joint whirlwind – *irimi*, taking the centre – and went for the throat – *he's down* – but the dropping man's head pulled the knife from Josh's grasp, so Josh used both hands to spin the bastard into the other knifeman's path.

The real danger was the handgun that the third man was bringing to bear.

Time elapsed in tenths of a second as Josh slammed the gunhand aside, while his first punch to the neck was simultaneous, and he pumped in more punches to the same place – *carotid sinus* – as the man's knees folded – *again* – seven or eight deep snapping hooks to the same target – *got you* – and as the gunman's strength dissipated Josh tore the handgun from his grip – crunch of broken fingers – and hammered with the butt to the back of the gunman's neck, just in case.

One of the knifemen was back.

Josh used the gun as a hammer, no time for anything else, striking the bastard's fingers but not hard enough. Their hands moved like propellers through the air at five times the speed of conscious thought and then the opening was there. Josh punched with his gun-holding hand, taking a cut as he parried with his left and then he had the sleeve, twisting to keep hold while his knee drove into the spleen – *again* – this time taking the bladder.

Something went out behind the knifeman's eyes as he dropped to his knees – *play safe* – and Josh stamped down on the exposed ankle – *yes* – to snap the Achilles tendon, then pushed away as the man collapsed with darkness at his crotch.

He was alive but his bladder had been full when the knee strike burst it. Lethal toxic shock was likely.

Another flicking glance.

Suzanne.

She was watching, frozen, but there was movement at the far side of Phoenix Gardens, the alley Josh had run in by. He needed to get her clear, but as he turned again two more men ran into the square and these two had guns.

Shit.

He was still holding the snatched gun round its barrel and he dived now, shoulder-rolling as he changed his grip – *Novaya Stechkin* – taking the gun two-handed, knowing he had fired a weapon like this before, one of the Russian reboots of classic design – *sight now* – and the first body was centring in his visual field – *yes* – as he double-tapped and then again – *slam-slam, slam-slam* – and both gunmen were down.

Then he rolled onto his back, raised head and shoulders as though for an ab crunch, and took aim between his feet. One of the opposition came into view around the garden wall, crouching as Josh pulled the trigger – *head shot* – and the guy's face exploded.

Josh rolled to his feet.

Get Suzanne.

As he jogged to her, his phone vibrated, the high-priority message already visible.

Trin is MI5. Details appended. L.

He thumbed the phone, returning Trin's earlier call.

"Hello," she said.

"I'm in a firefight. Suzanne needs pickup. Covent Garden asap."

Then he powered off the phone.

He watched as Suzanne stopped her muscle tremors, bringing the shock under control. She reached as if to hug him, but he stepped back, scanning the environment.

"Later," he said. "When we get clear."

If he gave in to his need to hold her, his senses would collapse inward, enfolding her, endangering them both.

"Yes."

The black iron railings stood half again as tall as Suzanne. If he could get Suzanne into the cemetery that lay beyond, she could make it to Covent Garden. Kneeling beside one of the fallen men, one whose clothes were not sopping with blood, he pulled off the corpse's jacket, then its dark blue t-shirt.

All the while, he made twitching glances in all directions. Others could appear at any time. As a bonus, the dead man carried a slim, extensible black baton clipped onto his belt.

"All right," he said to Suzanne. "You need to get over there. Get to Covent Garden."

"I can't–"

"Whatever your clients think they can't do, they almost invariably can. Isn't that what you tell them?"

"Oh, Josh–"

"Come on." He led her to the railing. "Now take hold." He dropped into a rock-bottom squat. "And step onto my hands."

He drove upwards, flinging her vertically, her hands moving fast to keep on the rails. As his hands reached chest level, he dipped and pressed high overhead: a second boost. Suzanne used the momentum to roll over the top.

"Slide down quickly," he said.

She descended the other side, shivering when she reached the ground. Josh passed the t-shirt through the railings.

"Wrap it around your head like a scarf." He flicked the black metal baton to first extension. "Use this as a walking stick. Walk like someone old."

He handed it through to her.

"Josh, we need to–Later, right?"

"Later."

Another series of flickering glances – the entrances still clear, the bodies still down, not moving – then he watched Suzanne move among the worn, lichen-stained headstones, wrapping the t-shirt around her head as she walked. Beyond the old church, she took the baton from her belt, assumed a bent-over stance, and began to shuffle along the ground and out of sight.

Good.

Final phase.

He had told Suzanne *later*, but that assumed his survival, while in fact the main thing was to cover her escape and evasion. The entrances to the square were still clear but – *go!* – he threw himself to one side in a lateral breakfall as shots smashed off the tarmac – *window* – and the bastards were inside one of the buildings – *shit* – so he rolled again on the diagonal and then he was up and springing into a sprint, towards the building because that was the safest place.

Two men launched themselves out of a fire exit, one aiming not at Josh but across into the cemetery, a long shot – but he might have an angle on Suzanne. Josh ran at him, ignoring the other bastard, because Suzanne was the one to save.

A percussive gunshot sounded, aimed at Josh but missing, and a man yelled – but there was no time to look as Josh smacked the other bastard's gun hand some hundredth of a second before the trigger-pull, shot crashing high. This was up-close and personal as the top of Josh's skull drove into the fucker's nose – a distant crunch – and he slammed both hands against the head and twisted it like a football, rotating his own body as he drove the head down, sprawling on top to smash it into concrete.

Dark blood was already pooling as he launched himself back up. The other man was clutching one eye, but recovering fast and raising his gun towards Josh.

Guns do things that are missing from the webmovies, and these were gunpowder bullets, which meant shell cases ejecting. Josh's guess was that a hot casing had hit the bastard in the eye – couldn't happen to a nicer bloke – and he drove a long kick into the body, blocked the gun arm, and hammered into the neck.

A downward stamp, bone against flagstones, to make sure.

This was a chance to get away, but if pursuers spread out they might find Suzanne, so the thing was to keep them busy. Someone leaned from a window – *second floor* – so Josh sprinted towards the alley leading to Shaftesbury – *two shots* – and he was still running – *missed* – and around the corner, then again, turning onto the street.

Chasing me like prey.

The reptile was annoyed.

Between two shops he found the narrow door they had used to get inside. Smashed lock, nothing subtle. They were professionals in panic mode and dangerous, but the question was, whose need was greater?

Josh ran inside just as clattering footsteps sounded, coming downstairs.

Two more.

The reptile was annoyed and wanted blood.

Josh's own knife was sheathed at his back so he ripped it free as he moved forward, closing on the bastards. They had guns but these were close quarters: a gun needs to be pointed at its target while a knife can stab or slash from any angle; and the most dangerous weapon in the universe was right behind Josh's eyes, and it was activated now.

The reptile.

His blade sliced hand and face, slid across sleeve and chest – *Kevlar fabric* – and whipped back across the throat, slicing skin, while the gun blasted a hole in the wall – *bastards* – using hard-nosed piercing ammunition because they did not care about killing innocents – *no more of this* – so he rammed his blade through the fucker's right wrist and twisted back the gun, jerking it so it fired at the other bastard, who spun away bleeding.

A shifting reflection warned him – *behind* – and he lost his knife as he drove to one side, through a splintering door and into a domestic lounge. There was a fruit bowl on the table and he whirled like a discus player in reverse, smashing the bowl backhand into the new bastard's face, then hugging the man's waist, driving his hips in low to make contact, rotating, both of them going down.

Josh used angular momentum to keep rolling, onto his feet once more, but now he had another Stechkin in his hand. He pivoted towards the doorway and fired.

The bastard fell with a hole in his forehead but still firing – *for fuck's sake* – with a bullet in his brain – *just die* – until Josh leaped diagonally forward, shot again, got close, fired into the back of the man's neck, and that was it.

No brainstem, no life.

In the shattered lounge, a gunman was on his hands and knees, so Josh drove his elbow downwards, dropping his hips, into the back of the neck. Down, perhaps not dead.

Get clear now.

Out through the front door, checking everywhere – *safe* – and he reached the staircase leading up – *check it* – scanning in all directions – *go* – then running up, keeping it as quiet as a hill sprint can be, slowing at every floor, then speeding up until he reached the uppermost landing.

There was a ceiling hatch.

He used rooftops, commando crawling across the top of a cinema, then descended to the rear of a tapas bar. From the open back door, a man working in the kitchen looked out, then stepped back inside, blinking.

Josh's phone vibrated.

Suzanne is safe. T.

Objective achieved.

[THIRTY-ONE]

They picked him up in Earls Court, after he had taken three bus rides to ensure he was not tagged. Their vehicle was a burgundy people-carrier with silvered windows. Josh climbed into the rear and found himself beside Suzanne. Sliding together, they enwrapped each other; and when they kissed it was soft, as if their lips and selves were melting together.

Rocking as the people-carrier pulled into traffic, they held on to each other, immersed in the moment. Then they disengaged, and Josh breathed out, finally checking his surroundings.

Two people up front. The driver was male, a tiger-stripe tattoo upon his face.

"That's Shane," said Suzanne. "He works for–worked for Steve."

Past tense because Steve was dead.

"Hi." Shane was concentrating on driving. "We're getting you out of London asap."

"And that's Shireen." Suzanne gestured to the dark-haired woman in the front passenger seat. "Also in the team."

"Are you OK, Josh?" asked Shireen. "Not wounded?"

"I'm fine."

He had slid his hands around inside his clothing, while sitting at the rear of a Number 36 bus, then checked to see if his hands came away red. The procedure had been drilled into him because in combat you can take a lethal stab – sometimes even a gunshot wound – and feel nothing. Only when the world began to darken would you realise that blood was pouring out of you, with no time for medical help before the end.

But he was alive and the world still existed. For a long time, in that bus, he had sunk deep inside himself as the shivering set in, the uncontrollable shaking that follows pushing everything to the edge. No one looked at him. If anyone had, they would have thought he was a druggie manifesting withdrawal symptoms.

A medic might have diagnosed shock.

Then it had passed, transmuting into something like sleep, though a brief one. Now, he was able to see the world clearly once more. Outside the vehicle, the afternoon was grey and cold. Bioluminescent snowflakes and stars decorated shop windows, surrounding *Merry Midsummer Christmas* messages.

"I was expecting Trinity Purcell," Josh said.

Shane scarcely reacted to his knowing her name.

"She prefers Trin," Shane said. "We call her Trinity when we're trying to wind her up."

The good old British art of the wind-up, closely related to taking the piss. He had tried to explain them once to some Epsilon Force troopers who translated them as torturing your buddies and making wisecracks, which seemed sort of correct and yet totally wrong, for reasons he could never work out.

"She's covering for you," said Shireen up front. "You took out more of the team who killed Steve."

The state does not sanction killing outside formal warfare. But then, His Majesty's Government would not own up to many of the ops carried out by Ghost Force.

"I'd rather take down the Tyndalls. Or is it this Badakian guy?"

Beside him, a vibration set up in Suzanne's limbs.

"Stay away from him, Josh," she said. "You can't know how dangerous he is."

"Like hypnotizing someone into killing himself? Something you told me wasn't possible, but I assume it's because–Are we going the right way?"

Shane had turned left when Josh was expecting right.

"We're not going to Thames House. The wrong people would notice."

"You mean your own superiors."

Shireen said, "We prefer to think of them as upward managees."

"Right. Um, I'm sorry about Steve," Josh said. "I should have said that first thing. And thanks for getting us clear."

He hugged Suzanne.

"We're cracking on because Steve would have wanted us to." Shireen looked back at them. "So we need to debrief, pool our thinking on this hypnosis stuff. You found out more in Paris, right, Suzanne?"

"Take this." Suzanne handed her phone over. "Everything's on there."

To a casual thief, private files contained in the handset or out on the Web would remain inaccessible; but to MI5, a DNA-tagged phone was no challenge.

"But it's still what we thought?" said Shireen. "Hypnotic software?"

"And targeting teenagers, who are especially vulnerable. Evolution favours fast learning, which is why young people have a propensity for believing what adults tell them. Add that to teenage turmoil, and it's the optimum time for installing paranoid fantasies and pervasive low self-worth."

"How about false memories of child abuse?" said Josh. "And how about doing all this to a fully functioning adult with a PhD in physics and a successful career?"

"You're kidding," said Shireen.

Shane steered west.

"We really need to debrief," he said. "Thing is, Steve used to have off-the-books safe houses, but can we trust them? Trin's facing our new bosses right now."

A replacement for Steve already. Someone allied with other interests, perhaps.

"Head out on the M4," said Suzanne.

"Going where?"

"Has anyone read Edgar Allan Poe?"

"Say what?" Shane's tiger stripes bunched up on his face. "Horror writer, right? *Carrie* and *The Shining*."

" 'Quoth the raven, nevermore'," said Shireen. "And never mind this Philistine."

"*The Purloined Letter*," said Suzanne.

"If you say so." Shane switched lanes to ascend the Hammersmith Flyover. "Sounds rude to me."

"A safe house means somewhere to hide," said Suzanne. "Right?"

"Sure."

Hammersmith was beneath them.

"So what about a house with a thousand cameras?" Suzanne took hold of Josh's hand. "If you were looking for fugitives, would you look in a house that's under twenty-four/seven realtime surveillance with millions of observers?"

"No," said Josh. "But that's because we're not geniuses like you."

Shane shook his head.

"For us Philistine plebs, you want to give clearer hints?"

"You're driving in the right direction." Josh worked his phone. "Continue west, exit at junction 5, and I'll direct you."

Shireen was scanning her own phone.

"Fuck off," she said. "You can't be serious."

Josh kissed Suzanne.

"Genius," he said.

• • • •

Flora McIntosh sat behind her too-large desk beneath print portraits of the King, the previous London mayor, Cowell, along with the famous Derren Brown caricature of Pullman painted on the day of the Holy Axemen incident. To the right of McIntosh's desk sat Davis Llewellyn.

As far as Trin was concerned that was where he should stay, preferably chained to the desk leg, because he was McIntosh's political pit bull. He was also supposed to accompany Trin back to Thames House as Steve's *pro tem* replacement, while his assistants tore apart the op-in-progress case files.

The problem was that Llewellyn's ferocity was of the bureaucratic kind. His idea of fieldwork was weeding his garden; his weapon of choice was the toxic vmail.

"You're a natural intelligence officer, Trinity," said McIntosh.

"Some of us have to be."

Llewellyn's face tightened.

"But isn't it true," said McIntosh, "that when you've a pet theory in mind you tend to perceive only the corroborative evidence? Isn't that what the psych guys say?"

She meant Steve's perceived persecution of the Tyndalls.

"Like homeopath believers who notice when people get better and ignore the failures," said Trin, "even though it always fails in double-blind trials."

In normal years, McIntosh suffered from hayfever, but had problems with antihistamine treatments. The rumour was that she saw a homeopath in Harley Street, someone who rented a consulting room by the hour – along with two hundred other alternative therapists – in a Georgian townhouse-turned-warren whose address allowed the "tenants" to claim they possessed a "Harley Street practice" like the genuine medical high-flyers up the road.

"Tell me what Steve was doing in Paris," said McIntosh. "If he's been trampling all over Six's field of operations, I need to know."

Trin shook her head.

"Paris was just a convenient place for the opposition to

make the hit."

"So they knew who he was." This was Llewellyn. "Is that what you're saying?"

Implying a leak.

"I wasn't," said Trin. "But you're right. Thank you for that. We'll look carefully at everyone who knew."

"No, you won't," said McIntosh. "Davis will head an internal team to—"

"With respect, we're focused on the Cutter Circles" – Trin blinked as unexpected tears threatened to grow in her eyes – "exactly as directed by yourself when I sat in this room with Steve. If you disrupt the effort, we lose the momentum."

Llewellyn waved his phone.

"Hello? Earth to Trinity? It's all over the news. TechDems using mindbending software to brainwash their young supporters. The whole thing blew up in their faces, because of a little accidental side effect called suicide psychosis."

"Right," said McIntosh. "The priority is finding other potential victims. Teenagers at risk because they've called the site. Meanwhile, the entire TechDems IT team are in Paddington Green."

The most heavily fortified police station in the UK.

"None of which," McIntosh went on, "requires MI5 involvement."

"The Cutter Circles have spread to France," said Trin.

"Then it's even more outside the purview of—"

"Which means many more teenagers will die if you derail the one operation that is focused in the right direction."

McIntosh's body tightened.

"What do you mean?"

"It's a specific targeted virus, but it's loose, and its *objective* is to make teenagers kill themselves. Suicide is the intent. If you start with the assumption that suicides are an accident, a failure in the brainwashing, then you'll only look at the evidence to support that theory."

Turning her own point against her.

"That's hardly–" Llewellyn started.

"No," said McIntosh. "She's right."

A vibrating silence filled the room.

"Davis," added McIntosh after some moments. "Would you leave us, please?"

Llewellyn's mouth clamped shut, then: "Of course."

He left without looking at Trin.

So I've made an enemy.

Tough.

"You and I don't know each other very well," said McIntosh.

That was true. All Trin knew was that she had given Steve a hard time.

"If I send Davis in to do what I had intended," McIntosh went on, "then I'll be expanding my political empire, as I'm sure you'd worked out. Taking control of your section."

"Could be," said Trin. "I hadn't expected you to say it."

Not even obliquely, certainly not this bluntly.

"But if you think I'm going to let teenagers die," said McIntosh, "just so I can get a bigger desk, you've totally mistaken me. So instead of putting Davis in charge, I'm appointing you as Steve's successor."

Trin pulled her attention inwards, holding still, before focusing on McIntosh once more.

"Thank you."

"I don't know why Steve had it in for Tyndall Industries, so forget that. Just be objective, Trin. Do your job."

"Of course I... Yes. I will."

No matter where the trail led. Mentioning Professor Badakian would be a mistake.

"And if you do it wrong," said McIntosh, "I will disembowel you in a civilised fashion, purely metaphorically. Then I really will own the section, but you won't be part of it. You'll be an office cleaner stationed in the Hebrides, and I'm not bloody joking."

"I can tell."

"Good. Now get out of here."

Trin pushed herself up off the chair.

"I'm good at my job," she said.

"So prove–"

"Because I was trained by the best. And I'll do my job objectively, because that's what Steve would have wanted me to do."

McIntosh's mouth twitched.

"Then prove it," she said.

Trin nodded, and left without more words.

Everything was coming to a head. Trin had already arranged for her parents to take Tommy for a few days, neither of them asking why, just as they had never asked precisely what she did in the civil service. Dad had been an ophthalmic surgeon before his retirement, his mind even more piercing than his eyes, and it was his continued failure to ask questions that reassured her: he understood and approved.

It's going to get tricky.

The team – *her* team – was loyal beyond doubt, but there would be others in Thames House keeping watch and reporting to Llewellyn or McIntosh. What she needed was off-the-books assets that were highly trained in the required skill sets, capable of working with minimal direction.

When this was over she might well offer permanent jobs to Josh Cumberland and Suzanne Duchesne, unless it all went tits-up and she herself was in charge of a broom cupboard in Shetland, far from the civilised heights of London, in exile with Scottish sheep-shaggers.

Could be worse. Could be Welsh sheep-shaggers.

Alone in the lift descending to the subterranean garage, she smirked.

Let Internal Surveillance make what they would of that.

• • • •

Unlike the fighters, Carlsen got to go home every night. Tonight, Sandra was with him. They were sitting on the couch, each twisted to face the other, one knee up on the cushions. He was trying to find words to explain what he felt about continuing with the *Knife Edge* series.

"It wasn't just the Durkee woman killing Anders," he said. "But up until that point, I could sort of ignore the way things felt wrong."

"They can't make you do it," said Sandra. "With or without a contract."

"I signed it, though."

"That doesn't make it–"

"I kinda like to keep my word, you know?"

"Captain Invincible," she said. "Man of honour."

"You're being ironic, but actually – yes. I try to be."

"I was being sort of serious. What about the training?"

Carlsen shrugged, conscious – because of something Sandra had said – of the mass of deltoid muscle involved.

"Siggy's covering for me, you want the truth. He's a better coach than I'll ever be."

"What about your own training?"

He always liked to work with guys hands-on. But he had agreed to fight Jason Krill at the season's end, so he should in fact be training with a purpose.

"Timing's kind of off," he said. "Fitness is good."

"Your head's not right, is it?"

That made him smile.

"I may not be intelligent, but I can lift heavy–"

Chiming indicated visitors at the front door. He reached for his phone, and pointed it at the big wallscreen. The porch view lit up.

"Who are they?" said Sandra.

Two men – one with half-face tiger-stripe tattoos – and two women.

"I recognise her." Carlsen pointed. "She was at Kat's funeral, and also at last year's–Well, fuck me."

Sandra looked surprised. She had not heard him swear like that before.

"What?"

"That's the rogue fighter from last year. The renegade." He rolled to his feet. "Fought his way through and I thought I was going to face him, then bam, and I was asleep."

"*Him?*"

Sandra was standing too.

"I can call the station for more officers," she said.

"Or we could just offer them a cup of tea."

She smiled.

"Open the door, then," she said.

[THIRTY-TWO]

An hour later they were on their second mug of tea each, a half-demolished plate of Jaffa Cakes on the low table. The six of them paused, their explanations made. What was surprising was how quickly they got on with each other. Or perhaps it was simply that they were on parallel paths, with no reason for antagonism.

Also, Shane and Shireen's false Special Branch IDs carried a lot of weight, as did the real IDs they showed to Sandra, who knew how to recognise and verify them online.

Josh stared yet again at the bereavement cards – the old-fashioned kind – ranged on a shelf. That was the other reason for their agreement: the dead niece, Kat, and the need for revenge.

"My daughter died," Josh said.

There had been no thought behind the words. No conscious intent.

Carlsen and Sandra looked surprised, as did Suzanne. In her case it was probably the fact of his talking about it that was unexpected.

"Aw, God," said Carlsen.

"Her body died less than two weeks ago. But she'd been in a coma for a year. Vegetative state."

"How old was she?"

"Ten when the car hit her. Eleven when she died."

But she had really been dead for a year.

"Car accident?"

"Running out into the street," said Josh. "Running away from a knife fight in the schoolyard."

"Jesus."

"Yeah."

No one said anything for a while. Then Sandra looked at Suzanne.

"You realise that us four, all our names begin with S?"

"Do you think that's an omen, or something?"

"No such thing," said Sandra. "Which I reckon you know, right enough. Just one of the things we got in common."

Suzanne tilted her head in a way that Josh loved, inviting further speech.

"And what else do we have in common?"

"We want psychos who could twist kids' minds to suicide to be locked up," said Sandra. "Unless someone guts them or cuts their throat first. And we want you safely out of sight, so they don't come for you again."

"Well..."

"So Matt's going to help you," she said. "Aren't you, Matt?"

Carlsen said, "Yes, dear."

The others smiled. The mood was still too serious for laughter. *Captain Invincible*.

Rock solid. Ultimate good guy.

"When I grow up," said Josh, "I want to be you."

This time they did laugh, though not for long.

Then Carlsen said: "Once Suzanne is tucked out of sight and these guys" – he gestured to Shane and Shireen – "have gone back to spookworld, what are you going to be doing?"

Josh took out his phone, and gestured towards the wallscreen.

"Can I?"

"Sure."

Two display panes blossomed.

"That's from a month ago," said Josh. "The Foreign Secretary, Reid-Browne, and her delegation meeting President Brand in the States."

"That arsehole," said Sandra.

"Well, maybe, but this guy" – Josh zoomed in on a shaven-headed, goateed figure – "name of Badakian, designed the mindbending software."

"But if he's with the Foreign Secretary–"

"Yeah. He's what you might call an establishment figure."

"Seems to me" – Carlsen smiled – "they're the kind you like to have as an enemy."

Josh smiled back.

"Funny you should say that." He enlarged the second pane. "Tyndall Industries' flagship power plant is just down the road from here. And Badakian's going to be there the day after tomorrow for the official opening, though the reactor's already online."

"I got confused," said Sandra, "by what you said about, um, Evans, was it? The scientist who killed himself. I mean, I get it that Badakian made him do it, but what's all this about power plants?"

Shane looked as if he wanted to speak, so Josh let him.

"When they do the big opening ceremony," Shane said, "and the prime minister throws the big switch and power goes into the national grid... The thing is, that's got to work exactly right for the realtime webcast, so in fact it's a fake. The power plant went online yesterday."

"But if it's already online–"

"It's in operation with some design flaw that Evans spotted," said Josh. "He also told Badakian under hypnosis how to fix the flaw, but they haven't delayed the opening. That can only mean they're going to wait for the next downtime period before they re-engineer it. At least the stolen redesign is being used for the other plants under construction."

Shane and Shireen nodded. En route here, Josh had phoned Lofty, and the MI5 officers now had access to the same GCHQ channels that Lofty had used. Together they were diving deep into the onsite systems at every one of the Tyndalls' nuclear reactor sites.

"So in terms of the power plant," said Sandra, "they're going to make it safe and–"

"The next downtime period will be in five years," said Shane. "At a minimum. Meanwhile, it's running twenty-four/seven, and because it's the so-called safe mesoreactor design, there are thousands of people living just a short jog away in every direction."

"Shit."

"Including the fighters' house, by the way."

"But if the reactor is dangerous–"

"It's not going to blow during the first few days of operation," said Josh, "or the Tyndalls and Badakian would be nowhere in sight."

"Right."

Everyone looked at each other.

"So you're going to the reactor to make a nuisance of yourself?" said Carlsen. "Is that it?"

"First," said Josh, "we get the other victims on our side."

"Victims? The other kids' families?"

"No, the *other* victims. The TechnoDemocratic Party."

"Oh," said Carlsen.

"Oh," said Sandra.

Suzanne smiled at Josh. "You didn't manage to take down the government last year," she said.

"Unfinished business," he said.

Shane put his fingers in his ears.

"La-la-la, I can't hear this treason plot, la-la-la."

Shireen patted him on the thigh with her fist.

"I think he might have voted for the wrong lot," she said.

Jack Hardin – former employer of Alex Rhys Evans, PhD, and a friend of the better-known Philip Broomhall – was a long-term TechDems supporter, an industrialist who had donated the maximum amount of money allowed by Parliamentary regulations. Those regulations were circumvented by Tyndall Industries in their support for the LabCon Party in general and Billy Church in particular; but Hardin played by the rules, which were designed to stop wealthy individuals having too much influence on politicians.

Still, he was prominent enough that when he requested a face-to-face interview with the party leader, Sharon Caldwell, she agreed, suggesting her Richmond home – rather than her utilitarian constituency office – as the venue.

But it was Josh Cumberland who walked up the path to the pseudo-Georgian front door, even though the security systems identified him as Jack Hardin. That door glistened not just from fresh gloss paint but from the underlying material: alternating layers of ceramic and steel.

Good. If she was security conscious, or used to doing what a good personal protection team told her to do – in terms of living arrangements and travel details – then she ought to be more open to his strategic arguments. That was what he hoped as the door opened and a slim man said: "Please come in, Mr Hardin."

"Thank you."

As Josh entered he passed another man, also lean and expensively dressed. Both looked like cosmopolitan young gentlemen unless you noticed the hardness of their knuckles or the watchfulness in their eyes. He altered his own stance, adding awkward muscle tension, holding back from scanning the environment, because he was supposed to be a civilian, not an operator.

"Please come this way, sir. Ms Caldwell will see you in the drawing-room."

The mistress will see you now.

He buttoned down his laughter as he followed the guy along a Persian carpet laid on a parquet floor. At the far end, an elegant cream door stood open. Josh entered while the guy remained in the hall. The door closed.

A woman's voice said, "Jack, it's good to–Who are you?"

"I apologise, Ms Caldwell," Josh said. "I'm here with Jack Hardin's agreement."

The Right Honourable Sharon Caldwell, MP, stood with a glass of fruit juice in her hand, beside an antique desk that faced twin rows of display screens, eight screens in all.

"That's not an answer to my question."

"My name's Josh Cumberland, ma'am, and if you watched last year's *Knife Edge* final, then you've seen me before."

"I don't follow sports like–Ah. I see."

She was fast. Also composed.

Trusting her panic button.

He kept his distance, while she remained beside her desk. Close enough for her to slap the button, which was probably above the drawers or under the top. If it reassured her, that was good.

No reason for her to know that he had disabled it.

"May I?" He pointed his phone towards the display screens. "Just to show you what I mean, ma'am."

"Go ahead."

He popped up still images: himself facing Fireman Carlsen; Zak Tyndall and his father Zebediah looking outraged; and the prime minister, Billy Church, his face blotched, staring at one of the big Barbican Centre wallscreens that showed him and the Tyndalls leaving virapharm labs in Africa. A montage of incriminating data glowed in secondary panes.

"Too bad you picked that particular day," said Caldwell.

Minutes after those images were taken, the screens were showing realtime aerial webcasts from the West Coast of the soon-to-be-former United States: mushroom clouds and plumes of volcanic ash, from Mount Rainier down to the destruction of Los Angeles.

He flicked the image from existence.

"Afterwards," he said, "the PM's influence engineers got to work, spindoctoring everything."

"It wrong-footed us," said Caldwell. "By the time our people had verified all the details about the virapharm labs – and maybe we were overcautious – the webcasts were filled with dire images from CalOrWashington, all of it real enough. Diverting the people's attention."

"And now Midsummer Christmas is three days away."

"Yes." Caldwell snorted. "That."

She had already denounced the PM's decision to inaugurate a holiday – associating it in people's minds with himself – and to hold the general election on the same day. Everyone stuffed with food and drunk with celebratory booze as they voted online for the guy who had given them the day off.

"The predictions for the TechDems aren't good," said Josh.

"Please. If we get any seats at all it will be a miracle."

"I didn't think you believed in miracles, ma'am."

"I don't."

She might not fully trust him, but she had not tried to use the panic button. Call it a measure of success.

"If you'd been convinced by last year's data straight away" – Josh pointed at the screen that had shown his image – "you'd have been able to get people to listen, wouldn't you?"

"With the West Coast blowing up? Maybe."

"And without that kind of disaster?"

"I'd have had that bastard's head on a plate," said Caldwell. "And if this is some LabCon trick and you're reporting back to Billy Church's people, then feel free to pass on my sentiments."

"The image of me looks a little different," said Josh, "because I used theatrical makeup as a mild disguise. Your people should be able to do the analysis and check it's really me. And do it pretty fast."

"Mr Cumberland, this is old news. Last year I might have been able to do something with your data; this year, frankly, we're going to get slaughtered. Teenagers have died and our IT people are in police cells, and if they're guilty of what the prosecutors accuse them of, then they deserve whatever happens to them."

"They're not," said Josh.

Still standing, Caldwell rocked back.

"I'm not relying on last year's data," he added. "You might want to sit down for this."

Gesturing with the phone, he brought up the video footage of Evans slumped in a chair, while the shaven head of Rashid Badakian leaned over him, reciting his hypnotic induction of self-destruction, building false memories of childhood horror and the rest, implanting an awful picture of reality in Evans' mind, along with a fixation on ending it all and making the world suffer.

"I recognise him," said Caldwell when the footage ended. "But I don't believe what I've just seen."

"Dr Evans, the man in the chair, threw himself off a Welsh mountain less than two weeks after this occurred. I was there when he did it. That guy with the bald head and the goatee is Professor Badakian, and this session is taking place inside the Burnham power plant constructed by Badakian's friends, the Tyndalls."

"The mesoreactor?"

Caldwell's degrees were in physics.

"I'll show you what Evans said about the reactor design in just a minute," said Josh. "That's part of the reason Badakian made him commit suicide, after Evans had spilled the details of his own new process. Evans was one of Jack Hardin's top guys before this."

"Ah." Caldwell relaxed, moving a little away from her desk and its panic button. "I see the connection."

"And there's another link that you'll really care about." Josh stared at her. "A man able to get people to kill themselves. Ring a bell?"

"No. I mean, it's an accidental–No."

"My girlfriend is a neuropsych specialist. She assures me it's possible, and also that Badakian is a sociopath according to the clinical definition. She's met him."

"So have I." Caldwell shivered. "At some function, somewhere. I remember shaking his hand and getting the creeps. Laura always says half of us, meaning politicians, have a touch of the psycho about us. But that man–"

Laura Collins was Sharon Caldwell's partner. They had been married for twenty years.

"Do you mean what you just said?" Caldwell went on. "This Badakian put the suicide software on our website? Infected those poor young people?"

"Yes."

"You have full forensic proof?"

"Official agencies are working their way towards getting the proof," he said. "Please do *not* mention that to anyone. The Tyndalls and Badakian have powerful friends."

"Clearly. But I don't believe anyone would deliberately kill nearly two hundred teenagers just to get at us. Church is stupid but not evil, not like that."

"Maybe you're giving him the benefit of the doubt," said Josh, "because you're a better person than he is. Or maybe he just wanted Badakian's help and washed his hands of involvement with the, um, means of its implementation."

Caldwell's face became hard.

"And now he's too shit-scared to say what he knows," she said. "That sounds like him. But the rest is still hard to believe."

"It *should* be hard to believe." Josh pointed at the screen where Badakian was hypnotizing Evans, with the audio now muted. "Without that footage, people would think what you did, that no one would kill teenagers just to turn the public against your party. But Badakian is exactly that sort of person."

She stared at the silent video.

"Leave me everything," she said. "A copy of all your data."

"Sure." He gestured with the phone, then sent the prepared archive file. "It's all there."

"Thank you."

Caldwell brought all eight screens to life and began to flick through data.

She's a fast reader.

But there was a huge amount to wade through. If she was going to mull over this before deciding, he might as well leave and contact her later.

"Ma'am? If you need time with this, I can–"

"No." She looked up, then pointed to another door, not the one he had come in by. "If you could wait in there, please. There's a coffee machine and a cocktail cabinet. Help yourself."

This was why she was the leader of her party.

Or she could be trapping me while she calls the police.

But that was not the way he read the situation. He moved to the door as Caldwell turned back to the displays.

"Brainwashing," she muttered. "Suicide cult. And that fucker *engineered* it?"

Josh stepped through to the next room.

It was a library devoted to hardcopy books. But it was the treadmill, and the long-legged woman walking on it, that caught Josh's attention. This must be Laura Collins.

"Right with you," she called. "I'm just finishing up. Four minutes more."

"Don't mind me," said Josh. "I'll just browse the books."

He did so, until he found a shelf of first editions, including a signed copy of *The Selfish Gene*. Losing himself in the lucid writing, he raised his head only when the sound of the tread-mill stopped and Laura Collins walked towards him.

"I'm Laura." She held out her hand.

"Josh. Josh Cumberland."

Her grip was sweaty and strong. In her left hand she held a water bottle, from which she took a swig.

"I was going to finish with a stretch and a little tai-chi," she said. "Do you mind?"

"It is your house, but even if it wasn't, I'd say go ahead."

"Well, cheers." Her smile was bright. "Take a look at that. It's the reason I fell in love with my sweetie. She posted it to a forum when we were both students."

Laura pointed at a framed text that looked like an excerpt from a textual script. It hung between photos of Richard Feynman and Jocelyn Bell Burnell.

```
ACT 1, SCENE 1
SETTING: THE BRIDGE
Krok: What are you doing here, Mr Spick?
Spick: Awaiting your instructions,
Captain.
Krok: Beans, how can Spick possibly exist?
Beans: Damn it, man, I'm a doctor, not a
philosopher.
Krok: Alien life is based on replicating
molecules-
Spick: Indubitably, Captain.
Krok: But not DNA, that's just Earth. And
for God's sake, Mr Welsh, why humanoid
aliens?
Welsh: Ya cannae break the laws of
biology, Captain.
Krok: Mr Spick, you cannot possibly exist.
```

```
 Spick: This does not compute. Does not
compute. Does not…
 (explodes in a burst of gamma rays)
 THE END
```

Josh read it and laughed.

"You can see why I was smitten," said Laura.

"Anyone would be."

Smiling, Laura went off to a part of the floor laid with exercise mats. There, she sunk into a Yang-style tai-chi posture. Then she stopped.

"What is it?" she said. "You're looking at me funny, and not in a get-this-lesbian-chick kind of way."

"I was just wondering whether you do this only for exercise."

"Why else?"

"There's a fighting art in what you're doing."

"Against slow-motion geriatric muggers, maybe," she said. "But I can't see it, myself."

"When you pull down with both hands like this" – Josh demonstrated – "what if your fingers were hooked inside someone's collarbones? The clavicles snap easily under downward pressure."

"They do?"

"Yeah, and the power comes from collapsing the hips, which you've already got down pat. So long as you keep your elbows close to your body, that is."

"Show me."

Josh grinned as he placed her fingers against his collarbones. "Careful now."

She dropped her weight, allowing her hooked fingers to relax, for Josh's protection.

"Oh, that's nasty," Laura said. "What else can I do?"

"You can start by speeding up, because you've already got the alignment and structure – if you're on balance in slow motion, you've nailed the biomechanics."

"Like this?"

She advanced into a lunge.

"Right," said Josh. "Think of your arms as whips."

"But what does this move actually do?"

"Here, let me show you–"

Some twenty minutes later, the connecting door opened and Sharon Caldwell started to step inside, then stopped. Josh and Laura were moving around the mats in a fighting dance that involved clawing eyeballs and striking the throat. Then Laura hooked her calf behind Josh's, and kept her centre of gravity low – as she used the strong muscles of her legs to power a double-hand push. Josh flew backwards through the air and slapped down as he hit the mats.

"Hey, sweetie," said Laura. "Look what Josh has been showing me."

Josh rolled to his feet.

"Excuse me," he said. "I know you've got your own protectors, but knowing how to defend yourself is always worth it."

Caldwell stared at them.

"I came in to tell you that I can't risk it. I can't risk the party being involved in this. If the authorities can vindicate us, that's fine. But if I try to publicise the Tyndalls' involvement and the forensic proof doesn't surface, we'll look guiltier than ever."

Josh wiped sweat from his face.

"Yeah, I understand."

That meant relying on Trin and the others in MI5 getting the information out there, which would be easy if they were not running their op off the books in defiance of their superiors' orders. Disobeying directives, for them, could mean more than the end of their careers: it could involve a prison sentence. The Official Secrets Act is a serious document; so is the MI5 Contract of Employment (Covert Personnel).

The situation would be even more fraught for Lofty, since the Regiment was under the control of the Prime Minister's office as much as the MOD chain of command.

"–thing is," Caldwell was saying, "even I can change my mind on occasion."

Laura was smiling at her.

"I'll do everything I can to help," added Caldwell. "And I mean everything. But you know the Tyndalls have considerable power. When the information gets out there, they'll do everything to distort it. Even if they don't manage it, you know they'll be in Rio or somewhere in hours."

Josh said: "Let's hope not."

For the first time he let something reveal itself in his voice, something that was not civilised.

"Do you mean you're going to do something?" said Laura. "Something to the Tyndalls?"

Josh waited a moment, then:

"I have no idea what you mean."

The three of them smiled.

[THIRTY-THREE]

Suzanne was part of Carlsen's secondary support team. She stood among the group she had ridden in the van with: Big Andy, Little Pete, and Angie, all from Carlsen's own gym. The other assistant coaches for the Bloods, headed by a big Viking type called Sigmund, had nodded when Carlsen said he needed additional help, and welcomed the four of them.

It verified what Suzanne had expected: Carlsen's mind was not on his own training, even though he had a fight coming up at the series finale, when he was due to face Jason Krill.

She could also tell, from the way the others spoke about Krill, that he was a deadly piece of work. They were worried for Carlsen's safety if he went ahead with the fight.

Careful of the camera angles, she slipped into a technicians' room, where four people worked in front of a large console, while another was pouring coffee from a flask.

"Hi," the guy whispered. "Who are you?"

"One of Carlsen's gophers, really," she whispered back. "They don't need me, and I wanted to check that it's OK for me to hang around with you."

Even with her voice low, she was able to use command modulation. This was ethical only because of the circumstances.

"Yeah." The guy's head nodded in time with hers. "Of course."

She watched the screens showing both training gyms, as the Bloods and Blades worked out at the same time with their respective coaches. Krill's people were drilling routines with plastic knives over and over, while Carlsen had his fighters running on inclined treadmills for sprint intervals, then working with kettlebells and big sandbags, hoisting and swinging them.

It was over an hour before Carlsen, his t-shirt black with sweat, took a break. Swigging electrolyte replacement fluid, he headed for one of the so-called dead rooms where no spy-cams were allowed. Neither were the fighters under normal circumstances.

Suzanne slid out of the techs' room and went to join him.

"I just got a call." Carlsen pointed his phone at a wall screen. "Guess who."

Josh's image appeared.

"Are you all right?" said Suzanne.

"Yeah. Everything OK there?"

"Sure."

Carlsen said: "I just heard Zak's coming here this afternoon. Poking around, having a session in front of the cameras. Discussing our impressions of the fighters, mine and Krill's."

"I won't be there in time for that," said Josh. "I'll just have to catch up with Tyndall later."

He meant at the Burnham reactor.

"You have to be careful." Suzanne realised there was something she had not done. She had not made Josh understand how truly dangerous Professor Rashid Badakian was. "I mean really, really careful because Badakian–"

"I know."

"I don't think you're afraid of him enough to–"

"None of that, darling. Commanding me to be afraid would be counterproductive if it actually worked."

After a second, she smiled at him.

"You have learned your lessons well, my young *Padawan* apprentice."

"Ha. Right." On screen, Josh grinned at both of them. "We have the politicians on our side. They'll be making a public fuss just as soon as we give them the signal."

"Good," said Carlsen.

Suzanne nodded.

"See you later," said Josh. "Out."

The screen blackened.

"Tsk, tsk," came from the doorway behind them.

Suzanne whirled.

"Who are–? Mr Krill."

"Cutter Krill to my fans." He was leaning there, arms folded, but the hands not tucked in: a fighter's stance, the kind of thing Josh might use. "And when I meet you in the arena, baby" – this to Carlsen – "you'll be finding out why."

Carlsen shrugged his big shoulders, looking calm – but no doubt getting ready for violence.

"What we get paid for," he said.

"Yeah. Meanwhile," said Krill, "you want to fuck with old Zak and his cronies a little, is that it? Like last year's fuck-up wasn't enough?"

Suzanne was observing the minutiae of stance, the harmonics of voice, the implied semantic structure beneath the surface words.

"And what do you think of that, Mr Krill?" she said.

"Why, it sounds fine to me." Jason Krill's smile was half-cold, half-nasty. "Never liked the little prick too much. I'll help you all you want."

"But we're still going to fight," said Carlsen. "Is that it?"

"Like you said, it's what we get paid for."

"Yeah." Carlsen's wide, flat chest expanded as he inhaled; then he let the breath out. "Yeah, it is."

Suzanne looked from one to the other.

"Ma'am." Krill tipped her a salute. "Fireman."

Then he rolled around the doorframe and was gone.

"Damn," said Carlsen. "I guess you think we're all insane, Dr Duchesne."

She smiled at the rhyme in his words.

"I'm not sure I know what sanity is," she said. "Not any more."

From the technicians' room, Suzanne watched the big limousine arrive. Zak Tyndall smiled often, but only when the cameras were on him. He made a speech before both teams of gathered fighters, as they looked at how the statistics would be displayed once the elimination fights began. He also announced a bonus for every bout that went with a clear win, meaning a defanged – disarmed – opponent and a stab or cut to a major artery, or a neck crank.

"Now that the medics can repair a snapped neck," he said, "and regrow the severed spinal cord with the new treatment, we're allowing full-on neck cranks and headlocks in the tournament. Plus there's a five thousand bonus for any fighter who pulls one off to win."

The fighters looked at each other.

"Bring it on," said one of them.

"That's fighting spirit," said Zak Tyndall. "That's what we like. What the fans want to see."

Until this moment, every bad thing Suzanne knew about Tyndall might have been rationalised, at least in theory: he was CEO of a vast conglomerate, he could not be expected to know how his commercial operations worked in detail, and he might not necessarily be cognizant of every evil act performed in his name. But this, happening now on screen, was direct corroboration, because she knew this kind of behaviour from her time working in a secure psychiatric unit filled with rapist-murderers.

And from conversing with Rashid Badakian.

Badakian.

Fear shivered through her in waves. Josh was highly trained

in combat and possessed the highest level of computer skills.
He had also picked up some basic applied neuropsych techniques to enhance what he already knew. But he did not seem
to appreciate that for him to go up against Badakian was like
her taking on Jason Krill or Matt Carlsen in a knife fight: no
contest, instant defeat.

Or prolonged and painful torture if they chose to drag it out.
Josh. You don't realise what he can do.

Tomorrow, at the Burnham reactor site, Zak Tyndall and his
father Zebediah were going to be accompanied by Badakian at
the opening ceremony. The prime minister, Billy Church, was
going to press the ceremonial button or whatever it was.

Josh had not yet shared his plans – the exact shape of them
being contingent on Sharon Caldwell's reaction to his proposal
– but Suzanne was pretty sure that they involved some kind
of special-ops incursion into the power plant itself, followed
by a disruption of the ceremony to catch public attention, just
two days before the general election.

Even Billy Church could not call off an election two years
in a row, not without provoking a backlash.

But Josh is in danger.

He had placed her here to keep her safe. In the service tunnels between the false and real walls, she could survive for
days on end, unobserved in the fighters' house despite the
thousand-strong array of spycams. But she had thought of the
location herself.

If she could find a bolthole and get it right, perhaps she
could also find a way of actively helping instead of hiding.

Zak Tyndall, his announcements to the fighters over, led
Carlsen, Krill and their assistant coaches to one of the briefing
rooms. They sat around a long oval table, some sipping water
or coffee, and talked through their impressions of their fighters.

Apart from diehard fans signed up for the premium-rate realtime webcast, viewers would see edited versions of the show

that would condense this kind of session to seconds-long cuts. Some clips would be retrieved later, after a fighter had won or lost an elimination bout, so the fans could see predictions that were spot on or a hundred percent wrong.

The technicians around Suzanne seemed to find it tedious, but they kept working the angles and performing cut-aways, switching from one spycam to another as the primary thread, for those viewers who watched the prioritised-panes service. The techs were professional.

So am I, allegedly.

What the hell was she going to do to help Josh?

Then Tyndall was wandering off by himself to one of the dead rooms, perhaps to make a call without a million viewers listening in. Suzanne was moving before she realised her decision.

I don't do damsel in distress.

Josh had it in for the Tyndalls, but Badakian was hers. He had to be.

She slipped across a dead zone in the corridor, into the room where Tyndall was sitting at a desk. His phone was raised halfway, about to bring a wallscreen to life.

"Hello," he said. "A pretty woman, looking breathless. The story of my life."

She smiled at him.

Left shoulder.

Keying in on someone's breathing was a learned skill, and the trick was to find the most obvious indicator at this moment in time, as presented by this particular person. Something specific. Right now it was the shoulder of Zak's jacket that betrayed his respiration.

"Stories are good" – she altered her voice – "because they allow you to relax now as you become aware of those sensations in your body that your unconscious dealt with before you are lost in the story of knowing who you are becoming more and more relaxed as you may blink – that's right – and blink again at any time – that's right – and close your eyes now as my words descend alongside you soften your muscles and relax deeper and deeper and deeper still."

The syntax of her induction was a single unbroken sentence that took some fifteen minutes to utter. It contained pivot words to blend one clause into the next in ways designed to bypass normal psycholinguistic filters.

Then she returned him to wakefulness, after reinforcing a posthypnotic suggestion: that whenever she touched his left shoulder and said "Trance now," he would slip back into trance.

Tyndall blinked his eyes open. His smile was sleepy, un-guarded in a way it probably had not been since childhood.

"Welcome back." Suzanne leaned forward to press his shoul-der. "And trance now."

His eyes closed, chin dipping to his chest. His breathing went shallow and slow.

"Because you like this relaxation and before you go deeper again than you have ever been wondering how deeply you can go does not matter as you descend further and further into deep relaxation of every muscle is softening as you–"

This time he went deeper.

The process was called fractionation. The easiest way to enter a profound trance is to go in and out again, deeper each time. She finished the trancework with a single-paragraph ver-sion of her favourite H.G.Wells, because ending with a metaphor is always a huge reinforcement.

It had taken twenty minutes, but no one had tried to interrupt.

She brought him out of formal trance for the last time.

"Thank you," she whispered.

Tyndall jumped.

Then he stood up, looked at his phone, frowned, slipped the phone in his pocket, and left the room, all without looking in Suzanne's direction.

Good.

She rubbed her face, trembling a little now, knowing she had used her skills in ways that went beyond the bounds of therapeutic ethics, hoping she had done the right thing for the sake of the world.

The world? How grandiose.

Biting her lip, she knew she was committed now. Having laid the groundwork, she would follow through.

For Josh's sake.

Only for him.

Carlsen was glad at first, watching from the front steps with the others as Zak Tyndall headed for his limo. Zak's entourage made their way to black-windowed 4x4s. But then a woman with chocolatté skin exited the fighters' house via one of the service doors, crossed the flagstones, and fell in beside Zak.

Suzanne.

Zak's security people turned to look at her, but Zak showed no reaction. Perhaps they were used to this: their employer gaining a female passenger en route.

What the hell is she doing?

If Zak was ignoring her, did that mean he knew her? That everything Suzanne and Josh had said was wrong? He started to step forward, to call out her name.

"No," said a voice beside him. A grip fastened around his arm.

"Leave her," added Krill. "Say nothing."

"What's going on?"

"I've seen something like this on a stag night."

"You what?"

"Stage hypnotist. Watch what she does."

Carlsen knew nothing about hypnosis or suchlike weirdness, but he knew everything about watching for the body-language precursors of violent intent, the specific twitches that signal attacks. Zak was paying no attention to Suzanne, as if she were not there at all.

As if he could not see her.

"Bloody hell," said Carlsen.

"On stage, they called it the Invisible Man Impersonation. The hypnotist waved objects around and scared the shit out of the ones he'd hypnotised. All they saw was stuff floating in the air."

"Yeah, but it's not really possible, is it?"

Krill nodded towards the limousine, where Suzanne slid inside ahead of Zak as a chauffeur held the rear door open.

"You sure about that?"

Carlsen shook his head as the limo closed up and the chauffeur climbed in. The whole group moved off, one escort vehicle ahead of the limo and two behind.

"She's a brave chick," added Krill. "Don't you think?"

"Brave, or scary?"

"Climbing into a car with fucknuts Tyndall and his crew? I'm going for brave."

Carlsen nodded. He and Krill would have been high on adrenaline, going up against Zak's people, yet you couldn't call it bravery – more like excitement, doing what they were trained to do. But Suzanne was no fighter; for her this must take courage.

"She'd better be OK," he said to Krill, "or her boyfriend will try to kill us."

"Uh-huh," said Krill. "You really think we could've stopped her?"

Carlsen shrugged massive shoulder muscles, enjoying the feel of easy strength in arms and torso, all the better for grappling a determined, thrashing opponent. How muscular power matched up against voodoo, however, he was uncertain.

"Maybe not," he said. "But I kinda wish we'd tried."

[THIRTY-FOUR]

Josh drove slowly through Surrey, ensuring his subversion ware was altering all traffic surveillance logs. The parks were bare and grey instead of rich green, but at least there was no snow. Everything felt strange, shimmering with odd perspective; but it was his mind, not the world, that was different, because this was the endgame and his nerves knew it.

Lofty's image appeared on the heads-up.

"I didn't tell you this, if anyone asks. We're readying for deployment, laddie. All of us."

"Shit." Josh collected himself. "Kick ass, take names, and the best of British luck."

Lofty would be too busy to work against the Tyndalls.

"Naturally I can't discuss the theatre of deployment," said Lofty.

"I wouldn't expect you to."

"But our friend Matt is there already, laying the ground."

Josh slowed the car.

Matt Carlsen?

Then he realised who Lofty meant: Matt Klugmann, cousin to Carol Klugmann, Suzanne's Texan colleague and friend.

"Jesus Christ," said Josh. "You're kidding."

"We're on standby. Pre-empting a pre-emptive strike into

Europe. Some people don't like other people taking their toys."

"Oh, no."

"If it's going to happen, we need to shut it down."

"Yes, you do." Josh blew a breath, but failed to relax. "Good luck."

"Yeah. Thing is, laddie, whether I should wish *you* luck is not entirely clear. We need strong leadership."

Now Josh had to pull over. He found a side street with a space, and parked.

"Maybe the right leadership, though. One with a brain and a conscience."

On the windscreen display, Lofty nodded.

"Agreed. Good luck."

"And you."

The display pane winked out.

Holy fuck.

Even with encrypted comms, Lofty had used oblique language, but the meaning was clear: the SAS and associated special forces were readying for deployment into the former United States, helped by renegade ex-Epsilon Force soldiers already on the ground.

Their specific mission objective remained unspecified; but the underlying goal would be to prevent President Brand ordering some kind of strike in Poland and other Eastern European countries that contained American nuclear missiles.

Whether it involved securing the missile sites, firing the weapons, or retaking the Romanian installations that the Georgia-Ukraine-Russia alliance had recently captured, perhaps even Lofty did not know.

If the pre-emptive counterstrike was a special forces op, then it was going to have to be a strike into the heart of Brand's government. Designed to kill him or perhaps bundle him into a stealth plane and fly him to the Hague for trial. When the former US carried out such actions, they called them regime change and extraordinary rendition.

Brand would have different words when he was the target. *It's too risky.*

Even if the op succeeded, Brand might have loyalist replacements capable of triggering all-out war. The meek shall inherit the Earth after the hawks have nuked it to ash.

If Trin and her team at Thames House could keep operating, then Josh's mission could still succeed. He had to ignore the fact that geopolitics might be moving in the background, far beyond his or anyone's control, with the capability of upsetting everything once more.

A strike against Brand, plus its aftermath, would be as overwhelming a news event as last year's destruction of the West Coast, and the subsequent global ash cloud.

And if the British voting public did not care about their government's corruption, perhaps they were right. Perhaps corruption was irrelevant against a backdrop of disaster. When everything is falling apart, who cares what a bunch of politicians get up to?

If millions were to die in another world war, a couple of hundred dead teenagers would be a footnote in some future history only academics would care about. Assuming culture survived.

He phoned Carlsen, expecting to have to leave a message, since the fighters should be training now. But Carlsen answered immediately.

"Suzanne went with Zak in his car," Carlsen said. "I'm sure you can find out where they've gone."

"She went with–?"

"It's voodoo. She rode in his car but he didn't know she was there. I swear he couldn't see her."

"What do you mean?"

"Jason says it's an old hypnotist's trick. I still can't believe it."

By Jason he meant Krill. Hadn't Carlsen and Krill hated each other earlier?

"Burnham," Josh told Carlsen, checking a secondary pane.

"He's just arriving at the power plant."

The footage was pulled from a public news site. Background text in a tertiary pane revealed that Zak Tyndall was sleeping in the compound overnight, in one of the managerial suites that allowed visiting engineers to remain on site if necessary. He was showing his solidarity with ordinary people and confidence in the safety of the mesoreactor, the major selling-point of the new design.

NIMBY had been the old term – Not In My Back Yard – which the Tyndalls' information engineers had propagandised into oblivion, making it something to be ashamed of. No one found themselves able to object to a nuclear plant just because it happened to be constructed down the road from where they lived.

In general, high-profile figures with good security people do not advertise where they will be staying on any particular date. But the Burnham reactor would be guarded not just by Tyndall's people, but by NPD officers.

The difference between the Nuclear Police Detachment and other police forces was the same as that between American Federal Air Marshals and every other US law enforcement department. Both NPD and the Air Marshals were counterterrorist in focus, therefore trained to kill suspects first, let the pathologists sort them out.

"We can't leave Suzanne in there," said Carlsen. "Voodoo is one thing, but they'll have full security, won't they?"

"The tighter the perimeter," said Josh, "the smaller the infiltration team."

"Which means–?"

"In the trade it's called a solo penetration." Josh grinned. "But I could do with some help in two departments: a diversion beforehand, some guys to help with heavy lifting afterwards."

On screen, Carlsen blinked.

"You want my help? Me and the guys?"

"If you want to give it."

"Well, of course I bloody do."

Josh smiled.

"With Fireman Carlsen on our side, we can't lose."

But Suzanne was inside the perimeter.

Why?

He had not counted on that.

There was one more piece of assistance Josh needed. Ever since he had seen Evans commit suicide by throwing himself over the mountain edge, a part of Josh had worried about this: the night before the suicide, he had blacked out because he had glimpsed the PulseTrance running on the wallscreen in Evans' room.

Plus there was his continued amnesia regarding the Armenians who attacked him in the forest, even though he had related the full story to Lofty, Jan, and Brummie while in trance.

With all that had happened to teenagers joining the Young TechDems as well as to Evans, he needed to be sure that his own mind was clear. He needed to know that none of his current actions were driven by something buried in his mind.

In the display pane, a voluptuous woman raised her eyebrows.

"Josh Cumberland," she said. "You're in love with Suzanne again, is that it?"

"Hello, Carol," he said. "I need your help."

"To increase your sex drive?"

"No." He exhaled. "But if you want to throw that in as well, feel free."

"So tell me."

Steel fences, the rearing polished domes of the reactor beyond, and the tangle of huge piping. This was the Burnham reactor, their destination, and it was just as well, because on the seat beside Suzanne, Zak Tyndall's eyes were beginning to flutter and shift.

She dared not drop him into trance again to reinforce the suggestion because the driver, up front, would notice something was wrong.

Another five minutes.

Long enough for the limo to get inside.

That's all I need.

The technical name was negative hallucination, the same neurological process that occurs whenever someone fails to see an object they are looking for when it is right in front of them. The brain fills in background by computation, not observation. No one is conscious of the blind spot in each eye, or the never-ending flickers of eye movement called saccades.

Just keep hallucinating, you bastard.

Mentally cursing her trance subject was far from normal practice, but this was not therapy: her goal was to destroy Tyndall's life, not heal it.

Several hundred metres inside the installation, the driver slowed, approaching a polished glass-and-ceramic building that must be the main administration block. There was an actual red carpet strip leading from a carport.

The chauffeur stopped, got out, and opened the door for Tyndall. Suzanne had long set up operant conditioning in herself to associate a gesture – four fingertips and thumb pressed together – with massive confidence. She squeezed hard now as she slid across the seat, then stepped out, careful not to brush Tyndall's sleeve.

He might yelp if an invisible presence touched him.

I'm scared.

Fright swirled inside her as she walked with Tyndall and his escort into the polished reception area, in full view of security staff and other personnel. And of the automated surveillance systems in place to guard the reactor site.

Inside the foyer, security personnel in blazers were dispensing badges to members of Tyndall's entourage. Tyndall needed no badge, but he must have been carrying some form of electronic ID, because he walked through the security barriers to the far side of the lobby with no alarms sounding.

Beyond, silver-haired men and women in good suits were waiting, and the glad-handing began. Several were politicians recognizable from webcasts, but not at Billy Church's level: the PM would not be here until tomorrow, for the ceremony proper.

Some twenty members of Tyndall's party were bunched up at the security desks. The number of badges laid out was greater than the number of visitors – some of the badges, clearly, being intended for others who would arrive later. Delays in clearing visitors were probably commonplace: hence the restrooms this side of the barriers.

Suzanne slipped away to use the ladies' room, passing through a three-metre steel oval to do so. Some kind of scanner designed to pick up weaponry. It did not react.

Hers were weapons of the mind.

She sat in a cubicle atop the closed seat, eyes shut, revisiting a sequence of stored and vivid scenarios in her mind, each associated with a particular strong emotion. The sequence was deliberate, a chain leading from calm through confidence to massive determination. Then she visualised herself penetrating deeply into the reactor complex: first as if in a movie, then floating inside her imagined self, experiencing it through her own eyes.

Approaching the desk for real, she headed for one particular security man, keying her gait to his breathing, phase-locking to his physiology. She smiled at him, pointed to one of the badges, and said with certainty: "You can see my badge is there, for me to check in OK."

"I'm not–"

Wavering.

"I like visiting here because you're so good to give me the badge now."

"Sure."

He handed over the badge and Suzanne clipped it on.

"Thank you," she said. "It's all OK."

An indicator flicked red as she passed through the gate, but only to her sight – the security man saw nothing untoward. With luck it was a minor warning that he could override by ignoring it.

As Suzanne waited, the icon changed back to green.

Good.

She went in among the larger group, smiling like them: professional, not casual. It was easy to avoid conversation. She picked up a champagne glass from a passing waiter. Presumably there was going to be food elsewhere, but the visitors needed drinks before proceeding.

There.

Beyond the group, a hard-faced man stood. His suit was cheap. Teardrop tattoos slid down his cheekbones as he watched for a while, then turned away and headed down a corridor.

Suzanne followed.

You're one of them.

She could enumerate the details she had noticed, but it was intuition that made the connection. The man up ahead resembled the Armenians, Nik and Kari and the others, who had come for her in Paris. The Gestalt totality was greater than the sum of its parts.

Scared but still functioning, she followed his route: left-right-right-left along corridors, to some kind of loading bay or garage. It was large and echoing, pipes everywhere. Three 4x4 vehicles were parked inside.

Besides the man she had trailed here, there were six men and two women, all with similar complexions, two with motile teardrop tattoos. One of them glanced at her, then raised his phone.

A heavy steel door rolled shut, closing off the loading bay from the corridor where she stood. She flinched as electromag bolts clunked home.

That told me.

The bigwigs were treating this as a networking opportunity, but these guys wanted to be left alone. Perhaps they were under orders to stay out of the way, since they did not fit in with

Tyndall's people – either the on-site security company or his personal protection crew – or with the police officers she had glimpsed at the outer gates and while driving through the plant.

If these people were who she suspected, then perhaps Professor Rashid Badakian was here already. Because these were Badakian's personal muscle, the ones who worked black ops – that was what Josh would have called it – that not even the Tyndalls' normal security would contemplate. Or so she guessed.

There was more she should have talked to Josh about. But he would have tried to persuade her not to do this. She would have had to use all her skills to change his mind; and that was not what their relationship should be about.

Get going.

Her feet did not move.

"How courageous of you to get this far."

A voice from nothingness.

No. Something else.

It was like an alien ship de-cloaking in the old movies. One moment there was only a bare corridor, then the air was rippling and a shaven-headed, goateed man dressed in an expensive suit was standing there.

Badakian.

She had time for intellectual understanding – what she had done to Tyndall, Badakian had done to her – and then the world was shivering into liquid, streaming around and around in a turbulent whirlpool as she fell down the centre–

I'm sorry, Josh.

–and drowned.

Suzanne's phone had a silent vibrate mode, so she should have been able to receive his call, no matter the circumstances. But no matter how many times Josh called, he not only failed to get a reply – he could not even track her position via GPS. He sat in his stationary car, trying every portal and backdoor hack he could think of, getting nowhere.

"Why the hell did you do it?"

But there was no way he could get angry, because there was only one reason that made sense, and that was to confront Badakian. Her motivation might have been to face her fears – she had surely been frightened by him during their first meeting – but that was not how her mind worked. She would not have seen it as a macho challenge.

Oh, Suzanne.

She might have gone for Badakian in order to protect someone else.

Protecting me.

Then he used an old psych trick taught to him at Fort Bragg on an exchange tour, though he could do it better now that he had learned so much from Suzanne: he constructed an imaginary box to contain his worries – a secure silver box with a peculiar sheen – and popped in a fluttering scroll that bore Suzanne's face and represented his worries for her.

Then the lid closed and he forced the box into a distant imaginary hillside, thrusting it into the ground and burying it, with a promise to retrieve it later, to open the box and bring what was buried back into the light.

Call it compartmentalization.

Badakian. Zak Tyndall.

Even the old man, Zebediah, if he was there.

I'm coming to get you all.

If Badakian had caught Suzanne, he could force her to tell everything she knew about Josh's plans. From what Josh had seen – and everything he had read and heard – the bastard would break down her defences – even hers – and get her to talk.

Under other circumstances, it might have been enough to cancel the mission and try something different at a later date.

Not this time.

For one thing, Suzanne did not know what he planned to do.

[THIRTY-FIVE]

Dusk, with bark and leaves appearing to glow amid enveloping gloom. Against a wooded slope of Burnham Beeches – an area of woods that was not quite forest and definitely not wilderness, not here in Berkshire – a clay-spattered piece of machinery started up.

It used a rotating cone with a screw thread, looking like some device created in the neighbouring rebooted Pinewood Studios. But the dented look and grinding vibration indicated it was well used, and real. If there had been anyone nearby to examine it, they might have dug beneath embedded clay to find a logo and asset tag: property of Hardin Construction Ltd.

Should anyone check the nearest Hardin premises, in Slough Trading Estate, they would find forensic system evidence to show someone subverting the gate locks and stealing a carrier vehicle with a tunnel digger, but nothing to suggest the thief's identity.

The borer churned into motion.

Now that it was activated, it would perform its function with robustness. There were more modern pieces of kit, but this design was proven and rarely broke down. Now, it flung soil behind it in some machine parody of a mole digging a tunnel.

But this mole was headed diagonally down then horizontally straight on a specific route.

Directly towards the Burnham nuclear reactor.

Krill's team were called the Blades. They already had what it took to step inside the arena and fight with live weapons, though few of them had fought totally unarmoured. But they were young and up for it, increasingly devoted to Cutter Krill as he fostered a mirror image of his warrior-psychosis inside their heads.

Perhaps that was why they had broken every rule of the Knife Edge Challenge reality show, and departed from the fighters' house en masse.

Krill drove one of the three people carriers, heading for the southern end of Burnham Beeches. They could have run from the fighters' house – they were fit enough – but the vehicles were quicker. Just in case some technician with a phonecam had filmed them.

Soon enough, everyone would know what they were up to.

"Ready for this, lads?"

Because that was the point of the whole exercise.

Carlsen and Sigmund looked at each other. In the back of their van, Big Andy and Little Pete were checking their weapons. Angie was giving little bounces up and down on her seat, as if she had springs in her limbs.

"They want to fight," said Sigmund. "They *so* want to fight."

"We have to be ready," said Carlsen. "It might come to that."

"But you'd rather they didn't. Not outside the arena."

"I'd rather they didn't have to."

Sigmund moved his ursine body, pulling his lips back in the pseudo-smile of a bear about to bite.

"But if they have to?"

Carlsen looked back at his students, who were also his friends.

"Then they're ready to win," he said.

Suzanne roused briefly, blinking at the sight of a winking red light and the piercing howl of an alarm. But she felt gorgeously warm as though in a hot bath, and her chin went back down as her eyes closed and she slipped down the long, easy slope into restful sleep.

Ten minutes after nightfall, Krill and his group appeared out of the woods like a band of warriors from a thousand years before. In place of shields, they carried rubberized mats from the fighters' house gym, along with ladders stolen from the house maintenance stores, and magnesium lamps that flared white as they were lit.

The group descended the slope at a jog, the mats bobbing with the motion.

As the first fighters reached the perimeter fence, they leaned the ladders up against it, then held them in place. Others clambered up with mats in hand and laid them across the razor wire on top. Magnesium lamps swinging, they swarmed over the edge and dropped.

Krill was among them.

Everyone rolled to their feet straight into a running gait, sprinting for the pipe-encrusted domes of the power station. The installation was lit by white and orange floodlights, around which tiny drone helicopters roamed.

By the time they were four hundred metres from the site proper, klaxons were sounding and vehicles were roaring. Drones overhead, in triangular formation, were heading for the group.

The final piece of equipment they had brought was a single container of Bonfire Jelly. Krill's assistant Chiang sprayed it in an oval on the grass.

The rest of the group came to a heavy-breathing halt.

"Hurry up." Chiang pulled out an old-fashioned lighter. "We've less than a minute."

He touched the lighter to the spread-out gel. Orange flames leaped.

"Why are we doing this?" yelled Krill.

"Because we're mad!" shouted the Blades.

Moving fast, they pulled their clothes off.

And tossed them into the fire.

"The choppers are closing in," said Chiang.

"Stop looking at my chopper," said Krill. "Come on, everyone! Time to dance."

They began to cavort around the bonfire, moving anti-clockwise, leaping with knees high while everything that could dangle or bounce did so. They yelled and laughed like idiots as they danced their music-less dance, hands high in the air, their buck-naked bodies orange in reflected flames.

Everything was on show: their nakedness, their lack of weapons or any place to hide one. Laughing and making noise, they were clearly no threat. When the NPD jeeps pulled up and the counter-terrorist teams rolled out in full armour with Heckler & Koch shrapnel guns locked and loaded, their training kicked in. They held back from letting loose.

Behind their masks, several NPD officers began to smile.

After the drones, three full-sized helicopters slid through the air over the cleared ground, heading some fifteen degrees away from a line between the main reactor pile and the naked fighters. The fighters were meekly holding their wrists out for binding, allowing themselves to be led inside the NPD vans.

But the helicopters were heading for a different disturbance, one picked up by the seismic sensors laid out in an underground array around the entire site. The new threat was below ground, heading for the mesoreactor.

Underneath each helicopter was slung a thermal sensor array. Every one of them picked up the heat signature of Josh Cumberland as he crouched in place amid the beech trees, ready to make his run. But although the sensors picked up the infra-red radiation, what they displayed on the pilots' consoles was entirely different.

All instruments indicated uninhabited woods, free from intruders.

Meanwhile, whatever was boring through the ground was coming to a halt.

Good.

Josh would have liked the borer to penetrate closer to the reactor, at least within the power plant's nominal perimeter, but he could not allow it to go further for the same reason that the helicopters had taken to the air so quickly: any under-ground incursion was a serious danger, regardless of whether the borer carried an explosive payload.

The machine was a diversion. Damaging the reactor was hardly the plan.

It still was not time to go. Josh checked the harness he wore, and the extending line wrapped around his waist, for maybe the tenth time.

What's keeping you?

Then he saw it: two more helicopters with white beams flaring downwards, heading into the opposite direction from the two incursions.

Well done, guys.

Someone had figured out that Krill's bonfire party and the burrowing mole machine were possible diversions. The two distractions were taking place roughly in the same place – some fifteen degrees apart, on radii drawn from the reactor core itself – therefore the obvious place to look for a quiet in-cursion was diametrically opposite, on the far side of the site.

Which was *not* where Josh was waiting.

Now he moved.

Zen and the art of infiltration. Timeflow dropped to zero as he moved over the fence – subversion ware running, so the cameras failed to report what they observed – his awareness totally in the world. He sensed the texture of every blade of grass as he crept across open ground in a commando crawl, and fetched up amid a tangle of piping on a heat exchange unit.

Then he moved through the installation, heading for the admin block.

It was wide but a modest seven storeys tall. Residential apartments for visiting board members and other VIPs formed the top floor. That was where Zak Tyndall would be.

The meeting point between a buttress and the outer wall formed a climbing opportunity, out of sight from roving patrols. Spyball cameras abounded, but his subversion ware was deep inside the system. No one could spot him now.

He pressed feet, body and hands against vertical surfaces, and climbed using counterpressure.

At the top floor, every window had electromag locks keyed in to the integrated system. That was why they clicked open as he drew level, tilted the pane, and crawled over the sill, coming down in a crouch.

Pressure pads beneath the carpet responded to his weight, but the building system ignored them.

Let's find out who's here.

An old man was sleeping in the bedroom.

Talk about harmless-looking.

Zebediah Tyndall's white hair was mussed and splayed on the pillow. But to the children kept comatose and used as virapharm factories in Africa, his current vulnerability mattered less than his vindictive manipulation of the world. Josh pulled a pad from his pocket, and held his breath as he tore off a protective cover. He pressed the pad down on the old man's face.

Tyndall's breathing quietened.

Josh stripped off his harness and wrapped it around the old man, trussing him, snapping safety catches into place. It was no effort to lift him up, drape him over one shoulder, and carry him back to the window. There, Josh propped the unconscious Tyndall on the sill, checked the karabiners, and took up a belay position.

He rolled Tyndall over the edge.

I should let you drop, you bastard.

Paying out the line, he lowered Tyndall to ground level. Then he redfanged a control code to release the catches, and hauled the empty harness back up. Tyndall lay in a heap below.

It was a cold night. If son Zak was not here yet, Josh would need to shift the old man before coming back. At this hour, Zak was probably drinking champagne with his cronies: the constant networking and manipulation of the high-flying tycoon.

But Josh had reckoned without some dependent or sentimental streak in Zak Tyndall's personality. A click sounded at the apartment's outer door, and Josh spun away to crouch behind a chair.

Zak came in, used his phone to switch on low orange lighting, and crept to the empty bedroom.

"Dad?" whispered Zak Tyndall. "Are you sleeping?"

Josh punched him in the side of the neck.

"Ach–"

Tyndall's limbs twitched, then he was out.

Josh used another narcotic pad pressed against Tyndall's face to make sure. Then he repeated the operation he had carried out with the father: harness, lock, over the window sill, lower to the ground.

That done, Josh followed, abseiling down the line in seconds. From the ground, he redfanged the release code. The top of the line came free, and it fell like a coiling snake.

Josh squatted down, grabbed each Tyndall by his collar, and

pressed up as he rose. The narcotic drug made their bodies stiffer than a normal sleeping person, making them easier to manipulate to an upright position. Then he dipped slightly to catch them, one Tyndall draped over each shoulder.

He rounded the building and stopped behind a van with the NPD logo on the side. The back of the van popped open.

Carlsen and his team were naked in the back. They grinned. A man in NPD uniform stepped down from the interior and nodded to Josh.

"Hey, Josh."

"Who are you?"

The man touched his ear. Immediately dark shapes moved across one side of his face and shivered into a static pattern.

Tiger stripes.

"Shane," said Josh. "I didn't realize–"

Again a touch on the earlobe, and the tiger-stripe tattoos dissolved to invisibility.

"Electric ink," said Shane. "I wouldn't be much for under-cover work without it."

"Good point. You're taking these fuckers off me?"

Carlsen and the others hauled the Tyndalls inside and began to strip them.

"This is so kinky," said Shane.

"No," said Angie. "It's bloody cold."

Josh tried not to stare at her nipples.

"No trouble getting in?" he said to Shane.

"Of course not." Shireen climbed down from the front. "You OK?"

"Yeah. I've Suzanne and Badakian to find, and we're out of here."

Once the panic was on, the NPD vans had begun going in and out. That was when the MI5 team had taken their own genuine NPD van inside the perimeter. With naked prisoners already on board, though the security teams did not know that.

They would assume, when the van left, that it was another batch of loony trespassers picked up within the perimeter.

"Twenty minutes," said Shireen. "That's our cut-off."

"Got it."

At that point they would bug out. The Tyndalls would have disappeared with no one knowing how or why. So long as the van got clear, the main objective was achieved.

Except that Josh's goal had changed, now that Suzanne was here.

Where, exactly?

Expecting nothing, he pinged her phone anyway.

The display flared.

"That's her location?" said Shane. "Back in there?"

The x-y-z coordinates should be accurate to within sixty centimetres. She was on the third floor of the admin block according to his display.

"Yeah. But she's been offline and shielded from resonance for hours."

"So this is suspect," said Shireen.

"Right. You might want to rethink the cut-off time and get clear now."

"We'll wait."

He climbed back up to the seventh-floor apartment and entered. There, he stopped to load false-image software into local cache, along with the double collection of interfaces – those it provided and those it expected the other party to implement – for driving the programs from afar.

This was for phase three, if he made it that far.

Out on a landing bigger than the floor area of most houses, he peeked over the steel banister, down into the stairwell. Clear. Subversion ware doing its thing with the spycams, he jogged without sound down to the fourth floor. Then he checked the doorway on level three.

Two security guards, looking stoic.

All right. Let's wake you up.

He worked his phone, checked the app configuration, then pressed the touchpad.

There we go.

Locks clattered everywhere on the second floor, staccato echoes in the stairwell as electromag bolts flicked open and shut at random, a thunderous click-clack covering Josh's moves. One guard was looking over the rail while his mate went downstairs.

Neither turned as Josh slipped through the door they were guarding.

Thank you very much.

Outside, the clattering died to silence.

Here, the space was open plan, desks arranged in groups, shadows everywhere. Illumination came from the floodlights outside the windows.

None of the shadows moved.

At the far end stood an inner office, a block-shaped room extending into the workspace. Its walls were dark, rather than transparent: tunable glass, set to opacity. Either Suzanne was in there, or the data that his phone was reading had been faked.

He sent an ultrasound pulse towards the wall, and read the returned signal.

Suzanne.

Two people were inside, sitting in what looked like armchairs. No traps waited.

Correction: no *electronic* traps.

Because this was Professor Rashid Badakian, sitting at an angle to Suzanne, whose weapons were words and a detailed understanding of human behaviour, coupled with zero empathy and reptilian determination.

But Josh had a reptile of his own.

Move now.

He pressed against his ears, then used his phone to work the locks. He walked into the room.

"Mr Cumberland." Badakian looked up from his chair. "How good to see you."

Josh thumbed his phone.

Everything you do.

Badakian's lips were moving.

Makes me want to run. Home.

Will you get me going—

Growing larger, Badakian's eyes.

—home. Will you get me going—

Kids in Glass Houses, an early number from Josh's youth, pounded in his earbeads. It was loud but not enough.

Badakian stopped talking, aware that his words were not getting through; but other things began to happen.

No.

Eyes like saucers.

Give me what I want—

Suzanne had talked about synchronizing breathing but this was something more. As Badakian made hand gestures, Josh felt his own body adjusting, whether towards or away from the hands he could not tell.

Eyes like plates.

Give me—

Music fading in and out, the world itself seeming to blink.

Badakian was making what you might call mystic passes but there was no such thing as magic, only phenomena subject to rational investigation. Josh *knew* that all the way down to his core but it did not seem to help as the world began to whirl.

Suzanne had demonstrated the power of non-verbal trance induction, but never like this. He was fighting to remain awake but his eyes were drooping, so hard to pull them up, to realize what he had to do.

Give in.

It was the only way.

–is it you want me to know?

I give up on you–

Eyelids pulling down.

Let it go.

Give me–

Allowing his shoulders to slump.

–what I want–

And he felt fingers fumbling at his ears because the only way to continue induction once the subject's eyes were closed was using words, and that was why Badakian was pulling the ear-beads out–

Reptile.

–in one smooth motion, his voice reverberating like that of God as he began to–

Loose the reptile.

–speak once more, the human-primate portions of Josh's mind under Badakian's control, totally at his–

Now.

–command, but the head snapped forward and the hands rose like claws–

Yes.

–smashing Badakian's face and ripping at his eyes–

More.

–and Josh snarled as his body leaped forward with the right elbow whipping high and arcing into Badakian's temple–

The reptile was loose.

–and the body's knee pumped into the adversary's testicles – first strike – then bladder – second – liver – third and out. Josh stepped back as Badakian dropped. Even unconscious, the bastard groaned, because a shattered liver hurts.

Josh's body stamped down once with the right heel to the adversary's head–

Stop now.

–and then he shuddered as he came back into control. The reptile bared its fangs in the evolutionary precursor to a smile, then curled back into its recess in his mind and grew quiescent.

Ready for the next time.

Good.

Now, only now, could he look at Suzanne. Before she had been an object in the environment, nothing more, because reptiles do not love. He knelt, kissing her, but she did not rouse. The softest of snores came from her. No way was she going to wake up.

No matter.

He retrieved his phone, thumbed off the Kids in Glass Houses, and tagged the phone to his belt. He had wanted to extract both Suzanne and Badakian with no one the wiser, but his harness and line were up on the seventh floor. The guards outside would not be fooled for a second time.

Then his phone vibrated, and he smiled.

There were no windows in this inner office, so he dimmed the lights and stepped out into the open plan area. He cracked open an outer window and peered down.

Carlsen and his crew, thankfully, were wearing clothes. Also, they were standing in a camera blindzone.

Josh grinned down at them.

Big Andy and Little Pete clambered up like orang-utans with an agility that surprised Josh: their pure strength was huge, but they were heavy with muscle. Still they managed it, with rappel-lines wrapped around their waists.

In minutes, they had lowered Suzanne and Badakian to ground level, and descended themselves. Carlsen draped Badakian over one shoulder.

"Back to the van?" he murmured.

"Yes," said Josh. "You get clear."

"You're coming with us."

"No." Josh glanced back to the top of the building. "I've evidence to get rid of. And I can leave the way I came."

"That's not the safest–Right." Carlsen shut himself up. "We're gone."

Big Andy carried Suzanne, and the three men – Big Andy, Little Pete and Carlsen – jogged off in silence with their human burdens.

Josh was alone again.

Good.

Phase two achieved.

He moved around the building's base until he came once more to the buttress where he had climbed before. This time he continued all the way to the roof.

There, he rolled beneath an overhanging vent some three metres wide, and checked the thermal readings on his phone. Combined with his subversion ware, escaping heat would disguise his thermal signature, if he used a heat-dispersing sheet.

From his thigh pocket, he took out a roll of flimsy-looking black material, extended it like a cloak over him, and settled down.

He closed his eyes.

After a while the shivering came, but it was an old friend and he welcomed becoming an observer in his own body as it shook and curled and tightened, reacting to the plummeting of adrenaline, the aftermath of action. Afterwards, as it s ubsided, muscle groups loosened while he made no attempt to regain control.

Instead he allowed himself to fall into sleep.

She's safe.

Suzanne was clear so everything else was a bonus.

Safe.

And so he slept.

[THIRTY-SIX]

At 7.30am, one of the Tyndalls' assistants made calls to both Zak Tyndall and his father Zebediah. Both calls were answered. Both men said they were not hungry and required no breakfast. Each agreed that he would be ready at 10 o'clock for the beginning of the ceremony, when they would greet the arriving prime minister – although it would be Billy Church who walked up to them, not the other way round.

Both Tyndalls said they had private work to engage in, and would take no further calls before ten. The assistant said, "Yes, sir," both times.

That done, Josh sent the kill signal, and his locally stored software committed electronic suicide, erasing all traces of itself. It had been Josh who had responded to the assistant's words, while the software changed Josh's image and voice to Zak and Zebediah Tyndall's in turn.

He settled back beneath the ventilator housing to rest some more.

At three minutes before ten, the prime minister's armoured limousine, with an escort of cars and police motorcycles, entered the power station premises and drove to the red carpet, where it stopped. Senior management and personal assistants stood there, unable to look anything but nervous.

Neither Tyndall was answering his phone.

Finally, an enterprising executive grabbed a security officer and ascended to the seventh floor. They used emergency lock-overrides to enter the apartments and look for Zak and Zebediah Tyndall.

The apartments were empty.

It was another five minutes before the klaxons sounded, and emergency teams poured out around the installation: engineers and officers of the NPD alike, all looking for the missing Tyndalls. Meanwhile, the prime minister's Special Branch protection team bundled him back into his limousine, and the whole entourage screamed out of the power plant, hurtling to London.

Reporters observed that Billy Church looked pale and sick inside the car.

Soon helicopters and miniature drones were everywhere, scanning the rooftops, while vehicles and people on foot scoured the buildings and grounds. The local encrypted comms net grew so busy that the connection pool became full. Links dropped or failed to form, forcing them to go to public cloud communications.

There, heavy-duty encryption was illegal – by the Enhanced Communications Act that Zebediah Tyndall had masterminded from behind the scenes. Within ten minutes, Google-Reuters journalists had the full story.

The reporters on-site were frantic to create their own reports, but the NPD took them into custody, in a paranoid reaction that would later backfire to create a public relations disaster.

At 10.17am precisely, the story broke worldwide.

Josh remembered watching a webmovie with Suzanne, called *The Sinkiang Executive*. The producers had not employed the same team as in the rest of the series. When the agent hero was tailing the bad guys, they spotted him. When he broke into the enemy HQ, he tripped an alarm. Both times, he got clear by fighting hordes of armed enemy agents with improbably poor aims.

"Why are you shaking your head?" Suzanne had asked. "Aren't the fights realistic enough?"

"It's the opposite to the book," he told her. "This idiot has shoddy tradecraft. No one should spot him tailing them. He should be in and out of the building with no one the wiser."

"I never thought of that."

The Ghost Force motto said it all:

GHOST FORCE

you didn't see us we weren't there

He tensed, then relaxed his muscles.

So far so good.

If they searched the roof in person, he might need to make a move. But for now, this was the perfect position to lay up in. He closed his eyes, breathed in slowly, then exhaled.

Relaxing deeply.

At around the same time, two people – an NPD officer on site and a member of the prime minister's staff in Number 10 – independently realised that there was one other person who had entered the Burnham reactor installation but not left, yet could not be raised on the phone or found in person.

His name was Professor Rashid Badakian.

The subsequent flurry of messages was confined to the encrypted net. Nevertheless, the conclusion was that the information should go public, given that the world already knew of the Tyndalls' disappearance.

One minute before the information was due to be released, a DA-notice arrived at all relevant communication nexuses, killing the webcast.

A member of the Joint Intelligence Committee called Flora McIntosh – accompanied by one of her officers, Trinity Purcell – had persuaded the other members that no purpose would be served by advertising the disappearance of someone with covert and questionable links to the British intelligence services.

Speculation about the Tyndalls' fate, from the least-informed commentators to political and intelligence service insiders, continued to rise.

By nightfall, desperation was showing in the faces of investigating officers, while on news sites, suppressed glee shone in the eyes of reporters. This was the best story since last year's West Coast destruction, and far more palatable.

Not to mention mysterious.

Lying still, and given the well-chosen food he had eaten the day before yesterday, there was no need for a bowel movement. As for urination, there were pads inside his underwear for that.

The glamour of special operations.

The pads also killed the smell, as an aid to avoiding detection. Otherwise the military would not have bothered to develop the pads, because comfort was not their top priority.

A true professional would slip out during darkness and leave them to it, leave everybody wondering what had happened. Here and now, his mission should be over.

Objective achieved.

He risked using his phone to check the local system logs. As suspected, he was not the only visitor to have remained on the premises once the official panic had commenced. The thing was, they were not truly official, no more than he was.

That meant that, whatever happened to them, their own people would hide the evidence.

Good enough.

If they slipped out before he was ready, then he would have to let it go. Otherwise, he was going to indulge himself, because they should not have tried to harm Suzanne.

Tomorrow evening.

If they were still here at that time, he would go for it.

So relax.

That was hours away, and this was the here and now: the hot ventilator housing, the darkness of the night, the roughness of the roof beneath him.

Relax.

He drifted into the kind of sleep he could jerk out of at any time.

Relax.

And sleep.

At 10am the next day, July second, it became official: Zak and Zebediah Tyndall had been missing for twenty-four hours. Shares in their companies had tumbled, and long-term corporate rivals were already swarming to the attack, starting with the most vulnerable assets.

No one mentioned Rashid Badakian.

Relax.

While on the rooftop, hidden beneath the ventilator housing, Josh continued to sleep.

Despite the chill weather, this was still the height of nominal summer. At this latitude, sunset was late. It was nearly 11pm when Josh completed his warm-up exercises on the darkened rooftop. Then he crossed to a maintenance hatch, worked his electronic magic with the locks, and slipped inside the building.

He descended all the way to ground level, bypassing human guards while his subversion ware did its usual work on the surveillance system. Then he followed a featureless corridor all the way to a heavy steel door, which he pushed open. Beyond was a loading bay, cavernous and cold, containing three large 4x4 vehicles with silvered windows.

A dozen men were inside, perhaps more in the vehicles. Several of the men had motile teardrop tattoos on their cheekbones.

"I don't know how to say hello in Armenian," said Josh.

"*Bozi txa*," said one of them.

"I'll bet that doesn't really mean hello."

He took five paces across the hard concrete, then stopped. Three of the men moved to take up positions between him and the door. The silence became solid, broken only by the rustle of clothing and the sound of quickened breathing.

The biggest and hardest-looking of the men took one step towards Josh.

"Trapped," he said.

Josh raised his phone. From the steel door behind him came the clunk of electromag bolts sliding home.

"Yes, you are."

The reptile was cold, computing algorithms of violence and blood; while the primate ran hot with outrage because of the things these men had done.

The organism that was Josh Cumberland drove forward with a single purpose, kicking through the big man's knee, but knowing that was not enough, that the big man could override the long-term injury long enough to strike back; so Josh's punches were a wing chun flurry followed by clasping the back of his target's head left-handed while his right forearm whipped in, elbow smashing the eye socket.

He used a double-handed grip-and-rotate while his body

revolved, using the bastard's head to spin the body to the floor, vertebrae crunching as they broke.

One.

A foot was curving in towards Josh's spleen – *too fast* – and there was no time to avoid so he lunged into the oncoming kick – *damn it* – taking the rolling impact on his ribs, slipping his right calf behind the kicker's support leg and reaping back. A judo man would keep his upper body in contact with the opponent but that increased the chances of going to ground, so Josh went with the shuai chiao version of the throw, thrusting with both hands.

As the man dropped, Josh continued his spin with a rear hooking elbow to another bastard's face, then reversed the spin to whip back with the opposite elbow. The third strike was downward to the back of the exposed neck.

The bastard he had thrown was getting back up, but Josh scoop-kicked his hands away, driving through, slammed in a knee, then dropped an axe kick onto the head.

Three.

The next man lunged for a single-leg takedown like a rugby tackle, but the reptile in Josh's brain picked up the precursor to the attack, reacting early, before needing to sprawl – *shoulder* – ramming the edge of his right hand against the guy's left shoulder to stop him – *got it* – then whipping his left forearm across the guy's face, encircling the head.

Josh leaned his chest against the back of the head, left hand in the crook of his right elbow, and drove up to push the neck crank all the way.

The snap was very loud.

Four.

He had established a pattern of attack so he changed it, blocking a punch, driving his crooked right thumb into an eye to force the chin up, then a left shovel hook into the exposed larynx, reacting as fingers felt for his shoulders, but he broke the grip to spin away.

Five.

If two or three reached him simultaneously he was done for, so he zigged and zagged across the concrete floor. Seven bastards likewise moved around, trying to close in and crowd him, their footwork like some homicidal basketball game on a high-speed court.

No firearms. Perhaps they were in the vehicles.

Impact against his head.

Blackening, the world spun, fluorescent streamers across his vision. He whirled, processing a distant shout, and the others fell back instead of closing in, which meant he was in danger – *gun* – so he grabbed the bastard who had hit him, the wavering silhouette which flickered in the madness of the world he was not back in synch with, not yet.

A double thump sounded, two shots fired through a silencer – *missed* – and then he spun the bastard again, keeping him as a shield. The third thump sounded and strawberry mist flew from the bastard's head.

The gunman – at the vehicles, a thirteenth man – must have realised his comrade was dead because he continued firing. Josh kept the corpse as his shield for two seconds longer before throwing himself headfirst through the air – *faster* – right hand at his left hip as his right shoulder rolled on concrete – wall-ceiling-wall flashing across his vision – and his knife was in his hand as he came up to his feet and threw.

Most knife-throwing is for show, but Soviet Spetsnaz commandos perfected the battlefield art, and these Armenians must have known that. Horror widened the gunman's eyes in the tenth of a second before the blade pierced his carotid artery.

Blood spurting, he was down with twelve seconds to live.

Seven.

Two men closing from opposite directions.

Josh went for the nearer, grabbing a sleeve to whirl the bastard onward, and they struggled to avoid collision, but not well enough. Josh kicked a knee and threw punches – cross-hook-cross – then a big palm-heel slam to drive one head into another, because both men were on him now.

It was an eight-limbed organism he fought, a tangle-limbed being, and he needed to get clear – *others coming* – but then he saw a target – *throat shot* – driving in a right hammer fist, a left precision punch – *got it* – then delivered the hardest groin kick of his life – *yes* – and knew from the gasp it was likely to be fatal.

Josh dodged the other man, back to the groin-kick victim, and a downward stamp to make sure.

Nine.

That left four alive but not for long because this was his time and the end of theirs, the bastards who had harmed so many. The next man was easy because a kind of fatalism had set in, seeing what happened to his comrades. His punches were weak or perhaps Josh's body was powered by greater adrenaline.

Josh's forearms beat the limbs aside to cause pain and clear the way, then he threw kick-punch-kick-elbow, an arpeggio targeting spleen-heart-liver-temple, and stepped back to spin through a three-quarter circle, effective because unexpected, heel ripping through the air: an arc that passed right through the bastard's head.

A knee-drop to follow, in case of doubt.

Ten.

Three left but these bastards were not giving in.

The first to close in had a knife in each hand, but that was not enough because Josh tangled the arms together, his wrists maintaining contact with the bastard's forearms, like the *chi sao* sticking hands he had shown Suzanne so long ago. His own knife was gone, but that did not matter, because the world was full of weapons and the loading dock was one of them.

Josh twisted in with the beginnings of an ankle-drop throw, but he drove the bastard horizontally over his outstretched right leg, head first into concrete.

Blood spattered from the skull.

Eleven.

He slipped a long curving punch, wrapped his arm around the puncher's throat and completed the triangle choke, turning it into a hip-throw, smashing the bastard into the ground and rolling clear, because another was on the attack.

Pain exploded in Josh's thigh and he was falling, but he went for the support ankle, hooking it, putting the side of his face against the lower leg as he shifted forward and the bastard fell back. But the bastard kicked out as he went, heel into Josh's face.

The world flickered as Josh rolled away.

The other man took hold of Josh's arm, going for the armbar – *go with it* – as Josh shoulder-rolled with his arm pointed straight out from the shoulder instead of curved – *free* – and he used his own feet in a leg-triangle, choking the bastard again, but the other bastard was on his feet, so Josh kicked out and rolled clear, retreating.

Both men were upright, coming for him.

You can do it.

The reptile and the primate were in agreement, but these men had reptiles of their own – and they were desperate as well as trained.

Previously, two had advanced so close together that Josh had been able to tangle them up. Now one led the other as they drew close – one to keep Josh busy while the other attacked from a blind angle – their success guaranteed unless he could smash through the nearer guy's defences before the other could close in.

Now.

The bastard was left-foot-forward as Josh stepped to his own right diagonal, ripping a hard left roundhouse kick high, cutting the angle for power. His instep blasted into the man's head, causing him to drop.

Josh used the fallen man like a small boulder, jumping one-footed onto the man's back and springing upward, driving a flying knee strike into the second man's face.

He pushed clear to assess the situation.

One bastard on hands and knees; one staggering, still on his feet.

Take them now.

He came at the standing man from the rear, forearm hooking under the throat from behind, then twisting into a classic hip throw but back-to-back, and whether the back-arching throw itself or the skull-to-concrete impact killed the bastard, Josh would never know.

Twelve.

Last man and it was easy, because the bastard was still wobbling when Josh's knee drove into his throat, a punch separated his cervical vertebrae, and a full body weight sprawl dropped him temple first onto concrete ground.

Thirteen.

Josh leaped to one side just in case, but no shots banged out. He zigzagged around the corpses to reach the 4x4 vehicles. He checked each one. They were empty. Every one of the Armenians was down.

Zero-sum unlucky.

Their bad luck was his triumph.

So what?

He needed to get clear before adrenaline withdrawal and remorse set in.

Thirteen down, and all those teenagers still dead.

He thought one of them twitched but it was an illusion, a movement of spreading blood. It did not take long to check their pulses and find none.

Good enough.

Time to get clear.

[THIRTY-SEVEN]

They put Carlsen and Krill in the same cell, the next one along from Big Andy, Little Pete and Lewis Chiang. All were dressed in prison-style coveralls, though this was a police station, not jail.

After some two hours, the cell door clicked open, and seven of the biggest police officers Carlsen had ever seen came inside.

"Uh-oh," said Krill.

Carlsen and Krill backed away together, so that a wall was behind them.

I won't let this happen.

Then the lead cop held up his massive hands.

"It's OK, guys," he said.

"Yeah, it fucking will be," muttered Krill, "if you take one step closer."

"No, no," said another officer. "You don't get it. We're all fighters. Actually, we're competing in the police nationals in Hendon next month."

"You're fighters," said Carlsen.

"Well, yeah."

Krill shrugged his shoulders, then rotated them out of phase, like bicycle pedals. Getting ready.

"So what do you want?" he said.

"Er... could we have your autographs?" said the first cop.

"Our autographs."

"Yeah, and maybe... How did you prepare for your fight with Mad Mick Foster?"

"And" – this was the other cop – "what about the time you took out Hitman Raye with a single strike?"

Krill looked at Carlsen, then back at the policemen.

"That was easy," Krill said, "'cause I knew that whenever he lunged with his right..."

Two hours later, the officers left bearing not just autographs but the memory of working out – in a cell – with two of the sport's superstars, plus open invitations to train in both their fight gyms, leaving reciprocal invitations for Carlsen and Krill to come and coach the police, as well as attend the Midsummer Christmas party being thrown by the Met at a hotel in Kensington.

Friends for life.

[THIRTY-EIGHT]

Midsummer Christmas, and they had a guest for lunch. Carol Klugmann raised a glass of champagne towards Josh and Suzanne. Her vast bosom jiggled with the gesture. Before her lay the detritus of her third portion of Christmas pudding and brandy custard.

Josh and Suzanne raised their glasses.

"To sanity and sex," said Carol.

"Sanity and sex," repeated Josh and Suzanne.

They drank the toast.

Afterward, Josh curled up next to Suzanne on the couch, and Carol took the armchair, while they watched the realtime general election results coming in on the wallscreen.

Ongoing exit polls indicated zero seats for Fat Billy's LabCon Party and over two-thirds going over to the TechDems, while the smaller independent parties gobbled up the rest.

"Jolly good show," said Carol. "Or fuck you and die, Billy Church, as we say where I come from."

Josh grinned at her.

Late yesterday, Sharon Caldwell had delivered a webcast that drew vast attention, highlighting the wrongdoings of the Tyndalls and their cronies in Whitehall, and delivering the details of the cyberattack on the TechDems servers that had resulted in so many teenage deaths.

She made no mention of Badakian's name. Too much to hope for.

"That Laura Collins is some kind of babe," added Carol. "If I was a lesbian, that's just the kind of chick I'd go for."

"Jesus Christ," said Josh.

"It would give the male half of the population a break," said Suzanne.

"Honeychild, I done wore them out already."

Yesterday's speech by Caldwell had fomented rising anger against the LabCons but with a much smaller increase in sympathy towards the TechDems than expected. Part of that, according to Suzanne and Carol, was Caldwell's poor choice of words, so that the public still associated their mental images of teen suicide with the TechDems despite consciously knowing that the party members were innocent.

But Caldwell's campaign meeting this morning had been different, when a huge-bellied man had leaped from the crowd swinging an object towards Sharon Caldwell's head, wrong-footing her supporters and security. The object would prove to be a bag of rotten eggs, but it might have been a lethal weapon. Caldwell might have been a fraction of a second from death.

Until Laura Collins stepped forward and ripped down with both hands, breaking the attacker's collarbones on either side, before hurling him off to one side with a thrust of her palms.

"Tai-chi," said Josh now. "Always good for restoring calm."

Within minutes of the event being webcast, Sharon Caldwell's electoral victory was assured. Soon after midnight tonight, when the online voting finished and the realtime counts were double-checked, she would be the new prime minister.

Fat Billy Church had already offered his resignation to the

King, before disappearing from the public view, with luck forever.

The only sour note for Josh was his inability to reach Lofty or anyone else in the Regiment. Whether they remained on standby or were already flying to the former United States, ready to deploy, he had no way of knowing.

Suzanne slipped from the couch and crossed to the table, saying nothing.

Josh looked at Carol, who nodded.

This better go right.

He shifted his sitting position, so his right foot was forward and his left foot was back, enabling him to move fast. He swallowed as Suzanne came back.

"Hi," he said.

But Suzanne said nothing as she leaped forward, fork stabbing towards Josh's eye–

Avoid.

–as he rotated away, trapping her arm and batting the fork away – it tumbled through the air – and pushed her back into the couch, the breath *whuffing* out of her as she went back against the cushions. Without a word, she tried to come forward again to continue the attack, but Carol was already beside him, her speed of movement surprising, and her hand was across Suzanne's eyes as she said one simple word–

"Sleep."

–and Suzanne fell back, dropping deeply into trance.

She began to snore.

"Don't worry, lover boy," said Carol. "I'll wash out the last of Bastard Badakian's little suggestions, and she'll be fine."

"Christ, I hope so."

The day Josh had gone over the wire into the Burnham power plant, Carol had hypnotised him over the phone, removing his amnesia concerning the Armenians who attacked him in the Welsh forest after Evans' suicide. She ensured there were no unpleasant psychological booby traps in his mind implanted by the PulseTrance.

For Suzanne the process would take longer – she had spent hours in Badakian's company – but interrupting a triggered posthypnotic behaviour was a shortcut, according to Carol, in accessing the full list of further suggestions – if any – that Badakian might have implanted in her.

"She'll be the same as ever," added Carol now. "Unless you want me to double her sex drive?"

"I don't think I'll be able to keep up," said Josh. "Although, I suppose you could double mine to match."

"What makes you think I didn't do that already, stud?" Carol smiled. "I had you in trance for half an hour, buddy-boy. You wouldn't believe what I can achieve in that much time."

"Actually, I think I would."

He went to the kitchen bar to make some coffee, while Carol commenced her work.

[THIRTY-NINE]

July twelfth, and Josh was pounding up a mountain slope. The air was clear, the sky bluer than it had been all year. The news sites all said that the climate had reached a tipping-point, that the ash was precipitating from the sky, promising a real summer for next year.

The pack on his back was heavy and the burning in his lungs was intense, because he had been on the go for twenty-eight hours on a mountain ultramarathon, and this was near the end.

Yellow beacon.

It was the final obstacle for Selection, the long journey under harsh conditions and the cut-off time of thirty hours. But the beacon that had shone in his mind as a visualization, drawing him towards his goal, was now very real as he pushed up the slope of Pen-y-Fan while all around the lay the magnificence of the Brecon Beacons, a wilderness he would be able to appreciate once the tunnel vision of stress had dissipated.

Once he had reached the objective.

Yellow beacon, and I've passed.

His phone showed the countdown, and he could slow a little and still have an hour to spare, but the problem with stopping was that it might be for good, because restarting was harder than continuing, however much it hurt.

Push it.

Pounding in what felt like an uphill sprint, but must look like a stagger.

Push faster.

Yellow beacon, bigger than it had been inside his mind's eye.

Faster.

And then he touched it, somatic reality impinging on pure visualization. So this was it: the end of his quest to prove himself.

"I did it."

"Yes," said the woman's voice. "You did it."

Mission achieved.

"With an hour to spare," she added.

Objective attained.

"Still got… what… it takes."

"You do, Josh Cumberland."

Gasping, but there was no need to collapse as he had thought he might; because this was victory and winners remain standing, so that was what he did right now.

"You always do," Suzanne added.

"I wasn't sure I could."

A private victory. Just theirs.

"I was sure."

He smiled at her. "Thank you, my love."

"You've passed *my* Selection, Josh Cumberland. You passed it a long time ago."

Their kiss lasted forever.

[EPILOGUE]

Eight days before Josh Cumberland passed his private Selection, Sharon Caldwell celebrated her own long-visualised victory as she posed before the door of Number 10, Downing Street, and waved to the reporters. Beside her stood Laura Collins, heroine of the moment, something that had definitely not been part of Caldwell's political dreams.

She was very, very proud of her sweetheart.

After the speech, the glossy black armoured door swung open, and she stepped inside to applause from waiting staff, all of them senior Whitehall civil servants. The door closed behind her.

So this is it.

Excitement pounded through her still, but stepping through that doorway changed everything. Before, she had been chasing a dream. Now she was the prime minister, and the world was different.

Now she had to live up to expectations.

"You'll want to see your private office, ma'am," said one of the private secretaries. "There are things that every new prime minister has to see on taking office."

"Really?" said Caldwell. "What kind of things?"

"Um, I can't say, ma'am. The specific contents are for your eyes only."

Well, this was the kind of stuffy old ceremonial procedure she would have to change.

Maybe I'd better see what it's all about, before doing anything drastic.

"Lead the way," she said.

"I'll inspect the living quarters," said Laura.

Her grin was wider than Caldwell's own.

Maybe I've achieved two dreams, not one.

"I'll join you later," said Caldwell.

She followed the private secretary to the office, where he showed her the desk, the wall safe and the display screen. Then he retired, closing the door as he left.

"Well," she said to the empty room. "Let's see what we've got."

The first files she opened on screen were simple text-only, which was no surprise when she read the dates. They were scanned-in copies of paper-based files, secret papers for the PM's eyes only. That lovely phrase again.

My eyes only.

It sounded romantic in her mind.

"Come on," she muttered.

Time to work. She began to read. After a minute, she leaned back and spoke aloud once more.

"No wonder we've a special relationship with the States. How could the idiot have promised *that*?"

She closed that pane and maximised the next.

After a moment she began to chuckle.

"Not him," she said. "And with a *donkey*?"

Seconds later, her howl of laughter reached the corridor out-side, where two grey-haired civil servants turned to look at each other.

"They always do that," said one.

"I wish I knew what was in those files," said the other.

"Maybe not *all* the files," said the first.

But the end of Caldwell's first full day in office ended in a very different mood. A senior police officer rang mid-afternoon to say that Zak and Zebediah Tyndall were in Paddington Green. Not arrested: they were suddenly, somehow, right there in a cell in the most heavily fortified police station in the country. No one could work out how they got there.

Nor did the Tyndalls have any idea what had happened. Zebediah remembered going to bed in the power station accommodation suite; Zak remembered looking in on him.

That was it.

Caldwell had managed to keep the joy off her face until the call was ended. Then she had a glass of champagne upstairs with Laura, before returning to work.

The second security-related call came just after 7.30pm, while she was still at her desk. It took her a while to agree to what they told her.

"Don't wait up," she told Laura.

No member of the public saw her leave Number 10. She walked through hushed and armoured tunnels through to a certain Whitehall building; there she descended some thirty metres in a lift. With a twelve-strong escort, she boarded an electric trolley-car that carried her along a subterranean thoroughfare whose existence she had not suspected.

That, despite eighteen years serving as a Member of Parliament, four as party leader of the TechnoDemocrats.

They fetched up below Thames House, headquarters of MI5.

Senior officials escorted her to an observation room, where she sat down in a comfortable chair, and looked through the transparent wall. Beyond, a shaven-headed man with a goatee was strapped into a hard-looking chair.

His cell was featureless save for acoustic tiles, guaranteed to deaden screams.

"Do I really want to see this?" said Caldwell. "And who are you again?"

The youngest-looking of the MI5 officers, a dark-haired woman, said: "I'm Trin Purcell, ma'am, and this is Flora McIntosh, my boss."

The two officers exchanged looks.

Something going on there.

This Trin Purcell might be junior, but she appeared to be in control. Caldwell would have to find out more, but later.

"So this" – she nodded towards the transparent wall – "is the famous Professor Badakian."

At that, Badakian straightened up in his chair and looked her in the eye.

"Shit," said Trin, and gestured.

The wall shivered into blank opacity.

"What was that about?" said Caldwell.

"Ma'am," said Trin, "that bastard can hypnotise people without using words. We have the video evidence to prove it."

It was McIntosh's involuntary shivering that convinced Caldwell.

"But how could he know I'm here? This is one-way glass, isn't it? Zero-way, now you've blanked it out."

"Our consultant Dr Duchesne," said Trin, "believes that Badakian has some characteristics of far-spectrum autism, including auditory acuity so great that he can hear subvocalised thoughts. Or he might be picking up some other hint, like a minute draught in the air caused by increased warmth this side of the glass."

"He's a scary individual, ma'am," said McIntosh.

"I see. But I thought I was here to communicate with him."

"That's the idea," said Trin. "He used certain keywords which indicated he knew how to specify information for the PM's eyes only."

Caldwell's mouth twitched, remembering this morning, and

the files she had read after thinking about that phrase.

"But I will need you here," said Caldwell. "Won't I?"

"For your protection, ma'am. If you agree."

Caldwell stared at the blank wall.

"Of course I do," she said. "If only half of what I've read is true, this man is hugely dangerous."

"He is that," said Trin, and pressed a control.

The glass changed colour. A blinking cursor waited at eye height.

"It responds to your dictation, ma'am. And to Badakian's. We can't risk you hearing his voice directly, you see."

Caldwell nodded, not speaking, understanding that her words would be reproduced on the glass, on Badakian's side as well as hers. She thought about what to say, and opened her mouth, but words grew on the glass, pre-empting her.

Congratulations, Madam Prime Minister.

She breathed in and out, then spoke.

"What do you have for me?"

A pause, then:

What time is it?

She looked at Trin and McIntosh. Trin said: "It's 19.58, ma'am." The system was keyed only to Caldwell's voice, not Trin's.

"Eight pm," she said.

Exactly eight? Or a little before?

"Less than two minutes to go."

Then I suggest you pop up some of the major international news sites.

Caldwell stared at the words.

"Why?"

No answer.

"Shall I do it?" asked Trin.

Caldwell nodded. Off to the left and right, a collection of display panes brightened.

"Now what?"

Wait for 8 o'clock.

They waited. As they did so, Trin said: "We've had him in sensory isolation, ma'am. It appears to have no adverse affect on him, unlike any normal prisoner."

There were questions Caldwell would have to ask about prisoners and secret chambers like these, but not just yet.

Several seconds after eight, the display panes began to alter. Soon most of them were showing the same image.

"Oh, my God," said Caldwell, forgetting that the system would reproduce her words.

Maybe I am your God.

"Like fuck you are."

Fine words to come from a prime minister's mouth.

You'll want to keep me, anyhow.

Caldwell was about to signal for Trin to cut the system link; instead she gestured to the display panes and said: "Maximise one of them."

"Ma'am."

The picture grew huge on the glass wall.

"Oh, my God," said one of the other officers, repeating Caldwell's words.

It's not possible.

There was no way it was going to happen.

It can't be true, can it?

But then she remembered that Badakian had been part of the Foreign Secretary's visit several weeks before. The visit where President Brand had been pleased to meet perhaps the only European politicians that would talk to him.

Perhaps he should have wondered why, exactly, they would want to talk to a renegade leader whom the rest of the world considered an insane liability and a threat to everyone.

These were the images the world would remember:

A press conference. President Brand and the whole of his Government Cabinet – the chief executive and his closest officials, whom everyone called his Twelve Apostles. By any means of counting that meant that thirteen men and women were on the blue-carpeted dais, smiling and facing the seated ranks of journalists.

Of course security personnel were present. But their attention was on the visiting journalists, not the politicians they were charged with protecting.

When President Brand drew the massive bowie knife from inside his jacket, transparent protective barriers dropped from the ceiling as they were supposed to, shielding the politicians from outside attack.

But it was President Brand and his Twelve Apostles who had the weapons.

Every one of them drew a knife, and every one of them was smiling as they gathered in a circle, each pulling up his or her left sleeve, before raising their knife right-handed.

As each blade cut into the next person's soft inner forearm, slicing up along the artery – did they smile or did they wince? It was something that amateurs and professionals would debate for a long time to come.

The Cutter Circle was complete as thirteen politicians dropped, blood gushing from split radial arteries, reddening clothes, darkening the carpet, and spattering against the transparent shields. Before the security team managed to raise those shields, all thirteen politicians were dead, including the most dangerous one of all.

The realtime report became the most-watched webcast of all time.

In the subterranean room, Trin was the first to speak.

"Bloody hell," she said.

But Caldwell simply stared at the screen, waiting for Badakian.

We should talk.

[ACKNOWLEDGMENTS]

Mille remerciements to Josette Sanchez-Reynolds for turning my broken French into the real, nuanced deal.

Massive thanks to rock band Kids in Glass Houses for allowing me to quote one of their best-known songs. Cheers to Aled Phillips, Joel Fisher, Iain Mahanty, Andrew Shay and Philip Jenkins.

Profound thanks to my niece, Emily Hill, whose insights as a mental health professional (working in a secure unit) informed my depiction of teenage suicide and its manifestation in clusters.

As with *Edge*, I owe a vast debt to the late Bob Bridges, software guru and former member of 22 SAS.

Again, the name and to some extent the concept of Ghost Force come from the book of that name, written by Ken Connor. I relied once more on *The Operators*, James Rennie's account of life in Detachment 14, and "borrowed" one of his experiences to create the scene with the unexpected exam.

I also nicked a fragment from *Working With Warriors* by Dennis Martin, who saw the renowned Lofty Wiseman, aged fifty-seven, running Airborne Rangers into the ground. Karate legend Dave Hazard's meeting autograph-seeking policemen, as told in *Born Fighter*, gave me Krill and Carlsen's encounter in the cell.

New insights came from *First Into Action* by Duncan Falconer and *Fighting Scared* by Robin Horsfall.

In analysing cult behaviour, besides personal observation, I relied on *Brainwashing: the Science of Thought Control*, by Kathleen Taylor.

The training cadence used by Josh – *the body is like iron* – came from an interview with the late Steve Cattle in *Fighting Arts International* decades back.

Both Nik Butler and Kari Sperring volunteered to die horribly, so I obliged them. Thank you for allowing me to kill you in Paris!

For copy editing above and beyond the call of duty, I gave Ann Zanoni a job in the Police Judiciaire. Thanks, Ann.

I hope Danie Ware of Forbidden Planet enjoys her new career in Ghost Force.

Hypnotic techniques as used in the book are real (and demonstrable with an EEG). Many thanks to Paul McKenna, who uses them as a force for good.

Limitless gratitude to every martial artist I have trained with since that first judo session with Alf in Slough College, on a Wednesday afternoon in September 1972.

Thanks to Hwyel Teague of the excellent *Fighters Only* magazine, for enjoying *Edge* and saying so.

Ongoing thanks and respect to Professor Jim Davies of Oxford University, who taught me the formal specification languages of Z and CSP mentioned in *Point*.

There are certain software folk (including a code ninja) with brains the size of Jupiter, to whom I offer respect. Every time I meet you, it's an honour.

Without John Parker – who started it all – plus John Berlyne and Marc Gascoigne, neither *Edge* nor *Point* would exist. It's Lee Harris's fault, too.

My wife Yvonne accompanied me on the journey as always. That's what made the difference.

[ABOUT THE AUTHOR]

Thomas Blackthorne is the pseudonym of science fiction writer John Meaney, author of *To Hold Infinity*, the Nulapeiron sequence, *Bone Song*, *Dark Blood* and the *Ragnarok* trilogy. His works have been shortlisted several times for the British Science Fiction Award, won the Independent Publishers' Best Novel award (in SF/Fantasy), and been one of the *Daily Telegraph* Books of the Year.

Now a full-time writer, in his time he has taught business analysis and software engineering on three continents, and is a black belt in shotokan karate, cross-training in other arts. A trained hypnotist, he remains severely addicted to coffee.

www.johnmeaney.com

JOSH CUMBERLAND'S GUIDE TO FITNESS & MAYHEM

Josh works by two principles: 1) combat-fit means combat-ready, and 2) self protection is not a martial art. He needs strength, power and endurance, and is often based in hotel rooms (or less hospitable locations) for long periods. When it comes to applied violence, his martial arts background forms the backbone of his response: he knows how to apply it.

When people ask him for advice, he advises a preliminary check-up with a medical doctor. This guide is for information only, and neither the author nor the publisher nor any other party is liable for any injuries or accidents resulting from reading the following information. (You knew we had to put that in, right? Be sensible, be safe.)

Component exercises
Let's start with bodyweight exercises (calisthenics), the basic conditioning method for wrestlers and boxers, and the mainstay of Josh's strength endurance training. The following two exercises made old-school Indian wrestlers the world's foremost grapplers. (The author has had his exercise form checked out by a graduate of an Indian *akhara*.)

Hindu Push-ups (aka *dands*)

With feet wider than shoulder-width apart (usually double shoulder-width), Josh places his hands on the floor so his butt is sticking up in the air. From the side, his body forms an inverted V. Then he curves his chest down to the floor (arms bending) and through (arms straightening) so he is now looking upwards at 45 degrees or higher, his hips close to the floor but not touching, legs straightened, weight on the balls of his feet.

This is like a dive-bomber push-up, but with feet wider apart.

Unlike a dive-bomber, he now simply pushes back to the start position. During the first motion he inhales (as the ribcage is expanding); when he pushes back to the start he exhales (ribcage compression). He routinely performs 250 repetitions in 15 minutes.

Hindu Squats (aka *bethaks*)

Josh starts from standing with feet shoulder width apart (or a fraction more) and toes forward (or a tiny bit out to each side). His arms are held straight out to the front, hands open, palms down. The first part of the exercise is to pull the hands to his chest, forming fists (the inside of each fore-knuckle touching a nipple) with the elbows flaring out horizontally as if rowing a boat. He inhales as he does this.

In the second part of the motion he squats down and comes straight back up to the initial position, all on one exhalation. His hands travel straight down (or a little behind him) until at the lowest point, in full squat, the backs of his hands face forward and his fingertips brush the floor on either side. At this point, his bodyweight is on the balls of his feet, and the heels have come up off the floor (different from weight training).

As he then stands, his heels go down and his arms swing up, returning to the start position.

This is faster than many people think. A repetition takes less than two seconds. Josh performs 500 squats in 15 minutes.

Neck Bridge (aka Wrestler's Bridge)

Some grapplers perform twisting manoeuvres from this position, but Josh considers it sufficient to maintain a static hold. His preference is to use a gymnastics mat, but in a hotel room he merely lies on the floor and puts a pillow on the ground just touching his scalp. Then he pulls his feet up so they're on the ground, touching his butt, and his knees are fully bent.

He pushes up with his feet, arching his back, and rolls onto the top of his head, but does not stay here. Because he's used to bridging, he shuffles his feet and rolls a little more (under control) until it's his forehead that is taking the weight, along with his feet.

His preference is to keep his feet flat, but some of his mates prefer to push on the balls of their feet or even the points of their toes, depending on footwear. Josh usually keeps his fingers lightly touching the ground for stability, but sometimes folds his arms across his chest.

He normally holds this position for 4 minutes.

Additional bodyweight exercises

Josh then performs abdominal crunches and (usually) standing side bends and twists. Optionally, if he wants to add a pulling exercise and he's in a hotel room, he opens the bathroom door, faces it end-on, takes a palms-down grip on the door handles and squats down, feet either side of the door. Then he pulls himself forward and lowers back – a rowing motion.

If he's not in his skivvies, he might find somewhere outside to perform chin-ups. He sometimes throws a towel over the top of the open bathroom door and hauls himself up the door in a chinning motion, but only if he's convinced the door is solid.

For a balls-to-the-wall workout, he adds burpees to the mix.

Kettlebell exercises

If Josh is travelling by car, he usually has a kettlebell or two with him. He mostly sticks to three basic exercises: one-hand swings, one-hand clean-and-presses, and one-hand snatches. All are performed with a shoulder-width stance, and he concentrates on pushing down with his heels throughout, differently from Hindu squats. He keeps both shoulders level, never hunched.

Swings are what they sound like: swinging the weight up to horizontal (or higher) and returning to the hang position between the legs. At the bottom, he is in a partial squat position. When he swings the kettlebell up, his legs straighten and his hips pop forward. As the weight swings down his legs return to the partial squat. Throughout, his lower back is flat but not always vertical.

Snatches involves swinging the weight overhead and then holding it there briefly, arm straightened vertically but not hyperextended. The kettlebell flips over to touch the forearm. Josh performs a slight dip at the top of the motion to "catch" the kettlebell and control its motion, if it's a heavy kettlebell.

With the clean-and-press, he hauls the weight up close to his body, so that as it reaches shoulder height he pulls his elbow down and in to touch his body. The weight flips over neatly to rest against his vertical forearm. Then he presses upwards to straighten the arm and holds it, before reversing the entire manoeuvre to return to the start.

He likes doing high-rep two-hand swings as well. (Sometimes he does the one-hand moves with dumb-bells, but the two-hand swing requires a kettlebell.)

● ● ● ●

Dumb-bell exercises

Besides substituting dumb-bells for kettlebells in the above lifts, Josh also does exercises that a bodybuilder would recognize. He has various routines, but the following is typical.

He supersets bench presses with deadlifts. (When lifting two dumb-bells as if they were suitcases, the distinction between squats and deadlifts disappears. Josh thinks of this as a squatting motion.) He usually works sets of ten or twelve repetitions with heavier weights or twenty reps with medium weights. His movements are fast but controlled. He performs four supersets (i.e. four two-exercise mini-circuits).

The pressing motion is obvious: lying on his back, he pushes the weights up from his chest, exhaling, then inhales as he lowers. The squatting is likewise obvious, a dumb-bell held suitcase-like on either side, squatting down (and inhaling) until his thigh bones are horizontal, then straightening up on the exhalation, always maintaining downward pressure on the heels.

If he's travelling with dumb-bells, rather than training in a gym, he lies on the floor to perform the presses. Josh is happy to train with benches but is not dependent on them.

He then performs one-hand dumb-bell rows, four sets, alternating sides, reps as for the previous supersets. Josh leans over with his non-lifting hand pressing down on a bench or other sturdy support. (He dislikes the knee-on-bench position some people use.) He raises the dumb-bell from the floor to his chest, elbow travelling close to his body, replicating the pulling motion that is part of many combat moves.

He typically finishes with a shoulder-triceps-biceps tri-set. Usually this is a set of shoulder presses (pushing the weights straight up from his shoulders while standing), followed by a set of standing triceps press (a single vertical dumb-bell, upper plate held in both hands, lowered behind the neck and then straightened overhead, the elbows above the shoulders and not moving position – they are the axis of the motion), then biceps curls or alternating hammer curls (dumb-bells held thumbs-up, curling one up, then raising the other dumb-bell while lowering the first).

Sometimes he will miss out the triceps exercise. Other times he will add stiff-legged deadlifts as a hamstring exercise, in which case he performs 4 shoulders-and-hamstrings supersets followed by 4 triceps-and-biceps supersets.

Josh has grappled with enough bodybuilders to know how strong they are, but his training differs from theirs. His moves are faster because he wants to work the fast-twitch muscle fibres. *Some* workouts are based on 20-rep sets for more strength endurance. He does only one exercise per body part because he's already performed hundreds of push-ups and free-hand squats before hitting the weights.

He performs full-body workouts (rather than split routines) partly because it fits more naturally with his travels. He does not schedule a particular workout for a particular day of the week, every week.

Lastly, he never performs a set to failure. Some of his friends have gained a lot of muscle with this approach, but in a fight, failure is not an option. He trains for success: whatever number of repetitions he has decided on at the start of a set, he always completes that number.

Running

Self explanatory. Josh's background means that he likes the aerobic endurance training of long slow distance running. He rarely does sprint intervals, but enjoys running on varied terrain.

He does approve of interval training (using various protocols), particularly with stationary-bike cycling, squat thrusts and burpees; and he has a love-hate relationship with Tabata protocol training: 20 seconds all-out, 10 seconds rest, repeated for eight intervals.

Putting it all together

His preference is to run first and perform a second workout later. If time constraints force him to do it all in one workout, he begins with the run.

Otherwise he begins with bodyweight exercises. Sometimes he does 100 Hindu push-ups, 200 Hindu squats and a 2-minute neck bridge as a warm up (slow on the first few reps), before launching into other training (e.g. bagwork when he has access to a gym, or the full-body dumb-bell routine outlined above). He may also perform this number of calisthenics immediately after a run, but if it's a hard training day he'll do more than this, as follows:

At least 3 times a week (up to 6 times) he gives more emphasis to the calisthenics and performs 250 Hindu push-ups, 500 Hindu squats, and holds the neck bridge for 4 minutes, often followed with a forward bridge (the belly-down inverse) for the same duration.

Some days he performs straight sets, other days he performs five supersets of 50 push-ups and 100 squats, while on others he mixes it in with fight training for intervals. Or he performs ten circuits of 25 Hindu push-ups, 50 Hindu squats and one minute shadowboxing (including kicks, knee strikes, elbows, takedown entries and sprawls) or jumping rope.

After this he may do a weights routine or bagwork or grappling drills.

On other days, rather than any of the above, he will make up a new circuit of weight training (dumb-bells, barbells or kettlebells) mixed in with fight training, alternating each set of weight-lifting with a fight drill. This means that he's performing all his solo fight drills under physical distress, operating under pressure.

Although it's not explicit in the books, Josh's diet is ovo-lacto vegetarian.

When Josh describes the above routines to his friends, he's careful to point out that the number of repetitions is something to work up to (or exceed). He thinks of the calisthenics routine and the dumb-bell routine as modules, and he has others (for example, two different sequences of ten different fighting combinations, each drilled for 20 repetitions).

Josh puts several modules together to create a workout, either sequentially or interweaving them. For example, he might do the ten-set circuit above, but interweave one of the combo sequences to replace the free-form shadowboxing.

If he were to do all forms of training in the same workout (which is *very* rare), and sequentially rather than interwoven, it would be in this order: joint-mobility warm-up; running; bodyweight exercises; fighting drills (including bagwork); weight-training; stretching. That's what suits him personally.

The real point, he tells his friends, is that they should learn routines from others but develop their own as their confidence grows. *That's* what will give them the edge.

Martial arts

Josh's training mostly looks like MMA (called ultimate- or cage-fighting by the uninitiated); but he began by training in traditional martial arts. Many people are in more danger from work-related stress and hypertension than they are from physical attack. In that case, the discipline and fitness of *any* martial art is excellent. The habit of controlled breathing and good posture – straight back, lowered shoulders, raised chin, centred bodyweight – pays enormous dividends in the workplace or at school.

Not only that, but Josh has met long-term dedicated practitioners of the least streetwise arts (such as aikido or tai chi) who are deadly in the street. In the evaluation of different arts and styles that follows, he points out that 1) it's based on the gyms/dojos he's trained at, so others might have different experiences, 2) the pros and cons are generalizations, and 3) are from the viewpoint of self protection, ignoring other benefits.

Every art can be made to work.

Karate

Features striking techniques, formal stances and strong etiquette. Pros: ambidextrous four-limb training, hard workouts, producing good spirit (if it's a good dojo). Cons: requires the student to do impact training at home (most British dojos lack punchbags), overemphasises traditional form (e.g. leaving the chin and throat vulnerable), may not experience contact.

Kung fu

As for karate, generally. But there is much variation.

Kickboxing

Features a lesser range of techniques than karate or kung fu, but concentrates on making them work, with live drills. Pros: very hard workout, effective techniques, bagwork and impact sparring. Cons: geared to one-on-one confrontation in the ring.

(From Josh's own experience – not a scientific survey – he believes that karate and some hard-style kung fu guys who are good fighters can defend themselves as effectively as kickboxers, maybe even more so. But the percentage of kickboxers who are real fighters tends to be higher.)

Boxing

Hands only. Pros: no-nonsense, impact training that brings out the required aggression. Great conditioning. Cons: too overwhelming for people who need a gradual introduction to fighting. (Boxers ideally need to add some barefist training on punchbag or sandbag.)

Judo

Grappling with heavy jackets, emphasising live drills and good conditioning. Pros: no nonsense, super effective throwing techniques. Cons: taught as a sport (and with reliance on the opponent wearing a jacket), not with opponents throwing punches.

Brazilian Jiu-Jitsu

The art that made everyone sit up and take notice. Judo-like grappling with more emphasis on groundfighting. Pros: proven grappling techniques, live drills, great conditioning. Cons: sometimes practiced as a sport (see Judo), despite its background as the root art of MMA.

(Josh believes that everyone should train in judo, BJJ or Russian sambo – or western wrestling, rarely practiced in Britain – to some extent.)

Krav Maga

Israeli self defence system, anything goes. Pros: usually hard training, realistic street-attack scenarios including weapons, often working closely with police forces. Cons: some students train only in scenarios and rarely spar.

Escrima

Fast-moving Filipino art that uses the same techniques empty-handed and with weapons. Pros: proven knife defences (uniquely so). Cons: complex skills, lacks pure power shots.

(If escrima is a person's secondary art, then Josh's opinion is that the complexity makes it hard to bolt the knife defences on to, say, kickboxing – even though he considers escrima to be superb. The basic krav maga defences, in contrast, are easy to add to another art.)

MMA

Everything together: grappling and striking. Pros: the closest to real fighting there is. Conditioning and confidence second to none. Cons: like boxing, may be too intimidating for some to train in – like boxing, it boasts more spectators than practitioners. Lacks multiple-opponent and weapon drills (but an MMA fighter is the best placed to add these to their arsenal).

Real-world self-protection

For most people, in Josh's opinion, the best approach is to pick a martial art they enjoy and use it as a core discipline. Then they can add a second art (a striker can add a grappling art, or vice versa) or cherry-pick from other styles.

He tells people to be responsible for their own training. He picks dojos that are challenging but not insane, ignores instruction that goes against common sense and biomechanics, and would leave any dojo that tried to stop him training with other instructors.

Josh has a large collection of fitness books, and knows exactly where an opponent's liver, spleen and kidneys are. A lot of his training involves techniques that are banned in competition. For example, his sprawling technique includes driving an elbow downwards to the spine (for emergency use only).

What martial arts don't teach are verbal de-escalation skills, situational awareness, and the legal ramifications of use of force (which varies according to whichever country or state Josh is in). All-out fighting is the last resort.

For Josh, avoidance is *always* the first choice.

Further information

For more on self-protection, including the psychological effects of experiencing confrontation, Josh recommends British authors Geoff Thompson and Peter Consterdine, and American experts Marc MacYoung and Loren Christensen.

The bodyweight exercises are explained in Matt Furey's *Combat Conditioning* book and DVDs. Pavel Tsatsouline's materials teach all there is to know about kettlebells. For bodybuilding, Dave Draper's writings are instructive, whimsical and motivational.

In MMA, Josh likes Bas Rutten's instructional DVDs.

Hardcore athletes should check out boxing coach Ross Enamait (sounds like *Eena-might*). Major thumbs-up from Josh!